FALLING OUT AND BELONGING: A FOOT-SOLDIER'S LIFE

S. Joseph Krause

Bloomington, IN Milton Keynes, UK

authorHOUSE"

AuthorHouse™
1663 Liberty Drive, Suite 200
Bloomington, IN 47403
www.authorhouse.com
Phone: 1-800-839-8640

AuthorHouse™ UK Ltd.
500 Avebury Boulevard
Central Milton Keynes, MK9 2BE
www.authorhouse.co.uk
Phone: 08001974150

First published by AuthorHouse 7/13/2006

ISBN: 1-4259-2579-0 (sc)
ISBN: 1-4259-2578-2 (dj)

Library of Congress Control Number: 2006903182

Printed in the United States of America
Bloomington, Indiana

This book is printed on acid-free paper.

Cover art by Matthew T. Swartz.

This novel is dedicated to members of the Fourth Infantry Division who served during World War II. I couldn't have written it without the patience and inspirational love of my dear wife Ruth (aka Soothie).

A number of the characters are composites of men I knew. Some situations are also composites. Most incidents are based on underlying accounts recorded in a journal written shortly after discharge, containing events either experienced or, on occasion, derived from fellow soldiers. I use authorial license, but on-the-scene details come from direct experience. Certain heart-draining images were as vivid to me in the writing as they were during the times they occurred.

SJK

ACKNOWLEDGEMENTS.

For their good counsel and encouragement, I want to thank my brother, David Krause, as well as Dan Waterman, and Nick Arvin. The constant assistance of Bob DeGroff at every stage of publication was indespensable. For their fellowship, I also want to acknowledge Elmer Glenn, who was a member of my Company, Bill Wilson, a member of a nearby Company in our Battalion, and Leo Jereb, a member of a Company in another Regiment of our Division, men with whom I shared reminiscences. I came to meet them at Reunions of the Ohio Chapter of the Fourth Infantry Division Association, a great bunch of guys.

PART I

1.

They marched us up the middle of the ferry where people drove their cars, and we stood there in ranks on the rock-smooth planks stained with age-old grease marks, each man leaning forward from the hips, his nose up against the pack of the guy in front of him, waiting for them to fill it and take us across to Pier Ninety-eight. Nobody said 'At ease,' or anything, and I guess we could have talked, except that our mood hovered between anticipation of the uncertain and wanting this sardine-tight feeling to be over with. As often happened in the Army, when we were assembled and being moved around like a mass of so much nameless *stuff* to be bulked up on a dock somewhere—as we had just been—we'd tend to shrink into our private selves. In this instance, I, for one, was feeling like we'd been shoved into a tomb, with the echo of GI shoes ghosting the beat of others clomping in behind them. Just the image to take with you, going overseas, destined to be assigned to a line infantry unit.

I turned my head trying to make out how near we were to being all packed in, but couldn't get very far around. Willie Dacey, who stood one man ahead of me in the next column, had just done the same thing, and seeing me, rolled his eyes back and chuckled nervously, sounding as if he had a mouth full of bubbles, a piece of rubbery tongue sliding through the gap in his sawed off yellow teeth. Ol' Arkinsaw. He said he fought an alligator once; bit him in the neck and ground his teeth down on the damned thing's backbone. He was a first-rate shot, though looking at him, so blubbery, you'd never think it. He said he wasn't worried about going over. They'd make him a sniper—good at 300 yards. ("Daddy took me huntin far back as I kin remember.") He had it all figured out. They'd throw a camouflage net over him, sit him in a tree just behind the line, have him fire at will, like on the firing range, and just keep on a-poppin 'em. His buddy, Rebel, wanted to know, while he was dreaming, did the Army ever give a body anything but what he didn't want?

In the mean time, the favorite target for Willie's kidding was his unlikely friend from Brooklyn, gravel voiced Gino, who stood just in front of him. Ever anxious Gino, a dead ringer for Chico Marx, craned his long horse face around following Willie's look. He was forever adjusting his straps and mumbled about his back, as he shifted the weight of his pack. He swore there had to be a loose "disc bone" moving around back there. "True," Rebel said, "but the loose bone's in the back o' yer head." Gino insisted that wherever it was, the pain would be his insurance policy if the Army had any idea of sending us stumblebums into combat. He cracked a half smile at something Willie said, and winced as Willie jabbed at his pack. "Hey, Mista Brooklyn. Talk about *backs*, that fella yonder ain't gonna be getting on *ours* anymore."

The testy Kraut-type sergeant, who indeed was a Kraut, had been riding us hard back in our former outfit ('I'll make soldiers outa you bastards yet!') when he practically apoplexed over finding his own

2

name on orders. He thought it was a prank, not realizing his fate was sealed when our unsoldierly Captain got wind of remarks Kraut made about him. Actually, there wasn't a great deal of starch in this Captain, who for one thing had a funny flat-footed step, even when we marched in formation. He somehow looked misplaced, more like a middle-aged businessman than an officer. We could see him in a double-breasted suit, sitting behind a mahogany desk, handing a stack of papers to his secretary.

As comfortable cadre, Kraut thought his status gave him a certain immunity, so, in the normal course of things, he'd sound off quite freely and think nothing of it. Unhindered, his mouth, we thought, might get a tad too free for his own good, as in time it suddenly did. "In what kind of army would you find a Captain who walked, no less marched, like a duck? Doesn't even square his shoulders. A civilian in uniform, the stupid American written all over him, and, of course, he's got a piss 'n vinegar name like Smith. *John* Smith. *Captain John Smith*, the original American businessman!"

Kraut might be ignorant about things he didn't want to believe— don't confuse him with the facts—but he wasn't uneducated. He had in fact read quite a bit of American History, and from time to time he'd let you know it, which at first made us wonder what he was doing in the Army, composed, as he saw it, mainly of the lower class element—by his standard, us. We'd find him a complicated guy, but the uncomplicated part of his enlistment was his sense that, in light of his heritage, he had to prove himself as one hundred percent American. Now, with his come-down, after those choice words about the Captain got around, Gino risked the reminder that many American Smiths were actually Schmidts ("Could be our Captain's one") which back in camp would have made trouble for him. Gino felt Kraut was especially prejudiced against "Eyetalians," with him

3

saying that since Roman times you couldn't find a helluva lot of fight in them, short of a promise they could go back to their eating, drinking, and screwing.

Gino laughed, "Well? Makes sense, doesn't it? Who wouldn't rather fuck than fight? He oughta know the whole goddamn Army is made up of nothing but Eyetalians. Might even be a few in the German Army." In our back-and-forth banter, Gino frequently had the feeling he was being picked on, usually by Willie, but he could give as good as he took. When Willie assured him that the real Krauts would go easy on him because the Dagoes were Hitler's friends, Gino said they'd sure go after hog-wild hillbillies. He also thought the reason this Cabbage Head (Kraut's last name was Kohlkopf) was so ticked off was that he was being sent over to fight his own. Rebel said, "Aw, can all o' that stuff. This fella was jest born angry." In any event, we liked the idea he was not happy with his current situation, and we liked it even more that he was bunched in with men he disliked, minus the prior authority he'd had over us.

We did a lot of laying around, waiting, there always being a wait in the Army, but the good part this time was that we didn't feel beat the way we did in training. We'd been at Camp Shanks (in effect, our POE) for over a week, mostly getting shots, the usual short-arm inspection (in raincoats), a new issue of clothes and equipment, and a second pair of shoes to weight our packs down a little more. In the midst of our card games, Kraut would be pacing the barracks and kicking anything in sight, a footlocker, a stray shoe, whatever, and, in addition to cursing his own rotten luck, he'd be pissing and moaning under his breath about how incorrigibly lax we were. How in hell were we ever going to face real soldiers? One of the card players exclaimed, "Who in hell said we would?" Undistractable, Kraut kept ranting about this, that, and the other thing, always coming back to

4

his outrage that in this poor excuse for an Army, he should be shafted by a business-man masquerading as an officer. "Probably bought his commission too." Rumor had it that our Captain belonged to an affluent ranching family in Texas and did the family's books, hiding what income he could from the tax man. Willie said that's how he got his waddle—from doing the dodge.

When Kraut wouldn't let up, Rebel finally yelled for him to take a hike. Would do him a heap o' good, us too. We got a kick out of his going after the de-fanged Kraut and getting away with it. But Kraut was too obsessed to pay it much heed. He kept pacing and he'd point a finger at anyone who looked his way telling him, "Wait!" Gino, cards to his face, stage-whispered, "Should we shoot him now or *wait*?"

It was a relief when he disappeared for a day, and it was an even bigger relief when he showed up in the mess hall next morning with his mouth zipped. That created all kinds of speculation. He'd found out he was going over because he could be a translator? "Meaning they'd stick this super-soldier behind the front squeezin info out o' POW's," Willie said. "And guys like us duckin bullets. The Army for yah." Others, wondered how come he was the only non-com among us, a tech-sergeant at that, and, as luck would have it, sergeant of the fourth platoon—ours. Or had he been broken? Most suspicious of all, was his packing a separate duffel bag.

With Kraut having all that military savvy, Gino put it together that, knowing the Germans are better soldiers, he might take a notion to go over to their side. "Be just the thing. He gets himself into a *real* army and finds out what he wished for." Willie figured that being with a rag-tag crowd like us would encourage him. As he saw it, the Germans would hear him talk, and looking at him, with that square chin, high cheekbones and yellow brush cut, they'd know he was one of theirs. Frank Kolhkopf—had the name too.

5

"Noticed him standin there chawin on a finger nail," Rebel said, "like he was doin some deep thinkin. Sure nuff, must've got him *somethin*. Sees me and he's grinin like a possum eatin shit." And on the talk went, some of it within earshot of the newly silent Kraut, whose grin only broadened.

One thing his new attitude did was to give us peace at our card games, but it also got Gino back to his old refrain that he was too old to be in the Army. He'd pull a bottle of beer out from under his sack, suck on it thoughtfully for a while, sigh for no reason, rub his mouth along his sleeve, and sing his usual refrain. "I'm too old for this kinda stuff. Look at me. I don't belong here. I oughta be home drivin a truck. This crap is for you young kids. I got a wife and kids livin with my shitty in-laws. I think about what they'll be like when I get back."

With the war dragging on and casualties mounting, it seemed that the Army was scraping the bottom of the barrel for replacements to fill the ranks. So they were down to the newly inducted eighteen year olds and drafting guys like Gino and Willie pushing thirty-eight, even some with more than two kids, depending on local quotas and who you knew on the Board. The older guys talked about finding a way out, some ways bizarre, some desperate.

Rebel claimed he was nearing forty. With those bags under his bloodshot eyes and brown spots on his balding head, he looked it, though he was a naturally well-muscled type, and, in training, more vigorous than most. He had us looking at one another when he said he had a notion to volunteer for the Rangers. We never took him for a loony. He said, "Leastwise, they'd find out mebbe I ain't fit for what's a-comin." Something none of us believed, and didn't think the Rangers would either. He came from a family that had always been pretty big on scrappin, both in and out of the military. "That

6

is," as Willie added, "When they weren't huntin, fishin, drinkin, or carryin on about how the Yankees won a War we didn't lose, and us a-fightin wars for *them* ever since…that they mighta lost."

Rebel laughed. "Oh, yeaah! Ain't that just like us."

"Well, matter of fact, a whole half o' yer lill ol' town just north o' the Alabama line, could be drunk a good part o' the time, which is why they already sent in more 'n their share 'o volunteers."

Rebel said his family was indeed about volunteered out. He had brothers and cousins who'd been killed and wounded, one a POW. So, he said fightin days should be about over for his whole damned clan. "One day, might jest tell 'em as much, and walk off, while I still got legs to do it on." That was Rebel all over. Making like he wanted out, when, not once, did he chicken out of the rough going, here or over there. Willie said there'd be just three words on Rebel's tombstone: 'He Was Tough.' And, as we'd learn, he was that and lots more.

Much as they'd want to put it out of mind, as you listened to their chatter, what kept nagging at this over-the-hill bunch was that the guy who was so gung-ho for soldiering seemed to have found himself a way out of the nasty stuff that miserable slobs like them were destined for. Kraut's only welcome command was the one for dismissal: "All right, fall out, men." Now *he* was the one falling out, was he? For the duration? It became even more aggravating when one of our young guys came down with the hives, and got himself a discharge based on allergies. *"Allergies,"* Gino moaned. "We're the ones that are supposed to have 'em, not that smooth chinned young squirt. After eatin this stinkin chow, I have a feeling the damn allergies oughta be comin on *me*. Any day now. Maybe that's why my nuts itch. Could be, huh, Willie?"

"Sure. But they'll say yah got a dose and stick yah in sick bay. You won't like the cure."

7

Like the rest of the young ones, not two months after my eighteenth birthday, I got the notice from my good neighbors on the Draft Board that I'd be reporting to Camp Dix. Like other late teen-agers, I asked for ASTP, which sounded like a real good deal—"Special Training," just the thing. We'd be sent to college to study engineering and wind up becoming the gurus of push-button warfare. We'd be wearing these clean GI lab coats and sitting behind some big plastic machine with all kinds of buttons, gauges, and lights; no bullets to dodge, none of the muddy fox-hole stuff. Hardly a week would go by that we didn't finger another battalion of Germans to be rubbed out, and, like the Air Corps, we'd never hear a scream. While getting ourselves prepared for all that, we'd be living it up like fun-loving college boys. Most of us came from Depression poor families, who would find it kind of hilarious for us kids to think they could send us to college, when there were times when they had trouble coming up with the rent money.

So we said, ASTP here we come! First, though, the Army insisted on making soldiers of us. We'd really *need* that?—considering? Oh well, a short six weeks. We were sent to Fort Benning, Georgia, home of the Infantry School, for a proper stint of basic training, which we had to really hump ourselves to get through. But a funny thing happened when basic was over. The Army changed its mind about push buttons. Somebody must have finally asked what the hell were they thinking. (In fact, what were *we* thinking?) Anyway, a light went on, and some genius must have seen that for the time being they would probably have a greater need for warm bodies than cool brains. It was the Army, after all. So they sent us to join stateside infantry divisions, located in the boondocks of the sultry South; safe outfits to be held back for post-war occupation duty. Not as good as college, but just the assignment for us, after shovelin shit

8

in Louisiana for the duration. The last thing to occur to us was that these pseudo-divisions would turn out to be available replacement pools—an educational experience that you woke up to only when it was too late to think about trying for an alternative, like, say, the Signal Corps, where we supposed we could guard a radio tower, or, better yet, man a strategic light-house somewhere in Maine.

It bolstered our confidence to hear the older guys complain, because most of us kids felt we had shown that we'd be able to cut it physically if faced with the real thing. We had no idea where those older ones had shipped in from when they joined the division, or what kind of basic they might have had, but throughout training—except for Rebel—they sure had a time of it keeping up. Hearing them bitch, we saw ourselves as rough and ready, even poised for combat, if it came to that, knowing how the mindless Army tended to change its mind. Hey, we might just have the guts to defy danger; when called upon, assault an enemy stronghold—or what have you. After all, as we obnoxiously let people know, we'd taken the training prescribed by the Mother of all foot soldiers, *the* Infantry School, where we'd done more than one staged assault, with live ammo too.

Before long, we found ourselves secretly looking forward to the adventure of actually going to war, imagining we'd be like guys in the movies, cheek to rifle butt, firing away as we crawled forward on elbows and knees to lob a hand grenade at those square heads behind the machine gun emplacement. Many of us, like myself, were younger brothers, who had been treated like kids all their lives, and here was our chance to get some respect. Hell no; I didn't want to spend this War sitting behind a big plastic machine, now that they said we wouldn't be. I had an aunt who, every time she visited, kept calling me the baby of the family, with an "Oh My," of late, surprised that the baby had grown up. For me, it became more than a way to assert my manhood. Yes, I wanted to be taken seriously, but, if so, I had to *be* serious, and about one thing I was. As I thought about how, had my parents stayed in Europe, they might have been dispatched to some concentration camp, there was enough raw animosity in me to want to be a for-real part of this thing. I had reason to be thankful for America, and grateful to be an enviable citizen thereof.

Besides, from the war movies we had seen, we picked up the notion that it was always the 'other guy' who got killed. There was this vision of fearless John Wayne urging the troops forward, "Come on, you guys; let's go get 'em." Hero that he was, he could wipe out the enemy single handed, and wind up with nary a flesh wound. You did earnestly believe it was the likes of good ol' long John who were going to win this damned war for us—the rest of us tagging along. Not quite as inspiring was the fact that he himself was sitting it out, so he could show us how to get it done. He said he regretted that. So did we.

The impression we took from war movies didn't greatly change until we got a taste of what an unglamorous thing combat was, cringing under fire, crawling past white-faced buddies, lips clotted with blood, thinking we might be next. We would have a different attitude toward a lot of things, especially when it came to all the talk about "heroes." As if you were one just for getting passively killed by virtue of being there, the miserable so-called heroism of which could be measured by how cowardly scared you were, thinking you might get yourself sawed open by enfilading machine gun fire, legs torn off by a mine, or had your guts ripped out by shrapnel. If, in a fire-fight you happened to hit some poor, weary, beat-up son of a bitch like yourself, you were not amazed that you didn't give it a thought. War was like that—impersonal. Most of the time, all you could say was you'd been there, went into the attack when called upon, got beat up like the rest of the guys, and, luckier than most, made it out.

When I looked back on those dreamy times, and all the bitching about the Army, in particular the complaints of the older guys, it seemed nothing short of amazing—indeed impossible—to imagine how combat experience would change us.

2.

I was able to get home on a two-day pass. My folks were glum and tight-lipped. It didn't cheer them up much when I said I was lucky to be going to Europe instead of the Pacific. Ma, who was a great instinctive cook, prepared her tastiest roast chicken dinner, nicely browned, the bird rubbed with just the right touch of butter and garlic. Along with it, she prepared one of my favorite treats, potato pancakes. She was so good at spicing—never too much—that Pa said she could be a French chef. He poured the wine and we clinked glasses somewhat more solemnly than on other occasions. Ma plied me with one goody after the other, bacon and cheese omelets, tuna salad, even a dish she didn't care for herself, like lintel soup loaded with peppers and onions. Unfortunately, there wasn't a lot I could do to raise their spirits. Little as they were impressed by my telling them I was really fit and ready to go over, they accepted it. There was much warmth just in our being together. I briefly visited some friends, who wished me well. We'd hoisted a few, talked about people we knew and what they were doing, like my cousin with an Infantry Division in the South Pacific, wounded a third time and coming home. The second day was gone before I knew it.

Pa kept saying, "Take care of yourself," as they walked me to the bus stop. His pigeon-toes seemed to point in more than I'd noticed before, though he walked, as always, with his head erect. Ma kept blowing her nose, and looking up at me over her handkerchief. Her brown eyes were bigger and rounder than usual, and they were red. She had a cold and hadn't been able to get much sleep. The old man gave me a bear hug at the bus stop, and I could feel the power of his shoulders and the girth of his barrel chest. Ma kissed me on the cheek. Dear mother that she was, she kept running her hand over the back of my head, as if to put a charm on it that might keep anything from going in there.

They were God's own people. I'd do anything for them, and they anything for me. But somehow we'd never been able to talk much to one another. In their day, worried as they might be, adults didn't share their thoughts with the kids, who were left pretty much to fend for themselves, and find their own way. That's how it had been with their own upbringing. Which didn't mean they were unconcerned about what went on with the kids.

They were immigrants, able to come here because they had skilled trades, my Dad as a silk warper, and my Mother as a cuff-setter, both expert at what they did, and hard workers, who never complained about being exploited—as they were, long hours at meager pay, like dawn to dusk farmhands they'd known in the old country. My mother's first job in this country was with the infamous Triangle Shirt Company, less than a year before they had the fire that killed all those boxed-in women. Depression hardened, they understood adversity, and, being frugal, they were proud that they didn't have to go on Relief, as was the case with some relatives. As a boy, I was fully aware of what it meant to be poor, but I'm afraid I didn't appreciate what it took for them to keep us afloat. It bothered me that they weren't very tall, spoke with an accent, and didn't look very American. My best friend was the boy across the street, only child in a well-off family, his father a judge. When I'd come home talking about things like Thanksgiving turkey and Christmas presents, my mother thought it would be better if I found other kids to play with. When I grew up, I knew the shame was on me for having felt ashamed of them.

There was no scene at the bus stop. They had guts, were stoical in their way, and likely didn't want me to feel bad. I thought they looked smaller yet than the last time I'd been with them. As they stood there holding one another, Pa in his shirtsleeves, the wind blowing his hair, almost white now, and Ma in her green cardigan and kerchief over her head, I thought I'd never seen two lonelier people in all my life. They didn't move. I kept waving to them from the back window of the bus, until they disappeared behind parked cars. My eyes were moist.

3.

In the one conversation we had of any length, Pa said he didn't want me to shirk anything, but he wondered how come, if the Army thought I was smart enough to be sent to college, they wouldn't let me try for something a leg up from being a lowly infantryman, there being technical skills I could train for, where I might better serve the war effort. I told him it happened to a whole bunch of kids, many of them brainier than me, who were now regarded as cannon fodder. He didn't get it. I told him no one understood the Army. The Army didn't understand itself.

Wanting to soften things, I explained that we fortunately acquired the ability to laugh at the impossible situations we'd find ourselves in, even when painful. Hurry up and wait was but a minor nuisance. When we stood in ranks for hours waiting to get loaded on the train taking us to Shanks, with those eighty pound packs getting heavier by the minute, out came the inevitable call, "Get these troops out of the hot sun."—which could be heard in darkness or rain, as well. For Pa's sake, I played up how well trained we were, that we'd come out of Fort Benning tough, rugged and nasty, a match for anything. I knew he didn't buy my assurances. Nor did I tell him the real reason I was put on orders.

The fact that it was Europe when I expected the Pacific had much to do with my initial excitement about getting into the real thing, that is, once I got over the shock of seeing my name on the list. That graveled me more than anything, because, as I watched the lists being posted every month—sometimes twice a month—I noticed it was mostly the fuck-ups that got put on. It was Pappy, old Sergeant Roberson, who decided our fate; justly or unjustly decided, he never felt he had to give a reason. If you summoned the courage to ask, that could get you gone a little quicker. Talk about guys too old for this stuff, if you looked at Pappy when he was tired, the toothless bastard looked like a withered old hag. He was just prime when he came into the latrine to shave late Sunday morning, with his thin patch of sandy hair screwed up into a baby curl, his slit eyes, half-moon chin mottled with gray stubble, and his small paunch hanging over a knotted towel.

We used to kid guys about finding a home in the Army; it looked like Pappy never knew another. You could almost feel sorry for him, and would if he weren't so lethal in the exercise of his power. He was our top-kick, after all, First Sergeant, wearing the all-potent three rockers and a diamond, meaning he ran the orderly room (indeed, the Company) for the Captain. He did all the paperwork for the Old Man (familiar for Captain), also his dirty work. He could give you an 'Atta-boy" one minute, and shaft you the next, which I was not the first to find out. All of the new Second Looeys toadied up to Pappy the first week they were in camp. He made a big to-do about taking them under his wing and Sir-ing them in an easy, familiar manner. The minute they got used to things and began to feel their rank and let Pappy know how things stood, his "Yes-Sirs" would be clipped off real short, and before they knew what was up, he'd have them shipped out. Platoon leaders—that is, Second Lieutenants—didn't last long on line.

For much of his skullduggery, Pappy relied on his crony and enforcer, none other than the notorious Kraut, Sergeant of our platoon, comprised of mortar and machine-gun squads. If you wanted a taskmaster to oversee recruits running the obstacle course and penalize laggards, Kraut was your man. He'd bark out commands that could make people jump at the far end of the Base. Believing Kraut thought well of me for a while (and, astonishingly, we'd find out there *was* another side to this guy), I failed to recognize that to make a mistake with him brought consequences from Pappy. Actually, I made a number of mistakes, one of which I got away with.

Every now and again, we'd have to do a forced march, in that merciless Louisiana sun, ten miles in two hours, loaded down with a full field pack, double-timing as needed, to get in under that second hour. Guys were barfing, wheezing, and hacking along the way— some, like Gino and Willie, plopping over to the side of the road —and then, around the wicked last fraction of a mile, Pappy would come trotting alongside our winded column, pumping his arm, when every shred of a run had long gone out of us. And there he was yelling, "Come-on, shag ass, men! Pick up the pace. That's it! You're doin good! Bring it on home now!" His style of encouragement, which was greatly appreciated by guys with chests on fire and legs about to buckle.

He even followed us—his mouth still moving—as we bolted for the showers fully clothed, our fatigues rimed with salt stains. Heads under water, we fortunately didn't hear much of what he was saying. What we gathered was that he wanted everyone to think we'd done well, as the forced march was considered his responsibility. But we also learned that Pappy was, off the record, telling Kraut (who could likewise forgo our fun and games) how straggly we looked coming in. Sad sacks that we were, how did we think we'd be ready to charge up a hill with fixed bayonets, the whole purpose of doing the damned thing in the first place? At least, we missed the stuff meted out to Gino and Willie, along with the others who didn't make it to the finish. After a day's rest, Kraut had them doing close-order drill till dark, calling out fast-change commands that were bound to have them tripping over one another. It went something like: "Detail! half right, march!; to the left flank, march!; to the right flank, march! Left oblique; march! *Ab-o-ut h-a-ce*! " And more of the same. Predictably, they'd get it wrong; so he'd call, "As you were"—with them not having the foggiest idea of where they were by then. When they thought they finally had it right, he'd have them take it one last time. On his finally calling for them to fall out, some guys literally did.

Talk about exhaustion, we were told that the next forced march was going to put us in position to attack the enemy where he least expected it. On paper, it looked great. A tactic that Pappy said had been used by Napoleon. Just our thing. Standing in formation next morning, we had to listen to his commendation on the march just done (pure bullshit), given to impress old Stoneface, our non-participating Captain, who had a stake in how many of us finished the thing, the number to be reported up to Battalion. As Pappy went on about how well it would serve us one day, Gush Gaetters, the guy standing beside me, forced a very audible cough, and, without realizing it, I did the same.

We were mortar gunners, a level up from riflemen, and sometimes able to get away with things. Cherokee Gush, ol' Oklihoma, was number one, and a whiz when sober. He had the Injin smarts and was definitely not a guy you could call "Chief." Next to him, I was a distant two, and Gino an even more distant three. That cough could have earned us a week of KP, ten-hour shifts of scrubbing pots and pans. So, waiting to get the message, I was surprised when it didn't come, and even more surprised that our names hadn't come up on shipment. I found out that Kraut wanted us held back—penalty deferred—and, unbeknownst to me, he wanted both of us on hand, fearing that, after a week-end pass, Gush might, as usual, be hung-over the Monday that we were supposed to be putting on a dog and pony show for the new battalion commander, a Major, bucking for Lieutenant Colonel. Guess I was better than nothing. In Kraut's eyes, barely.

On the mortar demonstration, our field exercise required us— ideally—to put nine rounds up in the air so fast that the first one didn't land till the last one was out of the tube, whereupon we'd break down the mortar and head for the woods before return fire came in on us. Once we calculated the range, the pattern consisted of three rows of three, which meant two cranks to the left from the start, one crank up, three back to the right, etc. A neat trick, rarely accomplished. The danger of going at it so rapidly was that you might send a round or two of live ammo over on the units to either side of us.

As it turned out, when it came to crunch time, fabulous Gush was in ranks, but barely functional. His hands shook so, he took too long getting his mortar set up and leveled, and after putting those first three rounds in the air, he extended his arms in frustration and gave it up. The Major was standing on a hill behind us taking it in through field glasses. Perplexed at the sudden halt, he handed the glasses to an aide and asked for the radio. Suppressing a giggle, Pappy had Kraut tell him that we were just doing a trial run, to see how well this mortar would zero in for us, which was nonsense. The new Lieutenant whom our Captain had sent out to get his first taste of command, moseyed over and asked Pappy some questions, which he brushed off with a reassuring wave of the hand.

He looked around, and out popped Gino, in need of doing something positive to make up for past lapses. Gone was the backache. But when he got down, and felt Kraut leaning over him, he lost his nerve, and tipped the tube as Willie, our ammo man, dropped the first round in, which sent it careening off pretty close to our forward riflemen huddled in a clump of trees over to the right of us. Kraut dragged Gino away by the collar and shoved him back in the bushes. Seeing Willie beside the mortar, he gave him a look, but Willie lifted his canvas yoke to show he was just the ammo bearer. Pappy then went for Rebel, but he backed away, saying he "ain't never done that stove pipe," and walked back to his machine gun. Pappy went palms up to Kraut, who, getting madder by the minute, was even more agitated when he looked around, and seeing Gush was in no better shape, pointed to me, the hopeless back-up. He spat, looked at Pappy a minute, said, "What the hell," and turned his back.

Pappy, who was giving the Lieutenant a line about these boys not getting out on the range often enough, said he kept telling the Captain dry runs weren't doing them a lot of good. "But we got another one here who's been out before. First rate. Watch him bring 'em in." At first, I thought he hadn't looked close enough and was mistaking me for Gush, but then I could see that he was simply doing his thing. He prided himself that he could make these green officers believe whatever he told them, and soon as they swallowed one line, he'd feed them another. If I messed up…, well, no sweat; he'd handle it.

As it turned out, the performance of Gush and Gino got my adrenalin going. I quickly hunched myself down and decided I'd pull it off the way ol' Gush-the-Lush did on his good days. I took a quick reading on the stake, and, looking in the sight, I was determined to forget hair-line accuracy; no need to keep the bubble cleanly centered. I'd just keep a-crankin and yellin "Fire!" to Willie, who had the nine shells neatly lined up and nodded that he'd be fast. And, by God, I did it, got 'em all up, and was dismantling when we saw the first puff of black smoke appearing noiselessly in the upper right corner of the target area, followed by the Ka-chunk, about which time number two fell some twenty yards to the left of it, and so on, real tight. It was a coup, the text-book pattern. Up on the hill, the Major was flashing a thumbs-up. Kraut was dumbfounded. So was I. It was also the start of my downfall; of his too.

Gush was instantly gone on KP, and for my performance, Kraut was willing to give me a bye. However, Captain Smith was skeptical about what had happened out in our sector of the field. He'd never heard of it being done. He had been off watching a more dramatic exercise—a line of infantry advancing on an enemy hill behind a screen of creeping artillery fire, which, like the mortar show, was part of our preparation for up-coming maneuvers. Though Smith might have thought it was a fluke, from Pappy's bluster about me having pulled off the "Nine-Up" drill, I got the impression I'd suddenly been elevated to top gunner. Stupidly, I began to feel a little cocky, and was late getting into formation the day after we returned to camp, falling in embarrassingly after Kraut had snapped off his salute to Captain Smith and reported, "Fourth Platoon all present and accounted for, Sir." On that one, there was no tolerance for 'almosts'

I went on KP for the week I owed, during which time Smith, still shaking his head, decided to order a repeat performance on the mortar, and he wanted it "Right now." When told where I was, he naturally wondered: This gunner did so well, and they have him on KP? Pappy got out from under the Captain's wrath by blaming Kraut, who took a considerable chewing out. The problem was compounded by their not being able to find me, as I'd been sent down to the Quartermaster Commissary for spuds and stuff, including the meat that would turn up in our billy-goat stew, which it took them a while to scare up, me taking a little snooze as I waited in the three-quarter ton truck. Since I'd pulled the truck into the shade of a big oak, they couldn't find me at first. So, more time elapsed.

That's when things started getting a little crazy. Just after Kraut's hearing it from Smith, he gave Pappy the arched eyebrows, which the Captain caught out of the corner of his eye, and Pappy tactfully ignored, his head arched back in sublime indifference. Obviously, no help there, so Kraut understood he'd be going it alone. The Captain began to suspect Kraut was putting him on about the whole deal; damned if he hadn't hid me in the kitchen. And—come to find out—I wasn't even there! So, hackles up, he went at Kraut a second time, a lot hotter, threatening to break him, something he'd long been hankered to do. Kraut made the mistake of snidely suggesting that he check with the Major, which got him one mean finger-shaking rebuke inches from his nose, as Smith icily reamed him out in a low hissing voice, lips twisted to the side.

For Kraut, that burst the dam. Tomato-red in the face, and barely able to conceal his hatred for this civilian fraud of an officer, he shouts an exaggerated "Yes-SIR!" and does a hasty about-face, not even feigning the requisite salute.

Nor does it stop there. First, he lets off steam to Pappy, saying just once, he'd like to give it right back to Smith, calling him every name in the book, fully aware that the Captain's orderly is standing right behind him. Then, still having some fury to work off, he looks at his watch, and claims I'm taking advantage of my gold-brick chore and might indeed have gone A-Wall. "Where the hell's the fuckin truck!" Actually, I'd taken the long way back. Without consulting Pappy—no less Smith—Kraut orders the MPs to go look for me. That was the last straw. … The list went up next day. We didn't even have to look for our names.

4.

The ferry gave a quick little toot—just enough to say, 'Here we go'—and with a low rumble of the engine, it quivered and began to ease out into the River. It reminded you of an overgrown turtle and moved like one, sliding past the black pilings edged with barnacles and green moss, which I couldn't see, but knew from my childhood, when we'd gone by train to Jersey City, then by ferry to the Canal Street pier on Manhattan and took the subway to Coney Island. I always managed to get myself a place at the folding iron gate, where I could taste the fresh salt air and feel the hissing spray on my face, as the old tub pushed at the water with its nose. The ferry ride was one of the high points of our excursions, along with the walk beside the train up to the puffing steam engine, and the wave to the engineer wearing a red bandana. But, nostalgic images flitted out of my mind as I looked out the mouth of this thing from the gloom of its belly, feeling like I was wedged in a moving cave. I tried to dismiss the sense of hovering doom, and thought instead of being snugly safe in the fox-holes we dug on maneuvers, when, dog tired, it was so good to take the smell of the earth to sleep with you.

The heavy August sun, a juicy red plumb, which appeared to be a foot high when we de-trained at Weehawken had slipped away behind us. A dark blue haze had fallen over the River, and, for the time being, I was almost pleased to be part of the olive-drab mass enclosing me. I couldn't have told you then why I felt that way; I still can't, looking back on that day. I wasn't sure how the others felt—you couldn't go by what they said, or didn't say—but, if you thought about it, there had to be some security in all of us standing together like that. It couldn't be that we were *all* going get killed. Little did we know that the outfit we would be joining lost almost a thousand men in a training exercise off the southern coast of England, months before they did the D-Day landing, a disaster kept secret for many years thereafter. A thousand guys gone, just like that. We'd find out on our own how meaningless loss of life was—all the more so if it was large scale.

In the waiting stage, as time lengthened, you had your ups and downs. You couldn't help feeling anxious, however much you tried to stay confident. I knew I was in better shape than the older guys and— great on push-ups—probably stronger than the average of the younger ones. Besides I wanted to be part of the Times, very particularly of the defining Event of the Times. I didn't think the others felt that way; like I said, it was hard to know what any of them felt. It was just that, among ourselves, the war wasn't talked about because there was nothing to be said about it. You surely couldn't get anybody to talk about the importance of what we were doing. It seemed like for most guys those "Why We Fight" movies afforded us a time to relax from the weariness of training, and be entertained, unless maybe the guys didn't care for the big talk about Nazis, and such, that they'd already heard too much of. We had a better recollection of movies like the one that warned us about venereal diseases, the showcase picture of which featured some long-faced guy, looking like he just walked out of a fun-house mirror, with a huge pear-shaped nut hanging down to the floor, which they called elephantiasis.

Unlike the single-minded Germans, we didn't have anything like a sense of Cause. Many probably felt we shouldn't be fighting the Germans. Luckily, we had no trouble going after the sneaky Japanese, so ugly looking and easy to hate. Only America—dear America—could fight a war, and, while giving its blood and riches, make like it really didn't know a whole lot of what it was about. Take a guy like Willie. An easy laugher and as amiable a person as you'd want to meet. There were times when I honestly thought the only things that got to him were canned peaches (best if "sweet ol' Elberties from Arkinsaw") and moon-shine ("You sure's hell better know somebody if'n you're thinkin bout goin up into them hills."). He had some great yarns about trapping, one about a lynx that chewed off his paw to get away. He used to get specimens of female urine derived from various animals—no telling how—that he'd sell at a premium, and, between the piss and the moonshine, he'd made himself a comfortable living. With help from the home folks, he tried to keep his businesses going long distance. When Rebel wanted to know if he ever got the two mixed up, Willie gave him a quizzical look and asked, "Y'all never heard of panther-piss?"

Willie and I liked to josh one another. I asked him one day, with all the stuff we'd been put through, how come there was almost nothing he couldn't slough off. "Well, we jess go easy on life back home," was his twanged response. "There er times guys jess sit around an drink beer 'n tell lies." He asked me how come I was always so serious, and I told him it was because I came from the agitated East, where life didn't go easy on *us*.

We exchanged mirthless Ha-Ha's. Then, he paused for a minute, his eyes narrowing, and he adopted a measured tone, saying, it made no difference what life was like where we came from. "Hell, we're all in it together now, and ain't nobody kin do anything about what's happenin, but, when the shootin starts 'n things git bad, we kin make some good happen if we stand by one another." He couldn't know how that got to me. From early on, I had felt that our family didn't quite measure up as "Americans." I often found myself wanting to share the feeling of belonging that came so naturally to others. I realized I had underestimated Willie, and probably the country as well. After all, Willie *was* the country. Outwardly, he might seem shallow, but that would fool you. You didn't have to go much beyond the ordinary with him to find out that he had a wholesome attitude toward his fellow man. We did indeed naively intend to look out for one another and meant it—-without having the foggiest idea of how in combat such a thing might play out.

While waiting for the train, we had kept hearing, "The train ain't come yet." As the ferry slowed down to dock, some wag was saying, "Our ship ain't come yet. They musta lost it on the way back." "Good," said another guy. "New York's the easiest place to get lost in at night." Things surprisingly seemed to be getting very dark, until we realized that we were moving along a solid black wall. It curved outward, and for a minute it looked like this monstrous thing might fall on us, if our ferryboat pilot didn't—come-on now, fella—move it—umph—a little more to this side. Then somebody yelled out, "It's the fuckin ship! A biggie." And one endless biggie it was. We were in the first embarkation "wave," and, from the size of the hull, it seemed that there was going to be a parade of ferries coming across behind us. Rebel thought they should have started us over two days ago.

As we marched out onto the pier, we saw it was somewhat lighter out than we'd thought. We came off blinking and found ourselves on the broad dock area spread out in front of a huge gray shed, likely a warehouse for goods in-coming and out-going. We saw a WAC band playing before we became aware of the brassy music. There were four rows of girls, and they were going at it pretty hard, their cheeks all puffed out like rubber dolls. They were mostly on the heavy side, thick in the neck and shoulders, and their tunics fit tightly across their chests. From a distance, they looked like men in skirts. They were playing "God Bless America," and, God bless them anyway, they put the kind of spirit into it that gives you the royal tinglies.

When they were finished, we went through a line where the Red Cross was handing out little canvas bags with toilet articles. (Oh, well, why fault good intentions?) We walked up to a desk, gave the Lieutenant our names, which he checked off on his list, and had a number placed on our helmets. We formed a long line at the edge of the pier and got our first real look at the ship, which was moored at the dock neighboring ours. The damned thing looked as if it would stretch all the way back to Weehawken. Willie confessed he'd never seen a ship before, except in pictures, and, taking her in slowly from end to end, he pushed his helmet back to mop his brow.

"Man, oh Man," he said, as if talking to himself, "Won't that thing haul a load of hay."

It was the "Queen Elizabeth," all 83,000 tons of her, the biggest hunk of metal afloat, and what a load of troops it would haul—us to be stashed in a jungle of hammocks down in D Deck, torpedo junction. Could a U-Boat miss a thing that size?

25

As we were being herded into the big warehouse affair, Gino managed to slip back to see who all were being checked in. Actually, he was curious to see if he could find one guy in particular and ran into another, of all things, Gush, who, we had somehow forgotten, was clearly vulnerable. Gush happened to be the one guy among us that Kraut would talk to, as he had some respect for him, and often tended to favor him, as with a week's KP lasting just a couple of days. He'd say he needed him back for training purposes. Gush was thought to be half Cherokee (though he claimed three-quarters, counting a half-breed Okie grandpa) and generally a quiet sort, unless riled. Then his eyes would take on an oriental cast and his leathery face, bronzed by a combination of Louisiana sun and firewater, would tighten and you knew he was out for somebody's scalp, and were glad it wasn't yours. Everyone wanted to be Gush's friend. Gino pumped him for information and came back with the mother lode.

First of all, he was so mad at Pappy for putting him on orders after telling him otherwise that Gush came for him at five in the morning of the day we were leaving, dragged him out of a warm bed, and, before the blear-eyed old bastard knew what was up, Gush horse-whipped him with his own belt. He was certain Pappy (also from the South) knew the rules of honor well enough that he'd take the indignity of a whipping as more hurtful than if Gush had up and punched him out. Here on the dock, Gush had been ducking every time he saw an MP, and, getting out of the way of one, he bumped into another that Kraut was jawing with, which was how they made contact.

Regarding Kraut, Gino learned that at Shanks, he looked over the roster of officers and found just the one he wanted, a Captain in the Adjutant General Corps with a long German name beginning with 'Von.' Kraut's big mad was over finding out that he *had* indeed been broken and, as buck private, was given the MOS of rifleman. Loosening up this aloof Captain by talking German to him, he related how he'd been sandbagged and by whom, and what he wanted was for Kraut-2 to get him his old rank and salary back, and, as one homey Geheimrath to another, Kraut thought he could rely on its getting done. He had raised holy-hell when he found he was being checked in here as a buck private, but that was the least of his problems. Through the grapevine, Kraut found out that Pappy had blamed *him* for the whipping, and, it seemed like once they caught up with him, he'd surely be brought up on charges. And who would the prosecutor *be* handling military justice in his case, but some Adjutant General's Warrant Officer wanting to impress his Captain. And hadn't Kraut given his Kraut Captain information that could be used against him? That answered one question. Like it said in the song: "There'll be no more promotions this side of the ocean."

But the grapevine was thankfully faster than the bureaucracy, so, when the MP got tired of Kraut's yak about missing official papers and walked off, Gush exchanged numbered helmets with Kraut—just in case, to confuse the AG's long enough for the two of them to be beyond reach. Gush convinced him that, instead of fruitlessly fighting the thing, it'd be better for him to be going over as a buck private than to be doing time at Leavenworth. Kraut raised his arm to shake a pointless fist at the MP post, but, faced with the dishonorable alternative, if recognized, he let it drop. Never did anyone see that guy so dispirited. Gino said he'd never be the same. Privately, I recalled how at Shanks I'd gotten up in the middle of the night to piss and saw a guy sitting on the edge of his cot holding his head in his hands and muttering to himself. I thought it looked like Kraut, but ignored it. Bringing it back, I knew it *was* him, which told me

27

there was a real person underneath all that outrageous bluster about soldiering.

Continuing with his story, Gino pointed out there was one big thing about Gush that, in the confusion of all this, we tended to forget: more than anything else, Gush was fiercely loyal; once a friend, always a friend. Still it was an eye-opener when Gush assured Kraut that, should they come for him, he'd tell them *who* truthfully did the whipping. Kraut would have none of it. However, it was clear that Kraut was the one Pappy wanted, and, as victim, Pappy would surely deny it was Gush. If Gush intervened, they'd be giving Pappy a two-for: Kraut court-martialed on felonious assault, and Gush on false testimony. A real bind.

Having had a look at Kraut, Gino said he seemed resigned (for maybe the only time in his life) but also moved and, for him, almost humbled by Gush's wanting to help. To lift any sense of guilt on Gush's part, Kraut maintained that one way or another he'd have wanted Pappy whipped, and would indeed have done it himself. Before God, if not the law, that made him guilty, didn't it? Gush had told us we didn't know how often Kraut and Pappy quarreled—like over Pappy's insisting on those forced marches which he didn't have to do. Gush said Kraut told him it was usually after he'd come from an ugly session with Pappy that he'd go pretty hard on us. (Maybe, but, as we saw it, he sure seemed to get his kicks out of it, anyway.)

Gino said that, seeing Gush's face untypically lined with anxiety, he wanted us to help him and Kraut both. "For Gush's sake, couldn't we have Kraut kinda join us, and, when guys asked, we could tell 'em why. Like, ever know a GI who would take the rap for somethin somebody else did?"

Rebel put a hand up and said, "Hold on." There was no sense in Gino letting his soft Dago heart get in the way of reality. Some guys

28

might be looking for a little pay-back, and it wouldn't be smart for us to get in the middle of that. With or without us, Kraut was going to have to watch his back. As we batted the thing this way and that, Willie brought us back to Gino's point that we had to stand fast with Gush *and* Kraut, since, when the AG guys got to the bottom of what happened to Pappy, Gush would be wanted for protecting Kraut, in which case, like it or not, we'd need Kraut to protect Gush. ... So we couldn't take one without the other, huh?

We groaned. Finally, Rebel conceded that under fire it might be good to have somebody around with military know-how. Willie agreed with that. "Who knows we might jess be savin a guy who could save our asses." It was beginning to look like there might be six of us bonded in a way we could never have expected, which had Willie marveling that—hallelujah—we found a reason to appreciate the formerly most hateful guy we knew, and for what lies ahead we might be glad we did. We wound up laughing at ourselves. Instead of Kraut feeling queasy over having to put up with us, it was the other way around. Life in the Army doesn't get much stranger. Or so we thought.

For his part, Rebel remained skeptical, reminding us that once we sailed out of here, there were still going to be guys who couldn't wait for the chance to hoist this bastard overboard. From what we just agreed on, were we supposed to be looking out for him? We were relieved when Willie indicated we wouldn't have to. Who could find him among the thousands of hammocks stacked maybe five high in the bowels of that monster ship?

Gino couldn't resist asking Kraut what was in his damned duffel bag.

"Oh that," he said with a wistful smile, "I'd stuffed it with a field jacket, fatigue tops and OD shirts that had my old sergeant's strips on them. I asked the MP to see if he couldn't find the bag and kick it in the River. He told me to find it myself. He was lookin for some guys with gang-plank fever."

5.

Looking back, it hurt to think of how unfalteringly innocent we were. The fact is, at the time, we couldn't know that innocence might become our best defense against losing our minds. For one thing, we had no idea that there could be casualties on the way over and the way up. Nor did we think such things would be considered routine, something you didn't get worked up over, much as it sobered you, even if you knew the guys who went down. We couldn't believe the returnees, who would matter-of-factly tell us, 'You get over it.'

Standing in formation back at Shanks, as we waited to entrain, we'd had the Articles of War read to us (stuff like, no more than name, rank, and serial number, if captured), much of which just flew by like leaves in a storm. Our thoughts were consumed with 'what's next?' But we faintly recognized the voice coming out to us in the pre-dawn darkness as that of First Lieutenant Hurley, Executive Officer of our old outfit, a stocky, knuckle-cheeked Irishman, thick in the chest, and known to all as Hurley-Burley. Graduate of a South Carolina military college, he was sick of make-believe, and impatient to join the real Army, in the field, where he could apply his misused training. He was also not a little perturbed about being four years in grade with no foreseeable prospect of a move up. Being steeped in Army know-how, he was all too useful to Stoneface to be given his wish, which kept being promised and withdrawn each time his name went up on orders, until, Pappy showed him how to write his own orders. He had much in common with Kraut, both being cut from the same mold: ingrained discipline a

30

way of life. And, knowing how Kraut had been shafted, HB continued to treat him as the two-rocker sergeant he'd known him as. Kraut, for his part, obviously had good reason to be seen with HB, who, being the lone officer in our group, liked having somebody to talk to.

Over by the big hangar doors where we'd been assembled, the two of them were having a little confab that Willie and I caught the drift of. Kraut had been asking how the German subs could let this big prize get by unharmed, loaded to the portholes with upwards of ten thousand troops—which was what all the rest of us were wondering about. For the naïve likes of us (surprisingly Kraut too), HB's ideas about the world of arms were the kind of things we were eager to hear—and sorry we did.

HB was saying the Army goes by an unspoken attrition ratio. In any given operation, it is understood that there will be a certain percentage of losses, officially under-counted, unofficially over-counted by realists. HB disagreed with the commonplace that in the attack, expectations of your losses required nothing less than a three to one advantage. Montgomery insisted on a greater number, and, though he was ridiculed for that (by officers who hadn't been there), HB thought he had it right. He pointed to the Normandy invasion, where Big Brass deliberately sent in an outfit green as grass, instead of veterans of North Africa who knew what it was like for an outfit to get mauled. The Green Boys sustained losses that reached an outrageous ninety-five percent. One hell of an attrition ratio. But nobody's going to *talk* about ratios, so long as the mission's accomplished.

HB was going on about the losses suffered at the St. Lo breakthrough, where the Green Division was greener yet, its ranks almost totally replaced and decimated all over again, when Kraut interrupted, "What the hell are you scarin the shit out me for?!" He wanted to know, "Dammit, what about us?"

31

"Well, on a troop ship, especially one this size, it's different. On land, we could afford to lose a fair number goin up, but on the high seas, it'd be the whole shebang, a disaster. The few that fall overboard are gone the minute they hit the water. Truly, a spit in the ocean. No way, this thing's going to turn around and pick up four or five goofballs floppin around out there, with minutes to live anyway."

"Sounds like the Army. Ever know it to go back and correct a mistake? Admit one?"

"Agreed. But it's every army, and it's warfare. Listen, the best generals won big, because they lost big. Napoleon was a butcher and so was Grant. Fact is, we've got another runnin loose. Hell, tryin to avoid flak, our Air Corps drops five hundred pounders on us at St. Lo, and it gets a shrug. So, some men are lost in transit? Wouldn't surprise anybody, wouldn't faze anybody."

"Wouldn't trouble you? I mean if it happens with us? Here?"

HB couldn't resist a little laugh. "Look, Big Brass One, the guy with the winning smile, wants replacements for the push over the Rhine, and he has to have a certain attrition ratio in mind. Do you think the loss of a few GI's here or there means squat? I'm not all that sure I'm gonna last very long."

Kraut was somewhat taken aback. "So you mean what's gonna be lost in the big push might be the size of us in this tub?"

"And then some. They always go back for more. And, like I'm saying, nobody—for sure not Big Brass—thinks this package has to get there attrition-free. Even if there's no free floatin booze, it takes no more than the usual boredom, recklessness, and yah lose a few."

Hearing him, Willie gives me the elbow. "And I thought, where we're goin, this guy'd be the kind o' platoon leader you'd want to soldier with."

All I could say was, "Yeah, scary. But don't yah think he knows what he's talking about?"

"Aw, bullshit. He ain't been there yet, has he?"

The big hangar doors had been opened giving us a view of the cordon of MPs, with their conspicuous white helmet liners, positioned along the line of march that would be taking us to the Big Boat. Pointing to the street end of the pier, HB asked Kraut to have a look at that pyramidal tent down there. "You happen to see the three Blacks they rounded up? Got 'em penned up in there."

"So *those* are the guys? The ones with the gang-plank fever?"

"Haven't seen any in ranks, have you? They'll be our first losses."

It turned out—as we'd learn from Gush—that Stoneface was in such a tizzy over the loss of HB that Pappy felt he had to find a way to pacify him, and, knowing what he thought of Blacks, he reached over to the Commissary and latched onto these three guys, who he claimed had delayed me and deprived Stoneface of the mortar demonstration. Pappy got their names put on orders, where everyone knew they had no reason to be. But, once on, try to take them off. Their best efforts at getting it done were bogged down in red tape. Pappy finessed the matter—actually complicated it—by putting them down as cooks. In the segregated Army, HB knew that, whatever assignment was given to them, their presence, among us, would make trouble for them. Rebel pointed out that he'd grown up with Blacks. He said he'd met these three guys and found them the most congenial fellas you'd want to know. Whatever merit there was to their appeal—a loser as waged by the Chaplain—it was doomed by their having made a break for it when they were sent over to the Twenty-Third Street Armory for a whole new issue of clothes, shelter halves, shoes, packs, and the rest of it, gear they'd never use.

33

The conversation came to an abrupt end, when commands were suddenly sounded out over a bull horn that had units identified and marched out in columns onto the street and across to the other pier. Once they started clearing us out, it went pretty fast. The clipped commands and sound of GI shoes marching in cadence soon worked its way back to us, and off we went past the MPs, looking strangely suspicion-prone and making you feel you couldn't cough, but they'd pull you out for questioning. All told it was about as fast as we'd ever seen the Army move. At the pace they had us going, we figured the guys up ahead were probably being blown on board the way a cargo of wheat is hosed into the hold of a ship.

Out of nowhere, comes the order for our column to be dispatched past a line of pyramidal tents and turned into a squared off area covered by bands of tarpaulin strung up on posts, much like how officers' latrines were sectioned off on maneuvers. Our first thought was it was sick bay hastily enlarged. Some guys had picked up the social disease? A number of us had, after all, been on leave. Anyway, before we knew what was up, we were at attention, eyeballs straight ahead, and were ordered to bring our canteens out for inspection.

Canteens? As we learned once on shipboard, there was more to the story of why Pappy was able to get these Black guys shipped out. He had to have had help, and he did. It seems the Commissary was stuck with an over-supply of raisins (whole bags of the wrinkly stuff from a California supplier with connections) that were supposed to be used for rice pudding, which we GIs detested and the cooks hated to make. Some Joker finds out about it, and has Willie give the Blacks his six-day fermentation formula for making up a batch of raisin-jack, which, when prime, said Joker puts into a whole bunch of canteens. He has done favors for Pappy, and, an opportunist, he thinks the Blacks can be of use to him, all of which comes out later.

Well, there we were, our heads spinning (What now?), as the Blacks were brought into our little compound and asked to point out the culprit. They said they never heard of any such guy, no less who might have put the jack into canteens. Furthermore, looking at us, they couldn't identify anybody they could see. Like they kept saying, they weren't Infantry.

The pissed-off MP Captain hauls some guys out of ranks at random, but none of those he questions knows anything about jack, which gets us a chewing out. ("You mean you dog-assed stupid sons-o-bitches never took a sip from your canteens all this time?!") One after the other of our canteens pours out water. Whoever distributed the jack was clearly unfindable, probably laughing it up, already stowed away somewhere in the hold of that monster ship. We got another collective chewing out and were sent back into line for boarding. It wasn't long before the jack would begin to work its mischief.

6.

As the ship pulled out, we were standing at the rail, sandwiched in pretty close by the crowd that had come up to have their goodbye look at New York, maybe the last we'd see of the good old U.S. of A. The tugs pulling from behind looked like bull dogs on a triple leash, while two others were nuzzled in against our port-side bow to get us turned downstream. The guys were waving at sailors on a low gray cruiser docked at the next pier over. Soon the tugs left us and we were going under our own power, cutting ponderously into patches of soft haze, as if Big Boat One was ready to take on the rising sun itself, which flamed up the southeast windows dotting New York's renowned ridge-and-groove skyline. You couldn't help feeling a sense of importance sitting there on top of a duck that took up almost the whole damned pond. Our one moment of fame. How little we counted in the scheme of things. We heard the blast from a ship's horn behind us, followed by an answering basso blast from our own. As we stretched our way past Ellis Island and beyond the ever-beckoning arm of the Statue of Liberty, the guys waved frantically. Weren't we the greatest wavers?

One jack-happy waver who hoisted himself up on the rail to say good-bye lost his balance, and, teetering over, he took with him the guy who was half way up trying to pull him back. Waving all the way down, they made a mini-fountain splash and got a rousing cheer from their fellow happy-jackers, who were corralled and shoved down the nearest stairway.

In a funny kind of way, it seemed more like that landmark harbor had moved away from us than we from it. When it was gone, and all you had to remind you of land was the top of the Coney Island parachute jump and the low gray shadow of Long Island, we wondered where our escort was. We expected to see a flotilla of destroyers out there waiting to surround us with hoops of steel and stay with us stroke for stroke all the way across. Why was that cruiser *in there* instead of out here chasing subs? What good was that goofy Coast Guard plane flying low up ahead? A destroyer did materialize on the horizon, but what protection would that dinky little thing give us against the hidden treachery below?

One of the officers from Transportation Corps overheard us. (Imagine being assigned to this thing as a regular ferryboat-man— sailing over the Styx, every two weeks or so.) He said we could go almost thirty knots and were too fast for the subs. ('Oh yeah. You mean the clever Germans don't know how to lay in wait as we sail into the jaws of their down-and-dirty wolf pack?') This big ship, he went on, and her sister ship always crossed on their own because nothing else could keep up with them. They'd change course every mile or so, and zigzag their way over, so the subs couldn't draw a proper bead on them. A likely story. Willie was all for sleeping on deck under one of the lifeboats. He'd use his Mae West for a pillow.

Once land had vanished and we saw that we were all alone on the high seas unescorted (the destroyer on the horizon might have been a mirage), we gave ourselves up to chance, though not willingly. It was the same sick uncertainty that we took to bed with us every night down in D Deck, as if the packed-in quarters were not scary enough in themselves. There we were, crowded into a hot, sweaty hold, with lines of hammocks strung four high between pipe stanchions, and aisles no more than two feet wide. A perfect place to give up the ghost in, when we were making bubbles at the bottom of the sea. Through the whole trip, I'm sure some guys never really fell asleep. I was one of them.

Cooped up in this low narrow compartment, with steel doors at either end, some three hundred and fifty breathing bodies in a stuffy oversized Pullman car that couldn't have held a dead whale (though we could imagine it smelling like one) guys at first tried to amuse themselves by telling what it reminded them of. One guy said it made him think of a picture he'd seen of long racks of dead fish laid out to dry some place in Siam. Another guy said it felt more like a disaster center set up in the basement of a country church after a tornado, with all these tiers of hammocks bearing the sick, the homeless, the dead, and the crazy. If you happened to wake up in the middle of the night, you were glad to hear the snoring because otherwise you'd think you were on a slab in the morgue.

By the second day, we were bitching about every little thing. A Transportation Corps non-com, dropped checkers and dominoes on us, which went flying. Some jack had made its way into our area. So it didn't take much for us to be going at one another. Guys in the lowers would jounce those above them with their feet. We were forever knocking our heads against the pipes and cussing up a storm, and heaven help the fellow who got fallen on as he edged his way down an aisle to the latrine—always full. It quieted us a little when we learned that a couple of guys high on jack had tried to make their way up to the main deck, and, not knowing how treacherous pitching and rolling could be, they'd busted their heads against a bulkhead. Not discovered till morning. First casualties.

So there was the Casino. Given an impossible situation, leave it to some enterprising GIs to find a way out. It started with HB being asked to take charge of our unruly compartment. First thing he noticed was the three Blacks, out of place chocolate chips in the cookie dough, discovered to be even more out of place when they didn't show up on the roster. So, in light of their previous assignment, HB, hoping to keep the Blacks out of trouble's way, had them dispatched to the ship's commissary. Next door to it, there was a neat little cuddy for them to bed themselves down in.

Back on our former base, come payday, these guys were known to have set up the hottest of all-night poker games. When confidential protection was needed, in stepped Pistol Pete, none other than the Joker himself, not only the secret source of the on-board raisin jack (ten gallon water cans of it prepared by the Blacks, commandeered by Pete, and headed for stowage) but it was also known that, as our wily Supply Sergeant, he did a substantial business in military gear of whatever saleable description, anything from OD blankets to carbines. Typewriters didn't have a long shelf life. No one knew how he got on orders—to say nothing of his bringing along two Henchmen. He claimed he didn't know himself.

38

He just wanted to get in on the ground floor when good old Uncle Sam started dispensing post-war largess to our European friends and enemies. Everyone instinctively gave him a wide berth. From his swarthy complexion and low simian forehead, Gino thought he was a Sicilian, but was relieved to learn his origins were Middle Eastern. He laid claim to a descent from Phoenician merchants going back to biblical times. We were impressed even without the pedegree.

In any event, what started out as amicable nickel-dime poker games were escalated to quarter-ante and up. It got to be considerably up when Pete took over and began taking a ten percent cut on every pot (a piece of it said to be due the lookout, his T-Corpsman flunky, familiarly TC). The Blacks were more than chagrined at being crowded out. Roscoe, their anguished leader, strangely disappeared, when, hackles up, he questioned the cut and thought he was owed more than he got for the jack in the first place. (Hadn't Pete bragged it was the poor man's equivalent of Amarone, which retailed for a cool fifty bucks a bottle?) Pete's friend, Heavy Henchman, said Roscoe was learning how to swim. After Roscoe's two buddies got into a bare knuckles wingding with Pete, rescued by the crowbar-wielding Henchman, we were told they also wanted to be swimmers. The T-Corpsman gave us the line that it had always been anticipated there'd be swimmers among us. With his round face, narrow-set pig eyes, and king-shit attitude, this portly TC—anything but a regulation GI—was easy to dislike. He wanted us to know that, in fact, there were others—sore losers and winos—likely to be testing the water. Anyway, to silence the squawking, TC observed that since the Blacks weren't on our roster, they didn't officially count as casualties. Rebel, who was a pretty big guy himself, walked up to TC with the taunting question, "So, you're sayin what's the big deal, huh? Well, some of us think it ain't small either. Hope you didn't have anything to do with it, Bub."

But was any of this blather *true*? Could it be? Could it be that no one wanted to ask? Rebel and I did and got stiffed. I was finding that Rebel was a principled guy; his accent didn't make him a racist. Having lived and worked with Blacks all his life, and befriended these guys, he let it be known he'd make trouble if these guys had really been done in. Concern—never deep—was gone overnight. I wondered if the general indifference might be part of the hardening we'd heard about. Banking on our gullibility, Command made it clear: the matter was under investigation.

The hardening was not diminished when we learned about another version of what happened—namely, that the Blacks had gone over in the midst of a drunken brawl provoked by their own raisin jack. It wasn't easy to ignore the image of them being so hopelessly alone out there, caught in the icy grip of those dark waters, their screams unheard. How were we supposed to believe that in the dead of night some bastard among us would physically deliver fellow human beings to that kind of fate?

Of course, when the rumor mill started circulating other accounts of what happened, guys didn't know what to believe. TC assured us there was always the chance that at docking time the Blacks would turn up in some obscure cranny of the ship's hold.

Meanwhile, down in the commissary cuddy, from which the Blacks had been displaced, business was never brisker. Anything to get out of what had become our least favorite hell-hole. However, as word got out about the "Commotion," as it was called, and the combination of poker and jack was said to be its cause, the action had to be moved. Needing more than anything to distract ourselves from the futility of finding out the fate of the Blacks—to say nothing of our own—Willie, Gino and I decided we'd have a look. Henchman-1, recognizing jack-man Willie, took us to a companionway running down a steep flight, at the bottom of which he said we'd find ourselves in a cargo well, and if we climbed down a Jacob's ladder, we'd find someone stationed there. It was Henchman-2, who guided us along the corrugated steel passageway to a recessed wall light, where he pulled aside some barracks bags in what seemed a solid wall of them and nudged us into a low, brightly lighted area which looked like an oversized trench, well-sandbagged and reeking of sickly sweet raisin-jack and cigarette smoke.

Our shivers were matched by the rumble of the ship's engines, seemingly next door. There were two improvised tables, consisting of tiers of C-ration cartons covered by a GI blanket, the tables surrounded by stuffed barracks bags that served as stools. Gino took the empty stool at table two. I told Willie I'd seen enough, but he said I couldn't just turn around and leave or they'd get suspicious. Besides, we had to hang in with Gino. He folded early on the first couple of hands, then stayed for four losing pots.

We thought it was a good time to say 'thanks' and leave, but Gino wanted to try to get his money back. They were playing seven-card stud and he came up with a five and six of diamonds in the hole and a seven of diamonds up. He was looking for a straight or a flush and thought he had a fair chance at either. The third card paired his queen, both black. His chances for the straight looked dim, the flush dimmer. Meanwhile, the dealer got a pair of eights, another guy a pair of fours. It didn't look good—the fours and eights were cramping his straight, but he was high on the board and stayed, then wished he hadn't when he had to meet the raise of the dealer, an older guy we called Grumpy, which he was. Gino's fourth face card was a painful four of diamonds, meaning he was suckered to stay in.

On second thought, he had a notion to fold anyway. However, since there were no raises, nobody else was helped, so, against his better judgment, he stayed for two bucks.

"Down with trouble," Grumpy said. The guy with the fours lifted the corner of his down card, thought it over for a minute, and folded. The guy next to Gino had just previously folded, so Gino got his card. He must have shuffled it with his down cards for all of two minutes before he squeezed off a peek, Grumpy all the while scrutinizing him. At first Gino couldn't believe it; the longest shot going—an eight of diamonds. He suddenly realized that the guy across from him was high on the board with aces. The aces guy threw in a weak buck. Grumpy raised him two, and Gino raised them three more. Aces saw the raise and said it was time they played for real money, snapping a ten spot and dropping it in the pot. So it was reasonable to think he had filled. But apparently wanting to find out if the aces were just paired, Grumpy silently cast a twenty in the pot, suggesting *he* had filled, likely with kings. Gino quietly wished it on him as he threw in his last forty dollars. Aces folded, meaning he just had two pairs.

A bit of a crowd had gathered around the table and the air was pretty close. Grumpy lit himself a cigarette. He let the smoke drift lazily up and, eyes squinting, sat there taking Gino in for what must have been fully two or three minutes. He went into his shirt pocket and counted out four crisp twenties, and let them float down on the pile, slightly lifting the corner of his mouth as he did, in what might have been a smile or just smoke in the eye. A long coil of ash dropped from his cigarette, as he continued eyeing Gino with a look that said no green punk was going to buy a pot from him. Gino looked back at us and we came up with three twenties a piece. Grumpy turned around with a look that as much as asked, who the hell were we?

42

"Hey, if you guys want in here, you gotta have a seat. Yah understand?"

"We're just lending him money," I said.

"You can't do that."

"We just did."

"Yer in the game or yer out, and so's yer money. Yah understand." He was about to reach in for our money and throw it back at us, when, someone grabbed his arm. It was the dark-browed guy, Henchman-2.

As Pete parted the crowd and moved in, Grumpy looked up at him expecting support. Gino could have gone 'light,' but only for the call. So we were probably in the wrong, but hoped Pete would remember Willie. Gumpy was impatient for Pete to say something. "Fer Chrissake, that's outside money. How about it, Pete?"

Never one to mince words when money was at stake, Pete was blunt. "It's inside now. Call him or fold."

Grumpy turned toward Pete again, hands on hips, looking for a reversal. "Come-on, man. Fer Chrissake, what kinda game yah run?" But Pete was unmoved, telling him to call or Gino takes the pot. Grumpy sat there for several minutes sullenly staring at Gino. Then, he testily side-armed in two twenties and laid out a pair of kings to go with the king and eights he had showing. His head to the side, he peered over at Gino's cards, the corner of his mouth lifting up again. Gino's fingers were shaking as he turned over the five of diamonds, the six and eight, and slowly lined them up with his four and seven. A murmur rippled through the crowd. We'd barely caught our breath when four lightning hands descended on the pot.

Exiting—Gino with full pockets—we had Grumpy on our tails, going down that corrugated corridor. He looked like the kind of guy who packed a gun. We felt he was about to say something—maybe

43

reach for something—but he went on by at the sound of Rebel and Gush thumping toward us. They'd heard the Casino talked about as dangerous and decided they'd better get us shepherded out of there. We thanked them and when we indicated what happened, they were all "Wow's." As we thought about it, we felt kind of lucky to get out of there with our lives. We could feel out hearts thumping all the way back to D-Deck. Gino wanted to give me and Willie a hundred each, but I said to just give us what we'd laid out and enjoy the win. Willie urged him to have the Chaplain wire a chunk of dough home to his wife and kids when we landed.

Knowing they'd be after us to re-visit the tables, our guts were in an uproar. No way they'd let us back out. But our good fortune became our misfortune, which unexpectedly worked out okay for us, though with not-so-okay consequences. Next day it was as if the whole damned boat knew about the big pot. While gambling wasn't exactly against regulations, if at any time the Army didn't want something, that, by itself, was enough to create a regulation. Reasons weren't to be asked for or given, but, according to flexible TC, who knew when to toe the line, it was simply said to be bad for morale. We could vouch for that.

We were required to have our Mae Wests with us at all times and had to have them tied snugly ('Under the arms, not at the waist, Dummies, or you'll drown!') for daily muster on deck. HB hauled the three of us out of formation and said we had to show the MPs where those games were held, since it was assumed news of the win would have them getting bigger. We told him that we'd only just found out about the games and honestly couldn't find our way again without a guide. He cussed us out and said, "Dammit, you're gonna find out how to find that Casino again and report back to me by six hundred hours tomorrow morning, or I'll have your asses in the brig."

44

Willie started to say he knew a guy who could guide the MPs down there, but was cut off. Luckily, Kraut was loitering around as we were being talked to, and he whispered something in HB's ear. HB nodded, paused for a minute, and said there was a T-Corpsman we'd have to take with us, since, as a matter of jurisdiction, those guys had to know what was going on, and where.

Snapping off our salute with an emphatic "Yes Sir!" we dared not look at Kraut, but thanked him later. He said all we had to do was just go through the motions and report. If Pete found out who told, he would surely take it out on his own paid help, before he went after the guys who had run up a big pot for him. We were skeptical about that part, but had no choice.

7.

The three of us were yanked out of the sack at 4:30 the following morning, and feeling our groggy way—as directed—along a wood-paneled hallway that led to the kitchen, were shocked into wakefulness by a blinding assault on our noses. The place was positively dripping with the suffocating, stupefying ammonia aroma of one hundred per cent pure piss. It was as if every blessed pot-full from every man, woman, child, cat and dog from Moses on down had been run through that kitchen. Our first thought was we were going to be doing latrine duty before breakfast. Gino complained that we'd pulled our share, but never yet had to lick out the urinals.

We gagged and gasped, banged on the wall, and hacked and barked, and sneezed, spit and stomped, and clapped one another on the back, walking round and round, wondering why this kind of punishment was being meted out to us. Gino yelled, "Gas," and, tears streaming down our cheeks, we bolted for the big double doors, but were met by TC, and behind him was a Limey cook, who shouted, "Back! Back you ruddy slobs!"

He apparently thought we were to be his KP detail and wanted us to have our breakfast out of the way, so he could put us on pots and pans. TC started to tell the cook what our assignment actually was, but got nowhere. A bunch of mad Limeys had crowded around us, and one of them signaled to an MP who ushered us toward the chow line. We remembered Kraut's advice and thought we'd just eat and run for it.

What we got was creamed kidney stew on toast. A rare treat we were told; the Limey version of SOS, their Shit-on-a-Shingle. I bit off a piece of the wet toast and tried a cautious bite of the creamed kidney. I dumped pepper on the rest and managed another bite. Amazingly, Willie said it wasn't as bad as it smelled ("Hell, I've had day-old mountain oysters about as strong as this stuff.") So I took a spoonful and washed it down with a gulp of coffee, which did little to smooth out the taste. A water chaser was no help. Willie was frowning. He'd changed his mind. Gino wasn't doing very well either. Seeing Willie and me in pain, he apparently wanted us to think it could be worse, by noting what a marvel it was none of us had been sea-sick yet.

That was all it took. We couldn't open our mouths to tell him to knock it off. The ship was pitching and rolling a lot more sharply than the day before. Willie grabbed his stomach, Gino his head, TC his throat, me my mouth, and, as if by command, we stampeded up those wide flights of stairs three at a time, one guy slipping on the drippage of the guy in front of him, and we spilled out on deck lunging for the rail. Puffing and heaving in unison, we held on for dear life. We finally came up for air, but, what with the slime and stink, we had it going again, till, tear-eyed, all we had left were the dry heaves. The nausea lasted a while.

We weren't the only ones in sick bay that day. One breakfast shift after the other was flocking to the rail, guys pushing and shoving to open up a place for themselves. The side of the ship must have begun to look like it had been hit by a flock of seagulls. Since the officers' mess was no different, HB shortly found himself among the rail birds, and he was still a little weak in the knees when Kraut next day brought him back to his point about the Casino being T-Corps business. Indeed, knowing the ship as they did, T-Corpsmen were, as he spoke, dismantling what there was of the Casino and blocking off the corrugated passageway. They also nabbed Pete and locked him away in the brig, though no one believed he'd not be able to find a way out.

We never did get a straight story about what happened to the three Black guys. HB wanted it known that he had tried to get them on orders to be sent back when the ship turned around, but they were not found. Oh, there was one account about the flashing of knives (theirs) suggesting that, if they went over the side, they might well have provoked it and have gone over unconscious—or dead, the more hopeful believed. In any event, it was a simple fact, we would learn, that, one way or another, guys simply disappeared. In addition to those lost on line, over a thousand unaccounted for on D-Day alone (like those washed out with the tide or vaporized by the direct hit of an artillery shell), there were the unidentifiable, as well as the yet to be dismembered, captured, or tossed into mass graves. And then there were those who were just plain lost in miscellaneous ways, some genuine, some not, and got indiscriminately classified as missing in action. Something none of us ever wanted to be, or think about.

8.

The Medic had given me something for my stomach ache, and I was laying in my hammock, curled up like a fishing worm, when guys went jolting by, yelling, "Land! Land! Hey, we're there!"

Getting myself up on deck, I came to with a start. Sure enough, ahead of us and off to the right, rising out of the water and shimmering in the sun were the lushest, sparklingest, deeply greenest hills I'd ever seen, just pouring their sweet life out to us. "Green, green, green. Life, life, life," they cried. It made you feel like you wanted to swim over to those meadows, roll around, and tear out mouthfuls of fresh grass. Somebody said it was the Isle of Man. Wasn't it though!

Guys were clapping one another on the back, pointing, and repeating, "We're there. Son of gun, we're there!" It was as if we didn't fully realize how stressed we'd been, in our unspoken fear of the worst, helplessly cramped up in the belly of that leviathan, till—lo—here comes this vision of the green breast of the Old World. The air took on a new freshness that made you want to drink it. My throat had been as dry as a hay bin, and the tender wind kissing those green slopes blew right out of paradise itself. But as the boat trudged steadily on, the hills shrank to a barely shimmering emerald sinking behind us, our glimpse of heaven about to close.

We began getting announcements about landing over the PA, and before long, we were laying off Greenock (sure was) in the Firth of the Clyde. Lighters were brought alongside to take us in to shore—mere dinghies next to Big Duck—and once on board one of those bouncy little jobs, Willie and I were on the barracks bag detail, along with some other guys. Up top, they'd swing these huge nets over filled with bags, and we had to quickly untie the net, jump in and pitch the bags into the hold, where other guys were stacking them. A

48

couple of times, I was last man out of the net and could feel the coils of it being dragged underfoot as I scrambled to avoid getting tangled before it swung back with a remaining bag or two that got smacked against the ominous hull above. The resounding clonk made me aware of the hazard I'd escaped. As it turned out, that hazard would recur at our next docking, with an outcome that left us astonished at how easily unwitting disaster might strike.

There wasn't anybody to wave to, so the guys waved at the crisp clean Scottish tug that had seen us through the submarine nets. The skipper looked out of his window, puffing vigorously on his pipe as he strained at the wheel in pulling away. He paused to give us a thumbs up. He had a big shepherd dog on deck who was frisking around, barking and prancing back and forth, happy they were going in. He had a right to be. Scotland was beautiful. Everything sparkled and looked so clear and bright under the afternoon sun, the harbor scene unfolding before us had a picture postcard sheen to it that almost seemed unreal. The whole world was lit up with color, from the jewel-blue water to the orange-yellow stone houses with their slanting red tile roofs. Red-haired, blue-eyed girls were looking out over planters with red, gold, and purple flowers. Wherever we looked we saw people with red hair, the result, we supposed, of their sharing a national gene. Behind the houses, fierce green fields, dotted with black and brown cows and fat sheep, rolled out into an ice blue sky. I was sure nobody died there. When the people gave us a hearty "V," I felt embarrassed, thinking how little, till then, we deserved it. Girls who came to the window to shake out a cloth, stayed to wave. Willie said he had a notion to dye his hair and get himself lost there. He wasn't the only one.

And who could blame the T-Corps officers for being eager to get us formed up and out of there, which, with the usual confusion, would nonetheless take a while, time enough for them to linger over their coffee at the Salvation Army tent, trying to get the eye of these nice, soft-talking British gals, standing by in their dapper uniforms. The more the gals stayed politely to themselves and were so pleasant and smiley and obliging, when approached by the T-Corps Major, a tall, handsome, Hollywood type, complete with tilted garrison cap, the harder he bit off his questions about papers they knew nothing about. We had seen him before telling HB that he wanted to get Pete off his hands, and preferably put back into ranks, which told us that, in addition to his strutting around like he was God's gift to British womanhood, he was also corruptible, a phenomenon taken for granted among the rear echelon staff. HB told him flat out he had nothing to do with Supply, and wanted nothing to do with Pete—that being precisely the way Pete wanted it.

Willie recalled Pete's telling Roscoe (the one Black we knew had survived) that he was going to have GIs driving trucks in France and might even have a place for one of his friends. No matter that they'd never seen the inside of a truck's cab. Once they were taught how to drive, it would be like they'd been born with a slab of horsehide glued to their asses. On the routes they'd travel, he'd be able to put them in for combat pay, and they'd get medals and cognac, and cigars and genuine French whores, so long as they kept hauling the merchandise. So far as we could tell, it now looked like he had recruited TC and one of his Henchmen to do the trucking. Or, could it be that, after all our sweat over the Blacks, Pete actually had them in hiding? Ridiculous as his plans for them were, that would be good to know.

They finally marched us from the loading platform up the cleated concrete ramp to the tracks, and, once on the waiting train, occupancy being six to a compartment, Gino, fast on his feet when he wanted to be, got us one to ourselves. It was really something to be riding on

50

a spiffy Limey train like the ones we saw in their spy movies. The seats were nice and soft, unlike the hard kind we had in the States, and they were covered with dark green mohair. Around the windows, there was real wood trim, with a lacquered finish that shone like a pool of water when the sun played on it. We figured that tourists would have paid through the nose for accommodations like this. As the train pulled out, we had our last look at the bright Scottish sky and the deserted red brick station, so worn and soot blackened, but still so clean too, real and unreal, much like a stage set. The luxury was too good for the likes of us. Knowing we were not likely to have this kind of treat again, we leaned back and soaked up the good feeling. Chow was K-rations and coffee, but what did we care.

We were going through Edinburgh, and wherever there was a group of people, they stopped to wave at us, some with flags, ours and theirs. Even the little ones, red cheeked, held out a solid thumbs up. As the train picked up speed, bridges, church spires, tile roofs and faded brick buildings swam by like they were being rushed downstream on a tidal river. I'd apparently dozed off, for when I next looked out there was the beautiful English countryside. Every farm, every thatched cottage, every field, every garden looked as if every inch of it had been tended by hand. The hedges were clipped just so, the trees neatly trimmed, both placed as if for picturesque effect. Everything was again so richly green, one benefit of all that rain. It was hard to believe that in the midst of a war the whole land could be so well looked after. We had places like that, mostly where the rich people lived. But it wasn't the same; here they seemed to make the surrounding landscape look good because they liked it to be that way. It wasn't done for show; it was a way of life. We noticed what a difference it was from the kind of view you'd see from our train windows back home: dirty factories with broken windows, garbage heaps, junk yards, broken billboards, litter, old tires, unpainted barns with faded Bull Durham signs. We knew how gutsy the British were, which was great, but seeing their land up close, changed a lot of the usual attitudes toward them.

After all, these people had been at war going on five years. They'd had their cities devastated by bombing raids intended to kill large numbers of civilians, the survivors left to mourn family and friends buried in the ruins of collapsed buildings. Of course, it inspired the British to retaliate, which wasn't very good either, but they did recognize how nasty it was to do that. No one was harder on the Germans for that kind of thing than Kraut, who said it was outright barbarism, not legitimate warfare. Germans he knew disowned the madmen in charge of the war. Mainly Hitler. I heard Rebel breathe, "Baloney. Wants us to believe what he actually don't." Rebel never cared for Kraut, no matter.

To pass the time, we got up occasionally and went to the platform outside the baggage car behind us to have a smoke, given up when it got mixed with coal fumes from the engine. Dusk was falling, giving everything a sleepy look, as we clickety-clacked through a blackened industrial city with clusters of smudgy brick factories and a string of tall smokestacks capped by ridges of low hanging brown clouds. A sign said Newcastle. We were beginning to get into the rain that would follow us to our destination. Kraut got an idea of where that might be when he ran into HB on the platform, and said we were headed for the south-west of England, a good way off, not far from a cross-Channel POE. So Willie went into his pack and produced a canteen of raisin-jack—a good way to break the monotony and get to sleep.

When they woke us at five the next morning, it was pitch black all around. I lifted the shade and ran my sleeve across the misted window, but all I could make out was the soft pat of raindrops hitting the pane and tear-streaking it. Though we'd apparently been sitting on some quiet siding for a while, the shaking and jogging felt like it was still with us. Since the engine had left, we were without heat. A chill rippled through me. "D-Damn, it's cold," I said to nobody in particular. Willie and I had slept sitting at the windows, our legs jack-knifed over an armrest. My left hip felt like I'd had it in a vise. Willie was slapping at his legs, saying they had slept sounder than he had. On the floor, the other guys began to untangle themselves, coming apart like they were an octopus. We were all feeling pretty achy, and those full field packs we'd been lugging had us mumbling about our backs. It wasn't long before we started running into the usual GI fuck-ups. Being used to them didn't sweeten our mood.

We had formed on the road and had ourselves a good hour's wait for the trucks—lost, so far as anybody knew—as we stood there with the rain plonking off our helmets and running down into our canteen cups of cold coffee. The guys who had drifted back to the train were rounded up by our T-Corps friends and prodded back into ranks. Of all people to be abused by. When the trucks finally did arrive, we hadn't gone but maybe a mile when the truck ahead of us, headlights off, missed a turn and slipped down into the culvert. By trying to avoid doing the same thing, the driver of our truck slid us off the other side of the road. A bunch of us tried pushing the truck out, and, huffing and cussing, we got some rocking movement. Our driver prematurely gunned the motor, which churned the tires and splattered us with mud. Who did the drivers turn out to be—great at yelling for us to push harder—but Pete's Henchman and TC, just broken in and given false confidence. Pete told them to just follow his instructions and look like they knew what they were doing, and no one would question them. They were told not to take any shit, least of all from MP's, who, when told to make way, would assume they were on a strategic mission and wave them on. Unbeknownst to us, we were to hook up with these drivers again in France. Had we only known.

We marched the rest of the way, a column on either side of the road—under the circumstances, not the worst way to go. The rain was coming down in a steady patter that could have continued at that rate for weeks without straining the heavens. There wasn't much of a wind, but it couldn't have made us any more miserable if there was one, because when we arrived at our new base, and stood around again awaiting orders, the wetness went through you and made you shiver till you thought it'd shake the teeth out of your head. Then came the news that those nice brick barracks up ahead were still in possession of the previous detachment going through. At first, we had an idea that we'd be pitching pup tents on the parade grounds, but since most of us had thrown away our tent poles, we partnered up and thought that, come night, we'd lay one shelter half down and cover ourselves with the other.

HB didn't take kindly to that possibility, and had some pointed questions for the Base Commander, a narrow go-by-the book type. Getting nowhere, HB scrounged around and had them make room for us in several storage buildings, one of which had cases of M-I rifles, K-rations and coffins. As an alternative to the wet ground, the concrete floors suited us just fine. We couldn't smoke on account of the jerry cans filled with kerosene, which was okay, and we could also put up with the heavy smell of cosmoline that the rifles were packed in. Besides, we got first choice of the K-rations, and, like everybody else, we preferred the breakfast cartons, with cans of bacon and eggs, plus coffee. To even things up, we also took some of the lousy lunches with the cheese and lemonade, as well as dinners with spam and bouillon. Yum.

With us having relaxed a bit and wanting to know where in hell we were, Rebel found out the place was a peace-time military school, but all the schooling the Limeys had time for was being gotten in France. The town was called Warminster, which produced predictably corny remarks. "Hey, just our speed. Like goin to war without bein there."

When we learned why our predecessors were still there, it looked like we might be getting a taste of war there, anyway. It seems that, after cleaning and assembling their rifles, those guys were taken out to the firing range. But, on complaints from France that the replacements being sent over were too soft, our good ol' Base Commander heard from higher-ups that the rain made conditions ripe for putting these green bastards through a muddy night infiltration course, rifles capable of being fired at the end. The trouble was, on the run-through prior to our arrival, one guy had panicked and got up right in line with the heavy machine gun firing overhead. Another guy tried to push him out of harm's way, and both got chopped down. So it seemed best to just send over warm bodies after all. End of toughening story.

But not of HB's grousing. When he was pissed off, he sounded off, and when he did, Rebel said not a dog in the kennel barked. But he also liked to have someone listen; us, since higher-ups wouldn't. He was carrying on about the lack of initiative on the part of junior officers, who in combat situations should be obligated to use their damned heads and countermand *orders* when they were at odds with realities on the ground. From Regiment on up, they looked at maps instead of the actual terrain for which they concocted battle plans.

HB remembered rooming with a stiff-necked West-Pointer when he was at Benning, who not only followed orders to the letter, but was hell-bent on proving them right. He went ashore at Utah Beach, got hit in one leg on June 7th, and, limping through the 8th, he got hit in the other leg leading his squad over an open field to his assigned objective, a machine gun pit dug into a hedgerow. Had he used a little initiative and taken cover in a draw on the way up, his squad wouldn't have been wiped out.

As fate would have it, we were destined for the same outfit that Stiff-Neck was in. He'd been hit a third time and rejoined us in the absolute worst of all nightmare campaigns, Hürtgen Forest, the battle plan for which was a known disaster and adhered to anyway—at all costs, which were great. (Just SN's thing.) It rained every miserable November day in Hürtgen, with the temperature hovering in the low thirties. The low-hanging fir trees were so thick in places you couldn't see more than ten meters ahead of you, often less. Muddy roads made it impossible to bring up armor support. The fight was all foot-slogging Infantry, and it seemed endless. Companies got badly chewed up; morale was low, casualties high. Tree bursts from mortar shells sent shrapnel showering down on us, meaning our foxholes had to be log covered, on the example set by the Germans. Mine fields were everywhere, particularly in firebreaks.

Stiff-Neck had earned captain's bars to go with his Bronze Star, and so he outranked our captain-to-be at the time. The night SN arrived, we were ordered to move up to a designated firebreak for an attack at first light next morning. We almost never moved in darkness, but SN had his orders. Up we went, and, ignoring the warnings of our non-coms, he decided to scout out the firebreak. The result was a disaster, for him and men with him. HB would probably have shot him *before* he went down that firebreak.

9.

Back in Warminster, since we had to have rifles issued, they couldn't cancel our trying them out on the firing range. It was a bit of a fiasco, beginning with the half day we spent cleaning the cosmoline off the metal parts and assembling the damned things. Each twelve-man squad was huddled around a couple of ten-gallon pails filled with kerosene, and was given rags, along with ram-rods and wadding for the bore. These were not exactly new rifles; in fact, they looked like they might have been battlefield discards put together by POWs at an ordnance junkyard. Usually the pieces fit together better if they had all belonged to the same rifle. The two parts you never fooled with were the trigger housing and the bolt. Sure enough, some guys found that, what with the cold cosmoline having congealed, their bolts didn't have the freest-moving firing pins. Whether they didn't want to be stuck with that kind of firing pin or they'd just as soon not have a functional rifle, a number of guys started disassembling bolts, so there we were ducking little springs that went flying every which way. The firing range chief, an Ordnance Master Sergeant with the bloodshot eyes of a boozer (likely treating himself to Scotland's finest) had some choice words for us. Cussing under his breath, he put the bolts back together, hammered them into the breech, pumped them four or five times and said they'd work good enough, better with use. I tried one of those rifles, and the bolt moved as if it had been dipped in taffy. Somebody made the mistake of piping up about whether they would shoot okay. The only part of the response we heard was, "And don't call your piece a *gun*, soldier!"

Out on the range, Boozer, assuming his most pompous in-charge stance, made a total horse's ass of himself talking to us as if we were raw recruits—like, "Men this is your rifle, a choice weapon, the semi-

57

automatic M-I, A-I. Watch out that you don't get a finger mashed when the bolt sends that first round into the chamber. And dammit, make sure you *squeeze* the rounds off. Don't jerk the trigger." Before we even got down to firing, he was telling us we had to make sure to clean our rifles afterwards, and, putting a little extra snarl in his voice, he warned that, if he found any dirty bores, he'd have us up all night cleaning them. We gulped because, sure enough, every one of those relics we'd gotten had a pitted bore. Some hadn't had a ramrod down them since the Revolution. Willie said his belonged to Methuselah. We wondered what it would take to shut this guy up, as he went on trying to impress us with the importance of the rifle. From now on, we were going to eat with it, shave, pray, piss, walk, talk, shit, and sleep with it. We'd do everything but make love to it; and he didn't know but what we might do that.

Standing there, listening to all this, we were getting wetter and chillier by the minute. The wind shifted and the rain was coming down in squalls, not all of it caught at the neck by our rain gear. To our relief, HB came barreling down the narrow road in his Jeep, bringing some cadre with him. He had a couple of questions and, impatient with Boozer's answers, cut him off in mid-sentence. "Fer Chrissake, Sergeant, get these troops over on the damned firing line. Yeah, right now."

Boozer got us over, but not without more explanation. There were four ranges, one for each of our four platoons. Each range had twelve targets, six on either side of a trench that sloped down to the pits. One squad would pull pit detail, while half of each of the other two squads came up to the firing line. Each guy would get to fire two clips—sixteen rounds—and the guys in the pits would record the pattern on a target card; it seemed like basic training all over again. If the rifle seemed to be shooting high or low, pulling left or right, the cadre non-coms would help us correct our sights, winding them this way or that. Then we'd get to fire two more clips to see how the rifle was hitting. If still askew, but close enough, there was always Kentucky windage. Instructing us—superfluously—on how to take the proper prone position, he asked Gush to demonstrate, and had him lay down, left elbow inside the sling, legs spread apart, cheek to butt, etc. Boozer didn't know how close he came to having Gush turn the rifle on him.

It took a good while to get all of us run through, and by day's end, our hands were about frozen, our feet numbed. Guys were getting tired and careless; mean as well. Injuries got to be more than powder burns and mashed thumbs. Here and there shots were grazing the concrete slab atop the pits and slugs went ricocheting down below, in one instance hitting a guy in the foot. More and more of us were missing the entire target—spitefully—which had the pit detail sending up 'Maggie's Drawers' (the red flag). A guy who had the 'Drawers' waved at him, shot the waver in the arm. A guy who forgot to lock—he said—shot himself in the ankle. We were denounced as a worthless bunch of good-for-nothin fuck-ups guaranteed not to last a day in combat.

We wouldn't have contested that comment; and, probably, neither would HB, but he said to forget about it. The more we were around him, the more we liked him and hoped he might yet stick with us. Especially since he unexpectedly got us into those brick barracks when we returned from the range, stiff with the cold. We were flabbergasted over the clean inside quarters with varnished floors, polished banisters, glistening tile-block corridors, bunk beds, even window shades. The barracks were still pretty damp and drafty, without central heating, like most places in England, but to have those four walls around us and real beds was no small potatoes. In

59

addition to being half-frozen, we felt pretty grimy, and with all the clatter we made going in and looking around, it seemed a lot like bringing the cattle into the living room. It took no time at all for us to claim a bunk and make ourselves at home; that is, after we'd finished scuffling for the bunks nearest the coal stoves that were spaced down the middle aisle.

Like most of the good things that came our way, this wasn't destined to last. We barely had time to warm ourselves a little when Boozer came by with that shit-eatin grin on his face to tell us we'd be shipping out next morning.

10.

When the non-coms came around with their flashlights at four that morning to roll us out, most of us were already up, working on our packs, getting all the odds and ends of toilet articles, extra socks, underwear and stuff neatly tucked in, and trying the packs on to make sure there was nothing hard sticking us in the back. Out on the parade grounds behind the row of barracks, the platoon sergeants were holding up muzzled flashlights and turning them in the assembly signal, as they called out numbers. Off behind us, we could hear the soft chugging of a switch engine moving cars on to a siding. The fog held on, which strangely lightened the darkness a bit. Once on the train, we were quickly on our way, and a leaden tiredness settled down on us. The swaying motion was just what we needed to get back to sleep, little knowing that we were being transported with trouble—which never slept. We had Boozer snoozing with us.

Southampton was a challenge in itself, and so was Boozer's assuming operational jurisdiction there. At first, we were amused as we watched him chide a hapless Port Authority Limey who had no idea of when the Lighters might be called up to our pier on account of the wind—as if he had anything to do with it. Boozer insisted he hadn't come along just to annoy HB, or us. He claimed he had a responsibility to see to it that badly needed ordnance got loaded on the Lighters, which also required ballast, and heavy stuff too, with the Channel acting up as it was. From the way he lorded it over us, which was beginning to rile HB, we could see that something was going to have to give. But, for the time being, *he* wasn't, knowing it hadn't yet reached the point when HB wouldn't.

Since he was in charge of Stores, he took the liberty, in HB's absence, of making virtual stevedores of us. He said the Limeys who used to do most of that work were either too old, too infirm, or in the service. Kraut hinted that when HB got back from PAH (our equivalent of their Port Authority Headquarters) he might take exception to us being taken over like that. Unfazed, Boozer pointed out he was benefiting us by bringing up protective ballast. Considering that HB was so eager to get underway—about which PAH was giving him a bad time—instead of our just waiting around, what better way to move things along than for us to run loads of ammo and ordnance down to where the gantry could swing that stuff into the hold. Even with the use of fork-lifts and dollies, that still meant manual handling of some pretty heavy hardware, at least four men to a crate.

We expected that HB would be fuming when he returned. All the more so because Boozer had clout with the logistic-minded Quartermaster officers at PAH, who ranked supplies ahead of personnel. HB's return being delayed, no one could deal with the use Boozer was making of us. Willie, Gino and me wound up on truck detail—not all that bad, as it gave us a glimpse of what life must have been like for these folks when the bombs came raining down on them.

61

The driver, Lloyd, said he was a "Lancashir" man. We couldn't understand a third of what he said, which he found strange. He nonetheless talked a blue streak and drove like a one-eyed looney—all on the wrong side of the street. On the first trip, our cargo of mortar shells and cans of fifty-caliber machine gun belts got pretty well jounced around. Willie asked this guy if he ever carried nitroglycerine. I sat next to Lloyd in the cab and every time he told a story, he clapped me on the shoulder. "Eh, wot d'yah think o' that now, Yank?" he'd ask. One story was about a fat lady who got buried alive in a wine cellar during an air raid that broke a few tuns, and every time the wine came up so high, she had to drink enough off to keep from downing. I tried to sign him off, but he kept leaning over and talked right up against the side of my head—foul-breathed.

"Well, she did finally drown, poor thing. She drank s'much, she caved in the tun she was sittin on."

We were on our second trip. Half the time Lloyd never looked at the road. "Don't worry, mates. Know it like me own parlor. Know this lorry like she was me horse." He'd been laying the gas to her, but finally slowed down some—enough to make sure all four wheels didn't leave the road at once—because we were riding a good deal over wet cobblestones. He had to avoid craters filled with no more than gravel and cinders, and swerved around occasional heaps of rubble still standing in front of bombed-out buildings. We saw row houses that had been caved in. Lloyd said that during the Blitz there were some that got "chopped off," revealing bedrooms with mattresses, chairs, and dressers, as well as clothes, and other personal effects tossed every which way and covered with shards of plaster debris. The occupants gone. Things had just stayed that way for a while. Noticing my expression, Lloyd remarked that people came before wreckage. "Should have seen Plymouth," he added. "Jerries flattened the place. Brought everthin down. Saved us the trouble."

In the gray light everything generally seemed fairly well blackened over. The most hopeful sight along the way was a brewery going full blast, with thick coils of white smoke churning out of its chimney and the smell of hops and barley hanging in the wet air. We didn't see any kids playing in the streets. The civilians we passed were mostly older folks, and they too seemed blackened. Most looked very thin and long in the face and walked like they had a stiffness of back and knees.

Lancashir Lloyd did a couple of fast turns, swinging sharply over one way, then back the other to avoid craters, then sped down a short street that he said had had all its buildings leveled. At the end of it was a fenced-in field with rows of camouflaged one-story barracks, the supply warehouses. What did we see this time, but some rather sturdy late-middle-age men moving all sorts of stuff that had been off-loaded from incoming ships. We discovered what HB was on the verge of discovering. The hell there were no available able-bodied longshoremen. They were just working on trans-Atlantic arrivals in another section of the harbor. So here was Boozer wanting to put one over on HB—revenge for prior ill-treatment?—by persuading PAH to reduce our loading priority, already low, as a matter of caution, justified by the wind.

When we got down to the pier, we found HB working some longshoremen that he had marshaled from Boozer's British counterpart at the Central Port Authority, and we were just in time to see him letting Boozer have it. Chewing him out, up one side and down the other, he tore the hip flask out of his back pocket, tossed it in the water, told him he had a notion to throw him in after it, and kicked his ass—harder with each shot—half the way to his Jeep. We let out a war-whoop.

We would recall the detestation HB had for the rear echelon. "Yeah, the *rear*, well named."

11.

HB was so worked up, he let anger get the better of judgment. Ironically, that impatience would, in the near future, lead to adverse consequences, which, however, might have happened anyway. HB was going to allow just one more day of delay despite reports that the Channel was still pretty rough. All he had to do was have a Lighter brought in and find a place for us to overnight it, each a tall order. We could have gone back to a staging area that had decent quarters, but, since he wanted us on alert for boarding next day pending a report on the Channel, we had to stay put while he drove over to PAH to get our shipping orders redone, subject to approval by the Brits, who hopefully would grant us access to nearby submariners' barracks. He said to fall out, and we bunched up on the lea side of one the dock buildings. Had it not been for his getting us relieved of trucking in cargo, we might have done a lot more grumbling.

At daybreak, we were glad to get down to the pier again. We'd been pretty cramped in those barracks, more like huts, which had been vacant for a while and were dark and dusty with loose window sashes that rattled in the wind. The guys in one of them said they had to roust out a parcel of wharf rats, some as long as your forearm, when they made up their sacks for the night. Our other neighbors in the next compound over seemed more comfortable. They were housed in barracks recently improved that had barred windows and were guarded by British marines. Peeping through the bars were guys with squared-off haircuts. Somebody in a hut next to the barbed-wire fence was quite sure that from what he could see, they had on the desert suntans worn by Rommel's Afrika Corps. Gino said, "Oh sure." He knew the dodo who sounded off, the kind who spouts the first thing that comes into his head and starts a rumor going.

It was a damp and murky day, and the wind was pretty strong, bringing in the smell of the sea. It blew so hard the smaller ships anchored out in the estuary were bouncing up and down like tin cans. The sky had a lead-blue color and it rained on and off. The strength of those waves splashing high against our pier made us think we'd for sure be going back to our cozy little huts. Although HB had privately commented on the mighty British Navy being unable to bring a dinky little Lighter up to a deep-water pier, he obviously let none of that show when he approached their Dock Authority. He'd be dealing with some prideful old salts who had attended the Royal Naval College at Dartmouth. In making his case again, he no doubt appealed to the Limeys' stoical side, unless they were saying to themselves if this damned fool Yank wants to visit Davy Jones's locker, why not let him have a go at it.

Towards noon there was a break in the clouds, and, as predicted, the wind, though still brisk, slackened off enough for the Lighter to come bouncing in. Until its hold was fully loaded, the Lighter was light all right, and not all that heavy after it took on cargo. Once on board, we couldn't have weighed it down by much. Refitted at the Southampton Dockyard, it resembled a small version of ocean-going ferries minus the amenities, but built high in the prow like a regular ship. It was late in the day by the time we sailed down the estuary and on past the Isle of Wight. The wind had a solid push to it, and with the force of the waves coming at us, we thought we must have been going out with the tide, or we'd have been shoved right back into port.

Now and then the wind would come up in gusts that made our little Lighter bob and teeter like it was an overgrown dinghy. Those of us lucky enough to make it up topside held onto the rail, white knuckled. Once we hit open water, as far as the eye could see, the black waves were streaked with white caps and our bow pretty regularly pitched so low that the whole forward deck was awash. The British sailors told us it had been worse. One thing in our favor was that the Germans wouldn't be having their little Schnell-Boote on the prowl, tough little MTBs (Motor Torpedo Boats) capable of doing almost 40 knots. "Gee thanks," Willie said.

We were shortly ordered down below, taking buckets with us to be passed around as needed. The only way you could get back up was if you were in such a bad way that you made it tough on those near you. Pails in hand, several of us looked green enough to pass, but there was no relief up there. Rough as the pitching was, the rolling was worse. You'd look over to the side and see the water rise up and go higher and higher and then see the horizon push it back down again. Before we knew it, the gathering darkness had descended on us. We pulled the GI blankets over our helmets, and, all barfed out, called it a night.

Arriving at the Normandy coast next morning, we came to anchor about two hundred yards off shore. The weather had cleared, the sun was shining brightly, and the air was crisp. Looking out, we saw the long stretches of white beach and intimidating dark cliffs that went straight up behind them. It was a sight to remember. How could they have picked this place for the D-Day invasion? Doubtless, it was accidental. Even the Army couldn't have been that stupid.

12.

The beach still hadn't been cleaned up, and, as with the destruction in England, probably wouldn't be for some time, depending on how the supply of scrap iron held up. As far as you could see in either direction, there was all kinds of wreckage. The surf broke over disabled LCI's and LST's, Jeeps, trucks, and broken-down artillery pieces. The beach itself was littered with knocked-out tanks and half-tracks. There were empty ammo boxes and shell holes all over. Just at the water's edge we could see strings of rusty barbed wire with seaweed hanging from them like so many wringing wet beards; and there were still a fair number of those cross-clustered rails peeping out of the surf; jolly ol' creatures calculated to rip open an LCI or hang up a tank, maybe snag a gut or two. Between us and the shore, there was a whole row of derelict ships rusting away. Anybody could see that we must have lost that battle.

An LCI had been moving itself slowly into position beside us, and our Limey crew swung into action. We were surprised at what young kids they were—thin, baby-faced, fair-skinned boys, maybe fifteen at most, who didn't shave the faint down on their faces. It showed how hard-pressed the Limeys were; everybody had to do his part. The boys were real lively, as they rushed this way and that securing ropes and things, jabbering away at the helmsman of the LCI in their clipped Limey accent.

Soon they'd made the LCI fast to the Lighter and threw over a rope ladder. There was a tangle in the ladder, so one of those baby-faced kids hopped lightly over the side like a little jockey, and, just as he was getting at the tangle, the LCI suddenly bounded up high against the hull of the Lighter and crushed him. One of the kids who saw it coming had gone over to grab an arm, but he was too late. There was the slightest cry out of the little guy—like that of a sparrow chick fallen from its nest—and down he slipped as the two vessels parted again, and the water splashed up between them white and green. The horror was how easily a life was snuffed out, human flesh caught between plates of iron. The boy had served as a buffer—the sort of thing old tires or balls of knotted rope are used for to spare the hulls of the two craft. Though he fell straight down, it was a certainty that the pure, white soul of that boy flew straight up. His buddies cried out his name—"Tim"—and one of their officers came up and leaned over the side looking fore and aft for some sign, but there was none, not even a smudge on the ship's hull. The officer turned toward HB and made him understand that he'd better get us moving.

The frail little guy who had tried to grab the one who got crushed was rummaging around in a deck locker for another ladder. The one he lugged out was pretty frayed and knotted where it had been spliced. He showed it to his officer who was about to ask him to find another, when HB interceded and had him throw the knotted one over anyway. The kid still had tears in his eyes and bit his upper lip. After he secured the ladder, he turned and looked straight out to sea. He'd seen death before in his young life and carried on. But we found out that the one who had gone down was his brother.

HB wanted to know if they could throw something between the boats. The Captain explained that it wouldn't do any good because a man with a pack could still get fairly well bumped before the hull of the LCI touched the rubber tires he had, and, if stacked, the gap made by the tires would be too wide to jump.

HB said that the longer they waited, the more antsy guys would get, meaning that a few would probably miss-time the rise of the LCI. He asked Kraut, as much a master of obedience as of agility, to show them how easily it could be done. Kraut looked around with a 'who, me?' smile, then deliberately took the ladder with the tangle, neatly side-stepping it, and continued on down with short quick steps, lifting his feet cleanly off each rung as he went. When he got about a yard above the top of the LCI, he waited for it to ride down and just as it started back up swung himself out and over, landing securely on both feet with a hollow bang. He looked up and laughed like a man who had just jumped into a cold pond and was rubbing his chest to get himself used to the frigid water.

The tremor in Kraut's voice wasn't lost on those of us crowded at the rail. Nor was it lost on HB, who instantly got the first platoon going over, one guy after the other following Kraut's example, and after an initial nervousness, guys started getting the knack of it. The LCI was still pretty bouncy and you couldn't always calculate its rhythm, so several times a guy had to scamper back up a couple of steps to avoid getting hit. But by and large the embarkation went very smoothly, so much so that HB had us going over more rapidly, two at a time on each ladder. Soon it was our turn, and Willie and I went over together. We timed the rise just right, and riding out and away like kids going into the lake off an inner tube, we called out, "One, two, three, the hell with me."

HB made himself last, so he could check and make sure everybody was off. One leg slung over the side, he abruptly reached back for a lone straggler, and extending a hand, practically yanked him over the rail. It was Pete, his face sickly white. HB couldn't help laughing. The two of them were coming down side by side, until HB got a little ahead and had to go back up a couple of rungs. The heaves had left Pete pretty weak, and, as he nervously responded to HB's urging, his feet slipped and he began to slide. HB caught him, carefully planting each of his feet in a rung, and down they started again, HB with a hand on Pete's cartridge belt.

All of a sudden, Pete began to panic. His one foot got stuck in the tangle, and he pulled at it like an animal caught in a trap. Thinking he was trying to crawl back up, HB grabbed his free ankle. Pete swore at him in Italian, and HB swore back. In those seconds that the two of them were struggling with one another, the LCI had been slowly riding up. It dipped back for an instant, held, and, with a huge lurch, started up at them again like a mountain on the move. Pete, who had his eye on it all the time, saw the lurch and yanked his foot free at the last moment. Then ripping his ankle out of HB's grasp, he stepped on his shoulder to get the boost he needed to thrust himself up and into the clear, driving HB down as he escaped.

Looking up from the LCI, we saw HB and Pete suddenly become very big, and yelled "Watch out!" as we felt ourselves being sent toward them by the force of a powerful hand lifting us up with an awesome free-gliding movement. We heard the hull strike HB's pack with the slightest bump and continue to the peak of its glide, just grazing the Lighter's hull as it continued. Slight as it seemed, that bump was enough. HB's helmet clanged against the side of the Lighter, and we heard one high-pitched, fading "Eeh!" as we sailed down and away again, with him slipping straight down like an anchor weight, making a plop and a splash. We were no sooner down than we were swung back up again, and on that sweep a whirling mass came flying down on top of Willie and me like a goose that had been shot out of the sky. We found ourselves catching Pete, who was swearing and frothing at the mouth. He had tried to make his way back over the rail, but the Captain had planted a boot on his chest. Pete had to back-track and flung himself out and away as the LCI came within jumping distance on the next rise. We were stunned. HB gone. So casually. How little it took.

The vibration of the motor came up as we pushed off for the pier. Willie, Gino and I had clawed our way up to the edge of the bow, which was just a large slanting steel door. Gino pointed to something and, looking down, we saw these oily red clots moving with the water. Other guys came up on the door to look. We wondered whose blood it was—the boy's or HB's? Or maybe the salt water was preserving the blood of the GIs who had been killed during the invasion that now seemed like yesterday. Willie allowed it was like the ocean had a storehouse of blood from those bodies shagging around in the depths below, and maybe when a body brushed up against something sharp, or a fish took a bite, the blood came out. It might be a year before all the blood was washed away—if ever.

The LCI let us off at the Mulberry pier, a steel affair, which we were told the British invented to make an instant harbor on the beach. We got a closer look at the shell holes and barbed wire and the lonely battered trucks and tanks strewn along the beach. The waves came rolling in boisterously and angrily, roaring, bumping and hissing and leaving a thick white foam as they spread themselves out and then made a long, gravelly rasp as they tore at the sand on their way back out. It looked like an unearthly place that is forever stark and strange, where there are no people, and a cold wind blows over the shells like they were the scattered bones of ancestors long gone. The whole damned place tasted of salt and rust and sand and sulfur and ashes. What an awesome beach this must have been when the hot lead was flying. Also a hallowed place where you said a prayer for the two just lost—and an additional one for all the others who had fallen there. HB once said, "Guys will be gone and you'll move on, knowing you can't dwell on it." But, for us, at that time, we also had a long look at the surf.

13.

We would lose others, the first being Pete; a loss, but, unlike those to come, a live one unmissed by us, which the Army would have been better off missing. He had taken an impulsive shot in the mouth from Gush and was lucky he got off with nothing more. Pete would, in time, get himself situated in a Replacement Depot located in a vacant Chateau, former residence of one of the Rothschilds in a once exclusive outskirt of Paris not far from the Bois de Boulogne. From there he would operate a thriving black market and, in his spare time, a network of whorehouses. Rebel had been all for finishing him right there and then, but Henchman intervened. Pete slinked off to the Aid Station to get some stitches in his lip and had his buddies sent to the motor pool, a matter prearranged with the Hollywood Major, and which, like Pete himself, turned out to be bad luck.

Meanwhile, we would have a good old-fashioned tourist look at this forsaken war zone. Down at the beach, we'd waited around so long it was dark by the time we got ourselves across that fearsome patch of sand in a long straggly column, hauled ass up to the top of that cliff, and filed past the pillboxes commanding the heights. We marveled at how anybody ever made it that good long stretch from the surf to the base of the cliff without getting picked off. Just walking was hard enough. The sand sucked at our shoes, which weren't even wet, and the straps of our packs dug sharply into our shoulders.

Going up the steep hill path, guided on either side by white tape, we heard somebody whisper, "Mines."

"Here?" another asked.

"Yeah, stupid."

"Why, in hell ain't they got 'em out yet? Somebody could get killed with them still layin around."

"No time."

"Aw, so they say. Yah know, maybe there ain't any mines over there. The Germans are smart enough they'd put 'em here on the trail, don't yah think? Not over on the side."

"Be easy enough for yah to find out."

We had to stop several times to catch our breath. The way we looked at one another, it was as if the thought went through our collective heads that you wouldn't worry about your breath if you were about to take your last. We were dripping sweat and cursing, and one of the talkers wondered why they hadn't found a better way in, at least then. We had a break at the top and threw ourselves down on the rough turf. Friend Curiosity (the rumor guy) called out, "Hey, look," and down below the whole blasted beach was lit up like it was Christmas. The Navy and our Engineers were busy working on the steel piers and on the ships and wreckage. Acetylene torches were sparking all over the place. It was amazing to think they'd actually been trying to clear all that debris away—working nights, too—and it still looked so bad. And all that light. It had to mean Jerry was keeping all his planes home to guard the Fatherland. We never had any doubts that the Germans knew what they were doing. Couldn't say the same for us.

Turning the other way, we found everything go coal black as we stumbled into a tented area. There was a lot of confusion, and we kept bumping into one another and tripping over tent pegs and ropes, as word kept coming: "No room here; move." So we pushed on a ways and were directed into a field bounded by hedgerows, where we were told to pitch tents. That's when we found out that our new CO was Lieutenant Finch, whom we remembered from maneuvers, back when. We also remembered he was a decent guy, long and thin, with sharp features, and eyes the color of washed denim. Because of his

73

sharp nose we called him "Bird." Willie said he'd seen finches that could be pretty feisty. Some guys thought Bird was so thin because he had sandpaper nerves that wore him down. Others said he got that way from eating our chow, wanting to make himself less of a target. In any event, he came through with tent poles and pegs when we told him our problem, having apparently jumped on TC to get them from Supply. He also got us some C rations, which we ate cold, and had ourselves a cigarette—also courtesy of Bird—before sacking out. His presence helped lessen the pain of losing HB. It seemed that the closer we got to where we were going, the more attentive the officers became, usually. Unfortunately, we were going to have to get used to losing the ones we got close to; something that was even more hurtful when we lost fellow GIs we'd become close to—buddies.

We got a better feel for where we were in the morning. It had clouded over again and was gray and drizzly. While the officers and non-coms were getting things reorganized and checking in the new men—guys who had been wounded badly enough to go to hospitals in England—we had a chance to reconnoiter, which Bird allowed us to do—not HB's style. We took in the concrete gun emplacements, most of which were pock-marked where they had taken small arms fire and shrapnel, for all the good either of those did. Quite a number had large black splotches, white in the middle, with cracks running out from them, where our guys had laid a dynamite charge, maybe a bangalore torpedo, up against their blind side or back. We learned from the veterans that that was enough of a door chime to bring them crawling out with the white handkerchief. "Flag or no flag, heaven help 'em if they had a weapon."

We also heard our first combat stories. We had three paratroopers with us who had made D-Day there. One of them lost his Tommy Gun on the way down. He cut off a piece of his parachute cord and sneaked up on a Heinie sentry from behind, choked him and took his burp gun, a Schmeiser, better than our Thompson. We heard from a Ranger who had been with the first group in, way before the landing craft arrived. He had scaled that cliff, then fell into a hole on top of a sleeping Heinie and fought him hand to hand with his knife. He was a slight blond-headed fellow with a thin mustache, very cool, also modest. His name was Andersen, from Wisconsin. He looked so clean and innocent, a sort of all-American boy type, that you'd think the meanest shooting he'd ever done was in the pool hall, if that. The way he talked, all the hand-to-hand stuff and crawling around in the dark was nothing, the dark being a GI's protection in his kind of combat. What impressed us was that the mean kind of combat these guys were in was survivable. Andersen told us but not by all that many.

Gino said, "If these guys are tryin to scare the shit out of us, tell 'em what a good job they're doin. Didn't Rebel once say he wanted to be a Ranger? See what he says now."

Willie said, "I kin tell yah what I'm sayin. If the Army's got guys like these fellas, what the hell do they need us for?"

"Yeah, that hand-to-hand stuff. Man alive. If a Heinie comes at *me* with a hand, I'll shake it, and say 'goodbye.' He goes his way. I go mine."

The paratroopers took us over to the hedgerows. The fields in between ran maybe forty feet wide, and at most two hundred feet long. What amazed us was those weren't the hedges we knew at home; they ran at least twenty or more feet high. The troopers knew what we were thinking by our looks; true, a helluva place to fight. They showed us the Heinies' standing foxholes, well made like everything else the Germans did, but their standing grave if somebody got them buttoned up and rolled a grenade in. The snug-fitting earth came right up around them like a stocking, no way to get out in a hurry. Did the Germans do that so their guys would have to stand and fight, no matter what? Those standing jobs were being used as latrines. Squatting over blood. One of those gems that Andersen liked to entertain us with. He said to think nothing of it; just something that happens. That kind of use he attributed mostly to the Germans, very practical people, also pretty rough.

It was during our two days there that we were introduced to Calvados, absolutely the next best thing to drinking pure untamed rubbing alcohol and feeling it burn all the way down to your toenails. Willie announced that it was good. "Compared to ol' Kiamishy Mountain Dew, it did sort of tighten your pucker string." Some wag was saying that if you had a bottle of Calvados nuzzled up against your belly, you could just softly fall out, forget you had a name, learn French, and stay fallen out till they came for you.

Fact is, we had such a guy with us, Raol, a returnee. To us he was a nine-day's wonder. He spoke fluent French, having been born in Quebec, and taught French in a Detroit high school. He had volunteered for the Normandy invasion, and the day he got hit, a farmer found him in his field and took him in. He offered to show us the farmhouse that was a couple of miles down the road junction outside our bivouac area, and off we went, armed with a supply of candy and cigarettes that we wanted to trade for Calvados. Raol got a big, chatty welcome and before long an invitation to stay for dinner.

We were amazed at how blond, blue-eyed and square-featured the farmer was. Raol explained that the family was descended from Vikings, going back more than ten centuries. 'Holy smokes,' I mused. There was all that history behind this place where we were standing. The farmer took us over to the stone fence that divided his pasture from his orchards and potato fields, and showed us with a sweep of the arm how our troops had come around the German positions, but not before the Germans shot a number of the GIs in hot pursuit, one of them Raol. All of this was said with a half-inch cigarette butt stuck to the farmer's bottom lip, except for which you'd have sworn that he came straight from the snows of Norway. He had on the same wide dull-brown pants that many of these farmers wore, and a different kind of brown herringbone jacket, but I could easily see him wearing a ski sweater. Looking out the doorway of the stone farmhouse were four unattached girls, in-laws and cousins whose men-folks had been lost. Though their clothes were faded and worn, the girls themselves weren't bad looking, except for their teeth. One of them came forward and gave Raol a hug. They got real chummy. The farmer wanted somebody around who could speak English and help with the heavy chores. That was the last we ever saw of Raol. He went into that farmhouse and dropped out of sight—plunk. You could just as well have sent his dog-tags home.

What impressed us was that nobody seemed to notice he was gone that first night, and, when still no notice was taken of it the following day, one of the returnees hopped into a jeep and said he was headed for Paris '*toot sweet,*' and would just as soon skip the scenery along the way. Hell, he'd been there for its liberation, but they had rushed his outfit out of town and let the Frenchies' Resistance take over. Paris owed him a little fun before he went back up on line, and off he sailed, his Jeep fishtailing through the mud. With him turning the ignition key off and on real quick, the Jeep let go with a loud backfire. We were dumbfounded.

It set some guys to thinking. Me too. I was laying in my pup tent, feet in and head out the flap end, looking up at the richly black sky, with the stars buried deeply in it like diamonds in velvet. It was the first clear night in a long time. I'd almost forgotten what a starry sky looked like. For a while I indulged the sense of being a part of the stillness and the soft blackness up there that went on forever and had no end. I thought about what had gone on here. It struck me that the Army couldn't be bothered about losing a GI here or there, whether dead, fallen out, or just plain gone. There was the matter of prosecuting the war. Losses were common and expected. Personnel, equipment—it didn't make that much difference; we'd seen the debris on the beach and knew about the GIs lost and wounded there. The generals had their objectives. It sure seemed strange that they felt their pride was on the line. Among us, the objective was survival. There was no thought about anything bigger than that, like, for instance, wanting to rid the world of Nazi brutality—by engaging in ours. Oh well, about some things, there was no choice. In this case, good thing.

The stories that these returnees told kept coming back to me, and I wondered if I'd ever have that throat-grappling instinct. Could I sneak up on a German and dig my fingers into his throat—or, in a frenzy for my life, find I had no choice but to fight him to the bitter end? Did these guys actually *see* a German lurking in the far hedgerow and pull the trigger on him? If so, we supposed they had put it out of mind—much as our fellows had almost nothing to say about HB, or the little kid, outside of the blood in the water, and the long look. Of course, Gush had let Pete have it. But hand-to-hand. You probably had to get mad, *really* mad, and, above all, fear for your life.

I could tell the rest of the guys were having their thoughts too, but before anyone could do anything more than think, we were rolling up our sacks and getting ready to move out. Bird needed somebody to talk to among the enlisted men, and, just as HB had Kraut, Bird remembered Rebel for his toughness and shared some thoughts with him. One of the things he shared was our travel orders, which Rebel told me. We were to be leaving for Le Mans as soon as some trucks could be freed up from the supply run. After that we would push off for Orleans and follow a route north and east from there that would take us through Fontainebleau, around Paris, and on through Meaux, Soissons, Laon, and then into Belgium, going by Dinant and Marche, and winding up in a wooded area outside of Bastogne, from where we'd be called up to join a line outfit.

14.

Rebel passed on word that, on the way, we'd likely spend a couple of days in Le Mans, and said he was working on Bird to see if he'd find a way to get us passes to town. That had us thinking about—what else—women. Waiting for the trucks, guys were already nervous with anticipation. They would go to the bushes, and out would float their little anthem, "Oh, the girls in France, they don't we-her any pants." And, by gosh, many didn't. There wasn't any need of them, which offered a girl the convenience that she could just squat in the field any time she wanted to. And pants cost money that was better spent on other things, like food. The anthem was sung so hopefully, like a guy in the shower thinking about his date, that you knew the singers were going to be disappointed. I didn't give it much thought; green as I was, I had no idea of what it might be like to be with a strange woman and didn't think I'd want to be.

But getting to Le Mans was another matter. The weather had become rainy again, turning some of those narrow roads we took into thick gummy mud. For some reason, they didn't send back enough trucks for all of us, even though the guys were being stuffed into those trusty six-by-sixes thirty to a truck, packs and all. Our little in-group was part of the thirty that had to wait for them to scare up another truck. Four of us volunteered to go over to the motor pool, where we did find an empty truck. The only trouble with it was that the driver was lying across the seat fast asleep. When he couldn't be roused, Rebel motioned for me to grab his feet. We laid him down beside the road, and he kept right on snoring, not missing a beat. "My, oh my," said Willie. "Ain't *he* gonna be suh-prised!"

"Probably not," Rebel said. "Sleeps it off an' gets him some more o' the good stuff."

Bird had meanwhile shaken another driver zonked out on Calvados, doused him with a pail of water, and stuck him in the driver's seat. Heaven help us, it was CT. He tried to beg off, saying he was waiting for another assignment, but when Bird made like he was reaching for his forty-five, he came wide awake. "This ain't a request soldier. It's is an order."

There were closer to forty than thirty of us that finally got squeezed into that truck. Gush got up on the roof of the cab and pulled another guy up with him, a fellow Cherokee he had latched onto. It didn't give us that much more room; we still had to just about breathe in unison. Since we were several hours late, Bird leaned on CT to keep the damned thing a-rollin.

We began to accustom ourselves to the squeeze and the drizzle, and the misty early autumn dusk had a sort of dreamy, settling effect on us. We had gone through some bleak, shattered towns, with torn-up houses and tart-smelling narrow streets with crooked stone buildings that echoed loudly to the sound of the truck. Then we'd come out into the countryside with its billowy trees and high hedgerows, and it felt like all the shadows of a foreign night were playing around us like ghosts on the prowl. Willie managed to get out his harmonica, and there was enough Calvados slushing around in us for him to get a chorus of "Home on the Range" going. We faltered a bit on "Roll Me Over in the Clover." But the one he really let himself out on was that mushy old "Londonderry Air" that he'd heard back in Warminster.

> *Would God I were the tender apple blossom*
> *That floats and falls from off the twisted bough,*
> *To lie and faint within your silken bosom*
> *Within your bosom, as that does now!*
> *Or would I were a little burnished apple*
> *For you to pluck me....*

That's when the hit came—the crack, the sudden jolt, the flying sparks and near-toppling swerve, the cries, the bump-bump-bump and the final jarring slam that brought us up short. We'd been going at a clip and got sideswiped by one of those three-quarter ton weapons' carriers with the wide truck bed. CT apparently thought he'd moved over far enough to scrape by, but his far-enough still got us scraped. We'd taken a glancing hit somewhere around the back wheels, which turned our front end and sent us careening across the road into a drainage ditch and out, until we slammed into a tree.

Gush and his Cherokee buddy went flying off the roof of the cab. Gush was hurled some twenty feet, landing in an open field, and awoke fogged over and achy, but otherwise unharmed. Didn't he tell us the Normandy firewater would give you a cushion? Not so lucky was his buddy who shot smack into the tree trunk headfirst and fell off to the side lifeless. Back at the truck there was confusion. Guys were groaning and asking what happened. The two end guys had fallen out onto the road helmet-less when the tailgate let go. One, having hit the gate as he went over, was all bloody in the face and was tossing and moaning. The other was temporarily out cold. It was Gino. Just before the accident he had refused to take the third light off a match for his cigarette. When he came to, he pointed to the bloody guy and said, "*See.*" Except for those complaining of ribs bruised by their neighbor's canteen, and those faking it—an easy way back—the only others who got badly hurt were CT and Bird in the cab. Bird, who went into the windshield, came away, thanks to his helmet, with no more than a nasty bump on his nose, a few cuts, and some neck pain, which he shook off. CT had had the steering wheel planted in his chest and was carrying on about the pain. Bird said he ought to thank his stars he was still breathing.

Andersen the Ranger looked us over and, seeing how many came through without a scratch—most, more stunned than hurt—he thought we ought to be able to cut it in what lay ahead. "Which is a pity," he added, "considering that, by rights, guys like you will probably deserve to be shot for dereliction." That is, except for Gush, he admitted, who obviously led a charmed life.

Rebel went back at Andersen saying that the way we came through was the "will of God." "Yeah," he added, "and don't think He ain't a-lookin." From time to time we were reminded of how strong Rebel's Bible Belt upbringing had been—not something he wore on his sleeve—and, as we'd find out, it served him well. Indeed, it gave Rebel a sustaining power that made an impression on guys less inclined to see divine influence in our lives—for example, guys like me.

I didn't realize how sore I felt until we'd been laying out in that wet field for several hours awaiting the truck that Bird had radioed back for. Looking around, I saw it was the same with others. In fact, there had been five of us in a row on the swerve side who had each taken an especially mean shot to the ribs. Kraut, who I knew had gotten it pretty good from my canteen, stoically said we'd all feel better in the morning. Not the kid sitting next to him who asked him to check out the place where he felt a piece of rib sticking out. When Bird came by to ask how he was doing, the kid scrunched his face up like he'd bit into a lemon and answered in a scratchy voice, "Kinda piss poor, sir." Bird doubted him, but put him over beside CT anyway, along with the rest of the guys who were hurting for sure. Kraut said it was just as well ("Be no damned good to us anyway.") and was borne out when the kid blew his nose and went to sleep. "Po Li'll ol' Barry," Willie observed. "Must be thinkin his Mama's gonna be around to take care o' him." In time, the innocent little guy would surprise us.

There didn't seem to be any way we could lay or hold our arms without feeling some pain. Resigned to put up with it, we wrapped our raincoats around ourselves and leaned our backs against a tree for the rest of the night, sort of sleeping and not sleeping. Willie produced a bottle of Calvados, but Rebel said the only way it would help would be if we up and rubbed the stuff on our bruises. We saw the ambulance come and go in the early morning dark, followed by the creaky wrecker that lumbered in to pick up the remains of our truck. Barry bucked up and stayed with us.

15.

It was a good while into the day before our new truck finally arrived. We felt every bump along the way, and, as Bird told the driver to go easy, it wasn't till well into the night that we finally arrived at Le Mans. With all of the jostling around we'd taken, our aches acted up again, and it felt like we'd acquired some new ones. Lack of sleep didn't do much to improve our mood either, as we marched in from the road stiff legged.

As we approached the Chateau grounds, which had been converted into a Replacement Depot, we somehow got mingled in with guys returning from a pass to town. Hearing them talk about it did make us perk up a bit. As we arrived at the gate, a bunch of Air Corps guys muscled in ahead of us, and one of their officers—a twenty-five year old Colonel—walked up to the MPs and told them all of his men had been cleared; no need to check passes, and so they were waved on through. That was the Air Corps for you. The fly-boys got all the glamour and were used to getting the warm chow, warm quarters, warm women, and access to everything else that was warm and good. Like Andersen said, "We liked 'em for whompin the Heinies, hated 'em for whompin us. And we weren't too keen on their attitude, regardless." One of his buddies in the hospital had been with a regiment poised for the attack at St. Lo, and his was one of the outfits that took the notorious pounding, when our planes got scared off by flak and dropped their stuff short. Our losses, he thought, might have been heavier than the Germans'.

So the likes of us being in with the Air Corps was not a good mix. We could sense there'd be trouble ahead, and it was not long in coming. Next day, all we could think about was getting into town, pass or no pass. We had seen how the fly-boys did it and thought we'd give it a try. We'd been hanging around the gate in the shadows of a rose arbor watching the guys going out by two's and three's showing their passes, and then, when a whole flock of them came up, with that boy-Colonel waving a paper at the MPs, we saw our chance and just fell in behind them, going out on the tail end of their column. The trick was to catch them on the way back, which wasn't difficult because we all wound up at bars in the same part of town. Gino gave us the high sign when it was time to go, and out we piled, beer bottles in hand, not knowing exactly who we were following as we made our way to the waiting trucks.

Once back at the Chateau gate, we bunched up so close that Andersen, who was pretty well crocked, stumbled against the guy in front of him and, looking up, caught the silhouette of those leather flight jackets and garrison caps given the infamous crush and worn back on their heads. He spat out a choice remark about the chicken shit Air Corps. One of the fly-boys wheeled around on him, but his two buddies quickly grabbed him by the shoulder and horsed him back and away. You could tell that that guy must have been shot up himself. That might have been the end of it, if one of the other Air Boys didn't get his dander up when told what was said about their ace. He went for Andersen, and we all piled in and had ourselves a kind of a brawl, more fists missing than hitting. The MPs pulled us apart, and the upshot was that our contingent was to be shipped out next day.

By an interesting fluke, it was the first of our group that went. Because of our separate arrival, the administrators at the Chateau didn't have us down as belonging with them, they being the only ones identified by our shipment number. We spent most of the next day being marched about, which we didn't mind since it was a way to warm up. The lousy part was having to stand around in the rainy cold listening to a long drawn-out talk about German weaponry in a dripping apple orchard. The T-Sergeant, strangely a Black guy, something of a clown, kept reaching back into his tent like a magician and bringing out first this prize and then the other. He had a regular grab bag of moldy old pieces of captured equipment. He showed us all the Germans could do with their Mausers, burp guns, P-38s, potato mashers, mines, and even the hobbled remains of one of their feared 88's, the best artillery piece in the world, capable of firing a shell faster than an M-I bullet. He saved a muddy and battered screaming meamie launcher for last, and said with a laugh and hitch of the trousers that it might not look like much, being just a cluster of nine tinny rocket tubes, but it was the only weapon that could kill you twice, first by the hair-raising scream and then by the concussion.

It was obvious that this guy would never be going up to a line outfit, as they didn't have any Technical non-coms in the infantry TO, none that we knew of anyway, unless he worked in supply, or the kitchen, behind the lines. Nor did we know of the presence of any Blacks among us, though they had their own combat outfits, as I would learn later on when I met a guy, whose all-Black tank battalion had seen quite a bit of action. Willie and I kept nudging one another, wondering about this guy, until it dawned on us, that he, for goodness sake, just might be Judd, one of Roscoe's cohorts, looking quite different under a helmet and sporting a scar across his neck. There were things we wanted to ask, but he indicated he had to move on, mouthing a voiceless 'Later.'

In any event, it was a mistake for us to be told all that in a wet apple orchard. Between the rain and the apple crunching, we must have missed some important points. Chilled to the bone we wound up hopping around like Injins when it was over, Gush in the lead, letting out a tom-tom beat. Andersen lifted a jerry can from the truck that came in with our chow, and he spilled some gas on the ground and lit it. We gathered round and stretched our palms out to the fire. Andersen said the drivers did it all the time; used more gas than the trucks did, so, if you were up on line and were hurting for chow, you knew what they meant when they reported the truck couldn't make it.

16.

Essentially, we were killing time until we got called up to join on-line outfits, and since the war seemed to be stalling, it looked like there might be quite a bit of time to kill. So what do a bunch of idle GIs in the heart of France think about, knowing that before long they might not make it to the next day? It all came back to the hots for that sacred triangle, cranked up to a new level now that it was at last said to be available. Thought of as a last time thing, it sent one great urge to rut rippling through the ranks. Gino had latched onto a map of France, and, somebody pointed to the enlarged insert of Paris with the river curving around either side of Le Isle de la Cité. To a man, guys saw it taking on the form of one big luscious mossy hillock that, legs apart, winked at us and called out, *"COME! COME! I AM WAITING!"* Guys were suddenly itching, panting, dancing, singing, laughing, crying, aching to go for it.

That is, some were. Some were not. A number of the kids were confused, like me. I'd read enough nineteenth-century British novels to get the idea that there ought to be some romance about it, with luck, love. Willie suggested I go talk to the Chaplain, and he'd set me straight, but, truth to say, though I liked his services, the embarrassment put me off. I found that Barry was feeling much the same way. He said that when he approached the combat fellows and asked why they were holding back, while everyone else had the itch, they just smiled and kicked the ground. Andersen as much as said, what could they tell a kid, if he didn't know what to make of it for himself?

Without blaming anybody, Bird put out word that we should be mindful that in the serious business ahead inner discipline would be helpful. Rebel got an oar in too, asking didn't some of us, for goodness sake, have wives and girlfriends at home? Besides, didn't it make a difference that we'd be going where the Germans had been ahead of us? Usually humorless Kraut surprised us by saying, if it was good enough for his distant brethren, well.... Gino yelled, "Whoopee!"

Overheard in the chow line, the map readers weren't very secretive about their anticipation. In their anxiety to know 'Where the hell do we *find* 'em?' they put themselves in a pretty dangerous mood. Gush, who had spent some time on the west coast, said it was like what they used to call earthquake weather in California.

But not to worry. Although this big estate we were bivouacked on did have a wall around the Chateau grounds, it was a wall that had had ragged holes knocked in it by our tanks. It could have been the tankers' calling card, or it could have been that they were just blowing out the tube. Barbed wire had been strung across the gaps, and since the Base Commander had gotten our identity straightened out, he volunteered us for guard duty at those holes, two hours on and four off per guard mount, through the night. Not that those places really needed any guarding; it was just a matter of keeping us busy, like the milk-can detail we were also put on. (Fresh off the farm for the officers, our milk being fresh off the boat, powdered.) The BC wanted to compensate for the mistake (his own) that got him stuck with us. The previous guards, realizing there wasn't any reason to guard, had brought a GI blanket along and fixed themselves a soft place to enjoy their moment of bliss.

That's how guys found out that if they couldn't get to the hillock, the hillock would come to them. Judd, the T-Sergeant, gave them a short history of the situation. There was a seven o'clock train from Paris every evening, and the conductor slowed it down just enough as it passed our estate for a contingent of whores to hop off. That train

88

was still running. Judd wondered that we didn't hear the whistle. He said it used to be that the whores would come charging across the tracks, rush the gaps, conveniently cleared, and sweep through the area tent by tent. Then, stockings brimming with francs, blouses with cigarette packs, they'd listen for the whistle of the 10:45 going back to Paris and take off like a flock of pigeons rousted out of their nesting places. When it got to be too flagrant, BC felt he had to shut it down. So the guys went out to meet their enterprising guests at the tracks, herded them into the woods just beyond an open pasture that belonged to the estate, and business was flourishing again. BC, expecting a cut, silently approved. Out of sight was more like it.

By Judd's account, any time after eight o'clock you had to be careful where you stepped out there. That's when the Organization (better known as Pete's Octopus) took over, and things went more smoothly. There'd be seven or eight lines—just like regular chow lines—all leading to some mattress behind a clump of bushes. Guys just waited their turn like they would for anything else in the Army. It used to be a hundred francs and a pack of cigarettes a throw, but, of course, the GIs ruined it for themselves, offering more for the better girls, so the Organization put the price up for all.

Gino interrupted, wanting to know how things were *now*, and Judd had an eager audience who, he knew, couldn't hear enough. On a busy night, guys would be run through at the rate of about six an hour, so, if you counted the heads in front of you, you could figure out when your turn would come. You couldn't see who you were getting (for looks, that is), but it didn't much matter in the dark, except that some lines were suggestively longer than others. The good ones expected a tip, and, to the GIs, francs looked like monopoly money and cigarettes were very trade-worthy. The ladies were bringing in musette bags. From time to time, the system had to be modified to avoid another shut down, but, under the new management, if guys would just quietly take their stints of guard duty, everything would fall into place.

Willie filled us in on how it went. Having drawn the short straw, he pulled the first stint of guard duty, and he was just smoothing out his blanket when he heard the train whistle. The wait practically unnerved him. But just as he was beginning to think Judd was putting him on, he heard somebody go, "Hsst," and two heads popped around the jagged corner, one lisping something in vulgar French. He jubilantly whispered "Hot dog," and yanked them in. The lisper had a leg that was some inches shorter than the other, and the idea of it was to take her standing and kick the rock out from under her short leg. The other was no slouch. She removed her false teeth.

As Willie staggered away, he bumped into Gino, who called out "Next." Behind Gino was a line, kept at a discreet distance. The efficiency of it all was amazing. However, when two nights later, guys started jostling one another for position in line, the commotion brought up the MPs, who got banged around themselves, and the action had to be suspended, which raised a considerable clamor.

It got bad enough for Bird to approach the Chaplain, Captain Hilfer, a worldly wise Methodist minister and misplaced intellectual. According to Bird, Hilfer allowed that he understood our plight, but thought the men might not want to hear from him on something like that. The best he could advise was for Bird to tell us it was demeaning and impersonal, and that, contrary to what we might think, it would not put us in a good frame of mind; quite the reverse. He could be there to counsel men about their regrets; though, better still, he'd prefer counseling them in advance to contain themselves. Bird said he had to think about the morale side of it, but conceded that, as a compromise, the clamp-down might avoid trouble. As a reminder that we faced serious times ahead, Bird made a point of having Hilfer's advice filter down to the troops in hopes that guys would come to their senses.

In the lull, we got a chance to talk to Judd. He told us that HB, good guy that he was, had seen to it that Roscoe was released from Pete's clutches and sent back to the States with the returning Queen Elizabeth. As for Budd (of course, Judd 'n Budd, the inseparable pair) he pulled a knife on Pete's goons, and they turned it back on him. He was gone when they threw him over. Himself, well, he didn't have much of a choice. He'd gotten stabbed and was in a real bad way. He was told he had his choice between a swim and a job. So this was the best deal he could swing—a pimp, with a front, but a live one, which wasn't too bad, considering he used to play the piano in civilian life.

Unfortunately, our guys were not in a feel-sorry mood. Impatience got the better of them, and they started making noises. To hell with what lay ahead; dammit, they wanted what they wanted—*now*! So, fearing chaos, BC let it be known that he was going to clear us out. Bird said he'd try to wangle passes to town before our now-imminent departure. Hilfer rounded us up for a farewell service. I reminded him that I was a Unitarian, which, as he'd told me, was a mere notch better than no religion at all, but he wanted to have full attendance, and he thought I had promise, regardless of my faith. I did believe in God, after all, didn't I?

He wasted no time getting to his point, regardless of what we might or might not want to hear amidst our turmoil. We were very shortly going to be coming face to face with our mortality. Fear of the Great Void being man's most discomforting thought, he reminded us of a previous service when he'd said that for Man there need never be a Void. Though we may die, we live on by the good we have done. For goodness is not just a nice way to be; once experienced, it perpetuates itself. It endures, survives death, survives evil. We found all of that somewhat cloudy. Besides, we didn't care to be hearing a whole heck of a lot about death. Not wanting to lose us, he clarified. Goodness is eternal: that is the meaning of Jesus's death and resurrection. His death defied Death, His love ennobles Life. He abides and abides with us.

Hilfer paused and asked us to think about it. Flowers die in the winter and come back to life in the spring. We come to life, we *live*, by virtue of our humanity, our feelings for our fellow man. That's where true manhood lay. He elaborated, indicating an awareness that "manhood" touched a nerve, and asked us to direct ourselves to its greater meaning. He went on for a while about what God does for us and what He wants *of* us. So we drifted off a bit. Finally, wanting us to come away with a simple idea that had some staying power, he said our experience of goodness would be in looking out for one another and quoted Ecclesiastes: "For two are better than one, because they have a good return for their work: if one falls down his friend can help him up." His concluding words, slightly modified from the same book, were given in an impactfully hushed voice, "Good men, follow Jesus, walk but in the ways of thine heart." Some of his points found their mark. He was something of an actor, but nonetheless inspirational. Guys came away feeling better. Me too. Talk about mood swings in the Chateau at Le Mans.

I knew Hilfer was too smart not to know that the high he gave us might not outlast our terrible distraction. But he was not without hope, which lay in the decision he'd made—unbeknownst to us at the time, but revealed later—that when we left, he was determined to go with us. So he might have the last word after all.

92

17.

I met Fleurette by the purest chance, the purest experience of my young life. It was like a dream, so brief, so sweet; though fleeting, ages rolled into minutes. So infinitely real, it seemed for days afterwards like maybe it had never happened.

Bird confirmed that passes had been promised, but not many were given, and those that were, somehow wound up in the hands of the Air Corps guys. However, we weren't to be denied. Let 'em go ahead and put us in the guardhouse. See if we cared. All the more impetus for our bunch to want to make a night of it, and as Willie said, "We're a-goin regardless, and I ain't just a-woofin'."

We took off in groups, seeping out of the infamous holes in the wall—-no longer guarded. We hitched a ride with one of BC's drivers running the empty milk cans back to the farm for an early morning refill, that also consisted of refills on eggs, butter, ham, fresh baked bread, and the French version of apple pie, also fresh from the oven. Made your mouth water. Service outfits sure knew how to seek out the goodies. The driver turned out to be Pancho the cook, who indicated he was now going in the night before the 5 a.m. pick up and sleeping over, that being better than getting up at 4 a.m. for the trips some of us had to take with him. Besides, he'd developed a friendship with the buxom milk maid, dairyman Pierre's daughter, who would be waiting for him in the hayloft. Elsie, as Pancho called her, happened to be a first rate cook herself and, ever so accommodative, could be persuaded to come out to the Chateau to prepare pork chops, steaks, and seafood coquille for the officers' mess, which she'd bring in with great éclat, as they say, a festivity greeted with shouts and whistles.

It was a good eight-mile ride to town, and we passed several civilians on the way walking along the dark road. They'd get well off into the drainage ditch when they heard our truck motors, like they'd learned a thing or two about how GIs drive. As we got into the outskirts of town, we came upon a slight girl who was bent forward, weighed down with a fairly heavy load that, by gosh, she was carrying in a GI field pack. I just got a flashing look at her face in the headlights as she looked up waiting for us to go by. A loop of brown hair swung down over her forehead, bordering soft round eyes, ever so sweetly strained. She was puffing and my heart went out to her. Her angelic young face came as a surprise, because, seeing her from the back at first, kind of hunched over, carrying that big load, I thought maybe she was an old lady. Two guys banged on the cab for Pancho to stop, but he paid them no heed. We were going uphill and Pancho had shifted into a lower gear, so one of the cab bangers, Mad Markoff, was all for jumping off. He kept calling, "Che-ri, wait for me!" until she was out of sight.

Markoff was a wild one even before he discovered calvados. He had gone back to the Aid Station after our accident complaining of sore ribs, and said he was given a shot of something, told he'd have black-and-blue marks for a couple of days, and sent on to rejoin us. Having spent more than his share of recent guard duty, he had told Pancho he didn't know about the rest of us, but the way he was 'itchin,' he wanted to be left off at the raunchiest whorehouse in town. Pancho laughed and said there wasn't one, but he knew where to take us.

The streets in town were empty and everything was blacked out, except for an occasional dull hazy glow balled around a lamp-lighted café. Hardly any vehicles were running, outside of GI trucks, and some rickety old trolleys that dragged themselves sleepily along with maybe four or five passengers. Pancho stopped at a main intersection and gave directions to Rebel who had ridden in the cab with him. He didn't know about other joints, but Markoff was bound to find what he wanted there.

It was a dingy, smelly old café with wide store-front windows and raggedy burlap curtains running across them halfway up, so you could look in if you got on your toes. The yellow enamel walls had several cracks in them and the plaster was broken out in some places. Dull wooden tables and chairs were stretched the length of the place against each wall and down the center, on either side of a stove and a grimy red jukebox. There were some clusters of GIs around the tables in back, where the girls circulated, and a couple of lone Frenchmen sat up front, sipping their wine and reading the paper. One well-painted gal with a frilly skirt sat on a stool by the bar facing out, patting one of the cats that was curled up at the corner of the bar. From time to time she'd go around to see if anybody wanted another drink. The door upstairs was just beside her.

I didn't like it the minute I walked in. The gals went pretty heavy on the rouge and mascara. They could have been wearing masks. I'd never been with a whore and wasn't going to be with any of these. But I was curious. What struck me was that they were choosy. A guy would walk up to one of them and she'd look him over, and maybe she'd go upstairs with him and maybe she wouldn't. So the guys didn't choose them so much as they chose the guys, who were mainly Air Corps and acted as if it was their place. Nonetheless, Markoff and Gino were all for this setup, and each found a girl who would accept them—asking payment in advance. A frisky, dark-eyed little gal brushed past our tables and giving Willie a roll of the tongue snagged him. A peroxide blonde came by and gave us a saucy wiggle. When none of us bit, she walked up close to Kraut, and, staring him in the eye, popped the buttons on her blouse. He scratched his chin and looked around self-consciously, but that did it for him.

They left hand in hand, with Gush calling after them, "It'll do yah lotsa good, man. See if she'll take yah round the world."

It looked like they were going to be picking us off one at a time, when in breezed this tall, broad-shouldered Air Corps sergeant (ground crew) with a bit of a swagger, arms outspread. He shook hands with the bartender and gave the girl at the bar a hug and a squeeze and whirled her around a couple of times before sitting her on the bar, where, cross-legged, she pulled her skirt up. The cats went flying, and the two of them had themselves a laugh. He set his crunched Air Corps cap on her head, pushed it back for effect, pinched her thigh, and jabbered endearments, half in French.

"Look, I'm back, like I told you. Ha-ha! You missed me, huh, Cheri? A lot, huh? Ha-ha, ha-ha."

He slapped a wad of francs down and ordered a bottle of cognac. Leaning in close to buss her ear, he slipped a hand under her skirt, which got him a mock slap. Each whisper was followed by a 'Ha-ha, haah!'

"All this over a whore," Gush remarked in disgust.

"Must be something he saw in a movie," Rebel said.

"Yeah, thinks he's in one."

One of our guys at the next table leaned over and said, "Now, that's the gen-u-ine article. *The* rear-echelon commando."

Rebel smelled trouble and, flexing his fist, figured he'd better stick around. Markoff had been eyeing the bar maid.

"See you later," I said and left. Gush came out a minute later, and, just as he did, we heard the rapid click of high-heeled shoes. The clicker appeared out of nowhere and, hooking Gush by the arm, whisked him off. He called for me to come along—"Oughta be enough here for two." I told him to have fun.

A trolley had just stopped in front of the café, and, when it pulled away, who should I see standing there at the curb, but our little friend of the road with the GI pack. I ran across to her and, using the words Willie had shown me in the phrase book, I asked, "Puis-je vous reconduire?" which, I thought, meant something like, 'Can I walk you home?' She looked up at me hesitantly, and, as I took the pack from her shoulders, she said "Oui" ever so faintly. I guessed I'd taken her by surprise, but my manner must have told her that I meant to be helpful. Whatever she had in that heavy pack had to be precious to her, particularly since she'd gone a long way to get it. She kept a grip on the pack as we went off, guiding me down a dark curving street that bowed out one way and then back the other. A couple of times she made me stop and pull back into a doorway. There was somebody following us—a civilian. He stopped when we did, slipping into the shadows on the opposite side of the street. He finally lit a pipe, so he wasn't especially trying to hide his pursuit. She hissed something at him—as much as to say, 'Get lost, will you.'

In any event, we circled the block and she suddenly gave me a tug as we rounded the big bend and drew me under a large overhanging archway which we entered by going through a small door cut in one of the great wooden ones that enclosed the arch. We came out into a cobblestone courtyard. She pointed the way into a kind of tower at our right, and we went up three steep flights to her cramped little room. She bolted the door, lit a candle, and heaved a sigh of relief.

When she emptied the pack, I was amazed at all she had carried. Bread, bottles of wine, cheese, potatoes, turnips, apples, a rind of bacon, and even some black market cans of C rations. There were also some pieces of cloth and thread that she set over on her sewing machine, which she gave a loving pat. She seemed to know rather little English, and I'd forgotten most of my high school French, but she was very clever. She acted things out and drew pictures, and, for the hard words, got down her dictionary. I acted and drew too. We got on just fine. To start with, she drew a picture of a little flower with a smiling face and pointed to herself. I fumbled for a name and stupidly came out with "Daisy." She wrote "Fleurette" and looked up at me with warm brown eyes. My goodness, the girl had a soul.

As she became more trustful, I discovered that she knew more fractured English than she had let on she knew. She was a seamstress and made her living by making clothes, curtains, and the like, which she bartered for food. Times were tough, and there weren't many people who were using a seamstress, so she sometimes had to go a long way to find work, recently from officers' mistresses at the Chateau. The advantage she had over others was her machine, which had belonged to her mother, who had been killed when their house was destroyed. Everybody had scattered during the bombardment, and Fleurette didn't know where any of her brothers and sisters had gone. Her father had been with the underground. He was captured, tortured, and killed. It was sad, but she had to carry on. Small in stature, but one stout-hearted person she was.

I remembered that all four pockets of my field jacket were stuffed full of cigarettes, soap, gum, and candy bars, and, when I emptied them on her little oak table, she clapped her hands and cried, "Ooh la-la!" I reached in my pockets to see what else I had and brought out my pen knife, dollars, a coin purse, and Ronson lighter. She didn't believe all of that was for her, and, when offered, she wouldn't take it. I insisted, especially when she'd told me she had to trade off some of the food for coal so she'd have warmth enough in her hands to work on cold days. The reason I had all of those goodies was that the guys loaded me up with their extras, figuring they'd be safe.

Hearing how tough things were for her, I reached into my back pocket and laid out what francs I had, which she wouldn't take. That along with all the other stuff? Oh no. When I insisted that she absolutely had to have it, since I was well provided for, she started to take her clothes off, but I stopped her. Poor thing, she had no way to repay me and just assumed that that was what was wanted. It really got to me. She saw how I felt and threw herself into my arms, and we kissed. I was surprised at how hard the skin of her face felt, but the rest of her melted in my arms and I held her tight. We were at the brink of tears.

She dabbed at her eyes and, straightening up, offered me some of her wine. I wouldn't have it, so she drew me a map showing where I could get some by rapping at a basement door in the corner house. I ran both ways, and, when I returned, noticed she'd put some perfume on. Her eyes twinkled in the candlelight. She cut some cheese, and I'd just taken my jacket off and poured the wine when there was a shuffle of feet in the hallway and a low knock on the door. My return had been noticed. All I could think of was that that spook with the pipe and trench coat had followed me up. I was relieved to hear a woman's voice. Fleurette opened the door a crack and then cautiously let in two girls with tight-fitting dresses. One of them was pretty big in the chest. They were obviously curious to see who she had. She introduced me as her friend, and they gave her a push on the shoulder and said some things in a low rapid voice that made Fleurette redden ever so faintly. We felt like lovers caught in the act, which broke our mood. However, after she shoved them out, it was restored and we had our little snack.

Fleurette told me that there was a "soldat Americain" who was staying in the apartment next door, and, when she showed me how broad-hipped he was and sour-faced, I snapped my fingers and showed her how his crooked mouth looked and she nodded. I said, "Son of a gun, it's Grumpy, on assignment from Pete." Sure enough, here I was right next door to the Honeycomb that we'd heard was part of Pete's operation. That was where those two floozies had come from. They'd been checking to see that Fleurette wasn't stealing any of their trade. She had taken this room because its location made the rent rather cheap. Under the circumstances, who would want it? Also, Trench Coat was there to offer protection, and if she was doing the floozies' business, he'd expect his cut.

All of this corruption behind the line. War was a money-maker, for all but those who fought it. Fought it because...well, because we were *in* the damned thing, wanting to be elsewhere; were told it was a noble cause, believed it, and didn't think much more about it. No regrets about what miniscule part I would play in it; in fact, I felt much better, in afterthought, to have been where I was, and with the guys I was with than to have been out here for the duration with the scummy backwash.

Fleurette showed me that behind her dresser there was a double-bolted door which led into the Honeycomb itself. She covered her ears and tilted her head to show me there might be a little noise later on. It came earlier than she expected with some caterwauling in the courtyard. One of the whores went down with a candle, and, looking out of the tower window, we saw three GIs skipping around like goats, their bottles held high. The Madam came down, took one look, and pointed to the exit door. "Pussy malade. Allez-vous en. Sapristi!" They circled round once more and the Madam went for a shovel. It was then I heard a familiar voice—Pete's—singing, "Hey, a where d'yah work a Jun?" to see if somebody would come back with "Ona Delawa Lackawan." It seemed like, before clearing out, he wanted to know if Grumpy was still there. I recalled Pete hinting that there would be stops along the way before he reached Paris. But we didn't realize how close Grumpy was with him.

I had a notion to clear out myself. All of a sudden a funk had come over me. To go from such a big high to this sort of thing made me feel sort of... I don't know—I guess creepy. Fleurette sensed it and put her hand on my arm. She was used to such stuff. That was how it had affected her at first, she told me. She was not only intuitive, she had the softest manner of any girl I'd ever known. I suppose that was the reason for my funk: her, here. Here amidst what we'd call all of this 'shit, piss, and corruption.' She came in close for a hug, and that brought me back. She wanted me to sit with her, and so we got down on the floor and leaned against her bedstead.

We sat in silence for while. She snuggled up close, and I took her face in my hands. She had the joy and thrill of life in her that overcomes a lot. She was beautiful. We kissed and I felt her becoming very warm. I brought her over on top of me. Soon the loving got very hot; she was moist and so was I. Shaking out of my pants and drawers I dove under the covers. She undressed too, and as she walked over to blow out the candle, I noticed she had a ring around her waist that looked like the ring on the bath tub. As she walked along the road, that would have been where the dust settled on her. I felt sad on her behalf. Of course, she didn't wear any pants—what use were they?—yet I wished she'd had something to cover her.

She had the loveliest little breasts. In the light that came in from the window, they had a mother of pearl, virginal sheen to them. She also had a certain kind of grace in the way she moved that made you forget everything else. Shaking her hair free, she came to me on tip-toe like a goddess in the night, and once I felt her downy little bare body, I was gone, and so was the world. Every knot was slipped. Ah, but she *was* beautiful, all warm and soft and eager and giving. Every little movement—her subtlest rub—jibed with my own. Life showered through us and spread its glowing wonder into our very being. I'd never had my soul opened up like that. We had barely rested when we embraced again. It became even bigger. She was so silky. A tide washed over me, and I tingled all over for the sheer joy of life taken into the beyond. The quiver of thunder shook us again and again. Glory be to God, I cried, for all the sweet, moist, silky, downy, mother of pearl wonders that come to us in the music of love. We were floating off the end of the earth.

I must have slipped off to sleep, for, the next thing I knew, Fleurette was pulling at me. There was a racket going on next door. She didn't like what the girls were saying, and those high-pitched voices pitted against an angry male voice did seem like real trouble was brewing. I got up on the dresser and, looking through the transom, saw one of the Air Corps guys, drunker than a coot, with his fly open, demanding that the floozies serve him. He wasn't leaving till they did. He had shot all his money and wanted them to do it—first one, then the other, for free. The ruckus had awaken the guy's buddy, a short tubby fellow who had somehow fallen into the closet and was untangling himself from robes, petticoats, and dresses. He got up, demanding the same, and started chasing after the big-chested girl, who screamed, while her friend fended him off with a clothes tree. They cussed one another back and forth, with the girls letting them have a ferocious blast in French. "Saloperie cochon," was all I could make out.

102

Fleurette indicated she knew there'd be noise, but this was the kind that was bound to get the attention of Trench Coat. He'd likely want to inspect her room as well when he came up, particularly as she had given him to understand that she wasn't into any of that. Hard as it was to leave, it was clearly the thing to do. No way I could make trouble for her. Bad enough she was living amidst all this swinishness. I was into my clothes in short order. We kissed and I came back to give her a more lingering kiss. She kept calling "Revenez" to me all the way down the steps.

I had told her I'd find a way to come back. But I hadn't been on the road very long till my head cleared, and, in the cold of night, I knew "Revenez" would never be. I also knew the warmth would always be. Looking up at the black sky, I called out, "Fleurette, God bless you!" I initially regretted that I hadn't told her I loved her, but was glad I'd had enough sense to refrain. How could we not know one another's feelings? Feelings that made the most beautiful night in my life the saddest. In time, you learned to accommodate yourself to sadness.

I fell in with a group of slump-shouldered GIs plodding along the highway, occasionally looking back for a truck that never came. It was a pretty heavy slog, but heavier ones lay ahead: trucks that didn't come, rations and ammo that didn't make it up, battle plans that didn't work—almost never as planned anyway, guys you'd come to know who didn't make it, guys who didn't need to die, and wouldn't have, but for Army fuck-ups, friendly fire that landed unfriendly, rear support units that didn't support, didn't care, didn't know pain or loss. When loss became part of your life, it could break you; and it could give you strength. You lived with it and accepted it and felt yourself fortunate for what you had—like your life. It made you cherish the good that you had had, which, even if lost, was never gone.

Sorrow I'd known, and would know more of, but had yet to know Despair. Looking back from our forthcoming dark days, I was, on the one hand, amazed at my innocence, my pathetic hope that, warmed by good feelings, I would somehow see it through. On the other hand, gladness of heart was a boon to be treasured, more so when lost.

PART II

1.

Recalling something Hilfer had said, I came to believe you could always save yourself. Not physically, of course. I felt you had to—needed to—believe you could, at least as an idea. Even amidst hellishness? Yes, because of hellishness. As I batted Hilfer's preacher ideas around in my head, that was the frame of mind, post Le Mans, that hung on for a while. However, I soon enough learned that good thoughts couldn't survive the knee-buckling shock of cowardice under fire. I say cowardice, because that would be the most nearly honest word to use. A fright that has no name, it's a feeling that can freeze you.

At the same time, however, you find out that everybody else is just as scared. It helps that you're in it together. You share it all, and you get a sense of belonging. You come to realize that that's a lot of what keeps you going, scared as you are.

As I looked back to relive events which produced that realization, I went to the journal I had written shortly after discharge, when the details of my experience on line were still freshly etched in my memory. Certain heart-draining images became as vivid to me in the writing as they had been at the time of their occurrence. There were memorable incidents that came out at me like it was yesterday.

I recalled one in particular of a guy who "froze" during an attack in Hürtgen Forest, as we were about to chug up a hillside uselessly firing our M-1s toward the Heinies' well-entrenched bunkers. There was a sudden wail of artillery shells speeding down on us faster, faster, faster, which sent us lunging real hard to the ground. Breathless, I flattened myself against a rock beside a young fir tree growing out of a crevice. Another guy had thrown himself down beside me and was clutching a branch of the same tree, like me, his face pressed hard against the rock. Our knuckles were cut, our fingernails bleeding, but, scarcely aware of the pain, we'd probably been clawing at the rock, as if wanting to scrape our way into it. Two more shells came down closer yet, exploding on the blazing green grass no more than twenty feet below us. The air was torn apart by a terrifying roar, and I felt a shower of dirt on my back as shrapnel zinged through the branches of trees overhead. I lifted my head to look about, grabbed my rifle and was about to rise, when three more shells came racing down, seemingly headed right for us. I threw myself violently back against the rock, one hand on my helmet. There was a succession of air-ripping explosions on the road just beyond the grass.

It was time to get the hell out of there and best to move up. The guy beside me had not moved. He was still clutching the branch of the fir tree. I asked him what was wrong. Was he hit? No answer.

He stays put, doesn't let go of the branch. The Medic, a slow and easy moving Mississippi boy, comes over and asks me what's wrong. He helps me as we try to lift the guy to his feet. He resists and continues to clutch the branch. The Medic keeps asking, "What's wrong, fella? What's wrong?" There is a blind stare in his eyes. As we get him up, his lips quiver, but no words come out. His arms are stiff, one held out about six inches from his thigh, his fists tight, and he still won't let go of the branch. He's one of the older recruits, looking like he doesn't know his whereabouts, much less what he is doing here. He is a fairly husky guy, starkly white in the face, with a mustache the color of straw.

As the Medic walked away with him, a long arm across his shoulders, I heard him reassuring the guy, "It's all right, fella. They ain't a-throwin any more o' that stuff at us. Yah gonna be aw right now." The guy was stumbling along, still clutching the branch that he had torn off the tree. I didn't know who he was, hadn't seen him before, never saw him again.

The further I went in my journal, the more I found myself recording experiences of guys that I got to know, however briefly, only to see them go down. Some, like the guy holding onto the branch, simply became crazed by it all. As I read, I came across more guys to whom bad things happened than otherwise, something that in itself heightened the fear under fire for those who carried on—God bless 'em, which He did. But that's the way it was in the life of a foot soldier, and that's the story I'm trying to tell.

We joined a division of the First Army. The group of replacements that went on ahead of us joined a division that would be engaged in the Aachen campaign. We were destined for Hürtgenwald, Hürtgen Forest. We heard from the other group that on their first day of combat, Smitty, a stalwart among us, was shot right between the eyes by a sniper. He was a square-cut guy, a farmer from upstate New York, with a wife and two kids. The guy we heard from, Slim, had been shot in the hand in the same encounter and went back with his lucky wound and might not be able to grip a rifle again. The company had taken a beating. Their CO cracked and had to be relieved. Slim missed us. He wished us well.

On the way up, going toward the Siegfried Line, which we were supposedly the first to breach, we went through St. Vith, a column on either side of the road. Funny, some of the things that stand out in what you recall. We were in Belgium, but darned if the people didn't speak German. I wondered about that, especially as the few we saw were grim-faced and not overly friendly. Some of their houses had taken hits from artillery—probably ours—and roofs were caved in, exposing splintered rafters and broken tiles. But what the hell gives? Weren't we supposed to be liberating Belgium? (I heard later that that part of Belgium had not too long ago belonged to Germany— legitimately or otherwise.) We had reached the outskirts of town where the houses were more widely spaced and were moving along when, without warning, the line of march came to an abrupt halt. In the countryside up ahead we were coming under fire from 88s.

We got down apprehensively beside the road, and, as I crouched there on one knee, a wizened old codger came out of the battered old stone house beside me. Our eyes met for an instant, and he said, "Dreckig Wetter." (Dirty weather.) He was hobbling over to the wood pile by the side of the house when his white-haired wife came out on the step and had some harsh words for him. As far as I could make out, she was scolding him for going out after wet wood, and he was rasping back at her something like, 'How is it going to dry if I don't bring it in?' She pointed in the direction of the incoming shells and said wet or dry wouldn't make any difference if he didn't get back in. He grabbed a hefty armload anyway, as if to spite her.

About that time, Barry, who was made Company Runner, came back, short of breath, urging Rebel to get his machine gun squad together and follow him. The CO, Guldine, a first lieutenant who had

108

newly taken over the Company on the loss of our captain, wanted him up front. Having been given this assignment, Barry had taken on a new awareness, and, seeing me, Gush and Willie, he motioned us to pick up our mortar and come too. We arrived at a semi-open area just beyond the town proper, and crouched down in a ditch at the side of the road. Just ahead were a couple of burned-out Sherman tanks from a prior engagement. A Medic was bandaging a sergeant who had taken a hit in the shoulder, but the shrapnel must have gone on through to his chest, since he was dribbling blood from the corner of his mouth. Another guy leaning against a tree, smoking a cigarette, had a bandage around his head, and beside him was his helmet with a jagged tear up the middle. Further on, two guys lay face down in the mud beside the road, dead. Guldine was on the radio, calling back for armor, preferably TD's (Tank Destroyers) with their lower profile and 76mm guns that had a greater muzzle velocity than our tanks, and, their bore being rifled, greater accuracy.

The 88s had us stopped, and the question was, did the Germans just want to slow us down while they pulled back, or were they setting us up for a counterattack, likely on our flank? It was starting to get a little dark. Rebel and his squad had just finished digging in their machine gun when there was a staccato burst of burp guns firing from the woods off to our right. In that instant, Barry had yelled 'Watch out!" and, by pushing Rebel back into the emplacement, he, on the rebound, was himself thrust into the line of fire and got tattooed right across his chest.

The fire-fight didn't last long. Evidently, the Germans had sent out a reconnaissance patrol with a trigger-happy non-com in charge who couldn't resist a machine gun target. We raked them over pretty well on our side with our Tommies and M-1s—Kraut even went after them with a BAR—and they disappeared back into woods, leaving one dead of their own, the burp gun non-com that Rebel went after. Guldine wouldn't let us go in pursuit fearing they might be setting us up for an ambush. We'd wait for the TDs to come up before pushing ahead, which wouldn't be till the next morning. Meanwhile, we had better start digging in. The patrol would confirm our location and approximate number. So, the 88s, already fairly well zeroed in, were certain to be coming for us again.

It was a little strange how Bronze Stars were sometimes awarded. We might be queried in a rest area if we could recall anybody who had done something special. In this case, Rebel spoke up immediately, and Guldine went ahead and put Barry in for one, poor little guy, an unlikely honor for the unlikeliest warrior among us. We didn't use words like 'hero.' Nobly earned or not, Barry's was not much different from others so awarded and written up as deeds bigger than they were. For us, what Barry did was big enough.

2.

We had a day's rest before moving up to the Siegfried Line, which we'd find was surprisingly lightly defended, since the Germans had evidently learned from the Maginot that a "Line" could easily be outflanked. Fighting from fixed positions, they showed by their Blitzkrieg, had become obsolete. Nonetheless, we didn't know what to expect, and the Siegfried name itself was pretty scary. We were told to clean our rifles and pick up sufficient clips of ammunition—a bandoleer would do—and boxes of K-rations.

Rebel and Gush called the guys in our group together, and Gush said Rebel had asked Hilfer if he wouldn't lead us in a brief prayer for Barry. Hilfer was doubtful. The Company apparently didn't make a practice of it, hadn't done that sort of thing on behalf of prior casualties, and probably didn't want to get something like that started when we were going to be facing losses enough in the campaigns upcoming. Hilfer didn't believe Guldine, as Company Commander, would think much of it either. Some guys might get spooked by it. Besides, what about those other two guys who lay dead outside of St. Vith, one of whom was Andersen, a guy who, after what he'd been through, could just as well have chickened out about coming back up.

Rebel was insistent. The kid had saved his life, after all. And he'd had him all wrong. He said Hilfer didn't have to lead us and Guldine didn't have to know, but he wanted our group to say a brief prayer together. It would do us good, him especially. Gino said he thought the kid was Jewish. Rebel said he didn't give a damn. "Hell, so was Jesus, and He loved all of us." We made a circle, went down on one knee, holding onto our rifles for balance, and Rebel asked Jesus to look after little Barry's soul and make a place for him in heaven. He wanted Jesus to look after the rest of us too, because some of us might be joining the kid before long. We said a quiet "Amen."

It turned out that prayer did help us negotiate a mean night, when we went through the Siegfried Line and got ourselves lost. We had gone out on a scouting patrol and located a couple of pill-boxes, but got turned around and had no idea of how we'd find our way back to our Company. Not that we'd be able to say, once back, where those damned things were. Before we could figure out which way to go, we heard German voices behind us, which—scary thought—we believed was the way back. Unable to find a hole or dig one, we just had to lay there quietly, soaked to the skin, unable to sleep and scared that one of those Heinies, who might also be lost, would step on us.

Rebel had taken charge and said, if it happened, we either had to shoot the bastard or play dead, the latter for sure if there were several of them. The only thing going for us was the fog, which meant they probably didn't know where the hell they were any more than we did. Rebel said to relieve our minds of uncertainty we ought to pray, silently. It would let us know we could make it. "Hell," he added, "even Germans have to sleep." They did, and we did.

Come morning, we had one helluva surprise. Treading ever so cautiously in the direction of our lines, we ran into four Germans coming out from behind the underbrush, hands up. One of them, a Sergeant, spoke English and told us they had been rousted out of one of those pillboxes by a tank that came up from behind and fired at their back door. They had emerged waving handkerchiefs, but all the tankers could do was motion them toward our lines. They'd been cautiously wandering around looking for some GIs they could surrender to. They heard us, but, because of the dark, feared they'd get shot and gave up making contact till in the light of morning they saw us coming their way. So, back we went with a bag of prisoners to show for our screwed up scouting mission. Gino conceded that you needed to have prayer, but it was even better if you had luck.

~~~~~~~~~~~~~~~~~~~

"Soldiers: *I expect you to defend the sacred soil of Germany to the very last.*" It has been pointed out that the last time armed enemy soldiers had trod on German soil in wartime was back in 1814. Were they ever waiting for us 130 years later.

3.

We were supposed to have had the tough assignment and the rest of the company the easy one. We found out that they were given a couple of tanks and artillery support, also maps, supposedly reliable, and, above all, they were moving out in force; namely, with numbers.

However, as often happens, with a wrong move or a miscalculation of the enemy's move, the expected can, in an instant, become the unexpected. We also discovered that Guldine said he wouldn't have been surprised if our patrol didn't make it back. That in itself would have told him something, which it was our mission to do. Instead, with those prisoners in tow, we came back smelling like a rose, while the Company took a beating and had to do a hasty withdrawal. So, in short order, the bloom was off our rose, and Guldine was looking at a pretty difficult situation.

Kraut, who knew how to nose his way around, picked up what had taken place and filled us in. It seems we had been sent out north of the Company, as a probe, but also as a feint to distract the enemy from the Company's major thrust. The errant tank had picked its way through the staggered dragon's teeth where the Engineers had blown a path, sending the tank our way and leaving the Company minus one visible cannon and open to withering machine gun fire and mortars from a ridge, just back of the pillboxes, a position that didn't appear on Guldine's map, which additionally showed an obsolete road net, not the one the tank would actually follow. A prior patrol had been sent out to find an opening in the German's main belt of defense which could be exploited, and that's where Guldine thought he was headed, but what he found was the main belt itself.

What, with machine guns that sent our troops reeling back to the trees, the element of surprise went to the enemy, and, with mortars showering down shrapnel from tree bursts, casualties were termed "significant." (Casualties were reported up, never down, as if we couldn't figure out on our own that some guys were missing.) Worst of all, as the Company pulled back, it had to leave some ten to fifteen wounded lying out there, as well as two Medics looking after them—with the SS around, all sure to be finished off. Kraut took that

113

personally and said he was going to do something about it. When calmed down, he was told to settle for recovering any of the wounded that could be rescued. Even for that, though, he'd need to bring along some dependably mean sons o' bitches who could put up a rear-guard fight, if called upon.

We did have a couple of particularly ornery grounded paratroopers in our midst, guys who had made D-Day and, having come up with knee injuries on landing, were eager to compensate for the action they had been deprived of. The one trooper, of German extraction, was named Heuer, and the other one, with an unpronounceable Polish name, Kraut renamed Unge—together that spelled Ungeheuer, the German word for "Monster." And they looked the part, both sporting crew cuts, with the high, puffy cheekbones and slit eyes of boxers, which they had been. Kraut knew he could get them to go out with him if told about the guys who had been abandoned and, above all, with a chance to punish some SS, should they appear.

Wanting a few additional guys to join in, he came to our group. Did we realize that Willie hadn't been accounted for? He might well be one of the vulnerable wounded. That was all it took for Rebel, plus Gush, Gino, and myself to sign on. A hillbilly friend of Willie's, whom he called 'Hound Dog' and had the long nose of one, wanted to tag along, and Kraut welcomed him.

But there were problems. While Regiment shouldn't be told (they might think we'd only incur additional casualties, with nothing gained), should we tell Guldine? Kraut didn't want to, but had to, in case we ran into trouble and needed to call back for—with luck—artillery. Guldine was skeptical, but, thinking of the guys lying out there and the poor Medics, he said he'd take the responsibility for our going. However, his maps were useless, and we'd need somebody who knew the terrain. Kraut decided to have a go at Hans, the

German sergeant we'd brought back, and persuade him to be our guide, no easy matter since, with him being as good as home free, exposing himself to getting shot by his own didn't have much appeal. Kraut threw the SS card at him, and that was enough to get Hans on board. (The SS had been known to shoot their regular army guys who didn't stand fast under fire.)

After the initial downer Kraut had gone through on being broken, it didn't take long for us to see a whole different side to the guy. We saw, first of all, how adaptable he was; ready to join the ranks of us common riflemen, and determined to be a good one. Now, given an incentive, his old time take-charge attitude was emerging, and, scared as we were to be going out, that gave us some reassurance, as did the Monster rear-guards.

Hans decided it was best to go out at dusk, when both sides were generally hunkering down for the night. We were following a tree line that sloped down to a creek, when we were stopped in our tracks by the drone of Bed-check Charlie overhead, their artillery spotter, looking for targets. Just over the creek was a path leading up a thickly treed hillside that would take us to a sort of round-top meadow where the Company had taken its major casualties. The path was surely mined, and indeed there was a wooden sign in German that said so, put up for their own protection. On occasion, we might roll live grenades over a path to explode the mines, but that was risky business, and no way we could do that now. To play it safe, Kraut had us walk along the uneven surface on the edge of the path.

We had just reached the crest when somebody stepped on a resonant twig that caught the ear of an outpost guard, who started peering through the bushes. Kraut instantly took him out with a shot to the head and motioned for us to get down and lay quiet. It was a risk that had to be taken. A lone shot in the night often didn't mean much, but someone raising an alarm would do us in. After a pause, we got up, but Kraut motioned for us to hold it where we stood. Parting the bushes and stepping on through ever so cautiously, he hoisted himself up top, rolled the guy over to make sure he was gone, then had us join him. It seems this fellow was no guard at all, but a battlefield scavenger. We would find out that he had come on the scene after the hasty departure of a couple of scavengers responsible for a part of the carnage before us. Beside the one that Kraut shot was a canvas bag with a collection of watches, rings, necklaces, gold crosses, St. Christopher medals, a forty-five, a trench knife, franc notes, mark notes, assorted coins, boxes of K rations, and brass second lieutenant bars. What a haul. This bastard deserved a slower death. Kraut shook the bag and out came a broken harmonica. Oh-oh—Willie's?!

Hans pointed to the ridge off to our right where the Germans were likely dug in. At the foot of it was a Sherman tank over on its side with a track blown off. Straight ahead lay the strategic crossroad the Company was supposed to have taken. It must have been holy hell for our guys trying to make it across the meadow in front of us to get a position dug in there. Kraut had Unge (Ungey by our pronunciation) and Heuer crawl over to the tank and ready themselves to open up with their Tommies if we drew fire from the ridge, particularly should they be coming for us as we pulled out. He assumed they could shoot walking backwards, if need be, but warned them not to—"fer Chrissakes"—shoot first, regardless of whether they had a tempting shot.

Once there, they motioned for us to come on out. We saw a good number of GI bodies lying about, and over on the left were several foxholes covered with tree limbs. When Kraut's shot went off, we were perplexed by a low groan coming from that direction,

116

and Rebel, who volunteered to have a look, swung an arm for us to come over to the closest hole. Looking up at us apprehensively was a Medic with a red cross on his helmet, and alongside him was the groaner with a shelter half pulled up over him. Then, a bowed head slowly rose up out of the darkness in back, and what did we see but the whites of somebody's eyes under a muddy helmet. It was Willie, like he'd never looked before, clutching his pocket Bible. The guy under the shelter half with a bloody leg was—of all people—Bird!

All of a sudden, we heard Tommies rattling from behind the tank. The Ungeheuers must have thought they'd been seen. Shortly they were taking return fire from above. We couldn't see all that well, but a gauzy slit in the cloud cover provided enough moonlight for us to glimpse several squared-off helmets slipping down the ridge. Coming around the back of the tank, they opened up on our Monsters, and got Heuer. Unge shot back from behind the track and got two of them. Out pops ol' Hound Dog, who moving up ahead, hits the third one, and a machine gun opens up from the ridge raking the edge of the meadow, taking out Hound Dog and grazing by us, inches over our heads. Hound Dog had been telling the guys he was "just a-itching to get where the real shootin is." And, poor guy, he got his wish.

Getting on the radio, Kraut had called in artillery on the ridge, under cover of which, when it finally arrived, we were able to get Bird out, fortunately quieted by another shot of morphine. We were told by the Medic that the rest of our wounded had expired, two, close by, shot in the head. He said for the few who had been crying out, delirious with pain, as well as those ebbing off with a moan, the executioners (probably SS, and prior scavengers) ended the annoyance with a well-directed bash from their rifle butts, which saved a bullet. That's what had happened to the other Medic. About as mean as it gets.

Unge rejoined us, heatedly cussed out by Kraut, who, while the lead was still flying, had gone out to warn him that our artillery would be coming in. Kraut let out a cry and fell grabbing his leg. We thought he might have been hit by a stray round, but, when asked, he said it was nothing; he simply tripped. We made our way back down the hill, Bird being hauled in a makeshift litter of double shelter halves, tree limbs serving as side poles, with tough Unge at one end, me at the other. No way we could have gone out to grab one of the vacant litters. It was a struggle making it out of there, but slowly and painfully (me finally being relieved by Rebel) we were able to find our way back to the Company.

Willie couldn't help shaking as he told us what had taken place during the original "thrust," as they called it. As soon as one of the machine guns on high opened up, he disposed of his rifle and pack and dove for a hole he'd noticed as they came over the hill and fanned out. When the mortar rounds started falling, he thought he'd just as soon wait out the whole damned show. Guys were scattering and falling all over the place, some hit, some not. It was more than he'd bargained for, a lot more than he could take. Unlike the movies, where the good guys were able to duck out of the way, Willie said it suddenly got to him that in combat, if you hung in, it mostly meant you were, flat out, going to get yourself killed. He had seen Bird's legs go out from under him as he was backing up, still shooting his carbine over at the ridge. When the firing stopped, he dragged Bird into the hole, with the Medic scooting in right behind him. He thought it was curtains when he heard Rebel crawl over. The wait had been a living terror. Unable to read from his pocket Bible for lack of light, he silently repeated passages he knew by heart and was in mid-prayer, when, miraculously, there we were.

Beating our way through brush and tree limbs, we were on edge all the way back, knowing that, with all the shooting the Ungeheuers had done, we were bound to be discovered. Even if it weren't for the Monsters, Hans warned us that the Germans, with their new sense of urgency, would likely have a patrol out anyway trying, at the very least, to size up what was going on. It wasn't till we got safely back in camp that we looked around and discovered that Hans was gone. Kraut speculated he must have decided at the last minute that he'd be the first one Germans on patrol would kill—a traitor for sure—if they found him with us. His safest way out was to beat it back to the German lines.

Often, you don't realize how terrified you'd been until you were out from under the danger, and even then the tremors would hang on. Willie was a wreck, and the rest of us weren't much better off. Kraut, who had to admit it was a crazy thing to trust those Ungeheuers to hold their fire, was no less shaken than the rest of us and made like he wanted to beat his fist against something. ("Those fuckin idiots almost did us all in. And, dumb me, I insisted on having them come along!") We would find out he was to be installed as platoon sergeant, deservedly reclaiming his former rank by replacing one of the wounded who had been done in by the SS. Unfortunately, we hadn't been back but a couple of minutes, when Kraut collapsed on his way to give Guldine a report. In addition to rattled nerves, sometimes you don't realize how bad a hit you've taken till you reach a secure area. We noticed that Kraut seemed to be limping, but he had let on that he must have twisted an ankle when he fell going out to warn Unge. As the limp worsened, I asked about it and he pointed to the rough going underfoot. However, the sloshing in his boot was blood, not mud.

Bad as this had been, it was nothing compared to what lay ahead of us in Hürtgen. After all, most of our patrol did make it back. We also had found Willie and, on our return, did get Finch properly evacuated to a field hospital. As Kraut was being placed on the litter, he dismissed what the Medic thought (maybe a bullet lodged near his tibia) and, giving us a thumbs-up, he vowed he'd be with us again, real soon. Those recovered stripes sure lessened the pain. All in all, though we felt bad about the guys we lost and bitter about what happened to the wounded, we ourselves had, after all, made it through a hairy situation, and, we secretly felt rather good about that.

Maybe the confidence it gave us was too unrealistic not to be shattered.

4.

"The doughs who went into that forest to fight—and to die in the thousands—had [a] name for it... never publicized by the media back home during that gray, bitter winter.... They called it simply 'the Death Factory.'

"...From September 1944..., every two weeks or so, a new American division of infantry was fed into those dark green, somber woods, heavy with lethal menace. Fourteen days later the shocked, exhausted survivors would be pulled out,...passing like sleepwalkers the 'new boys' moving up for the slaughter. Seeing nothing, hearing nothing, muddy, filthy, unshaven, they had somehow escaped the Death Factory while all around them their comrades had died by scores, by hundreds, by thousands."

"To what purpose?... The Forest could have been sealed off using the superior armor and air power at the disposal of the Top Brass. The Germans defending it would have been left to rot on the vine... But the Top Brass was not prepared to admit defeat once they were committed to the attack into the Forest.... ...So the generals got away with it....

"Even later, when the slaughter was over, the accounts of that ... battle, which was a major defeat for the U. S. Army, were neatly swept under the carpet and forgotten. In his Crusade in Europe, *Eisenhower mentioned the battle only* once, *[though] half a million of his soldiers were engaged in it at some time or other that winter."* Charles Whiting, *The Battle of Hurtgen Forest: The Untold Story of a Disastrous Campaign.*

We poor, dumb, unknowing, and anxious foot soldier pawns had no idea of what we were walking into, except that it was very dark, cold and relentlessly rainy in there. We had been standing around in the icy rain waiting for the trucks to take us on over to the Forest, and, wanting to relieve the weight of our packs, we propped them up on our rifles or leaned back against a tree. The mud was hub-deep on the arriving trucks, which drove us in convoy past fields of the pillboxes previously dealt with and through the dragon's teeth that extended right into the wooded area of our recent encounter and snaked their way in and out of view across fields. The debris of war was littered by the roadside: empty wire reels, burned-out tanks, ours and theirs, discarded ammo boxes, empty cartridge belts, a wrecked halftrack, a tilted 75mm anti-tank gun (theirs) its barrel dislodged, green ponchos covered with mud. Further on, there were abandoned gun emplacements with shell holes gouged out of the turf beside them that had filled with water.

We shortly came onto a rather well-paved highway with German road signs, pointing west, east and north, reading Eupen, Rötgen, Walheim. We went through Rötgen rather quickly, passing a red brick railway station. White flags (actually, towels and pillow slips) hung from several houses, and the few German civilians we saw were sullen-looking and hard in the face, with expressions that let us know, as we passed, that they weren't admitting we were there. A couple of old ladies standing at a church door did give us a look—askance—and one of them muttered something out the corner of her mouth, prompting one of the guys in our truck to lean back and call, "Aw, fuck you, too, lady."

Walheim had taken more of a beating; they apparently had put up a bigger fight there and were rather heavily shelled for it. Among the houses that had been struck, a few avalanched right out onto the road. There were shell craters alongside them and next to the road. A stream swollen by the constant rain ran swiftly through town. Just beyond it, the convoy stopped on a narrow cobblestone street, where the officer in charge entered one of the buildings that probably housed Regimental Headquarters. Out with him, came a slick little non-com several of us thought we recognized. "Holy smokes," Willie cried, "it's the Fly." He smiled and gave us a wave as he got into the cab of our truck to guide us through the outskirts of town and beyond. The road out was bordered by clusters of old stone houses, some having holes of the kind that tanks make with their high-velocity guns to flush out snipers.

(The Fly had been the Company clerk in our Louisiana outfit. He acquired an inflated idea of his importance and, wholesomely disliked, used his position to trade on our eagerness to get the latest poop or, better yet, finagle a pass. We all owed him favors, and he showed no reluctance about cashing in. I didn't know many guys

122

who hadn't lent him money. We found out that he would be writing stories about our gallant doings on line, stuff that was palmed off on news agencies as authentic. How often we regretted that we protected him from getting his neck wrung.)

Outside of our greeting for the Fly nobody said anything. This was about the quietest bunch of GIs I'd ever been with. I tried to strike up a conversation with the guy next to me, but no luck. All the way along, no one spoke more than a few simple words, except for the guy who greeted the ladies at the church door, and he was talking to himself, repeating, "No good fuckin Germany," which nobody paid attention to. He was sitting on the floor of the truck looking out backwards. Could be he wanted to remember the way back. Everything about the country seemed hard and uncomfortable. For friend or foe, it didn't look like a place you could relax in. Many years later, I would see a sign in the Commy part of the country (also a dictatorship) that said, "Wer rastet, der rostet." (He who rests, rusts.) The only immediate sign of brightness was the swollen stream running through town, foaming white where it raced around the bridge supports, and, going at that clip, it too seemed merciless.

The raw wind nipped at our faces as we slid off into the gray haze, past bleak brown fields and lone farmhouses, and we soon found ourselves enveloped by the densely wooded forest. Noticing the looped wires alternately hanging from trees and lying in muddy ditches in the spaces where there were no trees, we got the idea that maybe communication by radio from Regiment to the front wasn't all that good. What with the thickness of the forest and a terrain of sharp ravines and well-nigh perpendicular hills, radios, as we'd find out, weren't wholly reliable. We were stopped by wires that had to be lifted over the cab of the truck and shortly reached the point where the trucks weren't going any further anyway, not with the road ahead being a virtual river of mud. Shouldering our packs and rifles, we were gathered in a patch of fir trees to be addressed by a lieutenant from Battalion, who told us our outfit would be going up on line shortly, and that meanwhile we'd better disperse, buddy up and find a hole or dig one because Heinie knew we were there and his artillery would be welcoming us.

There were quite a few holes around, all covered with tree limbs. We also took note of the fallen trees that the limbs were hacked from and others that had been split by direct hits from incoming artillery. There was quite a bit of litter laying about, K-ration boxes, ammo boxes, grenade boxes, GI and Heinie equipment. A Heinie rifle (a Mauser) lay rather conspicuously in the path with a piece of white tape wound around it, an object lesson for those who didn't yet know the deadly game of booby traps. Since the holes were soon taken, I was satisfied to find myself a single slit trench, plunked my pack down by it, and broke open a box of K-rations for supper. Willie came by to tell me there was room for three in the hole he had with Gino. I said 'thanks,' but decided to stay put, as I'd laid out a shelter half and blanket covered with my raincoat, and figured I'd crawl under and make a night of it. I sort of wanted to be alone with my thoughts.

Our artillery was drumming intermittently through the night, as if to keep the Heinies honest, and they were doing the same to us. I was at the point of falling off to sleep when I heard a loud shrieking noise bearing down on us, coming closer and closer, followed by a jarring explosion, maybe fifteen yards behind me. There was the simultaneous sound of a tree cracking, then crashing down, accompanied by somebody yelling out amidst the clatter of logs. Another shell came in, striking further down, and a third, as I lay there expecting the worst, with nothing between me and the next one but a blanket and raincoat. I didn't know how I might find Gino and

124

Willie's hole. It was too black a night for me to be out scrounging for logs to cover my shallow trench, which was beginning to puddle under me. Shivering from the cold and fear, I didn't get much sleep, not the worst of my concerns anyway.

We were up early next day, and it was good to learn that nobody had been hurt. The tree had fallen across the opening of a hole, pinning its occupants in for the night. Nothing worse. A lieutenant got several non-coms to remove the tree, and he extended a hand to the guys encased overnight, who came out shaking their heads. Fully expecting a follow-up hit, they spoke haltingly about how scared they were. So was I. I also learned a lesson. There, but for the grace of German gunners, I might have been a casual casualty. ('Casual,' as we'd shortly find, also had another meaning.) You got the eerie feeling that the Germans were telling us, 'Wherever you sons o' bitches are in these woods, you're in our backyard, and we'll find you.'

We got another indication of how serious things were becoming when they issued us two bandoliers of ammo, two grenades, and three boxes of K-rations. Walking over a corduroy path that ran past the tents housing Battalion Service Headquarters, we felt like we were tunneling into a gloomy maze of low-hanging fir tree branches that swatted you as you passed, as if to mete out a warning. Alongside our path was a string of white engineer tape that you strayed from at your peril. We came upon an abandoned Jeep, axle deep in mud, its wheels turned sideways, a sign of the driver's frustrated effort to move against the sticky mass. Not a place for wheels.

Arriving at an assembly area which seemed less heavily treed, because most of the trees had been topped off and splintered by artillery barrages, we immediately ran into just such a barrage— likely the Germans' 105 howitzers—and, scrambling for unavailable cover, took our first casualties—the lieutenant leading our column along with two non-coms, the ones who had removed that log pinning guys in their hole, in effect, company leaders before we had time to integrate replacements and form as a newly functional company. We scarcely knew them, and there they lay, helmetless, bleeding through their hair and tears across their field jackets. Ever curious Gino inquired about them and found out that those three guys were 'casuals,' veterans who had been hit before and were coming back to rejoin their units. It was terribly *casual* the way they had gotten it—and damnable, after they'd already taken hits lucky enough for them to get promptly healed and sent back.

A group of replacements at the end of the column had run back pell-mell at the sound of the incoming stuff, tripping over one another as they went, and they had to be rounded up and brought back, and also told to rid themselves of unnecessary gear—gas masks that we were told to retain being the first to go. On the way, they walked into a follow-up barrage, which killed two of them and wounded two others, and sent a bunch of them running off every which way, one of them stepping on a mine that took his leg off at the thigh and left him screaming for help. There was a danger in going up the path to offer help, but a gutsy Medic was shortly bending down over him and applying a tourniquet. Several of the other guys who had run kept on running. And we hadn't yet moved into the area of an upcoming attack.

5.

But that was Hürtgen, and we weren't the first to take a beating in there, where you could get hit doing nothing, be awarded the Purple Heart and listed as WIA (wounded in action) without having seen any. As we had already found out, the Germans could potentially zero in on almost any area in the whole damned forest that their spotters targeted, wherever movement was noticed, noise heard, or suspicion aroused, and they were so much in command of what was going on that their artillery killed replacements getting off the trucks bringing them in. Other outfits had been ground up and pulled back to make way for the next ones, like ours and the one with the Bloody-Bucket patch, appropriate for all.

We saw some of the earlier casualties still laying out there when we moved up toward the assembly area from which we'd push off. To this day I can still bring back the sight of a little guy lying face down in the draw we went through then, sadly forlorn. He was wearing leggings and the short, old style, light field jacket, suggesting he might have arrived early enough to have made D-Day and been in the hedgerow fighting of Normandy. He had to have seen quite a bit of action since. Now gone, in Hürtgen.

Actually, I didn't see him at first. I was tired, not having had much sleep, and wasn't looking anywhere but straight ahead, anxious about when the Heinies would pick us up. I bumped into Gush and, following his outstretched arm, caught sight of a rifle with its stock split and spotted with holes, then a helmet liner with a jagged gash bordered by blackish dried blood about where a man's temple is. Sprawled beside a bush like a bunch of rags thrown on a garbage heap lay the GI himself. His head was angled down, showing the sickly white at the back of his neck and the blue-black hairline. One side of his face was sunk in the mud. The gash we had seen in his helmet liner was repeated on the side of his head above the temple. His one arm lay crooked above his head like a child's. His fingers seemed like clay, gray-brown. The most pitiful part of it was that he seemed so much not a human being anymore, just a thing that doesn't move and is becoming part of the earth. I was in such a hazy state, I at first hardly realized what I'd seen, being more worried about the open space we had to traverse before the 88s came bearing down on us. As I walked on, a vision of the dead GI completed itself in my mind, and I felt a disheartening weakness in my knees. I would see that vision again, like on our brief and joyless Thanksgiving break, as I was lying in my hole, looking out, eye-level, at the granules of wet dirt, small stones, and pieces of broken bark and evergreen needles, all strangely magnified, and there he was amidst the lowly debris, face in the mud, starkly blue-black at the hairline—forever.

Likely, he had been killed during an attack that must have gotten pushed back, or dispersed. There were lots of foiled attacks and lots of lost GIs like him; poor guys, they were but one sign of the terrible inconsequence of death in there.

Since it was difficult to bring up armor, combat in Hürtgen was almost exclusively an infantryman's fight of small arms, backed by artillery. What we encountered from the Germans was mainly machine guns, with the barbarous addition of concentrated artillery and mortar fire, supplemented by mine fields, always in places that seemed safely passable. And talk about being mine happy, we heard that the Germans might lay as many as 500 of the things in a strategic firebreak. The shelling was often at its worst after we had taken our objective, and, at times, it was the sign of an upcoming counterattack. I remember the aftermath of an attack later on when the stuff coming in on us was particularly hot and heavy. It occurred after we'd taken two hills in succession, surprising even ourselves. The shelling was incessant, like it wasn't meant to be survived; and for many it wasn't.

To this day, I can bring back the sound. The Eeeh—Ka-ruck! Eeeh—Ka-ruck! Ka-ruck! Ka-ruck! on and on, again and again and again, the sort of thing that grinds your livery guts till they turn into acid and water. The Germans might typically fire three rounds for effect, on a limited target, but when they thought they had you boxed in with nowhere to go, like the instance I'm thinking about, it was time-on-target, for maximal effect. The shells came crashing down on us like a descending freight train, one car falling on top of the other. Ka-ruck, Ka-ruck, Ka-ruck! Louder and louder. The concussions seemed to be chewing up the very air. Curled up and wincing in our holes, some guys were crying out against the ripping blasts, waiting out the whine of hot shrapnel, and expecting any second to get hit.

When the barrages finally let up, the Medics were seeking out the wounded and, going to the worst ones first, checking to see if they were still alive. In the lulls, we became aware again of the icy rain that came and came and came, soaking all the way through our clothes and feeling like naked Siberian steel against the skin. It was a rain that came day after bloody day, and wouldn't let you sleep for the shakes it gave you. Then there was the mud to contend with that gripped your feet and wouldn't let you go when you absolutely *had to move* and, try as you would, couldn't, fast enough. The Medics would want litter bearers to carry our wounded back to the Clearing Station. With us having done it before, Rebel and I would, on occasion, pitch in, back-breaker that it was.

At times we'd be clustered around the officer in command as he was totaling up the killed and wounded and, more importantly, how many survived for his report to Battalion. There would be the question of whether he had enough bodies to withstand a counterattack, which seemed mostly a matter of curiosity, since, regardless of the total reported, he'd be told he had enough to stand fast. He'd ask for the Heavy Weapons Company (M, in our case) to send up its water-cooled machine guns, and Cannon Company to give us artillery support. Fat chance with the latter, a lot of the time.

6.

But all of that was yet to come, as were the mounting casualties. On the other hand, regarding our first significant attack in the Forest, after several lesser ones that came to naught, save for men lost, we got the sense of urgency when additional replacements arrived. They were intended to bring our Company up to the strength wanted for an impending action, for which we had to be marched to a new assembly area. It was a hell of a torturous hike to get there, bending back and around, at one point passing a truck filled with standing prisoners, guarded by two MPs, holding grease-guns, each with one leg on the tailgate. This was our first up-close look at Fritz in his homeland, wearing dark, forest green, or blue-gray uniforms, their faces white and unshaven under gray field caps. In their midst was one exceptionally tall, long-necked Fritzie, looking like a stork, who turned around and faintly smiled when Gino called out, "Lucky stiffs." Darned if they didn't know English.

The only thing good about the hike was that it got us warm, in fact, sweaty at the headband of our helmet liners. We had no sooner eased off our packs than we were told that our battalion was actually to be 'kicking off' from another sector of the front. So up went the packs again, complete with horseshoe bed roll, and we swung into another sweaty hike, moving out dispersed at ten-yard intervals, which got to be spaced a lot longer as we went. But first we'd been told to fill our cartridge belts with M-1 clips, so, in addition to straps cutting into our shoulders, the weighty cartridge belts, feeling like they were lined with rocks, bore down on our hips. In places, there was shin-deep mud sucking at our shoes. It was a march of some five or six miles that left us heavy in the legs, weary all over, and generally pissed off. In great shape to take on Heinie.

Pulling off into a new bivouac area, we found ourselves in the midst of a platoon of Engineers hard at work on a road for trucks to enter the woods with supplies. A chore we were glad to see them doing. Our officers were glad of it too. So glad, we had no sooner shed our packs than a group of us got put on a detail to help the Engineers fell trees, Willie and I taking turns at the ax. One way to chase the leg aches, we were told—without so much as a smile. They looked at Rebel's broad back and had him using a pick and shovel to make a gutter where the water could run off. Gush and Gino were laying down logs for the roadway, guided by the Engineers who had a knack for knowing how to stabilize the roll of those things. What with those punishing marches and an hour's work on the road, we were pretty well beat and turned our chores over to the next detail, some of whom were hoping they might just as well stay on with these Engineers, which a few guys wound up doing. We'd already seen how some things could get pretty loose the closer you got to the front.

This was an area that had also been previously occupied, originally by the Germans and then GIs, leaving a good number of well-constructed holes, nicely roofed over with logs. An officer appeared out of a bunker, a tall bearded guy, who spoke to us in an unusually soft voice (first time that ever happened) like he knew what we were in for, him apparently sizing us up as fresh troops. We were once again instructed to trim down our packs for combat readiness. While everybody was cussing about how far we'd carried the lousy stuff—some of it newly issued—the officer told us to be quick about chucking it and disperse, because we could count on being shelled at almost any time. He also pointed to a pile of arctics dumped by the side of the road. Some had been used before, but we were satisfied if we could find a fit. Many a guy had to do without, especially those with the biggest feet, about the only time I'd seen the big guys get short-changed.

We threw away all clothing except what we were wearing, and that meant getting rid of mess gear, tent poles, tent pins, toothpaste, shaving cream, razors, our second pair of shoes, as well as extra socks, underwear, and ODs. Toilet paper and letters from home could be stored in the webbing of our helmet liners. We were also advised to wear as many items of clothing as possible, since it got pretty cold in here (no kiddin'!), and they wouldn't always be able to get bed rolls up to us. Didn't we know that, though? But we went along with it, necessary for the replacements. After adding an item or two, we had on our long-handle underwear, fatigues on top of ODs, a sweater, and a field jacket. By the time we were finished, we had ourselves padded out like Eskimo kids. In time, some guys would be disposing of their cumbersome arctics, when they found that they kept more water in than out. Before we knew it, it was nighttime, not that it wasn't dark enough to be night a good part of the day.

Since it was too early to get into our holes and sack out, we sat around talking as we ate our supper K-rations. Naturally, there were more complaints about having lugged all that stuff, made heavier by the wetness, only to get rid of it now, and those wise enough to hold back an extra pair of socks were putting them on. The stick-together five had lit up a social cigarette, when a guy ambled over and clapped me on the back, saying he thought it was me, and darned if it wasn't old "Buster, the Battler," whom I'd taken basic training with at Fort Benning. We had found ourselves together again in the Bastogne replacement pool from which I'd gone up to this Division before he arrived. He asked for one of our Luckies, usually the brand you'd get on line, our one luxury. (It was Raleighs and Chelseas elsewhere.) I was amazed to see him.

"Buster, you ol' bastard. For goodness sake, I thought you'd found yourself a Belgian girlfriend."

"Yeah. Trouble is, next day, they found me. Went out on the second shipment after you left."

Buster was a talker, which was okay with me, as it was a way of easing the mind off what was coming up. He reminisced about the nice little enclave we'd had, nestled in the woods outside of Bastogne, where, after LeMans, we were put in "tactical reserve," supposedly being held back for the push across the Rhine to finish the War, while we sharpened our skills, like in digging garbage pits, going through the motions for calisthenics, and chasing one another around for squad problems. The area was dotted with replacement pools of that kind. On the way up, we'd seen storage depots covered with camouflage netting, peeping out from the sides of which were sections of pontoon bridges. Buster imitated the buzz-bombs rumbling across the sky on their way to Antwerp or London, sounding strangely like tractor motors. The second time they went over, the officers made us dig in deeper, issued live ammo to the guys on guard, and put themselves in for combat pay. But the 'hottest' it got was when we heard the distant boom of our long range artillery—probably the vaunted 240's—firing muffled salvos into the night. They said those things could lob a shell twenty miles and more, and on a still night you could hear the report that far away. Buster's nervous ramblings were worth a wan smile, as when he mentioned the times we would ignite tins of shoe dubbing in our covered holes to get enough light to read by and write letters home.

Strange how far in the past all of that seemed. Buster was going on about the bartering they did with the neighboring farmers, like when they traded shoes for a little piglet that they put in a sack to slit its throat. The squeals, resembling human screams, still got to him. At that point, I stopped him and asked what he was talking to that new Lieutenant about, and he said he might be picked for some upcoming operation, meaning a night scouting party to blow up the double-apron barbed wire strung in the way of our attack. He said he had an idea he'd be volunteered, and he thought that Rebel and me might also be volunteered on account of our previous experience at the Siegfried Line.

"That's what you came over to tell us?"

"Well, yeah. But I thought you knew. You guys have seen some combat, haven't you?"

"If you can call it that. More like beatings."

"They were thinkin of Injin too. Liked the looks of him."

I told Gush to ignore it, fearing that that kind of talk might make trouble. I said I'd straighten him out.

That was just Buster the Battler for you, but different now— wanting to be friendly, and, with all his blabbing, unashamed to show he was not a little chastened and pretty anxious, seen in the nervous blink he'd acquired. He had joined our ASTP boys with a bunch of tough young Irish guys from Boston, he the toughest of them. They kept putting him up for fights, which wasn't hard to do with them hearing all kinds of jokes about the Shanty Irish. He looked the part of the battler too, with his sandy-haired crew cut, and underslung jaw. Part of the hostility was over guys asking, if the Irish guys were so damned tough, what were they doing in a sissy outfit like ASTP? And the first response was that being tough didn't make them dumb; the second lay in Buster's fists. But he also had a lighter side and could in fact be a practical joker. So, now here he was, supposedly wanting to be chosen for another kind of fight that he said he'd kind of been itching for. Itchers, I remarked, didn't seem to do very well. But I congratulated him, and it was then he told us we would in fact be chosen for that scouting party. It was like he wanted to congratulate us on the upcoming excitement, for which I returned the compliment in hopes he'd get his wish to join in.

"Never known to miss a party, weren't you?"

Obviously, he was putting us on—there had been no volunteering, of any kind—and it took some talking to from Rebel for Buster to get toned down; among other things, he was told, "Ain't nobody laughin up here, fella."

7.

We couldn't figure out how come, if the Engineers could clear the way to the barbed wire, they couldn't take it out, and were told they had, twice, only to find it restored each time. Okay, but, if the explosion of the bangalore torpedoes was to be covered by artillery, why not have the artillery take the wire out in the first place? The answer was that it was a matter of pinpointing and, more importantly, of knowing the stuff was gone for sure. We were to be led by a Sergeant from the Engineers who was experienced at this kind of operation. Could do it in his sleep. He needed riflemen with him for protection, preferably a couple with Tommies, in the event he was detected, or hit before he could get the job done. The more we thought about it, the more it bothered us, particularly the matter of going out at night. There might be occasional night patrols, even attacks, in the dark of Hürtgen, but not many. The Engineer told us not to think about it. He had personally marked the way. (And could see it in the dark?)

When it came time to move out, we had plenty to think about, the most startling part being that our all-knowing Engineer had been called away for assignment with the Company on our flank. Our new Platoon Sergeant—actually, the old one, freshly back from his second wound—said he'd take over, but he'd do it differently. First, he didn't know anything about bangalores, and didn't think they were the right ones for the job anyway. Too clumsy to carry, for one thing. He was substituting satchel charges, at least five of them, which were just canvas sacks stuffed with dynamite or plain old nitro, as the case might be. I never looked inside one. Also, to keep us together and in-line as we went, the Engineer was going to have us hanging onto a length of rope. Our Sergeant never heard of such a thing. He was for keeping it simple—good old-fashioned night soldiering (in *here*?!) which, as he had it, meant no more than silent stealth. We were scared shitless, as things were. The new plan made it that much more intriguing.

But, actually, without realizing it, we lucked out. The Sergeant who came forward as our leader, Abner Kingston, Ab for short, was the kindest-natured Sergeant any GI would ever come to know. He was from a small town in Alabama near Huntsville, where people felt very much at home with one another, and he treated you like you were one of them. He called you right off by your first name (unusual) and made you feel like you counted. Ab didn't so much give orders as ask you to do something (highly unusual). He was an awfully long son-of-a-gun, lean as a sapling, and maybe as tall as six-five, but he had a kind of stoop that bowed his back out and brought his head down (automatic for infantry) as if he didn't like being so much taller than anybody else—though he was also aware of the vulnerability of height. There were some white burn marks on his cheek and neck where his beard didn't grow in. The first time he'd been hit was by short rounds from our chemical artillery, firing white phosphorous, which gave you mighty painful burns.

The way Ab had approached us was typical of him. "Whyn't we jest go out on a li'll patrol, fellers?" That was before we knew of the change, so we thought it was yet another night patrol preparing the way for the one on the wire. Even going with *him*, that would have been asking a lot. He said there was no reason to be scared because we knew where we were going and the Heinies didn't, so if we made contact, they'd be the ones to be scared and take off. Hearing him talk like that, I'm thinking, here's a guy who could sell refrigerators to Eskimos.

In describing the route we were to take, he made it sound like a walk in the park. After going through the trees, we'd come upon a path taking us to a sunken road that was overgrown with shrubs, scrub pine, and stuff, an area plastered by our artillery to set off mines and whatever else might be out there, so not to worry about that. The road would bring us to a draw at the end of which there was a greensward with a brook running down the middle of it, and some thirty meters this side of the brook was a gate and, beside it, three or four double apron strands of barbed wire. There might be a problem if they had booby traps hanging from the wire, but he knew how to handle that. We'd have to be careful of trip wires, but, being in the lead, he'd see to that too. We just had the one elementary job to do: get that wire blown up, booby traps detonated, and report back. All practically blind-folded—oh boy. And, Ab, could we have those directions again?

It was slow, tense going, and a physical strain, each of us with a six-pound charge strapped to our backs and several percussion caps and a length of primer cord in our pockets. We were hunched over and measuring every doubtful step, wondering how we were ever going to find our way to the wire on such a pitch black night. Pressing through those evergreen branches was tiring—like having somebody intermittently leaning against you. The bigger branches we had to crawl under, nursing our satchel. We were all breathing so hard when we reached the tree line, Ab asked us to quiet down so he could listen for sounds.

As it was somewhat less dark in the draw, looking up from ground level, you could make out some things you wouldn't otherwise see. That was how I picked up the gateposts. Even with the several times that Ab gave us the halt sign, we got to the wire in less time than we thought it would take. Once there, I'd never seen anyone work as quick and knowingly as Ab did. First, clearing away some brush, he exposed a trip wire just our side of the gate, found, it seemed, by pure instinct. (Gush later said he had a magnet up his ass.) Next, he crawled to the far corner of the barbed wire, and, with an easy swing, he sent the first charge over like it was no more than the lead sinker on a fishing line. Working his way back toward us, he planted two more snugged up against the wire and threw the last two over like he did the first, allowing plenty of slack on the primer cord. Blow one charge and you blow them all.

We backed up as far as the cord would go, and he had us get down in a shell crater further on, then whispered a few words into the radio. The fireworks were something to see, beginning with a stream of 81mm mortar shells flashing inverted cones as they crept up that hill accompanied by echoing Ka-chunks, intended to keep the Heinies buttoned up. Then the artillery came screeching down on them with 105's that exploded with their authoritative Ka-roooms. You could almost feel for the Heinies in their holes up there, but not for long.

Ab crawled out to light the primer cord, and, after an anxious wait, our charges blew beautifully, making a succession of sharp Bams, along with secondary explosions that rocked the ground under us and showered pieces of earth and metal overhead. Ab thought

138

they must have had some anti-tank mines planted there in case we used armor to deal with the wire. Clever of them, but they probably didn't know how wary our tankers were of being trapped in mud. Ab went down to have a look and came back with word that there was nothing left but a few jagged wires shaking in the rain at either end of the draw.

The pounding of our howitzers tapered off, and, once it stopped, we started feeling our way along the bank of the sunken road to pick up the place where it met the path taking us into the woods. Then it happened. Out of the silence came the sound of a boot slipping on that muddy path ahead of us, followed by another such boot, like B bumping into A. Oh, shit; somebody—somebodies—coming to a halt, and, where there are an A and a B, there are bound to be at least a C and a D, maybe more. We froze stock-still and in slow motion lowered ourselves to the ground. Gush reached for a grenade tied to his pack harness, but Ab grabbed his arm. The last thing we wanted to do was get into a scrap out there. My heart was already going like a trip-hammer, when, with the silence ringing in our ears, we heard yet another sound, a clicking over to the left of where the boot sounds had come from, putting the clicker not very far in from the tree line and fairly well blocking our return route.

If they saw our forms in the light from the explosions, the fact that they didn't let us have it right then meant they might have automatically taken cover and stayed put, unsure of what might follow. The fact that they still didn't have at us when we came their way indicated they were likely out on a recon patrol, and, since our mission signaled an upcoming attack, that made it more important for them to remain undetected and get back with what they'd found out than to risk a shooting encounter. One helluva fix. We're blocking them, and they us.

Things suddenly became unblocked, when, with one more click, a carbine opened up from our midst like it was bent on pumping out the whole fifteen-round clip. In the next instant, a burp gun answered, and, amidst cries from both sides, we rushed back to the safety of the road bank, from where we heard some slithering through the woods, followed by the explosion of a mine, more cries, hissed orders (as only Germans can hiss), faster slithering, and the scream of incoming 88's, always sure to go after audible noise. Ab led us to some holes the Engineer had marked just in from the edge of the woods, and we slid down into them to sweat out the barrage. With the stuff landing all around us, our nerves were pretty well jangled, and we were overall too damned beat to get out and confront whatever else might come up on our way back to the Company.

Ab felt obligated to go, but first he wanted to know who the hell had that "danged" carbine. Front and back, he and Rebel had a Tommy and the other three of us M-1s, supposedly. Rebel finally spoke up. He confided that it wasn't actually him covering the rear, but Buster, who insisted on tagging along and begged him not to say anything. It seems when Buster turned out to be a little weak-kneed, he had taken some razzing from guys who recalled past bullying, and he felt he had something to prove. By opening up like that, he must have thought he'd be 'showin 'em' what he was made of. What he did make of himself was a perfect target for the burp gunner, and Rebel saw him go down, helmet flying, his face a bloody patch. I had always sized Buster up as a lot more insecure than he seemed; in this case, naive. I wished he could have known that he just might have taken a couple of Heinies with him.

We finally did get our asses out of those holes to follow Ab for the return, surprised to notice Ab's sleeve was dripping blood where his arm had been grazed by an errant slug, at his turning toward the sound of the carbine. He said it was no more than a scratch. He'd have it bandaged and be there for the attack; and he was. Gush said he'd like to get himself a scratch, but one that needed stitches, and maybe had a little infection, so long's it took a while to heal. He wasn't particular.

The rest of us? We'd seen some action, but not all that much compared to what lay ahead. Talking among ourselves, we were wondering how long you could keep going if every event took such a toll on your nerves, to say nothing of how it wore you down physically, when, often sleepless, with no time to recover, you had very little left to go on—some of which we'd already experienced. Getting beyond that was the key ingredient for survival, we'd been told. Buster evidently thought he was being courageous, and that was one way of looking at what he did. There were guys who selflessly did very laudable things in combat. Nothing should ever be taken away from them. But what passed for courage sometimes happened by accident, desperation (no way out), or whatever, possibly compounded by stupidity, cowardice, or both. And not a thing should be taken away from guys so circumstanced either. However, most of us had a simpler idea. From our limited observation, we had the notion that it took courage enough for a soldier under fire to risk doing all that was asked of him—day after day. But none of us ever used the word courage; it became obvious that hanging in was the real ordeal.

8.

Gino said he couldn't wait to talk to me. At three in the morning? Why the hell wasn't he sacked out?

"Willie's in a bad way."

"So am I. In fact, bushed. I ain't had any sleep. You know we're supposed to be pushin off in a couple of hours."

"That's the problem."

"For the whole damned Company. Doesn't look like you got any sleep either."

"Yeah. Like I'm sayin, Willie ain't right. Hasn't been for a while. Doesn't think he can make it."

"*Make it*? The attack, right? Hell, that's the way we all feel."

"It's different with Willie. Something more than just bein scared." Gino explained that Willie didn't say anything at first, but that episode with him and the Medic and Finch stranded in their hole seeing the SS guys doing in our groaning wounded was about a ton more than he could take. Waiting for the bastards to come for them next reached the excruciating point where Willie seemed about to call for those murderers to, for goodness sake, come over and get it over with. Sensing that Willie was losing it, and fearing the unpredictable, the Medic said he stuffed a bandage in his mouth.

The matter-of-fact way that those SS guys probed the pockets and packs of the GI's they'd killed, and then compared their loot, was pure agony for Willie. By postponing the inevitable, they increased his fear of its expectation. The only thing that prevented Willie from jumping out of the hole and yelling at the bastards was the sudden realization, as he described it, that time gained was a sign he was being offered a chance to make his peace with God before fate overtook him. Recalling passages from the Bible could do just so much for him. When his silent prayer was interrupted by the arrival of our patrol, instead of seeing that as God's granting him physical deliverance in answer to his prayer, Willie rather believed that, since he felt no differently, it only meant others couldn't intercede on his behalf. The Bible was full of prophecies, and he felt one had come to him, which couldn't be evaded. Why else was he placed where he was, why else shown such menacing brutality about to come for him? The Medic told us Willie was so much into his thing he was unaware that those scavengers had dropped their loot and beat it out of there, called away by their angry superior officer.

In any event, the more Gino tried to talk him out of it, the more Willie insisted that God wanted him; it was just a matter of how it would happen, as it almost did, which suggested that time was short. Gino assured him we all hoped God would be with us when our time came, but it didn't have to be now. Indeed—talking about now— Gino angrily put it to him that faced with a perilous attack, nobody ought to be deliberately courting danger, which, by giving away our position, might get some of us killed who didn't want to die.

We all knew Willie was the most fully religious one of our group, at times, a notch more so than Rebel, and we thought it would be a help to him. Mostly it was, but now that he had gone totally berserk, we had no idea of how to cope with the situation. One answer was to have him meet with the Chaplain, Brother Hilfer, but he was probably back at Regiment. Meanwhile, could we, in the little time left to us, when we were so anxious ourselves, find a way to get Willie over this fixation that had come over him?

Gino was at his wit's end. "Mama mia, I got my own ass to worry about."

I agreed. It was a bitch. I had no idea of what the hell to do, except maybe send him back to the Clearing Station and have him declared up to his ears in battle fatigue.

Gino shook his head. "No time for that. No way the Medics would do it. Don't think *he* would. Told him to forget about wanderin over toward German lines. Said he'd look suspicious and get stopped by guys on guard duty asking, what the hell's he *doin*. Ain't *nobody* gonna believe him. Warned him that instead of bein killed, he could get himself court marshaled for desertion, or worse."

"Well, yeah, maybe. And he'd make himself miserable for the rest of his life. His family too. You and me, Gino, we don't have a choice. We've got to lug him along with us, and have him stay close."

"And be responsible for what happens to him if he goes crazy?"

"Crazy already. ... But wait; got an idea. I'll find ol' Unge. He'll help. It's his kind o' thing." As I thought about it, that was exactly the way to go. Unge was a hell-bent daredevil, but he had no death wish. He'd get Willie to risk danger, and be smart enough to survive, which would put a whole different complexion on Willie's idea of God's will.

9.

Before taking off for the Company Aid Station, Ab reported back to the Captain, who had been wondering what the hell took us so long. This Captain, just recently assigned to us, was said to be meanness personified, having muscled his way up through the ranks for a battlefield commission. Given time, he'd change, but not a lot. Guldine, an easier-going man, was satisfied to go back to being our Executive Officer, though, with the new guy in charge, it put him more in the line of fire with us. Ab tried to convince the Captain that because of our running into the Heinie patrol, they probably would be waiting for us over on that ridge we were supposed to take, and, in that case, it might be best to either delay the attack, or change our axis of advance.

I was there with Ab, as he wanted someone to confirm what he was saying. Both of us were interested in finding out what kind of

CO this new man was going to be. It seemed like the Captain didn't hear a word Ab said. What he wanted to know was how come, if we ran into a patrol, we didn't take it out, so they couldn't make it back to their lines and do us damage. He told Ab, never mind how dark it was, and said, "They returned fire, didn't they? Then you *maintain contact*, dammit." Ab conceded that we should indeed have pursued them, and, to make sure we'd got 'em, called back to the Cannon Company FO, though considering how accurate they were, even with coordinates, which we didn't have.... Ab broke it off, aware that he wasn't getting anywhere.

Captain Starck (short for Starckwell) wasn't a very patient guy. But we also understood that he was under a lot of pressure, and would be under even more to keep us on the attack, when—looking ahead—we'd be attacked-out, depleted, and down to mostly replacements. In fact, come 530 hours, Battalion dropped a new truck-load of them in on us anyway, on Starck's request. With them came word from Regiment that, given Ab's report, there would be a change of plan. Instead of us starting out at 600 hours, the adjacent Company on our flank would get going, so the attack would be coming from an unexpected direction, and with the Heinies' defense oriented southwest, we'd go after them from our original western axis an hour later. From his bitching, it seemed that Captain Starck thought ours might be no more than a mopping-up operation. —Oh, yeah. Like Ab's walk in the park.

The tactical delay gave us time to assimilate the replacements, get their names (before they were gone) and have them assigned to platoons. They were a miserable lot, after lying out in the ice cold rain all night. And here they were pocketed in the blackness of a strange cove at the foot of the reverse slope of a hill they had just slogged over after coming off trucks. We could see them wondering, where were they, and where would they go from here. Facing a thickly treed, impenetrable draw that didn't seem very friendly, they looked around confused, afraid, and anxious about their fate. We weren't all that happy a bunch ourselves and didn't take kindly to their self-pity.

Gush and I overheard them complaining, mostly about being so ferociously beat up by the cold, something ongoing for us, but new for them. One guy was saying his hands stung so badly, he kept putting them under his armpits. If he could barely grip his rifle, how the hell did they expect him to fire it? They couldn't do a thing about their poor icy feet, except try to curl their toes under. It didn't help that they'd had been told to forget about digging in, so they huddled under trees, shivering together like the dogs in the rain that they were.

They had some questions and complaints. We weren't receptive to either, though we should have been. We had our own worries, and one of them was whether they'd be a problem for us—like in giving away our position, or running off. Fortunately, most of them went to the third platoon, to be held in reserve. Our fourth platoon was to be split between the lead platoons, machine guns going with the first platoon and mortars, our group, with the second, packing M-1s in addition to the tubes and ammo.

We had a returnee sergeant for our squad leader, Ronders, who, on account of his occasional squint, was sometimes called "Sleepy," but not by us. He was a lean, pale, sober- faced type, who favored a leg that still had some shrapnel in it. Gush asked him why he came back, when he could have opted out, and he said it was because he wanted to come back, adding, "And, frankly, I found that I didn't know any better."

He didn't seem like the type of guy who would be cracking jokes. Gush asked me whether *I* knew what Ronders was trying to say. So I asked him myself. At first, he said, "No matter." But when I told him it mattered to us, the guys in his squad, he gave me a better answer than he gave Gush, but I couldn't say we understood him any better.

"I wanted to be here because I knew I was needed. For me, that was better. Not a big thing. Just me. It's in the family. Goes pretty far back. My father's a third generation minister. I wasn't comfortable with life in the rear echelon. The slackness bothered me. There was no awareness—about anything."

I felt that was as much as Ronders would care to say about himself. Clearly he was different, which often made it hard to guess what he was thinking. However, on practical things, he could be very direct and unafraid to speak up—for example, questioning what mortars could do with all that canopy overhead. The more we knew him, the better we liked him.

He had some useful tips for us. Gino and I were ammo bearers, and he told us that instead of sticking our heads through the opening in those canvas yokes, which would distribute the forty-pound weight, with three rounds front and back, we ought to twist the bags and put them over our right shoulders, so we could get closer to the ground when we hit it. Gush had been carrying the mortar, which weighed sixty pounds, and as he started fastening the helmet strap under his chin, Ronders told him to snap it to the back of his helmet. If he had it under the chin, the concussion of a near hit would break his neck.

We couldn't complain about having to carry the extra weight, because it looked like lots of guys were laden with various kinds of heavy stuff, like our machine gunners and their ammo bearers. The three BAR guys in each squad carried a load, as did guys saddled with a bazooka, plus rounds, not exactly a necessity in the kind of fighting we were in for. The guy in the column across from me who had one strapped to his back said he'd never seen one in his life, no less fired the damned thing.

10.

The bombardment on our right that preceded the attack lasted a good twenty minutes and got answered when it stopped. We "stepped off" as scheduled, and, getting close to the tree line, our Lieutenant, a new guy, Olafson, a big blonde Swede, stopped us and pointed in among several splintered trees to a couple of dead GIs, their heads pointed rearwards. He didn't say anything, and neither did we; no need to. Like: Run, and you're putting yourself right into a targeted area, where most of their shells are falling with the intent, as Starck later observed, of cutting the front off from supplies and reinforcements. (Never mind that they're falling up ahead as well as behind us.) Some guys were a little resentful of Olafson, coming up as he did with new, practically clean clothes and a slicker-type raincoat which glistened with the raindrops that didn't soak through. Unlike the other officers, he wasn't loath to use the voice of command, even when it wasn't necessary. But he would change soon enough, and so—too late—would our opinion of him.

Coming on up in a double column, we saw Captain Starck standing at the gate in his long trenchcoat, waving us forward. We heard several shells swooshing through the wet air overhead, and some of our new guys hit the ground. Starck rotated his arm to show that they were ours going toward the hill, which loomed some seventy yards in front of us, its different shades of green barely visible in the haze that enveloped it. Beyond it to the left, a few miles away, was a fire tower that stood in rather sharp relief against the gray sky, so obviously useful for their artillery that we wondered why our own artillery hadn't taken it out. Having passed through the place where we'd blown up the barbed wire, we were surprised by yet additional double-apron strands of wire further on, rusted and looser than the others, but a strain to negotiate, requiring us to high step it on through with the full cartridge belts digging into our hips. Noticing breaks in the wire, we figured if there were booby traps thereabouts, our charges would have set them off.

That greensward was something to behold. I'd never seen a richer, lusher green—except on the Isle of Man. Amply nourished by rain, the grass actually glowed as if lit up from within, and it shed an unnatural, sort of neon radiance over the draw that stopped you in your tracks. It was so blindingly pristine—though guaranteed not to stay that way—that I noticed many a guy seemed hesitant when he came upon it, like a suspicious cat that puts one foot lightly down on new turf, and is ready to bolt.

Starck came over and began pushing at anybody who was too slow about moving it, and he had a way of picking on lead-legged Gino (older guys irritated him); however, he soon discovered that the way to the stream was blocked by fallen trees. Rather than have us bunch up, Starck, his irritation mounting, directed us to detour around them. Of all things, we once again came upon signs marked for mines, the Germans warning their own, and a little further, near the opening of a trail rutted by Jeep treads (no telling where that led to), there stood a faded wooden cross, at the center of which was a carved miniature of Jesus. Keenly religious these Germans were, the motto on their belt buckles reading "Gott mit uns." Didn't see how they could bring Him in on their side—or we, on ours. Nor could I figure out how come just that one cross—decorated, too—and why there.

Our mild astonishment at the unexpected immediately gave way to the expected when the shells started falling close behind us, jarring the air with a succession of blasts. Then, as if finding their range, the gunners were bringing the stuff in closer, the shells making their

149

eerie, inhuman wail, pressing, pressing, pressing, louder, louder, louder, followed by the booming impact, and zing of the shrapnel. There was a frantic rush for the bank of the stream, more like a brook that looked maybe two meters wide from a distance, but got to be more like eight up close. Some guys looking for a narrower crossing found themselves slipping on the muddy bank and sliding in up to their armpits before they got their footing. I was with the ones who plunged right in and, despite the frigid shock, was relieved to find the water no more than waist high. The crossing was one tough push, though, against the weight of current driven water; not made any easier by Olafson on the far bank waving his arms and chewing us out for not getting over any faster. The sort of encouragement that made you want to say, "Thanks, pal. Now, how about throwin me a rope."

What really got us going faster, additionally weighted down as we were by our water-logged clothes, were the snapping sounds up on the hill, followed by sharp splashes in the stream—holy smokes!—like an invisible hand diagonally to our right had thrown a hail storm of pebbles at us. Before I knew it, I was slip-slopping up the other bank, grabbed at the arm by Olafson, just as the screaming shells came bearing down on us. My God, it was like they could visually direct the stuff. There was a pounding in my chest that went straight through to my shoulder blades, and it was like my eyes were popping as I tried to get the stone feet I couldn't feel to go a little faster— *please.*

Next thing I knew I was throwing myself at the base of the hill, gasping for breath. With the shells coming in ever closer, up I went on all fours, kicking the mud and stones behind me and grabbing onto whatever offered in my way—logs, tree trunks, shrubs, rocks— skinning my hands as I went. At one point, I found I was hoisting myself up by somebody's leg. Whether he was dead, or whatever, I couldn't stop to check. I was intent on scrambling my way to a large, inviting hole that I saw halfway up the hill. With that machine gun on our right opening up again, I dropped my rifle and flung myself into the hole. There was someone else in there, and we began to struggle over his rifle. Summoning up every last bit of strength I had left, I finally yanked it out of his hands, and was about to beat him with it, when he yelled out "STAHP!" in perfect English, and I saw it was a GI. Was I ever a wild man. So was he, his breath steaming out of his nose and wet lips like he was a raging bull, much as I was steaming myself.

The shells were falling right over us and beside us, and the next instant after our death struggle, we were down on our chests, shoulder to shoulder, wishing we could scratch our way into the wet earth. The chatter of rifle fire and short bursts of machine gun fire began to pick up in tempo, ours sounding strangely like firecrackers. Two guys popped in on us and lit up cigarettes, and our hole began to cloud up with smoke. One of them asked what the hell kind of a bag that was outside of the opening, and when I told him it was mine with the mortar rounds, he reached out and pitched it down the hill. Good. I simply wasn't thinking. Let one of the incoming shells hit close enough, and there'd be nothing left of us but Swiss cheese.

The rolling bag was picked up by somebody, and he stuck his head in. It was Ab. He told us we had to move out of there. Too many guys were hanging back, and they needed more fire power up ahead, so we could form some kind of a skirmish line to take on those dug-in positions. If we didn't move up, their artillery was bound to be saturating this downward area, and, as it crept up, we'd be trapped, with not much chance of making it out. The smokers nodded, but wouldn't budge. Neither would the guy I'd fought with, saying, "I don't give a good fuck. Let 'em come fur us."

If it hadn't been for Ab, I might have stayed put too. As I thought about it later, had I stayed, I might have been killed doing nothing, just cowering in a hole. I'd picked up my rifle and mortar yoke, and told Ab I was ready. Going up on all fours, monkey fashion, puffing like crazy, the two of us made it to where a thin line of guys was spread out in a looping semi-circle. They were lying down behind tree trunks and firing for all they were worth, clip after clip, trying to button up the damned Heinies who were shooting out of the firing ports in their solidly constructed log and mud bunkers. A couple of times Ab made like he was going to get us all up for a charge, but each time he raised up the slightest bit, that machine gun on our right let go, the bullets cracking into nearby tree trunks. Nobody had the guts—or stupidity—to face that. So we were pinned down and feared we might just get ourselves chewed up, until Ab came up with an idea.

The slope was too sharp and the distance too great for us to be throwing grenades, and it didn't look like we could sufficiently screen somebody maneuvering over to flank the machine gun squad while we kept them occupied out front. I was still holding onto the mortar yoke, and Ab remembered that if you jammed the fin end of one of those shells down hard on the ground, you had a chance of creating the quick down-up motion needed to have the thing spit its safety pin out the side and become armed, making it point detonating. If we'd just keep shooting, he could crawl over laterally, spider-fashion, and throw the thing up far enough to explode it within maybe a few yards of the machine gun, and, when they ducked, we could rush them, and that would as much as give us the hill—maybe.

Olafson came over to tell us whatever we did, it had better be quick. He said Starck probably had their tactic figured out. When their shelling became more intense behind us, their aim was to cut us off from reserves and supplies, and, next, Olafson suggested they'd likely creep their 105s on up the hill to annihilate the forward unit, meaning us.

"Somebody's gotta make a move on that goddam machine gun over there."

Taking one of the mortar shells and giving me one, Ab called for a couple of other guys to follow him and provide covering fire. I was to hold fast and fire from there at my discretion. When called upon, I was to deliver the shell. The cover guys were stalled halfway over by a potato masher grenade that rolled down ahead of them, but ran into a low-hanging fir tree, which absorbed most of the shrapnel. I saw another flipping end over end toward the guy lagging behind Ab. As he picked it up to toss it back, the damned thing went off and blew him backwards, all bloody at the throat and chest. The guy who had been crawling along side him was hit as well and cried out in pain, whereupon the machine gunner started peppering the area, putting slugs right through the top of his helmet. I had fired off a clip, trying vainly to distract the machine gunner. But with Ab's cover guys gone, I became aware that I was all that Ab had by way of protective fire. I drew back a bit and flattened myself against the ground, wondering, what now?

I hadn't noticed till then that the machine gunner had a corridor he was firing down, where the hill fell off more gradually and the trees were sparser, giving him a pretty good line of vision, but one that only went so far my way, before his view got obstructed by a rise, crested with underbrush and fir limbs. While the Heinies were concentrating on Ab's two cover guys, he was able to slip through the corridor. He had signed me to start shooting the second he lifted up to throw the mortar shell.

In my nervousness, I was on my feet for a better view and must have opened up before he was ready, pumping out the whole of an M-1 clip and inserting another. But that worked even better than if I'd waited, because other guys on our end of the line joined in, giving Ab more time to inch his way up for a shorter throw. Meanwhile, as the machine gunner started firing indiscriminately in my general direction, but more to my left and shooting high on account of the rise, I heard the familiar Ka-ruck of the exploding mortar shell.

Before I knew it, there I was unaccountably calling out at the top of my lungs words I couldn't begin to remember, as I ran forward to heave my own mortar shell, hoping it could provide a diversion—at the least, a cloud of dirt—that might shield Ab from detection by Heinies in the nearest dugout. Hitting the roof of the dugout, the shell sent out a shower of shrapnel that created more confusion than damage. Seconds later, two guys with Tommies ran by me, firing from the hip and making a kind of rebel yell as they sprayed the dugout. The two madmen kept going until they were mowed down. I had gone down on my knees, in the follow-through of my throw, but sprang up and, as I ran, tripped over them and hit the ground face first. Except for a bloody nose, I found myself unharmed. By then, everybody had opened up all along the line. Ab, firing his grease gun, got the three Heinies at the machine gun as they tried to run off. Meanwhile, the rest of our guys were storming the dugouts.

It all went very fast. I'll never know how come I got up and called out like that, except that Ab left the mortar round with me because he wanted me to heave it, which I very much wanted to do, knowing it might go off *on me* if I had to hit the ground in a hurry. But, damned if I know whether I did much good, since those two madmen created more of a diversion than I might have. Regardless of who was more effective, them or me, or both together, I desperately hoped we gave

Ab the help he needed. Anyway, we did make the attack, an amazing feat in itself, seen at ant level, and, depending on how success was measured, seen at Brass's level, it could at least be said that we made our objective.

However, we paid a price—an awesome price. The last time I'd seen Willie, Unge had him by the wrist tugging him up the hill, and darned if it wasn't him and Unge making that crazy, out-of-nowhere charge that did them in. Like me, they probably saw how exposed Ab was. But, sadly, looking around for Ab, we discovered that he was taken off too. I found out that after spraying the machine gun nest, he went for the dugout Heinies who shot Willie and Unge. They had just come out in the open and were about to run off, when Ab caught them, but they were too many for him. I did see him drop two and slide behind a tree when they returned fire. However, Ab would himself be targeted by an unseen Heinie sniper who drilled him with a burp gun volley.

That hurt, badly. I got with Gush, who beckoned me from the dugout. We had a hard time believing Ab was gone. He'd had such a fathering concern for us. One soul of a man. Good natured and, as Rebel said, "good by nature." Gone too was our pal Willie, Country America at its best. I would ask around to find out if anyone saw what Willie looked like going up the hill, and one guy said that he plunked himself down well shy of our firing line, and wouldn't move until Unge yelled in his ear and started shaking him. Who could tell whether exploding artillery rounds were enough to shock him back to reality? If so, he consciously allowed himself to get talked into doing a courageous thing. I liked to think that. But to lose him and Ab was a double heartbreak, made even worse when we learned how many others went down.

During the final assault, with Willie and Unge going down, it took somebody to lead the men up, and the one doing so would be first to fall, because, so long as the Germans could fire down at us from that vantage point, it was suicidal to get out in the open. Still, the only way to take the dugouts *was* to overwhelm them with a *wave* of men moving on them, however irregularly, everybody firing as they came. The tough part was having that one man lead it off and bring on the rest. In this case, it was Olafson, who immediately got riddled, the Germans having a goodly number of sub-machine guns on their front line, their weapon of choice, which gave them a mobility they lacked with the heavy MG42 tripod-mounted job that Ab took out. Good ol' Olaf, a gutsy leader after all. He was still calling out for us to blast 'em as he went down.

We couldn't tell at the time who brought the wave back up after Olaf went down, but found out it was none other than Ronders, typically quick on his feet, his grease gun practically on fire going for those ports of the central dugout. Also typically, he shrugged off Starck's saying he'd put him in for an oak-leaf cluster on his Bronze Star. Most unusual for it to be spoken of like that. Ronders didn't care. They never got along. Ronders was too much his own man—also most unusual.

11.

What we found when we took over the Germans' position was that their dugouts were solidly built up and covered by layers of logs cemented with mud, an ideal defensive set-up. Those of the defenders we didn't kill had "melted away," as Starck whispered that he put it in his report to Battalion, something he wanted us to know. From what we could tell, it was more like instantaneous disappearance, leaving the four handkerchief wavers we took prisoner. When our losses were totaled up, according to Starck, we might have had almost forty percent of the attacking force killed or wounded. Some of ours had also disappeared. And there were lots more losses to come, as we got a full taste of what it meant to fight in Hürtgen. We didn't care for the promotional history from guys at typewriters, but it was said (likely by the Fly) that this Regiment went through a "more concentrated hell" in Hürtgen than at any time "during the 156 years of its existence."

The Germans were masters at bringing their artillery in on fixed positions they had just vacated, and, in our case, they were quick about it, and concentrated their fire. At the first sign of a let-up, there were guys who crawled out to have themselves a decent smoke. But suddenly, mortars descended on us, and, unable to anticipate how fast the hot shrapnel would come down on them from tree bursts, the smokers were, in short order, screaming they'd been hit. We timed the intervals so we could go out for those lying nearby; however, the ones who were sprawled this way and that were clearly gone. The covered dugouts offered some protection from the mortars, but they were followed by those shrieking 155s that had no respect for dugouts. They rocked the ground underneath us, and left us badly shaken, indeed physically shaking. And we had treated ourselves to the airhead notion that, by rights, our fight for that hill was over and done with.

It was easy for guys to get disoriented with the on-and-off barrages. Just when the first several rounds of that heavy stuff started to land, I looked out a firing port and saw Ronders shoving guys back into the far right dugout. He himself shortly had to dive for a shell hole, and at one point, he vainly tried to catch hold of somebody making a mad scramble to beat it down the hill, shedding loose equipment as he went.

The Germans' accuracy seemed uncanny, but that was because we also thought you couldn't possibly find anything in that directionless forest, small on the map, though seemingly massive on the ground, where it was impossible at any given moment to know where the hell you were. Occasionally, we did forget that nobody was supposed to get out of Hürtgen alive.

Once the barrages did for sure cease, we had ourselves another cigarette and thought about chow. We had a special way of warming our K-ration meals. It got to be a minor ceremony, and we didn't have many of those. For draft, we'd cut a slit in the low end of the waxed carton with our bayonet, set it upright, and after filling our canteen cups with water and sprinkling in the coffee or bouillon, we'd wind the key three-quarters of the way around our canned entrée, hang it over the edge of the cup by the key, and hold both over the lighted carton. If needed, we'd lay some resinous twigs on the box to prolong the heat. As long as I live, I'll never forget the smell of that burning waxed carton.

12.

It being almost impossible to carry the wounded out in the dark of night, the most critical ones had to be taken out before total blackness set in. Rebel looked at me and said we were experienced, weren't we? I said we were beat, weren't we? But, hallelujah, our Medics made the case that it would benefit the wounded, if they had a day's recovery before being transported. Even with rest, it would become a hard pull to go those 800 meters to the Forward Aid Station next day, but what the hell? Since the Company was being pulled off the hill, after a heavy barrage sent some guys running off, it shortened the distance a bit.

So off we went at first light. With us more than once slipping and falling and almost losing the litter along the way, the distance got a

158

lot longer. On the other hand, considering the shape those guys were in, and that we ourselves might one day be in, we did our best and forgot about aching backs. At the last minute, Ronders decided to take a litter too. The guy that he and our Medic would be carrying was Ronders' fellow D-Day friend, who had had his legs raked across by the machine gun that Ab took out. He was pretty well doped up, and, fortunately, also slight of build. Two other Medics took a third litter with a guy who had a well-wrapped head wound and was likewise out of it.

Going with us were the four prisoners, walking wounded, who were well enough to alternate at carrying a litter. I recalled enough German to get some information out of them. They said the reason that the rest of them who survived weren't to be found was that the Germans regularly had SS officers behind the front who were assigned to shoot deserters. The lucky ones managed to slip away, or get themselves captured, but hanging over potential 'traitors' were the threats of what would befall their families. As a self-respecting German soldier, the only condition under which you could allow yourself to be captured was if you were so severely wounded you couldn't shoot any more. Didn't I say the Germans were the most practical people on earth? If not, I just said it, and noted it more than once. Lots of times their 'practical' was pretty vicious, and sometimes practicality had nothing to do with it. We'd shortly find out what could happen when they got behind our lines.

It figured, because the Germans were rotten at the top. As my Dad put it: tells you something that they are being led by an Austrian. Dad recalled how the Austrians were scorned as bootlickers, and worse, particularly by the Prussians.

One of our newly arrived replacements had wanted to know what the Germans we fought were like, and Rebel said they were hard and mean when they were shooting at us, and when we caught them, they were like us, red-eyed, nervous, wet to the bone, and done in with the cold and fright. The SS were something else, of course, sporting their skull-and-cross-bones insignia, and the nasty young fanatics who idolized Hitler were no picnic either. "Take yer pick, but, when the shootin starts, yah hate 'em all—lots. Like they do us."

As a kind of warning, our First Sergeant had told us there were no really safe areas in these woods. Among things to be feared behind the lines were pockets of Heinies who had been bypassed, or had become turned around and plain lost; some might even have been planted there to punish the invaders of their country. "Keep it in mind, men." That was one reason the Medics taking the third litter were concerned about my carrying a carbine (just exchanged for my M-1) and Rebel his forty-five. Their red cross might get the Medics a pass, but not if the Heinies saw weapons. I told them, "Hell, if we meet the SS, it won't matter a damn whether we're armed or not. They'll just go for the bunch of us, no questions asked."

I was more concerned about having to ford the stream. It might pull the stretchers right out of our hands as we struggled across. It was tough enough on our arms and hands having to carry those poor wounded. We needed a bit of a rest, before the Medics took us upstream to where it narrowed; however, what we thankfully found there was a log bridge the Engineers—bless 'em—had put over the water. That was a big relief because, after our prior crossing, one of the first things we did when we had the chance was to lift our legs and empty the water out of our arctics. Ah, what we wouldn't pay for a pair of dry socks, like the ones we had disposed of.

After negotiating the bridge and wending our way toward the path, we saw some of the damage done by the downhill shelling. In amongst the shell craters were dead GIs, one lying head down in a pool of accumulating water, and another behind him was tossed sideways, head back, arms outstretched. A little further on, there were open Medics' kits, their contents strewn about, and protruding out of the bushes beside them a blood-soaked leg. Blood-spotted footsteps indicated there was a second GI lying in there, who was maybe somewhat late in finding cover. As we looked around a little more, it became apparent that this situation was somewhat different than what we thought. Seeing the pole ends of an empty litter sticking out from under a fir bough, we realized what kind of dirty work had taken place there. Mean bastards! We had heard about that kind of thing, and there it was.

I questioned one of our prisoners about it, and all he could do was shrug, and say, "Vor iss Vor." (Showing off his English.) Rebel thought I was going to shoot him on the spot. However, my rage would get partially deflected when, a little ways up, our attention was caught by something lying mysteriously on the path itself. Of all things, it turned out to be a dead doe, open-eyed, with gashes in its side. Can't explain it, but that large sparkling eye was so striking, it was an image that would stick in my mind long afterwards, particularly since, sadder yet, I would see the same reflective eye on dead GIs.

On rounding a corner in the path, we picked up a faint rustling behind us. The Medics said for us to freeze, and I told them "Bullshit." After what we'd seen, I was ready to blast away at the first fuckin German that came into sight. The Medics stood fast, but Rebel and I gave our litters to the prisoners, and, squatting down, we duck-walked into the brush and waited at the ready. I had taken the safety off my carbine, and was thinking the best way was to shoot first. But, lo, our Medics were shouting out a greeting, and who was it coming into sight, but the Graves Registration Unit, four guys with a stretcher carrying a dead GI wrapped in a blanket.

It was helpful that we ran into them because we were getting pretty weary carrying our wounded, and the Graves people knew a short cut to the Aid Station. Ironically, we were so concentrated on completing our mission, we had no idea that the guy Rebel and I were carrying had not just passed out, but died, something a Graves guy pointed out to us.

We were glad to be rid of our prisoners, whom we'd been prodding from time to time to keep up. They were even more relieved, and happy at the prospect of much better treatment than they would have gotten from their own Medics. As for us, we had a decision to make. We could stay and overnight it at the Aid Station, where we'd get decent chow and a chance to rest up, but maybe risk being chewed out for malingering, or, hellish thought, we could try to make our way back and get overtaken by the dark.

Ronders, being the non-com among us, said he'd be held responsible if we didn't get back. "Yeah, if we could make it—alive," Rebel muttered sourly. The issue was resolved when Ronders got with the Doctor who was CO of the Station, and he said our staying would afford protection for his less-than-safe location. Looking for holes to collapse in, we sure did a great job of protection.

13.

I didn't realize how exhausted I was until I crawled down into the hole Ronders located. I called for Rebel to join us. The Medics had given us a couple of blankets, and I no sooner got myself tucked in than I fell into one deep sleep. Groggy on getting up at six next morning, I felt like I'd been anesthetized. Equally unreal, was rising to the smell of pancakes, bacon, and hot coffee. What a big "Wow" that was. Not so cheerful was the sound of small arms in the direction of our return. Though one path looked a lot like another, we trusted that, if we went in the direction of the intermittent shelling, we'd get there.

We hadn't gone very far when we heard somebody off the path mumbling to himself and came upon some poor old son of a bitch with a torn sleeve and a bandaged upper arm, sitting on a rock. There was some gray in his beard, and, with his glazed eyes and incoherent talk, he was one strange bird. Speaking with a heavy accent, he claimed he was Regular Army, a cook, actually, and that, before being mustered out, he had wanted a taste of combat, something to tell his grandchildren. Ronders was skeptical, and asked, where the hell he'd come from in the first place to get here? He shrugged; damned if he knew.

Ronders doubted the Regular Army stuff, and the idea that this old clown wanted a piece of the fightin was nonsense. However, our Medic said one of the wounded told him about a phony-sounding story that proved to be true regarding a Company in our Battalion which was in danger of being overrun. Headquarters ordered a bunch of cooks, drivers, and personnel clerks to move up and help man the Company's defense. Some got lost. Ronders wondered out loud whether *that* was how this fellow wound up here and got a hasty "Yah-Yah!"

"So you got yourself a lucky hit and you ran, huh?"

"Yah-Yah."

Pressing him to answer a few simple questions, Ronders finally got it out of Mumbler that he was the lone survivor of the massacre we'd come upon and, despite his dialect, spoke German well enough to convince the SS he was one of theirs. Ronders wanted to know how come they didn't shoot him anyway. Arms extended, Mumbler made like he was dumbfounded, but speculated that being eager to get away, they couldn't waste much time on him. Ronders said

163

neither could we. Our Medic, on the other hand, supposed it could well have happened like Mumbler said it did. He himself had seen how fluid things got behind the line, another kind of no-man's-land. Anyway, traumatized this fellow was for sure, and our Medic showed him the way to the Aid Station.

As we moved on, Rebel, turned to me and, under his breath, said, "Guess we learned somethin, Buddy. The Top-Kick wasn't just a-scarin us."

I said, "Hope we keep learnin."

We knew we had taken a wrong turn when we came to a cross road, where off to the left there was a wrecked P-38. One of its motors had gouged out a muddy trough as it slid up beyond the fuselage. The plane itself was all twisted, its aluminum body and wings creased and wrinkled up. The trees that it came down on were split and broken off and some had burn marks. There was a wooden cross right at the cross roads, marking where the pilot had been buried. (By Germans?) Except for the little spotter planes, no aircraft ventured into the heavy overcast that hung over the Forest, so this plane must have come in early. If the sky was clear enough for flight, it was clear enough for the Germans' ack-ack, another use made of their deadly 88s. It was worth knowing we *would* send planes in if the clouds ever lifted.

A little further along, we came upon a couple of deserted Jeeps, stuck axle deep in mud, each with a trailer loaded with bed-rolls and marked H-Company, the heavy weapons company of the Second Battalion, somehow wrongly over in our sector, a not unusual thing, except that H should have been supporting the old codger's doomed Company. At least the Jeeps put us on course for the greensward and stream that we had started out from. It must have been well past noon when we got there, and, crossing over to the other side of the stream, we ran into a couple of stragglers. They said that what did their Company in was a surprise counterattack that sent guys running. It was madness. Looking around at the thick stand of trees, many broken off at the top, Ronders said he thought there might be additional stragglers adrift in the woods. The stragglers thought so too; half the Company.

Finally reaching the draw over the hill that we had taken, we ran into H-Company itself, looking, as infantry situations go, rather well set up, with deep holes well covered, and warm C-rations brought up by Supply. A detail would likely be going back to pick up their bed-rolls. They let us share a can of stew with them. Good ol' H.

14.

When we rejoined the Company, except for Gush and Gino asking where the hell we'd been overnight, no one said anything to us. The mood was too somber for talk. The order had come down that, at first light next morning, we'd be going on the attack to take the hill—almost vertical—where that other Company had been so badly bloodied. Under the circumstances, the non-coms were going to have trouble getting some guys out of their holes. Gino, for one, said he didn't care what they did to him, but damned if he'd go. We knew it would be rough when even Hardy Hardiman, the toughest of our non-coms, said it might be better if we tried it elsewhere, and was told elsewhere was no better.

Starck told Sergeant Blazor he was relying on him to make sure *everybody* got out of their holes in the morning. Blazor (his name a corruption of something else) was a wild ol' mountain boy and twice wounded casual, who in Normandy had grabbed a bazooka every time he heard a tank go rumbling by. Blazor knew who Starck meant by 'Everybody,' but, before Blazor could get to that guy, he was walking up to *him*, his platoon sergeant, and reporting that he was falling out.

"Okay, what the hell does that mean?" Blazor asked. When the fellow said it means what it means, Blazor wanted to know where the hell he was going, and the fellow said he didn't know, just back. When Blazor gave him a mean stare, he stared back for a second, then about broke down.

"I can't take any more. *Can't, yah hear! Can't! No way! No more!"* His hands were working up and down as he talked. Gush and me being within earshot, Blazor asked us to help calm him down. This was his second stint on line, after a suspicious minor wound. He continued talking, and his tone changed as he appealed to Blazor to—in heaven's name—let him go. He said he was so beat he had nothing left, only his determination to go no further.

Gush asked, "What if we all took off?" After a moment's pause, 'Everybody' composed himself and quietly said he was sorry. Taking in his long, dark Jesus face, Gush's attitude changed and he walked away. 'Everybody' might, after all, be any given body among us. We supposed he had to understand the risk, and nonetheless was saying, 'anything but more of this.'

Blazor finally said he wouldn't stop him. So with just enough presence of mind to tell him "Thanks," 'Everybody' gathered his things and, in that flat-footed walk of his, feet to the oblique, off he went, disappearing into the dripping firs. That was the last any of us ever saw of him.

We only knew him as Nick something. He had a long Greek name, which sometimes came out in variations of Papas-whatever. Shortly after he left, Boyd, our First Sergeant, told us the way he took off, he'd probably get killed, but he'd report him as missing in action to give him the benefit of the doubt. The funny thing about Nick was that his people were immigrants who couldn't read or write English. Back home, a cousin had to translate the letters Nick wrote to Ma and Pa Pappas. Aware of how worried they were, and fearing daily that he might get killed, Nick headed all of his letters, 'Somewhere in England.' He never told them he had gone to France, no less Germany. We wondered what his disbelieving parents would think when they received the telegram saying he was "Missing in Action."

We wanted to know how come Boyd was so sure Nick would be killed, and he told us he wasn't. But it seems that we had bypassed pockets of Germans on our last attack, as had other outfits that came through the area before us. So it could be pretty dangerous back there. We told him we could vouch for that ourselves and wanted to fill him in on the dead litter bearers, the Medics and their wounded, but he knew all about that.

We were told that, getting wind of what had happened to those helpless guys, Hardy had gone into a rage, just as we had when we saw it, and, taking along Blazor who was madder yet, he couldn't wait to have at the bastards. He found them cowering in a well-covered hole that we had bypassed, unaware it was there. Knowing that "Kommen Sie Raus" would get the message across, he repeated it. And, sure enough, out came the white handkerchiefs, but instead of their emerging, the Heinies (maybe SS, maybe not) seemed to be waiting for an "Okay,"—anything reassuring—and, when instead Hardy let go with a burst from his grease gun, they threw out a couple of potato mashers, which Blazor hastily kicked back, while Hardy sprayed their hole and made an end of them. So that was the small arms fire we'd heard from the Aid Station. Rebel said that when we left the Aid Station, he, in fact, had feared we'd have ourselves a fire fight on the way back, for which, his forty-five being next to useless, all we had was my carbine. Wow. Was I ever glad he kept it to himself. Boyd said, dangerous as it was out there, it was a real good thing we pulled night guard duty at the Station.

One of our Medic litter bearers was actually a fresh replacement. He came over, and, listening intently to Boyd's account, said it never occurred to him to ask what the name of this place was. "How's about telling me where the hell we are, Sarg?"

Boyd said, "Nobody knows. And the rest of us want out."

Having found that on line you could talk to any of the once-feared sergeants, I asked Boyd, while we were at it, how come Hardiman was called Hardy.

"His first name was Harrison. He went by Harry, but, seeing him in action, we thought that was too chummy a name."

Since I actually got an answer, I wanted to know how come they ever got a guy like Blazor, second in toughness to Hardy, to pull back off the hill we'd taken on our last attack, when there was every expectation of a counterattack.

"That was one time we didn't need to. Remember the bombardment that came in after we took the hill. Some guys ran off. Blazor was one of 'em. Didn't Ronders tell yah about it? Well, a guy who was off to the side of Blazor ran into one of those oversized 155s and got blown up. What's left is a big red splotch where the guy was chopped to pieces. Yah wouldn't think it, but when Blazor saw what happened, he threw away his pack, his helmet and rifle, and ran back down that hill cryin like a baby. Miraculously, not a scratch on him. At the time, he'd just gone for a shell hole and was callin for that guy out in the open to come over to the hole when the stuff hit. It was like that made him run him right into it. Blazor took it hard. But, like yah see, he gets over it. Yah suppose yah'll never get used to it. But yah do. Everybody in his own way."

We also had a better understanding of Blazor's attitude towards Nick.

15.

Starck knew we needed more than encouragement before we pushed off. The Brass at Regiment, who had no idea of how their troops were getting mauled in these damned woods, finally began paying attention to the casualty reports from line officers. Under pressure from Division to take that hill, Regiment agreed to Starck's call for an intense and sustained bombardment of the German positions, beginning with those still shiny 81mm mortars, and backed by 105s, which he partly got.

The barrages were so heavy and prolonged, they scared us, waiting to mount the hill. It was one boom after the other, as the stuff kept coming and smoking the top of the hill. The shelling stopped for a minute, and some guys were starting up, but got motioned back. Ah-ha, we'd pay them back with some of their own. The idea was to have the Heinies think it was over, so they'd come out of their dugouts to check on our assault. Whether they came out or not, after a couple of minutes, the 105s began pumping out their stuff again, and we got the go-ahead while the shells were still streaming overhead.

It was one exhausting climb, with us, once again, grabbing hold of shrubs, trees, rocks, the wet ground itself, anything to give us a little hoist, as we scratched our way up on all fours. Halfway, I noticed how some guys were stopping to catch their breath, and I did the same. It was one long, steep pull and we thought we'd never get there—hopefully wouldn't need to if the 105s did their job.

Uncertainty was a factor in our tiredness, but that rumbling in the gut was sheer fright. I could feel the pulse banging in my temples.

We blanked all of that out, once we heard some guys ahead of us open up, which in the wet air had that familiar pop-pop-pop sound of firecrackers. The rest of us did the same, having no idea of what we were firing at, with those heavily branched fir trees just about closing off our view. But, finally, the trees fell away as we came within sight of the crest where our barrages had practically shaved the place bald, leaving timber lying every which way, the good part of which was that it offered cover, the bad that it slowed us when we were about to make our move on those dugouts, built-up like bunkers.

The mist that had coiled around the hilltop was lifting, and the next thing I knew there was Guldine bent over beside a chopped off tree trunk signaling for us to be up and at 'em, as he clutched his side where he'd taken a shot from who knows where. We were on our feet making our way forward as best we could, some tripping over fallen trees, the rest shooting from the hip, until the Heinies opened up with their machine gun, which sent the center of our skirmish line to the ground in a hurry. There was quick movement on my end of the line, and the guy beside me was hit in the chest and fell over on me, taking us both down.

Just then, I heard a wild yowl followed by a fearsome Ka-boom where their machine gun had been firing. Rebel had attached an anti-tank grenade to his rifle, with the one idea of taking out their machine gun, sure to make its presence known. And did he ever do the job. That rallied the rest of us, and, pushing on up as fast as we could go, we overran the dugouts and started pitching grenades into them. Somebody came up with a smoke grenade which he lobbed down a trench between dugouts, and that got the remnant out pretty fast, arms up, coughing up a storm.

All told, we had a fairly good haul, fourteen prisoners. Carrying their wounded as best they could, they were marched down to our Company Command Post at the foot of the hill. Their helmets discarded, they were wearing their dark green field caps with the short visors. Dark-faced and bearded, they looked bedraggled, weary and generally as beat up as we were. The older ones, probably in their late thirties, were apprehensive about what we were going to do with them.

As Hardy and Blazor came over to search them, they drew back, saying they didn't want to be searched, "Wir haben nichts." Hardy grabbed hold of one of them, went for his pockets and pulled out a handful of "Blue Balls," small, round, French-type concussion grenades. "Haben nichts, huh?" He spit the words into the guy's face. Properly frightened, the rest of the Heinies gave in to being searched, which turned up additional "Blue Balls" and personal items. One of our young guys found a neat little vest watch and chain, but Starck made him give it back.

Prominent among our prisoners was an officer, whom we'd bitterly refer to as Lieutenant X. As Starck drew him aside, he asked, in broken English, to be released so he could persuade the rest of his company to surrender, which they'd be eager to do. Where were they? Starck wanted to know. When told they were less than a hundred meters beyond the hill hiding in the woods, Starck got on the phone to Battalion. Standing nearby, I heard him repeat to Hardy the answer he got: What did he have to lose, but one lousy officer, with the chance of getting some fifty more prisoners and likely another hill? Hardy was doubtful. The rest of us who had gathered around were even more so, having noticed the faint smile on X's face as he watched us digging in for a fall-back position in case of a counterattack. Out of the corner of my eye, I thought I saw him give a knowing look to his two Sergeants. Hardy must have seen it too, because he tried to say something to Starck, but got brushed off.

Up the hill we trudged, and, with X indicating the direction he'd be going in, Starck pointed to his watch and said he'd wait no more than fifteen minutes. A second later and he'd call in our big ones, 155s.

That was one hell of a mistake. Within five minutes of the officer's release, in came *their* 155s, huge boxcar sized shells, rushing at us with their demonic screech that ended in booming eruptions, ripping up the trees, the earth, the very air, and some of us—also our nerves. Luckily we had scurried down into their well-made dugouts, which could withstand much, but not a direct hit. They sent in one harrowing barrage that must have lasted well over fifteen minutes, and the stuff landed all around us as we lay there cringing, scared out of our wits that the next shell would be a direct hit. I was in with Rebel and Gush, but some dugouts had four or five guys packed in them, and, when we heard a shell bearing down almost on top of us, followed by an ear-splitting explosion and screams, we knew there must indeed have been a direct hit, wiping out who knows how many guys.

We had to get out of those dugouts and off the damned hill. The devilish part was figuring out when the let-up might come and how long it would last. We'd been told that there were times when the Heinies could intermittently blast away at a targeted area for half a day. That was the point Rebel tried to make when Gush crawled over to the opening of our dugout, and we had to wrestle him back. Shaking and biting off his words like we'd never seen him do either, he cried, "Goddam, I can't stand bein a fuckin sitting duck. Next time I go, you sons o' bitches, you better not get in my way, yah hear!"

At that moment, two random shells fell right next to us, and we heard a scream. Looking out the opening, we saw a kid all bloody down his back, and, of all things, Gino getting hold of the kid's legs and dragging him back into their dugout. Gino felt for the kid, he being the one who had come up with the vest watch and chain. Gino had asked Starck to let him have the things, since, when that Heinie was searched at the next level, they were sure to disappear. Starck rarely reversed himself.

As expected, the shelling resumed, full scale, and we knew we were in for one hell of a sweat. It seemed like the Germans had those hilltop dugouts all plotted out and had pre-registered fire set for the entire area. We couldn't help thinking about that fire tower. Yet another dugout took a direct hit, and, from the way those shells came in that had wounded the kid, it almost seemed like they were bracketing Gino's dugout. After an interval, there was a deafening BOOM, and it was his that took the hit. The sharp screams seemed like they were right in our ears.

Knowing we were bound to be next, we bunched up at the opening of our dugout feverishly hoping for an interval. Rebel was cussin up a blue streak. Gripping his rifle butt, he whacked away at logs that narrowed the opening. When two more close ones hit, Gush blurted out, "No good Mammy humpin, two bit whores, y'ain't gonna mash *me* in here!" And there was no holding him back. We bolted out right behind him, racing full tilt down the hill, stumbling and falling as we went. Others followed, some howling. On reaching the bottom, we ran around like raving maniacs searching for those holes we'd dug.

Once the shelling ceased, we slowly emerged and I saw Hardy go for X's two Sergeants. He said he was taking them on a little walk around the side of the hill. Gush was all for it and grabbed a Tommy, but Rebel held them off, "Fellers, that's the stuff *they* do, not us." I agreed; besides what good would it do us. As we jawed at one another, the commotion brought Starck over, and he put a stop to it. "Think of what happens, men, if they retake this area and capture some of ours."

Which we felt they just might do, but, for the time being, we were thankful that we'd had the foresight to get holes dug at the bottom of the hill. There was little else to be thankful for. And lots to be heavy-hearted about.

As we sat around in numb silence waiting for the order to move out, the thought of losing guys we'd been close with really sank in. It weighed on us to the point that some guys finally had to talk. Rebel said that, when you thought about guys like Willie and Gino, you felt like you had a stone on your chest. Ignoring the odds, we had counted on their hanging in with us. Whatever it was that got to Willie, I thought it must have started eating on him the day he got up here. Gush felt it could do that to you without your knowing it. Some guys thought Gino wasn't tough enough, that he was, in fact, kind of soft and, as Starck put it, 'risk averse.' But who the hell wasn't? Above all, he had a heart; which said a lot. Missing those guys, along with those we'd just lost, made the situation all the more gloomy. Not something we liked to dwell on, but, in a lull, it helped—briefly—to share what we were thinking anyway.

16.

Our outfit died in Hürtgen. One of its cemeteries was an attack that took us to the vicinity of a sawmill. Afterwards, the mere mention of it remained so great a terror to us, we shivered at word of it. The attack that got us there wasn't quite as bad as others. The reason was that we came out onto a kind of plateau clearing, not the best terrain for the Germans' typically devastating defenses, though, once they had us locked in there, they knew how to make it more than typically devastating. Ironically enough, as we came upon it, the place looked comparatively placid, a commercial area where the Germans had been systematically felling those long, slender pine trees—150-foot beauties—to be milled for lumber that was coveted, especially for building homes and other prime construction.

Talk about construction, when the Germans built a house—say, with the good clean, fresh-smelling lumber of these pines—I was told they intended it to last for no less than a hundred years. They were big on things lasting for years; the Third Reich was supposed to last a thousand. In addition to looking forward, they went back a long way in time as well, and, ignoring the Huns, they could see themselves as descendents of Charlemagne, another empire builder, whose Court was celebrated as a center of culture. And there we were, base-born upstarts, fighting his descendents in what was practically the old fella's backyard. Ah, the Germans. So good as builders, so good at making things last; and at eliminating what, by their pragmatic lights, wasn't supposed to.

Time and again, the Germans were a puzzle to me, so capable, so terrible; so good, so bad. I talked about some of that with Rebel and Gush, and, for them, the Germans weren't that much of a puzzle. Rebel said they were just very good at being bad, which I wouldn't dispute. I knew 'em; had some German ancestry of my own.

The real hell amidst those prime trees came with the incessant pounding that was meted out to us once we got ourselves in there; an enclosure which, after attacks that went nowhere, we could neither leave nor fight our way out of. It got so bad, one attack was literally taken through the rain-splashed blood of the previous one, it being too risky to bring out the dead and wounded. Guys were killed digging their holes, and in them.

As the stuff kept coming, we could just visualize their artillery firing away with that great German fury, as Battery Captains called out: "Feuer! Feuer! Wieder, Feuer! Und noch ein Mal Feuer!" There were occasional lulls, but they weren't always noiseless. With the terror of sustained shelling still ringing in our ears, some guys would be yelling out at the top of their lungs. "Get us the hell out of here! God in heaven, OUT!" You couldn't make out all they were saying, but it didn't matter. You knew and were saying the same unintelligible things. Much as we hated thinking about it afterwards, we agreed it was the worst battering we'd ever gone through in this life. As Rebel would put it (well afterwards), "If you went to the hot place in the next life, you could tell 'em you'd already been there." Having been soaked to the bone by that knife-like rain, we'd say we could appreciate a little warmth, anyway.

17.

The damnation amidst uniquely cherished pines lasted for a number of days. Don't ask me how many. It could have been a week for all we knew. At first, seeing the open space, Starck, wide-eyed, says, "Ah-ha, revenge. At last we can set up our 60mm mortars, and drop the shit down *their* throats for a change." The only trouble was that the one fully manned mortar squad we had was made up of replacements, Gush and I having been put in with the second platoon. Ronders wondered whether you could find a target out there, where one patch of woods looked like another—that being what he quietly remarked to the Lieutenant who had came up with the replacements and had the same question. It didn't take long for him to get an answer. The moment this new squad set up and fired a test round into no-man's-woods, their position being revealed, they were wiped out by a direct hit of return fire, getting all nameless four of them, and sending the rest of us running for cover. Unfortunately, the replacements weren't quick enough at judging the sound and direction of the shells bearing down on us.

Our first attack—in fact, our sole mission, as best we could figure out—was to clear some 500 yards of woods sheltering dug-in Germans on the flank of a fellow Regiment. We were quick to 'clear' the open space, but once we got into the woods beyond, we ran into an ominous firebreak, and, knowing how notorious they were for being mined, we stopped for a couple of minutes, which was just long enough for the Germans to open up with machine gun fire along the break, essentially pinning us down.

Five of us were sent out to circle around back and to the left, expecting to locate the machine gun, but, after circling, our first forward move brought their 105s down on us. Our two scouts were killed outright. Luckily, Gush and I, always on the lookout, had spotted an abandoned German hole, and just as we heard the familiar incoming wail, we dove for it.

The hell of it was, the Germans had sent out some of theirs to circle round and create havoc for us. Gush and I picked up the sound of them brushing through the trees. Our only chance of making it out of there was to create enough havoc of our own to scare them off. So we prayed, anyway. I'd always wanted to throw my first grenade, and as soon as I pitched it, I was pulling the ring out of a second with my teeth and pitching it. Gush followed with his two. Some of them had to have been hit, as we heard cries of pain, and we got a bunch of frightened howls out of the others. The next instant, our grenades were followed by the sudden burst from a grease gun opening up behind us. Looking out of the hole, we saw three of them go down for sure, and our combined firepower spread enough confusion for the rest to do a hasty retreat.

Scrambling out, we were in a big hurry ourselves to get the hell away, and who did we run into but ol' Ronders with that saving grease gun, more alert—and, in fact, madder—than we'd ever seen him. Darned if he hadn't come along to give us back-up. And we had the feeling it was his own doing. That made me wonder, Did he still claim us as his guys? He would have gotten a push from Starck, who knew what Ronders thought of the mortar situation. But, as Hardy put it together for us, Ronders, being aware it was coming, had the satisfaction of telling Starck he was going before Starck could tell him he was sending him.

We got with the Company just as they were pulling back to brace themselves for the sure-to-follow counterattack, which, thanks to Starck's finally calling in the 105's, got stopped in its tracks, though not before there was a brief, but bloody fire fight. Following it, there was the most astonishing thing. Pedro, our chief Medic, a great guy and always on the alert, went out waving his red-cross arm band and, by hand language, told the Germans to come and get to their wounded, while we got to ours. And, be damned if it didn't happen. Both Medics started tending to the wounded as they came upon them, ours tending some of theirs along with our own, and vice versa. But there was the matter of our carrying the wounded back, and, considering the difficulty of it, the German Medics were more prone than ours were to give up on guys seen as hopeless. Many of them, ours too, died in the night, alone, in varying states of pain. It was bad; bad as it gets, hearing them moan and, weak-voiced, still vainly call "Med-dic."

The carrying back was indeed a big matter. Before bringing the artillery in on their counterattack, Starck had ordered everyone with a grease gun up forward to have at their leading element, and Ronders became one of the guys who went up. In the midst of the fire fight, it looked, at first, like Ronders, with that bad leg, might have slipped and fallen, but, as he clutched his side going down, it became obvious that he had taken a hit as he ran left to get behind a woodpile, and he was lying there writhing in pain. Fearing he might get taken out by our own artillery, I wanted to go get him, but Gush told me to hold on.

Finding Pedro, Gush got his armband and out we safely went. As we got close, we saw Ronders had been ripped up the side by a burp gun. He being in too great a pain to be lifted, we had to improvise as best we could. I grabbed him under one armpit, and, with Gush grabbing him under the other, we slid him back to our hole. In agony all the way, he kept chewing us out. Pedro was quick about cutting away the blood-soaked clothes, which exposed the torn flesh extending from Ronders' hip to his rib cage and showing white-blue bone. Pedro poured sulpha powder on the raw area, gave him a morphine shot and 'wound tablets.' Ronders was, all the while, crying out in pain and wincing, especially at the awkward bandaging.

Pedro said that Gush had given him the idea to ask the Germans for a truce ("Worth a try") during which, since we hadn't gotten our bedrolls, Gush had run out and found a muddy Heinie blanket that luckily we could wrap Ronders in. With Gush on one side and me on the other, we snugged ourselves up close against him, hoping to provide some warmth. He did quite a bit of moaning, but, fortunately, a second morphine shot knocked him out, though he intermittently sighed through it. It was a long night, and we finally were able to fall off to sleep, cold as we were with fingers of icy rain seeping down on us through the spaces between the overhead logs. We knew the difference between the feel of somebody's cold hand and the cold of a dead man's. In the morning, one touch and we knew Ronders was gone. He'd lost too much blood.

A tough loss, and it lingered. You couldn't get Ronders to say a whole lot, but the things we were able to learn about him sank in. Rebel had asked how come he was out there covering Gush and me. And he had just said, "Something yah do." Rebel thought he knew what he meant, but he wanted to hear it from him.

"Okay. But not somethin yah had to do."

"Well, yeah, something I did have to do." Ronders wouldn't go any further with it, except to offer a reminder of what he'd said before, "It's a matter of caring. Something that takes hold." We thought that was pretty extraordinary, but the idea of what he was saying got through; like there's a code that when the Sergeant looks after his own, they look after him. Not always true, of course, though, for the time being, we were satisfied that he still counted us as his guys.

We knew Ronders was pissed off that Starck didn't have a dime's worth of remorse over what happened to those four replacement mortarmen. It was obvious that Starck wanted Gush and me to set up another mortar in order to show the skeptics, and we could see Starck was doing a slow burn because he couldn't risk having a second try go bad. It was also obvious that Starck knew Ronders was reading him, and since we weren't dumb enough to volunteer, he was doubly incensed. So how else to appease his frustration than by giving hot assignments to guys who angered him. It was done all the time.

Did it ever get to us—not only realizing that Ronders could put pressure on Starck, but seeing he was all that strong about following his own convictions—in this case, to our benefit, his risk. I recalled that when he first came back to the Company, we couldn't figure the guy out. Guys in our squad weren't the only ones who wondered how he ever made Sergeant. We didn't always understand him; however, like I'd said, the more we got to know him, the more we liked him. How little we really did know him, we just found out. Rebel said he was "good folks," the highest compliment in his part of the country.

I had gotten to know Ronders a little better than others did. I recalled the instance when we had teamed up digging in together, and talked a bit before falling off to sleep. Still bothered by how he answered the question Rebel had put to him, I wanted to know how come, with that gimpy leg, he wouldn't accept LA (Limited Assignment), and he said it was a matter of instinct, of being where he felt he belonged.

"Belonged?" I asked, incredulous.

"Yeah; preference." His matter-of-fact tone of voice suggested it simply made sense.

"Knowing us," I said, "you gotta know preference would be to relax and stay out of trouble."

"Well, I had trouble being back there. Guys had it made and no sense of gratitude for having it. Nothing mattered; they were livin it up, but didn't know life. Here life was hell, but it was real. Okay, life and death real, but we shared it and we cared."

I marveled. "You still came back despite what you know?"

"Because of it."

I had a hard time with that one. I knew there was depth to the guy, but I didn't realize how deep it went. He'd been close with

Hilfer, who had had a service for us the day before we pushed off for the sawmill. The fact of the matter is that like Hilfer, Ronders was an intellectual, as I learned when I found them talking about the "culture of caring." In civilian life, Ronders had been a high school English teacher and taught Sunday School at a Church where his father was the Minister. He took life seriously.

"But you are scared, ain't you?" I couldn't resist asking.

"All the time."

18.

Not only didn't we get bedrolls, we didn't get additional K rations—courtesy of our lousy complaining Supply Sergeant, big-mouth Harobi; but, actually, the worst of it was that we didn't get any water—the heaviest stuff to carry. You couldn't just stick a canteen cup out in the rain and, after a bombardment, expect to get it back. A guy who had gone out to a shell hole for water didn't make it back. So I gathered up a bunch of canteens, stuck them in my empty pack, and, running as low as I could get, went down to the brook in the draw behind us.

I was so intent on getting them as full as I could, holding them against the current, that I didn't realize I might have company, until I looked up and my cup dropped to the bottom of the brook. There, no more than ten yards down from me, were two damned Heinies also getting water. Not knowing what to do, I unslung my carbine. Goddamn, if those sons o' bitches were going to get me down there. Their arms instantly went up, and a third came out of the bushes, also arms up. There was nothing else to do but make them carry the canteens up, me following with my carbine on them. As we reached our clearing, I had to go first to make sure no one shot my three prisoners, and maybe me along with them. The Germans were middle aged and kind of pathetic, being blear-eyed, bearded, and bedraggled, as we were.

What else could we do but make them dig a hole for themselves and settle in while we sweated out the next barrage. Hell, if they survived, they were destined for Heinie Heaven, Stateside.

19.

Starck reminded us that we still hadn't taken a foot of the 500 yards we were supposed to clear, so, amidst more than usual grumbling, and officers having to literally pull guys out of their holes, 105s were called in again, after which we moved out. We were firing from the hip as we entered the woods, and, before we knew it, their stuff was coming in on us. I happened to be walking somewhat behind a three-man BAR squad, who amazingly tried to outrun an incoming shell, and, as I sprang toward a stack of logs, I felt a sharp stinging sensation on my left thigh. "Oh shit," I thought, "my leg's gonna be gone." I figured it was time. My luck had lasted longer than it should have. Looking at how the three BAR guys were thrown back, the face of one practically blown off, leaving a vicious splattering of blood and spilled brains, I felt sick at the sight and sick for them. Had I been a fraction of a second slower and several yards closer, the same might have happened to me. It gave me the shivers. There were times when it paid off to recall what they dinned into our heads about dispersion.

After I'd hobbled back to my hole and had a look, it wasn't all that bad, just a streak of torn flesh, bleeding, but not deep. I got out my first aid kit, shook the sulpha powder on it and applied the bandage. Had myself a drink of the good water I'd brought back, and waited.

Considering that it did to my thigh little more than what happened to Ab's arm, I supposed I could stay put, expecting at least some of the guys would be back, and if nobody showed, no problem. I'd find my way to the Aid Station, let it heal for a couple of days and catch up with the Company somewhere. The upshot was that the Company had pushed the Germans out of a portion of the ground they were supposed to take and proceeded to dig in and defend their gain. Hearing voices, I looked out and there were the litter bearers and the Medics Pedro had sent for, taking care of the recently wounded. They got me together with several other walking wounded and said to follow them back to the Aid Station. An assemblage of prisoners, including my three, was going along with us.

The Medical Officer found that in addition to the scrape on my thigh, I had a sore throat, was running a fever, and probably had trench foot. My poor, itching feet were wrinkled, and blue enough. He wanted to have me shipped out to a hospital, but I didn't like the idea. It'd be embarrassing to be going back with guys who were really *wounded.* So he let me stay on. I told him thanks and promised I'd be a fast healer. Our Medics were great guys; they took all the risks we did, had nothing but the red cross to defend themselves, and were generally sympathetic toward us, a sentiment we weren't very used to.

20.

The first thing Rebel said was, "Don't tell me you're glad to be back."

"Well, they told me you're gonna be havin turkey dinner."

"They kin shove it. We're goin into the attack at first light in the morning. You're just in time."

Just back from their ordeal at the sawmill, the guys had no idea that it was Thanksgiving Day—if it was—and were too beat to think about it. There were things we could be thankful for, starting with our lives, and lots we couldn't, starting with an attack that followed hard on a real dinner. Of turkey! Something to cheer up the folks back home. There'd be pictures in the papers.

After three days of ease for me, and the same number of continued hell for them, it was like I was seeing them anew. It looked like they'd just walked out of the grave. They were so gaunt and slope shouldered, their lined faces so dark and drawn, their pale eyes so tense. The whole wet, misty gray atmosphere of the place was depressing in itself. Myself, having experienced rest and knowing what lay ahead, I was feeling a tightness in the throat, and the old throbbing in the temples was coming back, particularly as I saw the shape those poor good guys were in after yet another assault on their battered nerves and stamina. They looked flat-out shot, unable to go any further, and another major effort was being asked of them.

"Dear God," I prayed to myself, "have mercy on us. And if it's to be an end, make it quick and painless." The next moment, I realized how ridiculous that was, but I wished it nonetheless. What I saw then was what those of us who made it out of the Forest would see again in one another: guys looking like scarecrows in the wind, who had nothing left and knew they'd be called on to give more. Shortly after the Forest, we caught the Break-Through in Luxembourg, and our defense there got written up as the "heroic action" of a depleted unit. We were depleted, all right, not just in numbers. None of us cared what it meant to be in a heroic action. Couldn't tell you what it was. Apparently, the people who wrote about it did.

It came as a revelation when I later on overheard Starck himself admitting to Lieutenant Robbenstine, in a soft, choked voice, that he never really expected to make it through this damned Forest in one piece—or any piece. Robbenstine (the name got shortened to Robbens), a First Lieutenant and officially our Executive Officer, was an amiable guy who had no problem mingling with us enlisted men. He was trying to buck Starck up, with good words about his hanging in and his sense of duty to the Company under the worst of circumstances for his command. Robbens was Jewish, so he had a certain commitment of his own, but, regardless, he was also very much of a soldier, and leader, who made the fight in Luxembourg, and was big for us there, when we were down in numbers and hard pressed.

In any event, there'd be more action before we got there. On that Turkey Day, I ran into a guy who, of all things, I'd taken basic training with in Benning, one of the Boston Irish, a good-natured, overgrown blue-eyed boy. Jimmy Mac we called him. It was not uncommon for us to find that neither of us had any idea of the other's presence in our Company. His apple-cheeked baby-face, now pale, was mud caked, and his once bright-eyes were red-veined and taut. Low helmeted, he had the look of a ghoul peering out of a cave—in a place darker yet. After we exchanged surprised greetings, he was muttering things under his breath.

I wanted to know what was eating at him, and he said that since machine guns had lost four men, they gave him a forty-five and were putting him in with them. He had never fired one. He was told that except for vibrations, the machine gun, being anchored, was easier to shoot than an M-1. I pointed out he couldn't be in with a better guy than Rebel. He said, he could be in with Jesus Christ Himself, and it wouldn't help. He'd had all he could take.

"And I got company, this whole goddam Company. Dammit, how many hours do yah lay balled up in a mud hole under bombardments

186

that don't end, get out for the attack and…. Man, you just fuckin break." With that, he slinked off, wanting to be by himself.

I guess I shouldn't have been startled when we heard a lone shot and yell that had us reflexively cringing and looking for cover, until Rebel called out, "Somebody help that soldier." Guys had circled around him, as he sat there slumped over in pain holding his leg. Jimmy claimed the forty-five just went off on him as he was putting it back in his holster. "Never had one." His torso bobbed up and down as he talked, and he didn't bother to wipe away tears. I had an arm around him. After cutting his shoe off, Pedro did his best to stop the bleeding with a tourniquet. Amidst the blood, it looked like the forty-five had chewed up bones. No telling if they could save his foot, and he said he didn't give a damn. It was a small price to pay.

Like he said, he wasn't the only one. The three guys who had taken over for those BAR men we had lost were talking quietly among themselves, and one of them, a big guy we called Samson, had his arm around the other two and was walking them off into the woods. An hour later they reappeared like ghosts out of the forest gloom with Samson holding his arm in a makeshift sling. There was a reddened bandage on his upper arm. He didn't say how it happened and we didn't ask. He was such a big, rugged guy we never thought he'd crack. We guessed his best buddy, a great shot, must have made a careful job of it, not to hit the bone. He was a thin, spidery type of guy, kind of hyper, who had a nervous habit of running a finger under his runny nose. Long back, when it was still possible to smile, a wag said he was the son part of Samson, so he got called Sonny. He had been the trusty BAR man in another squad, and from time to time he'd be called upon to be our designated sniper.

Somebody had gotten hold of a copy of *Stars and Stripes*, where it was reported that the General of Generals, had visited a field hospital and raised holy hell about patients with self-inflicted wounds, who were written up as suffering from combat fatigue. Even Starck had to admit that when it came down to finding out how such a demoralizing thing could happen, the General was generally clueless.

We weren't the only ones who knew the fight in this Forest was a disastrous mistake. It wasn't long before our officers and those above them all the way up the line came to realize what was going on. They had to do no more than look at the casualty numbers (for them, percentages), from which even the higher-ups could conclude this campaign was militarily unjustified. But no one had the guts to say so. Line officers were chewed out for not taking their objectives. Like: what was holding them up? Should we be accepting such a poor ratio of ground gained to the cost in casualties required to take it? Taking the overview—from back at Corps HQ—the worst that would be said of the campaign was that it was an early winter stalemate. But never admit a mistake, particularly if it's your own; the first rule of Army Officialdom.

Oh well, it was Thanksgiving, and we were getting a turkey dinner with all the trimmings. We couldn't very well say anything about the dehydrated potatoes. Nor did it matter that it was cold by the time we got it, amidst complaints from infamous Harobi about what tough going it was for him to get the stuff up here. A group of us were sitting around together, eating in silence, some on logs, most on our helmets, that being the best way to keep our asses from getting any wetter. The roast turkey really looked good, in fact, inviting, with that nice brown skin, and I got a big piece, the thigh, my favorite. To this day, I can vividly recall how the rain was steadily dripping down on me and it as I ate. Can't say it was particularly tasty. Maybe the rain diluted the taste. After a bit, it was like eating rubber, but that wasn't the reason some guys couldn't finish, or why some who did, like me, couldn't help bringing that wonderful feast rumbling back up, leaving a bitter after-taste.

21.

As attacks go this one wasn't supposed to be as tough as others. So they told us, and the first part wasn't. Had we only known it would be our last sustained offensive action in the Forest, we might have been able to muster up what little spirit we had left, somewhere down in our shoes. We met our jumping-off time at first light—with a lot less than a jump—and made the usual hard, sweaty climb up that first hill. It helped that there had been a rolling bombardment just ahead of us. Once we caught sight of those mounded dugouts on top, Starck was about to have us form in something of a staggered skirmish line as before, firing from the hip as we went, when, all of a sudden, their machine guns sent us sprawling for what cover we could find among the fallen trees. We were beginning to think we were in for it again, when, out of nowhere, a short, swift barrage silenced the machine guns. We couldn't figure out whether it was our stuff—incredibly efficient—or a Heinie battery dropping short rounds, but a second volley fell close enough to our line that it sent hot metal zinging down hill, and several guys were making the anguished call for a Medic.

It wasn't till some time afterwards that we learned those mystery rounds had been fired by tank destroyers whose mud-shy officers had been bullied into bringing them up a road where they had cannon access to the hill we were on. A rare event, we knew there was something different about the report of their guns. Fortunately, having spotted us, they didn't have to be told they'd done enough.

On Starck's signal, we crawled up and started pitching grenades at the dugouts, and as some of the Heinies eased out of the back entrances, trying to creep away, we peppered them with small arms. Sonny stood up, and, steadying himself behind a tree overlooking the nearest mound, he began popping them one by one, till they either went down or were gone.

Several of us moved up closer, with Sonny in the lead, wanting to see if anybody was left in the dugouts, when, over on the far left, we saw a white handkerchief being waved out of a hole, above a barely visible black helmet. Some of our replacements, finding it a chance to shoot at something they could see, opened up on the helmet, and it got creased before Lieutenant Robbens could make them knock it off. He went over to size up the situation, and, finding just the one Heinie, with a streak of blood running down his forehead, he told me to bring him out for questioning.

I had him remove his helmet so Pedro could have a look at the scrape he took. He was an unsoldierly middle-aged fellow whose bald head was fringed by light brown hair. I had him pegged for a bank teller. He told me his unit was mainly comprised of older men like himself and kids, and, for proof, pointed to the wrecked machine guns, whose dead gunners were mere boys with hobnailed boots. And the rest of his unit? He shrugged. I pointed to the ridge beyond this one, wanting to know, whether it too was defended by kiddies and papas, and he indicated there couldn't be many defenders up there, if any. Wirklich? (Really?) I asked. Well, at best, a small host of pretty much the same bottom-of-the-barrel troops, eager to be taken prisoner. Alle ganz feige. (All pretty cowardly.)

I was told to press this guy for more info. Robbens had caught sight of a good number of his comrades fleeing through the trees on his side of their defensive front, as opposed to those Sonny went after. What about them? Baldy says, "Keine Ahnung. Ausser mich, bloss drei andere Soldaten da." (No idea. Outside of me, there were only three other soldiers there.) And what about them? "Müss tot sein. Zahlreich waren wir nicht." (Must be dead. We weren't numerous.) Robbens said to ask again about the next hill, and this time the Heinie shook his head, doubting that there could be anyone there.

That was all Starck had to know. But Robbens was suspicious. This fellow might be setting us up. He could have been left behind for just that purpose. How come he alone was left? He had legs, didn't he? The two of them went back and forth for a bit, with Starck talking about the pressure he was feeling from Division. The going had been too damned slow in here to satisfy the Top Brass, sitting back in their French Chateaus. Robbens said there was a report that Top himself had been out on a golf course near Rheims. Back there, a slow slog could be pretty boring. Starck gave Robbens a petrifying look.

"Well," Robbens countered, "do they know anything about casualties up here? Conditions?"

"Fer Chrissake, man, don't be naïve. Does it matter?"

They finally compromised, agreeing to send out a recon patrol to see what the Heinies might have out there.

Sonny was circling around, wanting to be within earshot to learn if anything was going to be made of the thing he did with Samson. Starck had been visibly annoyed over it, but, at this point, too preoccupied to give it much thought; just one more thing to be pissed off about. On the other hand, catching sight of Sonny slinking off, Starck asked me to bring him back. Evidently, the idea struck him that he might just put that pain-in-the-ass to convenient use. Sure shot that he was, and known to run a BAR out of ammunition, Sonny would be just the guy for a patrol, giving it firepower plus savvy, the latter to keep him from giving away his presence, while, if need be, the other to assure a return with info.

22.

On Sonny's request, Starck assigned him a squad of nine men, almost full strength, and, edging themselves sideways down the reverse slope, they were shortly swallowed up by the fir trees. Knowing that, in time, the German artillery was sure to be heating things up for us, we decided to have ourselves a leisurely meal in the roomy dugouts we'd inherited. But, no sooner did we open our K-ration boxes, than the shelling started, and it was heavy stuff, likely their 155 howitzers, coming in quantity, not the sporadic kind mainly intended to keep us on edge and take a casualty or two.

Obviously, there was serious business afoot; word was passed to expect that a counter-attack might be forming. When their shells started coming in practically on top of us, we were pressing ourselves against the sides of the dugout, some guys with their arms across their chests, heads down, lips moving; others, likewise tensed up, had hands clamped on the edge of their helmets. The earth shook and so did we, fearing a direct hit, against which arms and helmets could give no protection.

Clearly, the idea was to keep us buttoned up until their troops were right on us. It seemed like the tables were going to be turned. Assuming they'd come in numbers, and do what we did, kill as many as they could, when they overran our position, we'd have no choice but to run, be shot, or taken prisoner. Scared stiff, some guys were already shooting out the rear openings of the dugouts, against orders, until we realized nobody was coming. What we heard instead was small arms fire down in the draw below, which could only be Sonny and his squad taking on the Germans' lead element—possibly unnecessary. But that was Sonny for you; if in doubt, shoot.

Surprisingly, the shelling let up, but there was no assault, only continued small arms fire down below. Could Sonny be holding them off? My God! Starck pulled us out, and down we charged, Hardy and Blazor out front, grease guns at the ready. When we got there, Sonny's squad was down to four guys, firing from behind trees, with the Heinies on the other side of the creek running this way and that, having been taken by surprise. There were about five of their dead that we could see, and not much return fire from those who were left. It wasn't a counterattack, after all, but their recon patrol running into ours. Sonny had met his stubborn match in their head scout.

Ignoring the fact that dusk was descending on us, with total darkness soon to follow, Starck stepped out and, cupping his hands to his mouth, he yelled out, "Okay guys, let's go for it!" And over the creek we went, Hardy quickly disposing of the two Heinies who didn't run off. We were laboring up another steep climb, and about a third of the way, there suddenly came an unexpected light spreading out above us. Damn; they'd fired a flare. For an instant we were stunned, and, not knowing what to do, like deer, we froze. But then, immediately recovering, we hit the ground, nonplussed as to whether we should be moving up or back. Either way we were probably targeted.

In that unnatural brightness, the hill briefly took on the look of an other-worldly landscape, pockmarked with lunar craters and dotted with partially shredded trees that stood out like diabolic harpies. There were quite a few dead lying about, ours, in something of an uneven band, likely from a prior attack that was beaten back before it could get any traction.

Abandoned equipment was lying about—raincoats, shelter halves, helmets, canteens, cartridge belts, arctics, mess gear, and packs that had been ripped apart and stripped. One more step and I'd have tripped over a dead GI lying half way out of a shell hole with a field jacket thrown over his head. Beside him was a sieve-like mess kit, pierced with jagged holes. Couldn't figure that one out. No need to. Another GI lay on the other side of the hole, where he'd apparently fallen backwards, knees up, mouth dropped open, his chest tattooed with dried blood bullet holes. Obviously, all hell had broken loose on these guys. We were supposed to do what they couldn't?

The first sound to come out of the eerie silence was the rattle of a BAR up ahead—unmistakably Sonny—whereupon all hell was returned, beginning with burp guns, as our forward element came within range of them. Our answering fire was immediately followed by one ferocious barrage that sent us frantically searching for cover that wasn't there, just shell holes, and fallen trees to crawl under where possible. Our only other source of protection was the scrub pine—ridiculous shield—and the few still-standing trees that the shells came crashing through.

Guys were going berserk, wildly screaming out, the wounded in agony. The shells were coming in louder and louder, closer and closer. Tightly gripping my helmet, I practically buried my face in the wet earth, quivering with each concussion of the shell bursts landing nearby, the metal shards twanging overhead, thanks to the slope. Certain that this was the end, I felt something heavy strike across my back, and, contracting, I drew my knees up, anticipating the worst had happened, but, in the next moment, my cry was cut short by the trembling surprise that there was no great hurt. Of all things, a stout tree limb had fallen on my back.

To save what was left of the Company, Starck waved us back, at which point our only available recourse was to run for our lives, which those of us who weren't hit did, sloshing back through the creek and, short of breath, scampering on up the reverse slope with what little strength we could still summon.

We must have left a good half of the Company out there. Sonny, who had been among the first to answer Starck's original call, was surely among the first to fall. No way we could go back for our wounded, a situation like what had apparently happened in the aftermath of that prior attack. So much for Starck's free-lancing. Hardy vowed that the next time we got a Heinie who agreed to talk, he'd shoot him before he could get a word out.

So our last all-out attack in the Forest became for many of our guys their permanently last, with us being caught out in the open on the wrong end of a counterattack. There was no way to describe the desolating effect it had on those of us who remained, which was about all that could be said about us: we remained, with what little of body and soul that was left to us.

23.

It was time for us to be redeployed to another sector, headed for lesser engagements, less cost, as Regiment would put it. We were guided back to a road where trucks were waiting. We were grateful, but getting there was a heavy go, wet, weary, and dispirited as we were. Still, there was enough adrenalin left in us that we lost none of our sixth-sense precaution. I was careful to step in the footsteps of the guy in front of me, knowing mines would hound us all the way, whatever direction we took in that Forest.

We came upon an overturned Jeep, just off the path we were on, doubtless blown off by a mine; one front wheel was gone, the other twisted. Wherever we went, we kept seeing the debris of previous engagements, some involving us. We were shortly out on the deeply furrowed mud road. It was tough marching, with that taffy-like stuff sucking at our arctics, and in places coming up almost to the tops of them. Somebody said we ought to fall out beside the road and make 'em bring the trucks up to us. What the hell. I was reminded of Rebel's saying that after a while, you reach an energy plateau, and your infantry legs keep a-goin, even if you aren't. At this point, even he must have been thinking, 'But not in mud, man.'

At a bend in the road, there was a break in the cliff to the side of us, opening up into a little hollow where we saw an array of Heinie medical equipment scattered about and mud caked, signs of what was left of a forward Aid Station, abandoned in haste. (So, trucks had for sure been coming up this damned road. Lots of them.) There were stretchers, medical kits, a red-cross banner partially obliterated by the mud, and you could see the outline of bottles likewise covered with mud sprayed by the passing traffic.

On the edge of the hollow, lay a dead Heinie completely covered with an even veneer of mud spray, a man no longer a man, looking, in fact, as if he'd been sculpted. He had short-clipped hair which stood up stiffly under its coating. His eyes were open, but blotted out, with a few little eyelash hairs sticking up. His open mouth and teeth had a fine spray on them. It was as if his head was a bust done in bronze. His legs were bent at the knee and his trousers pulled down on his shins. His loins were thickly coated over, and above his coarse navel hair there was a gaping hole. In it, you could make out his guts. We

196

had seen our fill of the dead and moved on, but this one got to us; no matter that it was one of them. We could each of us very well know what was going through the mind of everyone else.

The road bent sharply left, and, derelict in the middle of it, was a burned out half-track. Not far beyond it were two dead Heinies in the brush along the roadside, and, beside them, their twisted light machine guns. They were kids, maybe in their mid-teens, small of build, the one bundled up under a heavy overcoat, his hob-nailed heels sticking out over the narrow shoulder of the road. The other kid had his head buried in a tangle of bushes, his hair clotted with dried blood. The machine gun barrels were rusting where they were bent, as were the pocked barrel-guards. Putting the picture together, Hardy surmised that the kids had opened up on the half-track after it passed them by, probably hitting the gas tank, and those of our guys who jumped off would have gone after them with either a bazooka or rifles grenades.

It wasn't easy to sympathize with adversaries who had been putting such a hurt on us, when we were only doing to them what they were doing to us. But, in the fortunes of war, there, but for the grace of God, might *any* of us go. You just never knew how or when, and weren't consoled that you wouldn't know either. Stressed out, you often couldn't keep your thoughts straight. But, the way things were going, it didn't look like the Generals were any better at it.

24.

We were finally told to pull off the road and dig in, and Gush, Rebel, and I went at it. With all the roots we had to chop through, it was hard going, but one incentive to stay with it was the sight of some five tanks lined up just beyond our bivouac area, each of them starting to pull in as far as they could to get under the trees. They were a sure bet to attract artillery, which made us leery of being near them, to say nothing of riding on them when called upon.

Just as Rebel went over to the tankers to borrow an ax, there came the shrill roar of swiftly approaching planes that made a grinding howl as they swooped down on us, with the staccato of their 50 caliber machine guns going full blast. They were awfully quick, passing in the blink of an eye, but returned for four more strafing runs, coming in lower and closer each time, the whining, shrieking motors getting louder on each run. Through it all we were hunkered down in our half-dug holes. The planes clearly wanted to get a piece of those tanks, several of which were hit, with what damage we couldn't tell. It was only on the last two passes that some of those big slugs skipped by our holes. To the pilots, we probably were no more than an afterthought. The tankers had opened up with their 50 caliber mounts, giving them back some of their own, but with no visible effect. A miss-miss situation, but a warning that the Germans could still put planes up with the slightest break in the weather.

Rebel came back and told us he learned that those were tank destroyers, and, when they described how two of their TDs had pitched in on a recent infantry attack, he told them, to their surprise, that from what they said, it was probably us they were sent up to help. Their Captain had protested long and hard about going up in all that mud, but was overruled by Regiment. The tankers knew they'd be sitting ducks and they were. Because they did so well by us, they were sent forward to do the same for a parallel attack, got bogged down in the mud, and, unable to move, became perfect targets. Both TD's got hit with Panzerfausts (anti-tank grenades) fired by Germans who had infiltrated behind them. The TD's went up in flames, and the guys who managed to get out were mowed down by burp guns.

We might envy the tankers because they had mobility and seemed well protected—above all they rode—but the tankers thought of themselves as riding steel coffins. Hearing them talk about their tough losses sort of filled out the picture of how everybody was taking one bitch of a beating in there. Whoever you were and wherever you were in those woods, the misery was unavoidable, death routine.

We had not quite recovered from the strafing, when we had yet another eye-opener, as from out behind us came the roar of six P-38s. No sooner had they breeched the horizon of our clearing skies, than they were overhead rushing by in formation, and, after circling several times, they leveled off for their run. The first plane peeled off and started picking up speed as it went into its strafing mode maybe five or six miles in front of us, the thud-like pumping of its 50 caliber machine guns likely spouting revenge on Heinie tanks. In succession, each of the other planes followed the same pattern, and the Heinies began firing back at them. It was hard to know with what, but their 88 was a premier anti-aircraft weapon.

Several of the planes veered over toward the observation tower that we had ourselves looked on with suspicion. The pilots apparently noticed something, but they banked and swung away, supposedly having to keep their minds on other business. As the last plane made its run, there was a rocking explosion and the burst of a large fire-ball that seemed to have a liquid quality to it. We thought, hopefully it had hit something big, perhaps a gasoline tank, and looked for the plane to come roaring out of the flames, but instead what we saw was a trail of fire spiral down into the trees, sending up a rocket of flame as it hit. The other five planes had hurriedly sped off, becoming mere specks on the horizon. The pilot of the lost plane had made the fatal mistake of taking the exact same flight pattern as the others, giving the Heinie batteries a chance to get fully zeroed in by the time he came around.

Just as the scene quieted down again, there was an explosion in the near distance, and a cloud of white smoke enveloped the tower. A second explosion sent it crashing down. Talk about fireworks in one day. We speculated that the planes must have dropped some sort of timed device. What else could it be? Somebody would fill us in.

Once on the trucks, we noticed how sparsely occupied they were, giving us room to lean back and stretch our legs. We saw there was near emptiness in other trucks. We knew we'd taken a good number of casualties, but didn't have any idea of how many. As we looked around, the number sank in. Out of some forty in a rifle platoon, we were down to thirteen, a squad plus one, of grim dark-faced GIs. We got another sad sign later on, when, after a considerable absence, they brought up our bedrolls, and we saw how many went unclaimed.

We had taken on a few replacements, one on our truck being a casual machine gunner, and a bit of a talker, as we, just then, were not. He had a couple of half-pound TNT cubes tied to his pack straps, as well as an orange fuse and a cap wound into the netting of his helmet. So word had gotten out about how tough it was digging in, and maybe they were also looking ahead toward the winter freeze. At first, we let the machine gunner blabber a bit about the hospital, the good food, the so-so beer, the welcoming women. Then, as his voice started to become familiar, we had a second look, and of all things this guy was none other than old Markoff, the Mad Russian. He'd been with the outfit a while, had been hit, healed, certified to be combat ready, and sent back.

He said he had some news for us. Did we know we had a new CO? He was a West-Pointer, tough on discipline, more spit than polish, sent to shape us up. As the Russian rambled on, he really got our attention when he asked whether we knew that our Captain had been relieved of his command and reduced in rank, making him eligible for assignments given an ordinary shave-tail, that vanishing breed, always in demand on line. It didn't go over well with ol' hard-assed Starck, but, whatever he felt, he just sucked it up. Since he could stay with the Company, he decided he'd make the best of it. The explanation that came down for the demotion was that in the first place he technically was still a First Lieutenant, since his Captaincy was actually pending final approval for performance in the field, which obviously had been found wanting.

That was a bit of a shocker: Starck humiliated; with that explanation, in fact, insulted. But others up the line of command were also being relieved, including our Regimental Commander. Our Division Commander might be next. It was getting that serious. But, getting back to Starck, Markoff said there was something he had been real eager to do, but couldn't get at, since CO responsibilities kept him tied down. He'd been itching to go out and bring that damned tower down. Wasn't it plain to see that a Heinie FO up there was probably directing artillery on us? And nobody had sense enough to go after it. Seeing the guys coming in with those TNT charges, Starck commandeered a bunch of the stuff and got Robbens and Blazor to help out. When asked to tag along, Markoff begged off.

"Hey, did you see that goddam thing go?! They might bump the ol' bastard back up a rank or two. Fact is, some people believe that's what he was doing it for. Yah think? Might get him another company. Maybe this one."

Gush sighed, "Hallelujah."

Markoff had changed, but his mouth hadn't.

25.

As for how the change would affect us, we batted it back and forth, but, whatever our opinion of Starck, none of us thought this by-the-book West Pointer was good news—not for us beat-up riflemen anyway. Hardy talked about the stupidity behind it.

"That kind of change is the Army all over. Yeah, Starck did his share of fuck-ups. But Top Brass comes up with an impossible battle plan, and they take it out on officers in the field because those poor bastards can't make it possible."

Our more immediate concern was just how the interaction of these two strong-minded officers was going to affect us. Starck might be second guessing our new CO, and *he*, for that reason, would likely insist on having it *his* way, even if it was the wrong one. And what would a stiff-necked CO think of Starck's daring little stunt? Not a whole lot, if he thought Starck was sending a message. It didn't help much that some of the non-coms saw things from Starck's point of view. Hardy, continuing his defense of the guy, did it out loud, ignoring the West-Pointer's presence.

"He loses half the Company in a failed attack. So he should have lost the rest, but taken the hill, and Regiment would have given him the silver star."

Our new man, John Vander-something was an imposing fellow, a big, blond, wide-shouldered Dutchman, brought up in the conservative Reformed Church, who was second in his class at West Point and, according to him, should have been first. In combat, he was a model officer, leading his men by example, thrice wounded and decorated for valor. By his standards, Starck, next to him, qualified as a pushy plebeian on the make, all for advancing his career, undeterred by an occasional set-back.

We wondered less about what Vander thought of Starck than what he thought of us. Did he have any idea of what we'd been through? Would he care? We being, as Rebel put it, 'plumb tuckered out,' how were we going to respond to a leader who was well rested, full of piss and vinegar, and all for push, push, push? Other officers had learned that any leader who followed orders literally, regardless of conditions, was bound to mean trouble for his men. It wasn't long before we would find out.

On information that was passed down, we were supposed to be moving up in reserve behind the First Battalion in the event a counterattack broke through their lines, an easy enough defensive assignment for a beat-up Company. But, with our new CO, Division decided it was possible to use us in a more ambitious scheme, which would give us a chance to redeem ourselves. In effect, why not have us fight our way through an enemy stronghold to close off the exposed flank of a fellow Regiment? It would also help align Division's front. All it would take was for us to 'clean out' some 500 yards of enemy infested woods. (That again.) I guess it looked simple enough on a map, but we never saw one, and those who made the maps probably never saw the woods.

26.

So, next morning, we were back on trucks and had ourselves a bit of a tour, of landscape all too familiar. We rode along a winding road between two hills checkered with shell holes, and on either side of the road there was abandoned equipment of one kind or another, much of it ours, some of it big stuff, like demolished howitzers, 57mm anti-tank pieces, and Sherman tanks rolled over on their sides. There were the usual spools of wire and the wire itself lying in ditches and strung out in trees, the reason for which, we were told—as we already knew—was that radio communication being unreliable in this hill and dale terrain, they had to resort to phones. Of course, they usually went from one CP (Command Post) to another. On line, it was radios or nothing; in a pinch, runners.

Descending a hill, we passed through a farm village with roughly built, gray stone houses and barns bordering the main road. Several of the houses had been hit by artillery, their entire sides caved in, and a number had holes in their roofs; typical of what we'd seen before and would see again. We saw a large bay workhorse limping painfully in a farmer's vegetable garden shakily gorging himself on cabbages. There were gashes and dark bloody holes in his buttock and rib areas. Further on, beyond the houses, were a couple of artillery batteries on one side of the road, their barrels facing the hill we were headed for, where the solid growth of evergreens was broken by gaps, the result of shells landing in their midst. We took note of the amply barricaded dugouts the artillery guys had made for themselves. We also spotted a number of the heating units that we were supposed to get on break, but never saw; no break being long enough. So, all in all, they must have had a cozy enough setup, except for when the Heinies returned fire, evidence of which we had just seen. Despite the netting they had on their guns, once their position was revealed they might have taken some hits. If hit, best with a little comfort.

The skies had clouded over again and the rain resumed as we dismounted from the trucks. The change of plan meant we had to return our bedrolls, unused. Off we trudged about a mile up a muddy road and pulled off beside a fire-break. We didn't have to be told to dig in. Night would soon be upon us. It was one tough dig, with us yet again having to break our way through a tangle of roots. I was in with Gush, who was a relentless root breaker; he had great angry

204

hands. About halfway down, Markoff came over and said he didn't have anybody to dig in with. We were glad to have a rested arm, and, after taking the hole down far enough, we had him get some logs to put over the top.

All sweated up and tired, we were lying there in our nicely fashioned hole, when we heard some conversation over where the officers had been dug in. We were getting ready to break out our K-rations, when we heard Vander's voice come up. He was on the radio to Regiment. At this time? In the dark of night? On that static-prone radio, could he make out what was being said? Blazor came by and dropped off bandoleers of ammunition. Whatever that meant—and we could guess only one thing—we knew that it made no sense. A night attack? Vander or no Vander, would anybody go?

As word filtered down, we heard we were to be moving up in position for the attack to begin pre-dawn, giving us the benefit of both surprise and dim light. If we could make the move now—usually considered out of the question—the Company's being solidly in place at the time of attack would increase our effectiveness. Starck was opposed and let Vander know, some of which was meant to be overheard. Did Vander have a map that corresponded to the terrain? Could he use a flashlight; send up a flare?

"Lieutenant, we can't just sit here on our ditteybox and expect to get this thing done helter-skelter in the morning."

"Sir, nobody moves in the dark in here. Regiment is telling you we have to take up a position at some specific spot? Do they know what they're askin? No offense, but do you? Night-time in these woods, you can't go to the bushes without gettin lost."

"We'll have no better light at four in the morning either. I've actually got a good description of where to find our jumping off point. And, by the way, this ain't the first time I've scouted out rugged terrain. The order is that we go."

And that was it. With no time for a K-ration supper, several of us began chomping on spare D-ration bars. Abandoning our hard-earned holes, we shouldered our packs, slung our rifles, and got ourselves out on the road, where, minus the thick canopy, we could do a little better at making out where things were. But from there on it was one helluva a trek. We bumped into a couple of Jeeps with equipment trailers stuck in the mud. From a stranded driver, we learned they had been headed for the First Battalion and veered off course. They didn't seem to be unhappy with the result.

Starck grumbled, "Sounds about right. We'll probably do the same."

Out of earshot, Vander was in the lead, taking the First Platoon with him, and, determined to make his point, he was moving faster than the rest of us. Trying to catch up, we arrived at another road, and not knowing which way to turn, or, if we should turn at all, we stopped, with Starck trying to recall the instructions. Hardy thought Vander was looking for a certain fire-break, and we could very well have passed it.

Confused, we slowly retraced our steps, sending a couple of guys ahead to see if they could locate the fire-break. At that point, an out-of-breath runner from the First Platoon came upon us, telling us to follow him. With guys getting angrier by the minute, we slogged our weary way to the fire-break Vander had cut off on, but didn't find him. The kid said Vander was further down the break, where orders were for us to turn left and follow directions from there to link up with F Company.

"Where in the fuck do we find the place to turn left?" Starck stormed. "And what's this about F Company? The Second Battalion. *They're* in here? I thought we were linking up with the First."

"The Captain's expecting you, Sir. I gotta get you back with him."

"On the double I suppose. Damnation! We look for a turn we can't see and find a different Company we don't know the whereabouts of."

Starck had a look like he wanted to ring the runner's neck. Firebreaks were treacherous territory, not easy to negotiate even in the faint light of dawn. Turning to Hardy, Starck grumbled that any delay and Vander would be on us for hanging back. So we had no choice but to follow the kid, who had strung white tape markers on fir limbs as a guide to the invisible turn—and Vander—who actually wasn't too far off. It still took us a bit to get there; distance growing longer, our steps shorter, in the dark.

On reaching the turn, Starck got a less-than-friendly reception from those shadowy shoulders and slightly tilted head. Vander at his impatient best. There was a hushed, but mainly one-way conversation, which Vander concluded by insisting, "There's a distinct place we're supposed to be and we *are* going to get there. Orders, Lieutenant, not something you and I can debate. I've given you the directions. You have your doubts?"

"I told you what I thought, Sir."

"You know of a different way, do you?"

Starck paused, as if trying to control himself. "There ain't no other way than your way, John."

"You don't think you can camp out here and find us when we push off, do you? I want to radio back to Regiment and make sure of my orientation here. We'll be a couple of minutes, but my orders—they're not going to change."

The call made, we fell in behind him and made the turn. Our eyes having become more accustomed to the dark, we could see far enough to move on to the intersecting fire-break he wanted us to take. It also helped that there was no canopy over the break. One look told us it spelled trouble. It was wider than the others, grassed over, and dotted with occasional shrubbery, which meant it was untraveled. In addition, the Heinies had placed logs down the center of it, so, if we went, we'd have to go where they wanted us to, on a path likely strewn with those "S" mines, the Bouncing-Betties.

There was another pause, and Hardy walked up to make a last-minute appeal, "Sir, I can tell you this is not good. Those logs. They're tellin us we oughtn't to be goin in there."

Several of us went forward to back Hardy up and Vander hesitated a moment. He squatted down and took another look, a close one. "You know what men? I see it differently. That's so obvious a signal, I think they're trying to scare us off—on the cheap; it saves mines. Also clever. If so, Sergeant, that's telling me this is exactly the way we ought to be going. You think Regiment would send us this way if they thought we couldn't make it through? Remember, there are men up ahead who are counting on us."

Under his breath, Starck was commenting on the tactical brain-trust at Regiment. Vander addressed his radio man and the First Platoon's new Platoon Leader, a Lieutenant he'd made his Aide (even Starck never had one of those) and, giving them the follow-me sign, he did an about face, smartly executed. We had to go along, hearts in our throats, stepping ever so gingerly at the outer edge of the break,

208

brushing past swooping fir limbs and pesky shrubs, anticipating a jump to the side at the slightest disturbance.

Surprisingly, we did make it through and, emerging onto a path, came upon H Company's 81mm dug-in mortars, beside which were the mortarmen themselves looking out of their secure holes, probably amazed at the sight of Raiders of the Night. Vander's Aide nudged Starck, saying Vander wasn't one to gloat, but this showed that the rest of the Second Battalion was within easy reach, and we'd be there to push off with them according to plan. Brimming with confidence, Vander didn't disguise his eagerness to forge ahead.

This time, Starck came forward, wanting us to verify directions from here with H Company, as he knew one of their Platoon Leaders, but Vander anticipated him. "No sense in stopping now, Lieutenant. We're right on track. The sooner we get there the better. Wouldn't you agree? And, with us pushin off early, they won't know what hit 'em."

And onward he gallantly strode, the bugles doubtless sounding in his head. He couldn't have been gone more than several minutes when there was a loud pop and explosion, followed by an unearthly howl. Vander had stepped on a mine, which jumped up and caught him just below the hips, blowing both legs off. He cried out for his Aide to shoot him, and kept rolling around hysterically. Before anything could be done, he'd rolled onto another mine, evidently a bigger one, which came up with a piercing burst that took out both the Aide and radio man, and wounded an approaching Medic.

Glimpsed at first light, it was a terrible scene. Beside dismembered body parts, there were patches of blood and pieces of flesh, bone, and guts scattered about, with additional bloody innards hanging from adjacent trees. Nobody said anything. There was nothing to be said. There was enough to be shared in silence.

27.

We had no idea whether we were protecting F Company's flank, or anybody else's, but our attack next day went off later than expected, and it worked out better than expected. The stronghold amounted to a huge concrete bunker commanding the road we came up, about half a mile from where we had stopped the night before. Starck was able to get through to the artillery unit we had passed on the way in, and, since they had already been pounding the bunker the day before we arrived, they knew the coordinates and let go with a barrage that landed on top of and right next to the hulking thing. The truth is those 155 shells could do no more than put surface cracks in that monstrous bunker, probably constructed of three-feet thick, steel-reinforced concrete. It might have been part of the Siegfried Line complex. All we could expect is that the shelling would scare the occupants.

When the sulfurous smoke cleared, we circled around back and blasted the steel exit door with rifle grenades. That was enough to bring out two lowly, helmetless corporals, white faced, trembling hands overhead. Obviously, it had been a major CP, and with our slow advance finally making progress, a decision probably came down for their brass to take off. We had no idea of what these two useless clowns were here for, unless it was to call back and let them know what was happening.

Further along, there was harassing small arms fire from a knoll on our flank, which didn't hit anybody and shortly ceased. So Starck kept us moving. The only other obstacle of any significance was a three-man machine gun nest that we managed to pin down with dual BAR fire, till we could crawl up to heave our grenades. But, remarkably, as we waited to see if they might have come back to the gun before we made a rush at them, there was silence. When we approached, we saw they were gone; not dead, but had disappeared, just like that.

That hill, so ominous from a distance, shrank a bit up close, and the small arms fire we took, soon tapered off; then it too was gone, suggesting the Heinies weren't intent on holding this position. When we came upon their dugouts and opened up on them, there was no return fire. Hardy and I went up cautiously and called, "Kommen Sie Raus." And that did it. The few who came out of the dugouts we sent back, telling them to surrender to the first GIs they met. It was common practice. I suggested they find the artillery batteries.

Having thus arrived at what Starck thought was our objective, we crowded ourselves down into the string of recently vacated dugouts, prepared to sweat out a howitzer barrage—but nothing came. Apparently, we'd been dealing with a delaying action, but it looked like the delayers didn't think they should pay for it. After all that Vander put us through, the tension, that fearsome maneuver in the night, his stepping on the mine, our anticipating the unexpected in the morning, it was—all of that—for naught. Unexpected it surely was. Thank God! Which we did.

Prematurely, as it turned out. Next day, just as we were forming on the road to our trucks, we came under a withering barrage of 105s that caught us in an unguarded moment, and, lacking cover, we lost a number of guys. Why they didn't instantly dive for the muddy roadside ditch, like the rest of us did, I don't know. How could anyone go slack in there? Ironically, it might have had something to do with how easy we'd had it in the loss-free operation we'd just gone through. Further evidence, that we didn't need, of how treacherous this Forest could be, especially when you felt it no longer was.

In three days, we started our exit from Hürtgen. We were marching in double column between columns of the incoming troops. From the looks of them in their spiffy clean uniforms and shaved faces, we, with our begrimed, bearded faces and mud-caked pants and field jackets, must have given them something to think about. One of our guys, taking them in with a mixture of sadness and relief, quietly wished them well. They seemed too stunned to say anything in response.

The trucks drove back by way of the village we had passed through on our way up, and we saw the cabbage patch horse lying there on his back, his stomach well rounded, all four legs straight up.

PART III

1.

We might have left the Forest, but the Forest never left us. As a parting pat on the back, a Commendation came down from Regiment, courtesy, we learned, of that little guy we called the "Fly" and had briefly seen at Regimental HQ as we rode into the Forest. He told them he could write, so they made him Propaganda Minister. — Ah, yes, the pat, which was headed "Unit Citation": "Regiment Command is pleased to commend each member of Companies in the Third Battalion. The splendid manner in which they utilized their tactical ability, courage and determination to accomplish an extremely hazardous mission, is worthy of emulation." We wondered if even they believed it. Casualties weren't publicized. For us, sparsely occupied trucks and missing buddies told that part of the story. For the record, though, we later found out that average losses per rifle company were well over 100 percent of authorized strength.

The Citation poured it on, taking note of the constant "precipitation and damp, penetrating cold…which alone called for heroism and physical stamina of a high degree.…" And the praise was not above a lie or two, saying that despite all that and our having to withstand the enemy's withering artillery, mortar fire, mine fields and overall punishing defense, the Regiment, often "under strength and without rest, [nonetheless] fought as a cohesive unit and carried the fight aggressively to the enemy." Hard to swallow.

But, then, it was on to dear slumbering Luxembourg, which, according to the outfit we were trading places with, was a very quiet front; and for about three or four days, it was.

Reverend Hilfer, our good chaplain, held a much-appreciated service for us, a large part of it devoted to remembering guys we had lost. His sermon contained appropriate expressions of sorrow, reverence, and thankfulness. He read from passages of "Ecclesiastes," which he had quoted before, this time beginning with, "To every thing there is a season, and a time to every purpose under the heaven. ... A time to kill, and a time to heal; a time to break down, and a time to build up." He really reached us when he spoke of fellowship, and going back again to the powerful thoughts of "Ecclesiastes," he read passages that reflected how we were knit together. "Two are better than one; because they have a good reward for their labour. For if they fall, the one will lift up his fellow; but woe to him that is alone when he falleth; for he hath not another to help him up. Again, if two lie together, then they have heat: but how can one be warm alone?" Though he was reading us some passages he'd read before, they now had a bigger impact. As I listened to Hilfer working his sermon around those good words, divine wisdom brought down to earth, Ronders came to mind. It gave me a better idea of how he looked at things. An outlook so hard to come by seemed to fall in place. Easy enough back here. Remarkable that it could stay with him up there. But, he *believed.*

We thanked the Lord for our deliverance, and Hilfer consoled us over lost buddies with the reminder that they were with Jesus now, just as His Eternal Presence embraced us all now and forever. Hilfer ended the service with a vigorous singing of "Amazing Grace," led by his Assistant, a guy with a good tenor voice. We were moved. Something we needed.

2.

We had some heartening things happen during this break, and some not so heartening things. Number One heartening was our being out of the Forest, out from under the unrelenting fear that seemed like it could go on till Doomsday. Hilfer's service was heartening, as was his presence among us. He was a man of feeling which showed in his eye contact and reassuring voice that told us faith could see us through the rest of it—something he got across even to the less trustful among us. Of course, our gratitude by itself gave us a lift, along with plain ol' R and R.

For Starck, it became a time to deal with unreconciled matters that couldn't be handled on line, for lack of time and inclination, to say nothing of morale: like, what was to be done about the guys who wouldn't go into the attack—called "misbehavior before the enemy"? There were two in particular whom he had harassed and all but threatened to shoot. One was a friend of Gino's, Rissoto, a Brooklyn Dago, who had been wounded and returned; and, until he got that unshakable block, was as good-natured a guy as there was in the Company. Ribbed about his accent, he'd respond with a Southern drawl. He had been a good soldier and was actually awarded the Bronze Star for going after a sniper who was holding up the Company in Normandy. But Hürtgen took it out of him. Each time he stayed back, he'd promise he was gonna for sure make the next attack with us, if we'd just let him alone. But, of course, when the order came down again, there was no getting him out of his hole. Robbens wanted to send him back so he could talk to an Army psychiatrist, but that got nowhere. All red in the face, Rissoto yelled, "I'm not crazy. You guys are!"

We had a common understanding that, if you didn't show up, you were letting the rest of the guys down. We couldn't reach him with that, either. Starck, once more in command, took the unusual step of bringing a group of us together and straight out told us that, like it or not, he had to put it to Rissoto. Taken by surprise, Hardy nonetheless gave him the nod, saying if it was done in this case we wouldn't have to go through it again. Grudgingly, most of us agreed, though it meant having a friend court marshaled for something that, under certain circumstances, we ourselves could have been capable of. You never knew what unrelieved tension might finally do to you. How do we walk away from agreeing with what had to be done, when we hated to think that it really had to be? It rankled.

When Starck indicated he had to consider other guys, we wondered how far he was going to take this thing. He brought up the case of a kid who, after missing one attack after the other, had miserably brown-nosed his way back by helping out with Supply, and Harobi, finding he'd do all the lousy stuff he didn't want to do, took him under his wing. The kid was good at cleaning up abandoned bivouac areas, which, among other things, required filling in slit-trench latrines and such. We didn't know his name, but when he got called Weasel, and accepted it, so did we. In part, it was possible to feel sorry for the kid, in part not. Nobody made anything of it when he reappeared a couple of weeks after he'd supposedly been sent back to face charges. Actually, nobody believed Harobi wouldn't reclaim him. Since Starck indicated he'd just as soon let the thing slip—not something worth batting around after the painful situation with Rissoto—we went along with it. The kid's humiliation was probably enough.

There were two other guys, both Sergeants, who had fallen out near St. Vith, where each managed to shack up with a Belgian girl. They had heard how things were in Hürtgen, and, with them having it so good, they decided they'd just as soon stay on and didn't come back until we arrived in peaceful Luxembourg. Prior to that, they'd been decent enough guys. But, when they tried to worm their way back into our good graces, most of us turned away. We might have cut them some slack had they joined us in the Forest. As things were, we didn't appreciate their wanting to be accepted as before, particularly when the one Sergeant, somewhat fatter than when he took off, returned our glance, with the joshing remark, "Hey, don't look that a-way, fellers. What's Army life without a little cheatin here an' there. Army does it all the time."

The other guy as much as said any of us would fall out, if we thought we could get away with it. *"Any?"* Rebel exclaimed and, without addressing them specifically, he added, "Yah know, there's such a thing as bein able to look at yerself in the mirror, come mornin."

The fact that the Sergeants seemed to be getting away with it brought back our misgivings over what had been done with Rissoto. However, Starck, continuing to show a new kind of awareness, came forward and let it be known that he was going to have Regiment deal with the Sergeants. He'd just lay out what they did. He also said that when Regiment took account of Rissoto's record, he might get leniency.

We would find out that Big Brass One was not only fed up with guys hospitalized for battle fatigue, but that he'd *had* it with desertions.

So he had one guy singled out to be put before a firing squad. Just that one guy, supposedly chosen at random, when the Army knew desertions ran into the thousands? Okay, maybe that was one way to stop it, but we weren't sure it would work, even though we had used the same reasoning. We heard that the deserter had been with the 28th Division, an outfit that got beat up along side us in Hürtgen, the Battle they didn't want to know about at the Top. Even though the guy got charged before that Battle, since his execution took place not long afterwards, with memories still fresh of guys who went out of their minds in the Forest, for us, the prior connectedness made a difference.

Some officers didn't like what was done, but they naturally kept quiet and went along with the official line. On the other hand, there were veteran non-coms among us who could speak more freely, and they thought the real problem was that Big One got pissed off with the 'Winter Stalemate,' when by rights he should have felt bad about it, and probably did, but wouldn't admit it. Who knows?

More importantly, Headquarters Brass was said to have been asleep at an unattended switch when it came to the Break-Through. Signs of a build-up had been summarily dismissed. How could the Germans, in their weakened condition, mount a major offensive at this stage in the war? So, as a totally unanticipated thrust—part of it shortly to erupt in our sector—the surprise attack worked real well for the Germans. An unreported report had it that, at the time their attack kicked off, Biggie's cronies were toasting him with champagne and oysters to celebrate his fifth star at a lavish pre-Christmas dinner party. The star—needed to get Montgomery off his back—was, on political grounds, well earned. But, with the attack rumbling through the weak Ardennes front, badly bloodying—more like obliterating—the green and under-strength divisions that manned it, diary accounts have it that Headquarters at Versailles (usually awash in 'spirits') was unperturbed, confident that the Germans were only capable of conducting a futile diversion.

3.

We were quartered in a small village not far from a group of towns near the Sauer River—bordering dreary ol' Germany—places that we'd be moving up to when the shelling started. We were assigned houses near the center of town. All of the civilians had fled, taking most of their portable belongings with them, packed in carts, some horse drawn, which we'd seen in towns we rode through on the way in. It made us wonder what kind of *rest area* we had come into, if the people had to abandon their homes and leave valuable furnishings behind. —Like *beds*, "Boy-oh-Boy!" which made it easy for us to cast aside doubts.

We were stiff and chilled through and through from the cutting wind that whipped in on us in those open trucks. Disembarking, we were still hearing the echoing roar of truck motors that reverberated down the narrow streets we traversed between old stone houses, yellowed by age. And here random collections of GIs were entering those houses.

I was with the group assigned to one of the bigger houses. Our weighty footsteps made a strange hollow sound as we clomped in over the wooden floor. I couldn't help feeling we didn't belong there. We were, in fact, under orders to be careful of the people's things. In addition to the beds, there were dressers, chifforobes (like the kind we had in my own home) tables, chairs, mirrors, curtains on the windows, multiple pictures of Jesus on the walls, crosses in every room (it being a very Catholic country), and, above all, stoves.

It wasn't long before our Alabama cowboy (who only raised the horses) had uncovered a couple of cases of hard cider in the basement. We had our shoes off for the first time in a long time and with the warmth from the cider, our long-numbed feet (probably in some stage of frostbite) were beginning to sting. We had gotten the stove rigged up with a stovepipe and, on finding the coal bin in the basement, had a nice fire going, which made it hot enough for us to start shedding clothes. We made a pretty raunchy bunch, roaming around barefoot in our baggy white long-johns, long since turned gray. Between the heat and the cider, the one whose feet stung the most was the cowboy, Billyboy (pronounced Billibaw by an Alabama buddy). He was half gone on the cider, and, hands gripping his feet, was soon rolling on his bed, crying, "Oh ma feet, ma poor li'll feet. Ma poor li'll *feet!*"

Mail had come up for the first time in a long while and, along with it the supplementary payroll. The guys who didn't have their pay sent home had money enough to set up a good old-fashioned poker game, dealer's choice. There was quite a bit of merriment, with Billy carrying on about his feet and the poker players throwing pillows at him. Before we knew it, evening was upon us, so the guys stuck a number of candles on the card table and kept dealing and drinking. Our fun was interrupted by the stomp of heavy boots laboring up the staircase. Of all people, it was Harobi, and we were in good enough spirits to offer him a bottle of cider, which, in sour-faced annoyance, he waved aside.

When Harobi shook his head at Gush's invitation to have a seat and take a hand, everybody just carried on, except for those of us who were reading books and writing letters. We brought our eyes up wondering what the strange visit was all about. Billy's cries had toned down to a whimper, but got cranked up again when he had himself another bottle of cider, which brought him to the brink of a crying jag. The card players threw corks, candles, and knotted socks at him.

At first, Harobi, simply peered over at the bucket filled with coal briquettes. He picked one up and turned it in his hand, before pitching it back down in disgust, as he looked around, taking in how nicely we were set up in these warm quarters. Those head movements made the candlelight dance in his hyperthyroid eyes, which, bulging out of a darkly bearded face, had him looking like the wild man from Borneo. We thought he was wanting to make himself at home when he walked over to the stove, took off his gloves, warmed his hands, and alternately propped one boot against a stove-leg, then the other. He started talking about the bitter cold outside, in which he had been making runs back and forth to Regiment all day to bring up our chow, blankets, mail, pay, and fresh underwear. (Regiment was supposed to offer us two-minute showers, after the officers got theirs.)

At the second offer of a bottle, he took it, looking fixedly at the stovepipe. "Yah know, some som-bitch stole my stovepipe while I was out freezin my ass off on the supply runs. Cold as a bastard in my room. No fuckin fire."

I told him I had a small stove in my room and he was welcome to join me and Gush, provided he brought his own mattress. The guys laughed, but Harobi was not amused. He wanted to know where we got the stovepipe, and Blazor said that Billy picked it up somewhere.

"That's what I hear. Fact is, somebody said he thought he saw Bill here walkin out o' my place with a stovepipe, just this afternoon; me bein gone."

"Zat so?" Blazor sat back, hands on hips. "Far as I know, didn't anybody see Bill goin near your place. Ain't that so, Bill?

Billy sat up, rubbing his nose the length of his sleeve. "Whoever he's talking about wasn't me."

"Okay. Where'd yah get the pipe, then, if yah didn't get it outa my place?"

"I didn't take your pipe. The town's full of 'em."

"Come on, where'd you get it, Bill?"

"Took it out of a house down by the kitchen. Nobody was stayin there."

"You're full o' shit. That's *my stovepipe.* I damn well know it is." With that, Harobi walked over to the stove, put his gloves back on, and sized up the angle of the pipe entering the back of the stove. Gush laid his cards down and turned toward Harobi as he began to jar the pipe loose.

"I froze my ass off outside today and damned if I'm gonna freeze inside tonight."

Billy rushed him screaming, "Get the hell out of here, you bastard! Leave that rotten pipe alone. It ain't yours!" He grabbed Harobi's arm and got a swift elbow to the gut that staggered him back against the bed, his heels striking the steel bedstead. Clutching his feet, Billy, began to go into his "poor li'll feet" refrain, but cut it short and angrily pounded his bed, shouting, "You rotten bastard."

Anticipating trouble, I was quick to grab him as he got up, bent on having another go at Harobi, who meanwhile had removed the pipe from the stove.

With the smoke filtering into the room, Gush got up and striding very deliberately over to Harobi, clamped a hard hand on his shoulder and turned him around. The stovepipe fell between them, knocking the ash door open, which jarred out several hot coals that rolled onto the floor and began burning into the wood.

"Dammit, Gush. You keep your nose outa this. I'm takin this stovepipe with me and you guys are gonna have to find yah your own, like I did."

As he bent down to pick up the pipe, Gush had that hand clamped on his shoulder again, straightening him up. He moved in toe to toe with Harobi, and, swaying ever so slightly from side to side, his cold eyes fixed on Harobi's, he spoke very slowly. "You ain't takin nothing outa here. I don't give a good Goddam where that fuckin pipe came from. It's here an' it's stayin here. If yah think it's too cold for yah, go on out and dig yourself a foxhole in the snow and see how warm it is out there."

Harobi made another move for the pipe, and Blazor rose, but Gush motioned him off. The rest of us formed a loose semi-circle around Gush and Harobi, who seemed very insistent on having his way. Behind us, Billy was mouthing off again.

Harobi ignored him. "Dammit, I'm telling you guys Weasel was packin up, an' he told me he saw Bill stealin my stovepipe. So gimme room, now. I'm gettin what's mine, an' I'm outa here."

Billy cried out that the kid was "a lyin worm." Gush pushed him back down on the bed and told him to shut up. Setting himself up once more in Harobi's face, Gush spoke through clenched teeth. "A-rab, I said the pipe stays where it is, and I mean it. You're wantin out, an you're goin, cause I'm asking you to get the hell outa here right now."

Gush wasn't exactly what you'd call an imposing guy, standing just five-ten in height and somewhat slight of build, but, when he got riled, he could look pretty big, the picture of ferocity, in fact. He paused, waited for Harobi to move, and when he didn't, Gush dropped a hand to the side of his belt where he carried his trench

223

knife. His voice came up the slightest bit as he continued, but his enunciation was precise.

"I just told you something, an' I'm gonna tell yah just one more time—real clear. I don't give one flyin fuck to the moon where that pipe came from. What I'm sayin is the pipe stays…an' you're gonna get that fat ass o' yours the hell outa here. Yah hear me? I'm sayin *out*…and I mean *now*." He paused again, and, speaking more slowly yet, his face warpath red, he went on in almost a hoarse whisper, "Or, just as sure as you're standin there…I'm gonna kill yah."

Harobi glanced hastily at Blazor. But getting a cold stare, he took a parting look at the pipe, then, head down and wordless, he brushed past our semi-circle and left.

Open-mouthed through it all, Billy sprang to his feet at Harobi's departure and chased down the stairs after him. I followed in hot pursuit and grabbed for Billy's undershirt, just as he was making a stab at Harobi's jacket. In the next instant, all three of us were tumbling down the remaining stairs, one on top of the other, each cussing up a storm. Harobi was quickly to his feet, out the door, and into his Jeep. Billy careened out after him, and I found him barefoot in the snow, hands cupped to his mouth, a raving maniac, hurling one volley after the other at the departing Jeep, its rear wheels churning up spokes of snow.

4.

It seemed like we had the worst of both worlds during our fall-winter combat, icy rain in Hürtgen, and deep snow plus bitter cold during the Break-Through. Hard put in both cases and chilled to the bone, we hadn't the foggiest idea of what the big picture was in either; and the immediate picture usually wasn't that clear either. Regarding the Break-Through, for some time, we had no idea that that was what it was. It began on our front with what seemed random shelling, as if Heinie wanted us to know he was out there and knew where we were. Indeed, the stuff was coming in precisely in the area where we were quartered.

The first shell hit into the barn right next to our house, igniting the hay, and it was perfectly centered at the level of our upstairs poker room. The accelerating whine sent us flying down the staircase, wildly jumping over the last ten steps. Some guys bellied down in the ground floor hallway, but most of us headed for the cellar. No sooner did we get there, looking up in expectation of the next rounds, when sure enough in they came, three in succession, crashing into the poker room, exploding the stove and setting the whole upstairs afire. Number one shell had burst through the floor, and the next two spewed shrapnel down onto the hallway catching two guys who strangely remained frozen in place. Nothing serious, just leg and ass hits. They were new and already had their million-dollar wounds.

Some wake-up call. But, after checking with Regiment, Starck said they weren't worried back there. At most, it was just the usual harassing fire. Word had come down from Division that, like we'd been told before, no way the Germans had the ability to get anything going. On the other hand, what bothered us was that Heinie was apparently firing 88s, and they seemed to be coming at us in direct fire, which meant they couldn't have been very far out, and might at least have binocular vision on us. Hardy speculated it might be tanks. That 88 was the greatest all-around artillery piece, and, as we well knew, lightning fast. Often by the time you heard the report—if you did—the damned shell might be right on you.

Up to that time, we had been doing regular guard duty, three men to a mount, on a rotating schedule of four hours on and eight off, later compressed to two on and four off, but with everything having been so neatly quiet, our only problem was how to pass the time and move around enough to fight off the cold. We had guys posted at the crossroads leading eastward out of town, and a machine gun squad was set up in the second story of the last house at the other end of town.

While pacing at the crossroad, I saw a Jeep come up bearing, of all people, our Regimental Commander, map in hand. After his talk to our officers, we went to outposts, a squad at a time, some 600 yards out in nowheresville, and, in town, we spent time being instructed on winter warfare, which included using the dynamite cubes to help us get our holes dug. On the outposts, it was three days out, and no fires. To get in out of the wind, we scouted out a ramshackled woodshed for our in-between snoozes. So long as Heinie didn't think we were a significant enough target, we didn't have much to bitch about.

The only less boring thing we got into before things became serious was doing a recon patrol over the river. We had a new second lieutenant come up, a little chubby in the face and young looking, probably a ninety-day wonder, obviously uncertain of himself, particularly as he took us in, to him no doubt as ornery as we looked, and not very trustful of him. As we took *him* in, he didn't look like much—an overgrown kid with pale blue eyes and a high forehead; nor did it help that his name was Gessner, which we shortened to Gesser. Again it was a squad assignment, and he was eager to go, so he could right off show us there was something to him, regardless of what we thought. He took nine guys across the frozen river with him and had the remaining three take up positions on our side to cover their return, if cover was needed.

They were to be gone three days. I was with the cover group, and, when we saw them return a day early with just seven guys, it didn't look good, and it wasn't. Snipers in a lone farmhouse—*their* outpost—had picked off two guys, the ones who didn't want to wear snowsuits because they slowed you down. No way to go out for them. Afterwards, we got the idea they had probably run into sharpshooter lookouts, whose assignment was to keep us from finding out what was going on over there.

Again, we were told it was nothing to be concerned about, except that our outposts ought to make sure they stayed awake enough to fire on any of their patrols that wanted to have a look-see over here. Next day, the stuff came in pretty heavy on us and pretty darned accurately, and so Starck figured maybe it was time to be a little concerned, after all.

A group of us had moved down the road to a house that looked like it might be out of what seemed their preferred line of fire. But not long after we had bedded down, Hardy came to wake me for my stint of guard duty, and I was barely on my feet when there was the sudden scream of an incoming shell, instantaneously accompanied by an explosion and flash of light, and I was under the bed. The hit had grazed the side of the house, carrying enough force to carve a hole in the far wall, shatter windows, and send shrapnel flying in against the wall beside my bed. I got myself down to the cellar in nothing flat, and it was like that damned 88 had followed me down, as two shells landed not far out from the cellar door, where Rebel had mounted his machine gun, which got buried, killing the guy with the ammo box, newly assigned to Rebel's squad. He had gotten up to run for the door. Rebel had had Billy along, and he followed Rebel's example by digging a shallow oblong trench back from the gun, where they assumed the prone. They shook off the snow-wet dirt and, other than the scare, were okay. We were amazed. They should have been gone. It proved a point Rebel had made with Billy.

Earlier, when Rebel had asked me about the quarrel over the stove pipe, I told him what was going on with Billy's feet, and Rebel said he was going to shape him up. He found us looking for a place to sack out after we'd come off guard duty. Billy hadn't been a machine gunner before, but Rebel told him he'd be a good one. Billy had his doubts. Despite his boyish name, Billy was a strapping six-footer, who on occasion had shown real guts, which, as with most of us, got drained away in Hürtgen. Hearing that Billy wanted to have our generous Medics send him back with trench foot, Rebel asked to see his feet and said they didn't look any worse than his.

"They hurt, do they? Hell, ain't nobody don't have hurtin feet." Did he know that the Medics were being told to watch out for malingerers? They'd send him right back to the Company, and, considering what we just went through with Rissoto, Starck wouldn't go easy on him. Billy protested that bad feet would slow him down, and he'd up and get himself killed "fer not bein able to git a-goin." But Rebel was waiting for him on that one. Billy remembered, didn't he, what Hilfer said in his last sermon about losing one's life.

"Like he said, yah could lose yer life up here. Yah could lose it behind the line too, and not jest by gettin killed. The thing is to find yer life before yah lose it."

"Oh, to hell with that." Billy flat out didn't want to hear any more from a sermon. For him, once was enough, and it didn't make any sense the first time. Rebel grabbed him before he could get away and reminded him of practical consequences.

"No way hurtin feet er gonna get yah back to the hospital."

"I don't care. I'm goin tell 'em how damn bad I'm hurtin, show 'em calishes."

"Listen up. Starck's been told we're losin too many men that way. Our Medics got instructions to look close, and, like I said, unless you got the *real* trench foot, they'll figure yer tryin to chicken out. That puts yah on Starck's shit list. An ugly assignment comes up and yer the first one he looks fer. Don't like ridin tanks, do yah? Goin on scoutin patrols? Worse yet, combat patrols? Remember in the woods, L Company was cut off, and we sent our First Platoon over?"

"I got me lost before."

"Listen up, friend. Like Hilfer put it, yah find your life when yah mind your heart. Yah feel for guys that get hit don't yah? On back, don't nobody give a damn. Gotcha a pass to Paris and went to Pig-alley. You jest get yerself back there, and, that's *all* you'll do. That's livin, huh?"

"Dammit, I had me a great time. Fact, I thought I deserved it. Guys deserve gettin killed up here? What's decent about that?"

"Nothin. But every time we make it through up here, we sure appreciate it we're alive. Don't we pray to God we're all gonna make it?"

"Maybe." Billy paused, his brow wrinkled. "Dunno about that."

"Aw, baloney. I've seen yah with yer hands clasped. I've seen yah lookin around to see who's there with yah."

Billy insisted he didn't need another sermon. But Rebel said he knew damned well what Hilfer meant, and he aimed to keep Billy with him, regardless. In the end, he'd see that bad as it was staying with the Company, just the same he'd know guys were looking out for him.

"If I'd live to see the end."

Dropping into his deep voiced southern drawl, Rebel came back at him, "Billibaw, y'all kin do what yah want, but jest stay with me an I'm gonna make yah the sojer yah once was. Yer gonna be fine. Fact is, I need yah."

So spoke our collective conscience, our tower of strength. It was like he personified what Hilfer preached. I'd been looking after Billy on my own after the thing with Harobi, and I knew Rebel would do him some good. Afterwards, when I asked him about what Rebel was saying, Billy walked away, but he didn't go to see the Medics.

I had to admit I might have wished I was of one mind with Rebel, but I wasn't quite there, and you couldn't find many in the Company who were. As Hardy put it, you could like what he said even if you weren't fully convinced of it. On the other hand, we did agree with Rebel's insistence that, whatever lay ahead, we'd hang together and stick it out as a Company. Rebel knew how to reach us. It also made a difference that he'd been promoted to Staff Sergeant and became our squad leader.

5.

Next day, at noon chow, which was set up in the courtyard of a spread-out, prosperous-looking house (Officers' Quarters) the stuff came in pretty heavy. To get to the chow line, we filed down a hallway leading out to the flagstone courtyard facing the road, and just as we emerged, Ca-boom! Ca-boom! Ca-boom! Guys were yelling and charging headlong down the stairs going to the wine cellar, where we'd sweat out the rest of the barrage in the dark. As I was crossing the courtyard to get to those stairs, another shell came in, and I had to hit the glazed flagstones real hard. Billy's buddy, Huey, who was next to me, had done the same thing, but, panicky, he was barely up when he slipped down again, and I helped him get up, surprised that neither of us had been hit. Good ol' thin-as-a-rail Huey. They said he was so skinny bullets couldn't find him. It seemed he was pretty good at dodging shrapnel too. A good guy to be near.

In the cellar, there was a hum of voices as guys wondered what this was all about. The only light came from the orange glow of cigarettes in quivering lips. One thing for sure was that the Heinies were practically looking us in the eye. It wasn't long before the eerie screams of another succession of shells came down on the house, shaking the ceiling above us, while yet another set landed in the courtyard. At each explosion, we reflexively hunched-up, thinking with one more pounding, the ceiling would cave in on us. Luckily, the Germans took their fire elsewhere.

When it was over, we piled up the stairs and got sight of the courtyard, which sported three fair-sized shell holes. Amidst the thick smell of sulfur, a big pan of pork and beans was sluggishly dripping its contents down on the flagstones; the cylinder of coffee looked like it had sprung a number of additional spouts; shredded bread was strewn about; and various chunks of other food—carrots and what looked like it might have been that nasty rice pudding—along with sticks of margarine, were spattered against the stuccoed side of the house. We couldn't figure out how come all that artillery wasn't followed by an attack.

It had started out harmlessly enough, with rounds that had fallen out in the field where we had our outposts, and gradually crept up towards us in town. Though we were mostly curious at first, we sobered up in a hurry. As we made our way back to our respective cellars to get our helmets and rifles, we noticed that the Heinies had apparently hit just about every house in town, many of which showed holes in their roofs exposing bare rafters. Enough. It was time to get our bed rolls tied up, shoulder our packs, sling rifles, and form on the road. We were good and ready to move out and see what this was all about, little knowing what lay ahead, and wholly in the dark about the scale of what was going on.

6.

But, at last, we began to get some information. Robbens, who was good about telling us what little he knew, said he'd be leading us on a march some six miles up the road to the towns of Dickweiler and Osweiler, taking off from this village, sign-posted Herborn. A fog hung over the snow-draped fields, which was both good and bad; bad because we were liable to not know where we were going—nothing new—and good because the Germans wouldn't know either. We couldn't have gone more than a couple of miles, when Robbens pulled us off the road. He'd gotten instructions by radio from Battalion that if we continued on that road up to Osweiler, we'd be running into a superior German force, reinforced by tanks. Also, the Company was to be split into two groups of a platoon and a half per, with a machine gun squad attached to each and mortarmen available. One group was to swing right for Dickweiler, on tanks, the other to go left and then turn right on a smaller road towards Osweiler. Robbens was taking the Osweiler group, and I was his available mortarman, to serve as a rifleman until otherwise called upon.

The route to that other road was cross-country in shin-deep snow, over fields and through several patches of woods, the snow part not very easy going. And, evidently we weren't exactly invisible, because our arrival in the first patch of woods was greeted by the heart-stopping whine of screaming meamies bearing down on us, the scariest of battlefield sounds. It was like a bunch of howling banshees were coming after you. Fortunately, they fell short. We had barely breathed a sigh of relief when another volley came in closer, landing with belching thuds. The damned things were rockets and came in clusters, some said nine at a time, which could be; I never thought of doing a count. There were various unpleasant descriptions of what they could do to you, like squeezing your brains out, sucking all the air out of your lungs—whatever. Concussion was certain, but if you were within a certain radius of the things, you wouldn't have to worry about what they did.

Curious to learn what was going on, I moved up close to Robbens, who didn't have much luck recontacting Battalion on the radio. He tried Artillery and got no more than static. It was no better with Cannon Company, who we learned already had their hands full, having to fire point blank at Germans advancing on them unimpeded. It looked like the Germans had had no trouble infiltrating, since we didn't have enough troops to set up anything like a substantial line of defense.

Our radioman, a guy called Curtan, whose name, after our initial experience with meamies, we changed to Curtains, was tinkering with the damned radio, a large square job that covered almost his entire back, but so far all he got was frustration. So Robbens had to do some fancy guessing, which was that the Germans might be trying to prevent us from making the right turn we wanted to take at that point. We were the relief column, it seemed, for the Company at Osweiler, and the Germans, having slipped behind our forward positions, were going to make us fight our way up—and, as they saw it, get wiped out, so they could do the same to the Company we'd fail to help.

We went through to the other side of the woods and, looking out at an open field some two hundred yards wide, Robbens decided we'd cross to the next patch of woods and make our crucial turn from there. Of course, there might be trouble in those woods, but we had no choice. The situation was so fluid, trouble everywhere. We couldn't have been more than twenty-five guys; nonetheless, Robbens wanted us to spread out at least twenty paces apart, making it difficult for them to find a desirable target among those snow beetles tracking up on them. Robbens also wanted us to pick up the pace (the less exposure the better), but fear had already put a little spark in our heels, so, halfway over, we were sucking wind and thinking it wouldn't be a bad thing if we had to hit the ground and sink down in the fluffy snow. Our lead man wasn't thirty yards from the woods, when we heard a series of sharp cracks. The lead and two other guys were immediately picked off. The bullets spun them around, and they staggered a couple of steps before falling down in a lump.

We hastily burrowed down as close to bare ground as we could get, but snow was meager cover. We returned fire, and it was answered by additional cracks and puffs of smoke coming from the woods, their shots kicking up lively spurts of snow here and there. Things got worse when two Heinies stood up and started spraying us with their burp guns, hitting three more guys, one of them not far from me, who was feebly crying out, "Medic. Medic, over here." I didn't think we had a medic with us. Looking over, I saw the guy had a gash at the side of his throat and was bleeding freely. He had raised up too far. There was no help for him, no hope.

I was over on the left wing, figuring an oblique angle would give them a lesser target when we made our dreaded run at them. Robbens being close by, I overheard him saying to Blazor we couldn't just lay out there pinned down for the meamies to wipe us out, a thought that made me go dry in the mouth. At that point, we got a temporary reprieve, when Rebel and Billy had their air-cooled machine gun mounted on its tripod and took out the burp gunners. The staccato chatter of that thing, different from the smoother sound of the Germans' machine gun, was music to our ears. Thinking out loud, Robbens supposed we could make a go of it if we timed our assault so everybody was up and firing at once, but he wanted to make one more attempt to get back to Artillery. While our 105s weren't exactly around the block, they might concede it was worth a try. Talk about desperation. Literally shivering, like so many cornered rats, we feared the worst. Pinned down out in the open, you don't have many alternatives.

Knowing none, we looked at Robbens, and Blazor asked whether we could chance a mad dash at 'em? I asked, could we survive it? Robbens said nothing. We needed help, even to pull back.

But, in a moment, it looked liked we could buy some time, as I heard a Heinie officer banging his radio and cussing that he couldn't get through to whomever at his Command Post. Robbens heard it too, and he told Curtan to keep trying to get through to Artillery—the static wasn't a bad sign—and, if he couldn't connect, to try Battalion again. That provided a sufficient interval for me to cradle my carbine and crawl on elbows and knees over to a slope that led down to the road below, where I'd spotted two guys manning a lonely 57mm anti-tank gun. As I reached the edge of the field, I heard Gush yelling at me. Where the hell was I going and what for? "Fer Chrissake, Buddy, yah cain't take off on us!"

I asked the guys at the gun to fire several rounds up into the woods. They could elevate the barrel enough to drop them in there, couldn't they? Since I couldn't get my nervous tongue untangled, I thought they didn't understand me, so I said it again. Incredulous, they cried, "No way." Their orders were to deny the road to enemy armor, which was a major objective of our defense if we were to save Luxembourg City.

"Good Christ, what kind of bullshit talk is that?!"

They didn't take too kindly to my remark, and told me to get lost. But I came back at them.

"You've seen a whole lot o' tanks here, huh?"

235

No answer. I told them never mind about what ain't there; just help us out with what is. They simply shook their heads, saying that, besides, they didn't have that many rounds. Dumb bastards; I told them the incoming would get them too, and there'd be *no* rounds. The spaghetti that Quartermaster scraped off the snow would be their guts. They looked at me like I was a maniac. Who the hell was *I* to be giving them orders anyway?

Gush had been scrunched down in the snow several yards behind me, and my voice carried far enough to bring him rolling down the slope. Short of breath and huffing, he was on us in a second. When I told him the problem, his face tensed up and reddened like he was ready to eat somebody alive. He told these clowns that he was our Battalion CO and I was his orderly, so they better snap shit and shoot the goddam gun. Dumbfounded, they wouldn't budge, which was enough for Gush to aim his carbine at them and holler, "Fire!" Stiff with fright, they couldn't move, so he put the carbine to the one guy's chest and said, "Listen, I've already killed one artillery gunner. And unless you fire this fuckin thing…." Before he could finish, the four of us were hitting the ground, as another set of meamies came in—lots closer than the others.

The Heinies had gotten their range. But it was the woods they hit, killing a number of their troops and sending the rest of them running back out of the woods, stumbling over one another and scattering every which way. —*Wow*, us saved by them taking out their own. It seems *we* were too late, the *meamies* too soon. Like Robbens said, if you're at a tactical disadvantage, it's good to have luck. And did we ever need it; most of us had been thinking we were done for, whether we stayed put or attacked. One thing we found out, though, was that, considering how these Heinies took off, maybe they weren't exactly those tough-as-nails Germans, steeled for the fight, that we'd faced before. Nobody was ready to sing Hallelujah, but our relief was the closest we ever came to levity on line. It was good to know that the Germans could screw up like we do, particularly when communication goes haywire.

Robbens was so grateful and preoccupied with our next move that he forgot to ask me and Gush what we were up to down on the road. And we didn't tell.

7.

So it was on to Osweiler, where we took up a position in yet another wooded area about 800 yards outside of the town itself, which had partially receded from view when we moved up beyond it. We looked out onto a parallel wooded area, also on the diagonal, that was somewhat up and to the left of us. Having circled around the town through a draw to get there, we had a brief view of the pummeling those people's houses had taken, a good number bearing jagged holes in their walls and skeletal roofs, with rubble being strewn about on the walkways and gardens and into the main road.

We went through a freezing night out there, and those who made the effort to dig in had to give it up. The ground was rock hard, and, since we couldn't detonate those dynamite cubes without giving away our position, we faced the morning darned well numbed. Banging our boots together didn't help; we couldn't feel our feet. That was quickly forgotten, as, dimly visible in the morning mist, a string of Heinies were cautiously moving down along the edge of the parallel woods, looking this way and that, rifles at the ready. We readied ourselves, having been warned, and for a change we didn't have to worry about ammo.

We did get some on the way out, when we stopped at the Company CP to get instructions, plus what additional clips we could scrounge, along with a lone BAR that Billy laid claim to. We were told that we could expect a Heinie patrol to come our way, and if it looked like we were going to be flanked or encircled, we had best do a careful withdrawal—whatever careful was.

The Heinies stopped and their officer got out his binocs to have a look. We were down and motionless, except for Robbens. He was squatted behind a tree, indicating for us to hold our fire until he gave the command, when, at just that moment, a couple of shots came our way. One whizzed by Robbens' helmet and whacked into a tree trunk. His arm movement must have been picked up. Billy instantly opened up with his BAR, and the fat was in the fire. "Flanked, hell, men!" Robbens called out. "Everybody open up, or they'll have us."

And open we did, cutting down several of them, and taking some return fire, until Billy bolted out to chase after those running off, firing his BAR from the hip as he went. Rebel kept yelling, "Get down, you idiot; get down!" But it was too late. The officer whipped out from behind a tree and peppered him with his burp gun. That got all of us firing away, and we peppered the officer. The way the rest of the Heinies took off, they must have thought they'd run into an ambush, possibly company-sized. There were just nineteen of us, but we had fired so quickly and furiously, also abundantly thanks to the extra clips, that they could have misjudged us. A few laggards hoisted handkerchiefs and came over to surrender. We just waved them on back, where they could be interrogated. They'd be a burden to us.

Rebel was sick over losing Billy. He'd been coming on like the Billy of old. We saw a flash of temper when he told Rebel off, saying he didn't need to be taken under anybody's goddam wing: What the hell did Rebel take him for, anyway? Having got that off his chest, he said Rebel obviously needed help, and he was ready to give it, as he did with those two burp-gunners. He claimed he wasn't trying to prove anything; he was simply eager to do something on his own. The thing he'd just done was stupid—twice over—but he also saved us by opening up first. Robbens recognized that when he called in his report to Battalion and asked to have Billy put in for the Bronze Star.

We wondered what Robbens might have been talking about when he said they'd "have us." It wasn't till later that we found out we were in real danger of being surrounded and captured. As it turned out, this group of Heinies wasn't up to getting it done, though they did have numbers, good weaponry, meamies on call, and armor not far off. Before disposing of the prisoners, we got it out of them that their offensive called for them to take key towns along the Sauer River, such as Osweiler and Dickweiler, clearing the way for their armor to move down main roads to Luxembourg City. A tall order for them; a taller one for us to resist. Just north of us, they were supposed to cut off and storm Echternach, which, in force, they would do.

8.

We were naturally interested in how things were going for guys in our other Companies, but, lacking a map, we were hard put to get our minds around the big picture. The small piece we had was big enough, and we weren't all that clear about it. Our radio had become functional again, and we were told to proceed through those woods across from us, make sure they were cleared out, and then await further orders. We were about to pull out into the open, when it looked like the Heinies were coming back, probably having been chewed out and *pushed* back. We waited for them to come further down, then, taking my cue from Billy (hit 'em quick with the unexpected) I was the first to heave both of my grenades, and others did the same, giving them the impression we weren't the depleted rag-tag they'd been told to go on out and whip. The grenades made a series of pops, and the lead Heinies were close enough that some of the shrapnel zinged overhead, but their shrill outcry, sounding like they were as much surprised as in pain, told us all we needed to know. Our follow-up was swift, giving them all we had. Clips were being shoved down into breeches almost as fast as the empties flew out. As the Heinies ran back, we directed our fire at the opening where they were slipping into the far woods.

There was an uneasy pause. Then, with burp guns putting up random bursts, they were moving again. We made out a line of them who were slouching back and around probably wanting to circle behind us. We opened up again, and, with Rebel's machine gun pumping out a streak of red lead right in their path, the Heinies finally had to pull away again—as before, leaving their dead and wounded.

Robbens figured they came back because they were supposed to have cleared us out, and, since they didn't, either they'd be thrown at us yet again, or their Command might just bring on their artillery to get the job done. The latest Robbens had heard before the radio went out again was for us to set up a defensive position. But poised which way?

Blazor told him that we did have the option of making that "careful withdrawal." Robbens, however, thought that, once we were out in the open, with no place to go for cover, they'd for sure drop the heavy stuff down on us. Couldn't he radio for help? Blazor asked. What help? Everybody was stretched thin. Evidently, Robbens made the right decision, at least just then, since another thing he didn't pass on to us (disclosed later) was that the Heinies had taken a number of houses back in Osweiler. Where would we have been able to go if we withdrew? Robbens wouldn't say we were trapped, and we, fortunately, didn't know enough to think so. Our thoughts were on what might be immediately ahead of us, which made us anxious enough.

Something else we didn't know (also disclosed later), that Robbens probably did know, was that among units recently captured, some were nearby. It was bound to happen; we were few, the Germans numerous. That, just then, was a situation we couldn't have begun to think about. But, when we were finally filled in, I, for one, believed that, faced with capture, we'd surely try to make a get-away, maybe shoot our way out. An idle thought, shared by Rebel and Gush, that made good whiskey talk. Actually, there were times we might have been put to the test, and with what we were shortly to find out, this could have been one of them.

For the time being, we were stuck with a typical Army situation: if you don't know what to do, try anything, and make believe it's right. We'd been watching Robbens nervously turn his map this way and that and scratch his chin (like, what if we have to run for it?) when who should pop up, breathless and stuttering, but ol' skin and bones, invisible Huey, the only guy who could have gotten through, with a message from Battalion. On being shot at as he crossed the open field, he had plunked down and played dead. It took a couple of minutes before he could talk straight. He reported that Dickweiler and Osweiler were both surrounded, but so far were holding the Germans off. However, confirming what Robbens had learned, he said one of our squads that was hunkered down in a Dickweiler outpost had been taken prisoner and led away under guard, which, to us, sounded like they might get shot. We didn't have much time to digest that.

Huey said the Heinies that we had encountered were probably supposed to support the squeeze on the two towns, and, considering where he got shot at, they, in fact, seemed to be on their way. But they'd soon enough find out that tanks had been called up, TDs too, and with our artillery ready to pound away, they should get pushed back in our direction, so we were supposed to be on the alert for them. We'd dig in a blocking position on the downhill perimeter of the woods, establishing a field of fire from which to take out all that came our way when dispersed by the artillery.

However, none of that happened; at least not the last part. What did happen was the maddening scream of meamies heading right for us. The first volley fell short, and the next fell long, each with shattering explosions. Murder! Were they bracketing us? Not likely; the German were more thrifty than we were in the expenditure of ammo. In any case, it made sense that the Heinies we'd been tangling with would call back coordinates to their rocketeers. The orders Robbens began shouting were instantly drowned out by another volley that fell so close we could feel air waves from the concussions. We got that terrible sinking feeling. One more and we'd be gone.

Gush and I had been flailing wildly at the ground with our entrenching tools, and, in frantic confusion after that close call, I rushed behind a stout pine, and, face to bark, I was holding tight with all I had—for whatever good that might do me. Looking the other way, I didn't realize at first that Gush was there with me doing the same thing. On recovering, we saw that the only thing to do was move back from the perimeter and start digging all over again—like mad. After a lull, all hell broke out. I could only begin to piece things together in the aftermath.

First, we heard our 105 batteries open up down below with one savage bombardment, sending over volley after volley without let up. They could have put out over a hundred rounds. The sound alone was awesome. Huey had said that the plan was for artillery to go after every German in sight, and those out of sight as well.

Robbens regarded that as bringing us into play, and he corralled Blazor, Curtan, and several other guys to move up to the perimeter with him, so they could check if there was anything like a fleeing remnant. He asked Huey to go back for the rest of us. But Huey told us it suddenly occurred to him that the perimeter might be the worst place to go, since our artillery would take it as far as they had to, and then some. Just as Huey ran down to get with Robbens, a horrendous ear-splitting barrage of meamies came screaming down on the perimeter, and then another, even louder. Gush and I, on the flank, some thirty feet back, were shaking all over in our half-dug hole. For sure, nobody up front could have lived through it. There wasn't even time for them to yell out—if yell they could.

The artillery had meanwhile let up and, in the eerie quiet that followed, there was the call for a Medic. Pedro being long gone, the new guy just assigned at Battalion needed us as much as we needed him. Utterly confused, he called out, "Who wants a Medic? Where?"

"Up to the edge of the woods, you moron! And hurry!" somebody answered. Unsteady on his feet and stumbling over rocks and broken branches hidden by the snow, the scared Medic finally oriented himself and went forward. But there was nothing for him to do. Rebel had gone up with the Medic, and the two of them came back carrying Blazor on a make-shift stretcher of snowsuits. Blazor was bleeding profusely from the nose and mouth, the eyes too, and his face had that dirty tallow whiteness to it we didn't like to see. He died on the way to the Aid Station. Robbens, Huey, Curtan, and two other guys had been killed instantly.

Moving out of those woods, we found the road that Robbens had evidently been looking for on his useless map. We ran into a couple of communications Jeeps with Signal Corps guys stringing wire from one of those huge spools we'd often seen abandoned along a muddy roadside. It seemed so strange, like they were in another world, quietly doing a work-a-day civilian job. We put Blazor across the back seat of one Jeep and had the Signal guys take two walking wounded in the other, one of them, silent Eugene, an uncomplaining guy who had been limping around with a slug in his thigh. In the emotion of the moment, I made the suggestion that we bring out Robbens, Huey and the others, only to realize how ridiculous it was to talk that way once I heard myself say it. Rebel put a hand on my shoulder. To make me feel better, he said the same thing occurred to him. Watching those Jeeps bump down the tracks of a snow-crusted road in the dusk of a dark winter's day, I was struck by what a dismal study in black and white that made. It was one of the lasting images we took away from our insignificant part in the outfit's attempt to hold the Germans off on the southern hinge of the Break-Through. (Truth is, we didn't know that that was what this fight was, until later, when somebody got hold of a *Stars and Stripes*.) The most intense action was over in several days, but the sadness lingered. Some real good guys were gone—yet again. Often the best of them. Officers didn't come any better than Robbens.

PART IV

1.

Losing men that we knew wore on us. Time and again you got the feeling that an infantryman's life was hopeless, in fact, worthless; clearly, so regarded by the Brass. Unknown to them, you could get battle weary in a day. When those days kept coming, you could feel you were just waiting for the end. You tried to think of that as little as possible.

Anyway for a short while, we had it good. Given several days rest, we were billeted in civilian homes in a quiet little town, and even had ourselves a one-day pass to Luxembourg City, which was nice. Sitting at a shiny little round table in a clean, well-lighted café, sipping my wine and watching the nicely dressed European civilians walk by, city dwellers intent on going about their business, I felt like I was a Human Being, after all.

Back at the town where we were billeted, some guys got themselves drunk on cellar Schnaps and stayed that way until it was time to roll up our packs and fall in on the road to be carted off for the push to send the Germans back to Germany. However, first, we had to clear more of them out of Luxembourg.

The civilians had returned to their houses and hosted us. In the case of Rebel, Gush, Hardy and me, the family we were with threw a couple of mattresses down on their living room floor. Appreciative, I managed to snag a pair of shoes from Supply for the man of the house. We thanked the people, hoped the drunks hadn't caused too much trouble (which they did) and left money, sweaters, long-johns and whatever else we could dispense with. They didn't want to take it, saying we would be needing that stuff to keep us warm, but we indicated the less weight the better.

I had become friendly with the elderly couple's niece, Maria, and we had ourselves a pretty warm good-bye kiss in the hallway. As I turned to go, she came back to me, and all that she had held back before under a shield of discreet modesty came out in a surge of passion. Her open-mouthed kisses took me by surprise, and I responded in kind. We drew so close that my helmet fell off and went clonking down the stairs, which brought a bit of muffled laughter from the living room.

Maria and her aunt and uncle joined the rest of the townspeople who lined the main street to wave good-bye, calling out to us in English. There was an overflow of good feeling on their part, which I thought gave us more of a celebration than we deserved. But they were mighty happy the Germans weren't coming back. Some of the girls broke into our ranks to get yet another parting kiss. Maria threw me several from the roadside. She got a letter to me afterwards and enclosed a picture, with a note on the back, "Please, do not forget your little friend from Luxembourg."

The night was clear, the air crisp, the long-lost stars were sparkling again, and the light coming off the snow brightened the whole town, especially the happy roadside faces—ours too for a change. In that sweet moment, the scene took on a kind of Christmas glow which gave us a short-lived feeling of nostalgia. Oh boy; not a good thing to dwell on that. And it sure wasn't, for the mood was abruptly pierced by the roar of a plane, its motor becoming increasingly louder as it swooped down low over us and, zooming back up in a flash, it swiftly faded into the night sky. From the shadow it made on the snow in passing, we thought it looked like a Messerschmitt. Could have been that the people spared us a strafing.

2.

Reality was not long in returning, not very far either. We had held the Germans off in our sector, but the fight wasn't over in others. After a tortuous ride over narrow roads, we dismounted from our trucks and trudged some five miles or so to a town with lingering fires, where we were coming in on the heels of what must have been a fairly active fight. A good number of buildings were in ruins, shooting ghost-like flames up into the black night, a spooky situation. Nobody liked nighttime action, and house to house was even less fun. We'd been given a report from the outfit we were relieving that they had run into a spate of small arms fire at the far end of town, either rear guard to stymie our pursuit or a patrol probing for possible resistance to a counterattack. Most likely the former, we thought.

Before our mission could be decided on, we had to determine whether that rear guard was still hanging around, and if so, it would help to get an estimate of their number. A designated group of us that included Gush and me were assigned to find out, best without actually taking them on, which made sense, though the guy with the bazooka didn't. Out front, giving us directions about walking close against the walls of houses still standing, was Eric-the-Red, a crafty old Sergeant, called on in place of the barely sober Hardy.

To get to the far end of town, we had to traverse the center. The main square was all broken up by shell craters, amidst which were three burned-out Sherman tanks with two dead GIs hanging over the side of one of them. Four additional GIs—maybe infantry—were sprawled around beside the tanks. Armor was an instant magnet for fire. Further on, we came into full view of two administrative-type buildings afire on either side of the road, between which, up against a curbstone, were four dead Heinies. Not far beyond them was one of their huge Tiger tanks, also burned out. All that remained of the other flaming buildings, already practically burned to the ground, were broken walls and blackened chimneys.

When we came upon what seemed a chancy intersection, Eric halted us at the corner and pointed down to where the Heinies were supposedly barricaded behind blown-out windows of a smoldering building. Eric always had an ornery streak. He said, never mind the recon. How in hell were we going to find out how many Heinies were left there just by looking? If the objective was to clear them out, he'd just as soon do it, and how many wouldn't matter. Starck obviously knew what he was doing when he chose Eric to lead the patrol.

Eric admitted he was the one who asked for the bazooka guy. And, wasting no time in using him, Eric had him blast one through the wall, while directing the rest of us to open up on the empty windows to deprive them of firing ports. There was enough yelling from within to indicate the exploding round might have gotten some of the Heinies. It rousted out others, whom we shot at as they flew out the back and into the woods. Everything happened so fast, we had no idea of whether we hit any of them.

A little guy awkwardly trying to crawl out the side of the wreckage fluttered a handkerchief, and I went over to pull him to his feet. When I asked about killed and wounded, the kid, stuttering with fright, told me one was dead, and everyone else was gone ("verschwunden") except for him. How many seemed a moot question, but I asked it anyway, and he said he didn't know. Typical. That seemed to be it, but Eric thought we ought to make sure that it was, so cautiously making our way down the side of the building, we heard boots scurrying over fallen roof tiles, and, for a fleeting instant, we glimpsed several Heinies flying off into the darkness behind the house—probably well gone by the time we fired after them. Not much of a rear guard, if that. So whatever they were, it looked like we'd gotten rid of them anyway, a little more than we were asked to do.

As we walked back down the narrow street, Eric, ever alert, said to wait a minute. He thought he heard the click of a bolt sending a round into the chamber of a rifle. He reminded us of the damage a lone sniper could do. Tony, Starck's runner, said he didn't hear anything, but Eric insisted the Heinies had probably left a deadly sharpshooter behind that barricade to detain us long enough for all of them to get away. I looked at our little prisoner, but, without my asking, he shook his head. ("Keine Ahnung."—no idea. That again.)

We had moved back to the street and were standing there on the wet cobblestones, trying to figure out how best to go after the sniper, when, before we could make a move, there came a sudden crack that pummeled Eric over backwards, his helmet flying off, blood spouting from his throat. Aware that the sniper might be reloading, we quickly pulled Eric over behind a garden wall that angled back from the street, and Tony opened his aid pack. We tied a bandage around the wound, but, even with pressure, couldn't stop the bleeding. Eric was limp; the bullet had apparently gone through to his spinal column.

This, after all he had made it through. I faulted myself for not talking him out of the need to go after the last fucking man. We should have dragged him the hell outa there—period. With me sounding off like that, Fred, the bazooka guy crawled around the wall, and just as he was setting up to fire a second round, there was the crack of another shot and over he went, low as he'd hunched, hit squarely between the eyes. Poor Fred was a good guy, but not very swift in the head. He was close with Eric, who kept a watch on him.

This time Gush got riled. "Bastard. He's showin us what a great shot he is, and he's got himself a shootin gallery. Knows our way back is down this street, and he's just awaitin for the next one to stick his head out."

We were getting pretty anxious, and one of the other guys we had with us wondered if we shouldn't dig in. Tony pitched in with unwanted hindsight. "Why in hell are we muckin around like this, about to get ourselves picked off one by one, when we shoulda had a damned radio."

The thing to do was, of course, to call for a tank—common practice with a sniper, who otherwise had the advantage, which Tony was quick to add.

Though, in this case, Gush swore, not for long. Taking Eric's grease gun, he said he had an idea of where those shots came from. I cupped my hands to give him a boost up the garden wall, where he could get some light from the fires. He no sooner got to his feet than he let go with a sweeping burst over the brick barricade that he said caught the shooter looking down the street for his next victim.

The following day, when we assumed a defensive position on the long hill that looped outside of town, darned if we didn't hear shells swishing overhead toward the shattered buildings and empty streets behind us. Not a doubt the stuff was ours, from who knows where, on whose orders. Looking for the remnant we chased out? Or just trying to keep the fires burning?

We couldn't get Eric off our minds. He was a real loss, so skilled at soldiering, and always quiet about it. Scandinavians could be pretty solemn types, and he was comfortable being that way. He'd been given assignments they would entrust to nobody else; did what was asked of him, and that was it. He was fully as scared and beat up as we were. You could see how tired of it he was from those sad, dark-socketed eyes of his. I remembered one of the things he said to me on the truck as we drove out of Hürtgen, with me looking so damned mopey. "Not good to look back, Buddy. You won't like what you see." After we lost him, I did; and I didn't.

At noon chow, we had a briefing at which Starck had some interesting news for us. It seems that if you had been in combat for a specified period of time and had at least two decorations, you could be sent back to the States for a thirty-day furlough. We thought Hardy would qualify, but, due to his hospitalization, he was short on time. It came as a surprise that Boyd, our First Sergeant, did qualify. He had pulled a couple of guys out of the surf in Normandy. The commendation read "under fire." Thereafter, he managed to steer clear of trouble. The furlough was as unexpected to him as it was to us. When we congratulated him, Boyd averted his eyes. He said he didn't think he deserved it. Blazor told him to keep his mouth shut or they'd take it back. He nodded and tried to say something, but all he could get out was a quiet "Thanks, guys," quite unusual for him.

Hardy clapped him on the shoulder and said, "Hey, live it up, man. The thirtieth day is gonna be a bitch."

What hurt was that Eric would have qualified.

3.

Our role in the Break-Through was over. As I thought about what our clutch of GIs might have contributed during that campaign, I couldn't have told you that we'd done a whole helluva lot. Yeah, we hung in like we were supposed to; didn't let 'em get through like *they* were supposed to. But with the downer we were in, big words about our "role" in this thing ("valor," and "epic defense") flew past us. There had been times when we were stressed to our hair roots, and in a few hot "engagements" we had feared the worst. Many guys got killed and hurt. We were sad for them; grateful that we survived. We'd also had ourselves a rest—which seemed like a year ago—woke up, and were being returned to our usual role, which would bring back the usual grinding in the gut.

Of course, the Brass, who put out those statements about valor, saw things differently. For battles they saw maps, for casualties, numbers. No offense; we didn't hold it against them, just the blind planning, which we knew nothing about, and they should have.

Our outfit was trucked up the road that Patton had sent his tanks on to break the siege of Bastogne. Patton had the reputation of showing no mercy, which gained him much respect from the Germans. (Both he and Top Man had smart PR Aides to suppress their mistakes and build up—sometimes make up—their virtues.) What people who read about Patton didn't realize was that, tough as he was on the Enemy, he showed little mercy toward his troops—none toward his favored tankers. There was a good stretch on that road to Bastogne where, just about every ten to fifteen yards, we saw a wrecked tank pushed off into the ditch. They were our Shermans and, by rough count, said to have been at least a hundred, probably more.

I said yards, did I? Okay, but when I said good stretch, I was talking about mile after mile of wrecks on either side of the road, and not just tanks. There were also TDs, half-tracks, trucks (large and small), Jeeps, Jeep trailers, field pieces of various sizes, anti-tank guns, ambulances, bulldozers with frozen winches, and doubtless other equipment buried under the snow, to say nothing of the frozen corpses lying out of sight, some in among the vehicles they had manned. The equipage of war peacefully rusting in the snow. Ah, the snow, which put the smoothest coating over everything, leveled shell holes, drifted evenly onto roadside houses and dusted over the holes blown in them. It was like an old Norse Snow-God, himself shocked, had rolled a batten of cotton over it all to soften the impact of the carnage. As the scene kept unfolding, we kept following it in silent astonishment.

Since we had been through here on our first thrust into Germany, some of the wreckage might have come from prior engagements, but, by far, most of it looked new enough to have been torn up in recent action. In any case, having been shifted from the First Army to Patton's Third because of the split made by the Break-Through, we had an idea of what to expect, and, in case we didn't, there it was in plain sight.

On the way up, we saw the big-chested bastard himself, sitting erect in a Jeep that sported a fancy three-star shield projecting upward from its front bumper. His fleshy face was impressive, puffed up like a horny bull frog's and reddened by his ample whisky allowance. The MP blew his whistle, instantly stopped traffic in the other three directions, and got off the snappiest salute, unreturned by the immoveable hulk, who was wearing an airman's padded jacket with a fur collar. After all, the temperature was well below freezing, as we well knew, worse in the wind. Must have been something for him to get in and out of a vehicle that, for his size, looked like a kiddy car. On our one-day pass, we saw the address that we thought he might claim for his Third Army HQ in Luxembourg City, nothing less than the Prince's Castle, surrounded by a grated iron fence, and guarded by MPs in spiffy dress uniforms, sporting white helmets, with matching gloves and puttees. No wonder he gave us a Unit Citation for saving the City.

4.

A couple of additional items, on the way up to a little episode that stayed with me for some time. We were marching toward a town (still in Belgium) from which we'd move on to our jumping-off point, and, unexpectedly, it looked like we were going to have to fight our way up to that point. Just like the Germans; they want you to pay for every inch of your progress toward, as much as going into, the Fatherland, artillery doing the most harm.

To get to the town, we had to make our way through woods and snow-covered fields, pretty much hill and dale, which was hard going. The town had been hit by sustained artillery during the initial Break-Through, and, so far as we could tell, all the civilians had left their houses, most now in ruins. Bitter cold as it was, we couldn't wait to get on into them. However, we had just descended into town and come within reach of a few houses when the shells found us, the first of them landing closer than we expected, and from their distinctive sound in hitting—Sheee-uck! Sheee-uck!—we knew they were 88s.

I dove for a ditch beside the road. We had picked up replacements to bring the Company closer to full strength, and there were two new guys just ahead of me. I called to them to stay down, but in their eagerness to get to the house beside us they got up and both ran smack into the next two shells, exploding just a few yards ahead of us. Both were killed, the one right in front of me taking a good share of the shrapnel, and, in so doing, certainly saved me. You can get pretty superstitious about things like that. I took it as an omen, that the end might not be far off for me. You know there's just so much time left on your fuse. The air was still heavy with the smell of gun powder from the craters left by the 88s, as if it were smoke from the Great Pit—which reinforced the Judgment image.

Those two guys were mere kids, probably about my age. Getting up, I walked by them kind of tentatively, and, taking in the one in front of me, saw his back was riddled, like the stuff had gone right through him. His helmet had been blown off, and he was still bleeding quite a bit from the back of the neck. His skin was stark white and his blood was turning dark red. I'd seen my share of that, but this time it was like seeing myself, as I'd never be able to.

Of all things, we had a European newspaperman with us, along with a cameraman, whose film was rolling. The two of them had all they wanted and took off. Meanwhile, as more shells started landing in the same area, a bunch of guys scattered into a grove of trees, me being one of them. Some of the replacements had also scattered, a few following the two newspaper guys, and Hardy, running around like a sheep dog, had to round them up. Additional shells went their way, and a couple of the replacements were wounded. Hardy came limping by and asked me to see if I could gather in some of the missing replacements. He had a tear in his fatigue pants and walked with a limp. When I asked about it, he said he thought he might

255

have picked up a shrapnel splinter, but shrugged it off, indicating it couldn't be more than a flesh wound, if that. No way he was going back. He'd had worse.

Joining us in the grove of trees, he was cussing us out, saying we'd grown soft on our break. No sooner did he finish chewing us out, when the 88s came into our grove of trees. It was like their FO had his binocs right on us. Several more guys were wounded, one that I recognized. He was sitting beside a tree, holding his side, a dazed look in his eye. I lit a cigarette and gave it to him—lucky stiff. The Medics might be a while getting to him, but his worries were over—for now.

One of the new Lieutenants suggested we might as well bed down for the night where we were. (Bed? Never heard that before.) Digging in was real tough (where were those cubes when we needed them?) but, tired or not, we kept at it, furiously, also cussin furiously, as we struck at the hard unyielding dirt, thick with tree roots. Early next morning, we sent out a recon patron. Because I knew German, I was chosen to be on it, but was pulled back at the last minute. There might be a call for mortars. The patrol—what was left of them—didn't get back till late afternoon. The leader, another of our new Lieutenants, blue in the face, his grimy hands shaking as he puffed on a cigarette, haltingly made his report. He'd had an eight man squad and was returning minus five, two having been captured, three killed. I took it to heart: another omen.

5.

Every outfit has at least one outright Shit. Ours was the genuine article, a four-star specimen. He was a Pennsylvania Dutchman, who spoke a terrible hick German, actually a bastard Bavarian accent. It was so bad none of the Germans we captured could understand him, much less recognize it as German, so I was called up to do the talking. His name was Klug, pronounced with a long u, which I privately expanded to Klugscheisser, a colloquialism that I believe means a dumbbell who thinks he's real smart. And Klug was dumb enough in how he related to the rest of us, though smart about everything related to himself, thinking no one would notice, but he was so obvious about it, we all did. He'd be the first one at the cartons of K-rations, making off with all of the coveted breakfast menus he could squirrel away. Back in Herborn, where we had the stovepipe incident, he found an oversized corrugated wash basin, took it to his room, heated buckets of water on the sly, and took a bath without letting anyone know what he was up to. When his secret got out, he claimed it was for bunions. At the time, we were still waiting for our two-minute showers.

There was lots else, not the least objectionable thing being his obviously brown-nosing Starck, who made him squad leader of mortars, the normal complement of which was all of twelve guys. We groaned, but put up with it—to a point. It's like having a cousin you can't stand, but you're stuck with him. First thing Klug wanted to do was make me his runner. I couldn't believe it. He had the position, but minus the stripes to go with it. So, as one Pfc to another, I told him to shove it, pointing out that no other squad leader had a runner. Rebel, who did have the stripes, wouldn't think of it.

We had to clear some Heinies out of a bunker just outside of town before we could settle into the houses. A couple of guys had wandered out that way, and there was a rattle of small arms fire. When Hardy arrived at the bunker with his grease gun putting out its streak of 45 caliber slugs, out came a small tree limb with a handkerchief at the end of it. I was told to bring the Heinies out, and all it took was to shout, "Kommen Sie raus, hände hoch!" Two of them ran out the back of the bunker, and we instantly brought them down. Of the four left, one was fearful. He indecisively stuck his head out the opening and didn't move until someone fired a shot that grazed his helmet, knocking it off, so out he came arms stiffly raised, his matted hair showing streaks of gray, a tic at the edge of his eye. Up steps Klug to question him, and the poor guy has a bewildered look, like maybe he's on the Russian front. I took over, and to each question, the poor guy comes out with "Keine Ahnung." And a damned-if-I-know look. I asked how come they were there, and it sounded like it could have been us: "Ich glaube Die Schweine haben uns ganz vergessen." (I think those swine completely forgot about us.)

Klug took offense; I had interfered, just when he wanted to burnish his new status on this pathetic specimen of the Wehrmacht. So what does he do, but pull rank, saying the non-coms are going to be quartered in houses, and the rest of us slobs would have to settle for barns. Most guys were too tired to make anything of it. Looking at a long cold night, all we wanted to do was get ourselves under a sufficient layer of straw and go to sleep, rats or no.

Gush said, "Fuck Klug." So, we went into the next house over from Klug's, little Tony, the Company runner, trailing after us.

The house had taken quite a beating. There were holes in the walls and roof, the chimney cut in half. On entering we found the living room bare, except for a few broken-down rough wood chairs and shards of glass and plaster on the barren floor. Then, taken aback, damned if we didn't hear German being spoken, but the voices were frail. I pushed Gush's carbine aside. Up from the basement came an elderly couple, well into their eighties, white-haired, stoop-shouldered, a stagger in their walk, the feebler one being the man, who used a cane. Gosh, we'd seen the same thing in a similar town, the first time we came through this region. It was really pathetic, in this case, touching. In many instances, old people simply didn't have the strength or means to vacate when the shells started landing. Some wouldn't leave their lifelong homes, regardless. Where could they go?

They were hard of hearing, and, at the sight of them, I seemed to forget half my German. But we managed to communicate. I asked if we could stay for a while to get out of the bitter cold, and they gave us a hearty welcome. With a sweeping gesture, the woman seemed to be apologizing for the pathetic shape of things. You could tell much from their looks. They were grim faced, but not beaten, determined to hold onto life. Our entrance had scared them down to the basement, where they had put up beds for themselves, committed to sticking it out. This was home, and so it would remain.

But we wondered how they managed to get themselves something to eat. They looked so gaunt, the man particularly, and hollow cheeked. His bony hands had a slight tremor. We sat down on the floor beside them and got out a box of K-rations for each of them. They were most thankful—imagine, for our ratty K-rations—and we had dinner together, they very intent at eating this gifted food, nodding to one another between bites, like they thought it was pretty tasty. I wondered if they were being polite. Gathered together like that, we made an unforgettable scene. As I took in the five of us in a semi-circle, these sweet old folks in the middle, heads bent over such meager fare they were glad to have, the poignancy of it got to me.

We hadn't noticed that there were a few hot coals left in the grate. The man picked up a piece of wood from the corner of the room, but finding it too big, he went into the hallway where he put it in a vise. Tony took the saw from him, but his arms were too numb to do much good, so the old man took the saw back, waved me away, and, to our embarrassment, his feeble motions got the log sawn through.

We went over to the fire and sat with them for a while. The old man got up and shuffled back into the kitchen from which he produced a bottle of apple Schnapps. The woman got some glasses, and we toasted one another. We had us a festive little time, and, with an outstretched arm, the woman offered us an overnight in their living room. But I said we couldn't stay. (We could make a pack of trouble for them if a German patrol got loose in town.) We exchanged hugs, and those dear folks were moist eyed. I didn't look at the other guys, knowing they too might be affected. We gave them the rest of our K rations. They were touched; so were we.

As we left, they pointed to their barn, where there was an ample supply of straw and said we could stay there. A couple of guys had in fact come over from the neighboring barn to take some, as they had more guys and less straw. Cold and careless, they had left a trail of straw on the snow, and, when I took a last look out the barn door, what did I see but the old woman, heavily shawled and bent over, very earnest about picking up every last blade of straw. I went out and joined her.

6.

We were going back over ground previously taken, and while not all of our Companies were pushing through exactly the same places again, in some cases, we were, at least so we were informed. On the other hand, I couldn't recall that we had previously crossed the Our River, but was told that some of our units had. That's where Tony came in. We thought it might help to know what we were supposed to be doing—once in a while, anyway—and Tony liked to tell us how

Corps HQ sized things up, as he'd heard Starck read their briefings to the other officers.

However, since what we'd heard and what happened weren't always the same, mostly we'd listen with half an ear. Like, what was it to us that our attack over the Our "was intended to plant us solidly on German soil again, poised for our tanks to make a run for the Rhine and strike at Germany's industrial heartland." Much of what Tony overheard had the bluster of press releases, like, with our attacks being "supported by armor and withering artillery, our troops would show the Krauts we were back for good this time." Tony lapped all that stuff up and had a knack for spouting it out in dead seriousness. Rebel would walk away in disgust: "Aw, tell 'em to blow it out their stackin swivels."

But, ignoring our skepticism, Tony knew we were curious and would give us more, some of it useful to know. "As they withdrew, in some instances the Germans resorted to skillful harassment, which raised our cost in casualties, with minimal cost to them. In other instances, their resistance could be rather fierce, raising the casualty figures on both sides." In our crossing the Our, we would get some of each, beginning with the first. For me, one particular loss was the worst—indeed, devastating.

Trucked up again by the trusty six-by-sixes, we passed a number of our M-5 light tanks, which told us not to expect much in the way of armor support, and, as for artillery, except for some killer short rounds, we got the feeling they were saving it for later. Markoff said he didn't like the look of things. Talker that he was, he nonetheless shook off questions about his second hospitalization, which we thought was why he was so antsy. Talking behind a cupped hand, Tony couldn't resist sneaking in a remark about which way he was running when he was hit and almost got pitched off the truck. Whatever it was, as we'd noticed, it didn't affect Markoff's mouth, nervous but otherwise robust as ever. Looking at the tankers' 37mm guns, he called over to two of them who were glumly standing in their open hatches, "Hey, you guys, what da hell you tink you're gonna do wit dem tin cans—kill mosquitas?"

Between them, Tony and Markoff managed to take the edge off our anticipation; at least, until we actually got going. Markoff didn't need anything to loosen him up, as he had filled his canteen with Schnapps, something we didn't do going into the attack. But canteens were a problem to us, because with us overnighting it out in the weather, they could freeze up and weigh like a rock. I know that Rebel carried his at the chest inside his field jacket. Others decided they'd just eat snow. Often enough, water became a big thing for us, no less here than in Hürtgen. We not only worked up a helluva sweat digging an urgent hole or running through the snow on heavy legs, but, when you were under fire, you sweated it out literally. The sweat band in your helmet liner would get soaking wet, your mouth parched, like you'd eaten sawdust.

Getting sight of the broad open slope we had to cross, sure to be slow going as we plowed through knee-deep snow, all other thoughts vanished. Walking into a biting wind, we had our heads down. We couldn't have been more vulnerable. A string of lumpy black figures against that white background, minus so much as a sheet for cover, we fully expected to be targeted. But as we'd drawn no fire halfway to the woods ahead of us, we relaxed a bit and just concentrated on making it across. Hardy was about ten feet ahead of me, grumbling to himself about "the stupid Russian." Walking along a fence in the draw below was another line of guys, Markoff in among them.

Before I knew what was happening, I saw Hardy suddenly fling himself down, and I did the same. In that instant, the air was split by the familiar sound of an explosion that hit just below us. The 88 came on us so terrifyingly fast that the shrapnel was zinging inches over my head before I even hit the snow. Down by the fence, the Russian was dancing around in pain, bleeding, his helmet blown off. He wrenched his pack off, threw his M-1 away, and with his arms flailing and knees pumping, he was starting to grope his way back, when the second round came pounding in. Hardy and I had crunched ourselves as far down in the snow as we could get waiting for the third round we knew would be coming, after which we made a mad dash for the woods. Damnation; to be sniped at by an 88. It occurred to me afterwards that, since those rounds had to be point detonating, we might have been saved by the snow we cursed.

Once in among the trees, we burrowed down into the snow as deep as we could get, and waited Sweat was running down my forehead, and I could feel my heart beating in my temples. A direct hit and we'd be pulverized; there'd be nothing left to be buried, nothing to report, except missing. The thought had occurred to us before, in horror. I could just picture their FO following us with his binocs, and, in a foul German rage, growling back to his gunner, "Du Arschloch! Zwei rechts, eins runder, un mach's schnell!" (You asshole, two turns right and one down and be quick about it!)

He evidently had something to show the first time around (our Russian probably wasn't the only one he'd snagged), but it must have burned him that we got away. I had the feeling he'd looked into our very faces, tight with fear, and said he had to get those gutless swine.

We didn't have to wait long for the damned things to come bearing down on us, louder and louder like madhouse demons crashing through the trees. I cringed with each Sheee-uck, as if it was right on us. I marveled that we weren't hit. When a branch or lump of

263

snow fell on our backs, we thought we were. Thanks to the observer's rage (half a turn down and he'd have had his wish) it seems that the shells landed further ahead of us than we thought. As we moved up, Hardy said something to me about how scary it was—an 88 singling us out like that. And, dammit, the FO *followed* us. Things are bad enough without them going for you personally. It made me feel better to know how Hardy took it, he being our on-line version of blood and guts, the real article.

7.

We spent the rest of the day in place, huddled against the snow, like it could give us some warmth. The German artillery kept pumping away at our position, but, lucky for us and bad for the Company up ahead, most of it was going overhead. We broke out our K-rations while we waited for orders. The sunless air was getting icier by the minute. I had the lunch ration and, already frosted to the bone, I could look forward to eating a chunk of cold cheese and crackers with a lemonade chaser. I was saying, 'Klug, you bastard, you even made off with the lousy Spam rations.' But I was alive.

At dusk, we finally proceeded up a winding trail, and, on the brow of the hill, just off to the side of the trail, we came upon a sight we hadn't seen before, a frozen mound of four dead GIs curled up real close and almost on top of one another. How they could have gotten heaped that way, I didn't know. Could they have been buddies, clinging together protectively when they heard the stuff roaring in, and get blown almost on top of one another by the force of the exploding shells? It was one of those things you didn't want to try figuring out, but not knowing still bothered you. They were from a different Company, so I didn't know them, which in a way made it worse. Gone in such a haphazard way. I felt bad for them and bad that we brought it on them.

It was dark by the time we arrived at the actual top of the hill, a flat bald area, and we found a good number of dead GIs strewn amid the shell holes, some lying beside the holes they had started digging, entrenching tools still in their hands. One guy was doubled over as if grabbing his stomach, another lay with his face turned sidewise, his open glassy eye reflecting the whiteness of the snow. God, did they ever take a beating. The same that was intended for us. Earlier, as we lay down below, we had seen the medical details coming up for the wounded and bringing them down on sledges. Fortunately, the shelling had slackened off.

This position put us above the west bank of the Our. We immediately went about getting our holes dug. Jumpy as we were, somebody thought he heard small arms fire in the distance. A patrol? Could be. We knew their whereabouts; they knew ours. But they might want to find out how big a force we were. A kid who had come up with the last batch of replacements said maybe it was guys from our fellow Company wanting to get even. We were too anxious to be annoyed.

Once again, we were half-way dug in when we got the order to make our way down to the river bank. Thankfully, we found some well-dug foxholes, actually deep bunkers, nicely built up—German style—with logs on the sides and top. We were tired, but tense; not much for deep sleeping. Next morning, at first light, the shells were hitting all around us. It was hard to tell, but it seemed like that stuff was coming from behind us—namely from our own artillery told to soften up the Germans over the River, but not getting it there. Some thought it was the Germans wanting to soften *us* up. I thought it was both.

We heard hurried footsteps outside our hole, and in stumbled Tony, white in the face, clutching his stomach, and crying out how bad it hurt. I scurried out and got the Medic who gave him a morphine shot and put a bandage on him. He wanted water, but most canteens were frozen, so I scooped up a canteen cup of snow for him. A piece of shrapnel had made a hole the size of a half-dollar in the middle of Tony's gut. It scarcely bled, externally. Maybe it was the cold. He said he'd been coming to tell us it was time to move out. We wished him luck, and he said, "I think I just got it." He asked the Medic to make sure somebody knew he was there.

When we started peppering the hill on the other side of the River, the most active fire was coming from our two machine guns, Rebel on one and Calvin on the other. Calvin was a ruddy looking, hoarse-voiced kid from Minnesota. They grow 'em big up there, and we liked to have a guy his size lugging the gun part. The night before we got on trucks, I was having a smoke with him and Rebel, and Calvin was talking about this being Minnesota weather, in a way his thing. Rebel, looking back on the balmy South, had a bit to say about that. Calvin had taken off his knit hat, and, as we talked, he was scratching his head with a trench knife. There weren't any of us who didn't have that pesky itch, but the sight of him going after it with that knife somehow didn't sit right. Jinxed for sure, I thought. One look at Rebel, and I could tell he had the same feeling.

Just as we were getting the order to move on over the River, I glanced in the direction of the rise where I'd last seen Calvin, and he wasn't behind his gun. I looked again and his ammo man was pulling a motionless body back under a tree. Calvin was gone. Gush said they for sure had one of their sharpshooters over there. Rebel couldn't have been more than twenty paces off to the other side of us. Just as I hollered for him to get the hell back in the brush, we heard a sharp metallic pop. The sniper had hit Rebel right in the canteen he stored up against his chest. The red water gurgled out, and Rebel fell face down over his gun. "Oh *Noo!*" I cried out in pain like I'd just been hit.

Hardy let go with one burst of his grease gun after the other in the direction of where that shot had come from. The replacement kid said he'd seen a Heinie ease out from behind a tree trunk and steady his rifle on a low branch. But no telling.

Somebody yelled over at me, "Hey, fella, get movin, fer Chrissake. What the hell's wrong with you?"

"Everything," I mumbled. I was frozen to the spot until somebody yanked me by the arm. It was Gush, coming back for me. One minute he was there, the next he was forging ahead. From the look in his eyes, I pitied the Heinies he met up with. Myself? I was going, but scarcely aware that I was.

The snow was pretty deep on top of the frozen River, and our haste made us stumble all the more as shells started falling in among us, breaking holes in the ice. Fall through and you didn't have a chance. We stopped firing when we noticed it had become quiet on the bank ahead of us. Once there, we found that the Germans had taken off, leaving their dead and some wounded. We hauled several of the wounded out of their holes—one sorry lot—wet-faced, and calling out in spasms, "Nicht schiessen! Bitte, nicht schiessen! Keine Gewehr." (Don't shoot. Please don't. No weapons.)

They had cast their helmets off, and their gray uniforms were torn. Their pants were wet at the crotch. One guy was bleeding down both sides of his face. Another had a bloody hand over his side, and the third was holding his thigh. I did a little scrounging in their hole. It was not above their comrades to leave a booby trap or two to reward the scrounger looking for a Luger. But they had probably hauled ass out of there too fast for any of that. Next to the helmets and rifles was a half-eaten tin of Baltic sardines, called Spruten, I think. It struck me as kind of sad. Nothing else to eat, and so unnerved they couldn't eat what they had. My father told me he used to eat Spruten—poor man's caviar. Only he had them with black bread and beer.

Hardy was thinking about taking these whimpering clowns around to the other side of the hill, unless someone would take them back. I told him not to look at me. What? Give that Observer another chance? Other guys shied away too. It made no sense to risk life and limb on their behalf. I suggested, why not just leave them there for the Medics to take back when they came for our wounded? Hardy shook his head, pointing to their rifles. "No Gewehr, huh?" I thought they were harmless, nonetheless.

Later on, as we thought about it, we had an idea of what probably happened to them, and knew enough not to ask. It was that kind of world.

The heavy-hearted spell hung on. But, dammit, I had to be scouting out a hole, or digging one, since the Germans were usually zeroed in on a position they'd just abandoned. Where the hell was Gush? Hardy pointed over to our Medic kneeling beside a GI who was banging the ground with his left arm. In his eagerness for revenge, Gush had leapt out front and got hit in the shoulder. A beaut, as wounds go. I told him so and said he was going to be all right, which wasn't the smartest thing to say. But he sloughed it off, paused, and wished me the same. "Only don't go lookin for it." He was so pissed off, the Medic wanted to give him a second shot of morphine, which he hotly rejected.

I went off by myself wanting to say a prayer, but couldn't get beyond, "Please, dear God, look after...." I was afraid I'd break down. I took my helmet off and slammed it against a tree. As I looked around for somebody to dig with, I realized that there were fewer of us left than I'd thought. So, who did I bump into but Klug, the last guy I wanted to see. He couldn't find anybody to partner with, so he came looking for me. He asked so awkwardly, I gathered he must have lost his chance at those Sergeant's stripes. It wasn't hard to see through him. He went on about me being a pretty steady guy, and I told him, "Bullshit. Let's dig." As it turned out, for the time being, he wasn't the worst guy to be with. In fact, just as well; I couldn't talk to anybody. I surely wouldn't want to say anything to him. Unless you bottled up your grief, you were going to come to it.

But, son of a bitch; me teamed up with Klug. Just the way that kind of day should end. On the other hand, Klug did have a strong arm, and I went at it with him, stroke for stroke. I could at least take it out on the unyielding soil of the Fatherland.

8.

Hell, we had to go on. Though all of the signs pointed to me being next. You can't defy omens. We had gone into a German border town, Winterspelt, with little opposition, just the usual shelling, which was actually harder on the civilians, who hated us for it. Along with everything else. I wanted to get water from a pump in front of an old stone house, and asked the Hausfrau for permission. She gave me a curt, "Ja," and a look that said she wished she'd put vinegar down the well. We didn't stay long before going into another uphill attack, a mean one, the worst of it being the shelling that pounded us after we took the hill. The stuff just kept coming. Exhausted as we were, Klug and I were feverishly digging in together again, and didn't rest till we got down far enough.

I was told that, when found, my legs were sticking out of a collapsed foxhole, and I'd been given up for dead, until a Medic checking somebody nearby heard a faint moaning sound. The Medic said that they pulled me out, sat me up against a tree, and he put the smelling salts under my nose. My head felt like it was being gripped by a pair on tongs; my nose hurt and I had a salty taste in my mouth. I spit out blood and felt dizzy.

As well as I could recall, I had heard shells coming in close, caught the sudden roar of a deafening explosion with a flare of light, and it was like I was hit by a wall. It was hard to account for anything else that happened beyond a piercing shot to my head, immediately gone, as, in almost the same instant, things went blank and I knew no more.

The Medic speculated that I might have been thrown up against the log top of our hole and, in coming down, grazed my face on the helmet—all in a split second. Who knows? From the size of the crater, the Medic thought it might have been more than an 88 that landed a couple of yards from my hole. He told me to be thankful for dirt. I vaguely recalled that Klug had said he was going out to take a piss. He must have been the dead GI they found down from our hole. I guess I blacked out again, because the next thing I could recall was looking up at the arched ceiling of a railroad car and hearing the clickety-clack of the train carrying a load of us wounded GIs back to a hospital in Bar-le-duc, France.

9.

Last time I'd seen what life was like in the rear echelon, it left a bad taste in my mouth. This time it didn't get any better. The litter bearers carrying me from the ambulance to the hospital were talking about high times they'd had with the women (screws past and present) and their prospects at the forthcoming dance. With the bearer up front having his back to the one behind, they had to raise their voices. I had the impression some of it was for my benefit, their way of letting me know their job was a bore, and I was nothing but shit to them. What was a litter case anyway? Hadn't they'd lugged enough of them? So much for their contempt. They couldn't know how little it meant to me.

Jonesey, the guy in the bed next to mine, said he'd had the same experience. Angry a good deal of the time, Jonesey, with his wide-set eyes and thin lips, looked like he needed to bash somebody. As he saw it, the lousy bearers were covering up for the fact that they should have been shamed by how good it was for them, when it was so bad for us. He got worked up at the thought of them. "Yeah, I wanted to roll off and kick their asses. You noticed they had those brand new combat boots, didn't yah? The ones we never got."

The doctor had been digging shrapnel out of Jonesey's arm and hip and said there were small pieces, some no bigger than granules, that might have to stay unless they made their way up to the skin. It was something of a sport to grab 'em before they got away. Jonesey said that when he got better, he was going to look for those damned litter bearers. They graveled me, but not as much as they did him. I said to forget it. "Fuck 'em; they ain't worth the trouble." The truth was, having made it out with nothing worse than what I had, I was too grateful to get real stirred up by the likes of them. Jonesey made a fist, so I added, "But if you get to 'em first, give 'em one for me too."

After their pretended indifference, once the bearers deposited me on the examining table, they had themselves a quick curiosity gawk. I hoped I didn't disappoint them. The nurse gave me a mirror, and all I had to show for my pain was a swollen face, black eyes, a nose that looked like it was going the wrong way, and dried blood on my upper lip and at a corner of my mouth. The doctor was a really nice guy, Antonino or something like that, a kidder who said, "Hey fella, next time pick on somebody your own size." He worked on my nose with his thumbs, then backed off a bit to see if he had it straight enough. I asked him if he ever did sculpture. He said, "Usually in clay." It figured.

They didn't want me to be walking around, since, in addition to my being a little wobbly, they found I had trench foot. I knew I had a sore throat and cough. They said I was also running a fever. As I thought about it, there weren't many guys in the Company who didn't have a cold or cough. The long willowy guy who became the new Sergeant of the machine gun section always had snot running down his upper lip. None of us ever got so much as an aspirin, never thought to ask. But time to forget about that.

When I got well enough to make my way around in the wheelchair, I went past the ward where they had the wounded Germans, and the care they got was no different from what we received. The doctors were just as concerned. In fact, I saw Dr. Anonino leaning over a young kid who had the same concussion that I had. Since the Doc was shining a pocket flashlight in his eye, the kid might have been in worse shape, and was still pretty much out of it. I heard him repeating one word, "Bilder." Worried about his pictures, he sure as hell didn't know where he was.

They must have done one super job of taking care of the Germans' wounds, because they not only looked in fine fettle when I saw them walking around, but there was a platoon-sized contingent of them who were being put through close order drill in the courtyard. They had a demanding, bad-tempered Sergeant barking out commands.

272

The phrase he used to call them to attention seemed sort of funny, but I supposed it was just how they did it: "Hände auf die Hosen Naht!" (Hands on your trouser seams!) The way they snapped to and sharply executed his commands it was like the Sergeant was telling them they better damned well remember that they were still Deutsche Soldaten, best ever. I hated him.

He was one arrogant bastard and walked around the corridors like he owned the place. I tried to run him over with my wheelchair when I had the chance. He got the point and did a nonchalant evasion; like, 'Don't get your knickers in a twist, fella.' Jonesey also had a run-in with him in the corridor. He gave the guy a dirty look and got one back. The nerve of the son-of-a-bitch. The nurses were scared of him.

I didn't know why he wasn't cut down a notch and, overall, couldn't help wondering how come the Germans looked in such good shape, getting fat on the rest and abundant hospital food. We thought that, except for the drilling, they couldn't be just lying around; or could they? For one thing, it went against their temperament. But seeing how considerate we were of them, it would be just like us to adhere to the Convention about treatment of POWs, regardless of whether the Germans gave a darn for ours, who, we heard, were in many situations damned near starved. Just as Jonesey wondered whether we could put them on a work detail, in comes a quick-footed little Heinie, an older fellow, graying at the temples, and, head down, he does a really efficient job of cleaning up the ward, even does the latrines. He was a modest type, somebody's Daddy, who somehow had wangled himself a job. I didn't mind him getting the work, but as Jonesey put it, we couldn't help wondering, "Who knows what all our generous Uncle Sam gives 'em? Tells 'em how stupid we are."

Mostly we ignored them. But every now and again another guy in our ward would get pissed off at how good they had it and ask, "Don't anybody remember we're here because o' them?"

Whatever—to hell with them, especially that son-of-a-bitchin Sergeant and the bearers too. As we used to say when it got to be too much, "Fuck 'em all." What I liked to hear was that the Doc said my head would get better; and, in fact, the pain was beginning to ease. They just had to do a check on my hearing—which they somehow didn't get around to, and, though there were voices I had trouble with, I didn't say anything about it. The less foolin with me the better. Many guys would never have their teeth checked by an Army dentist. Neither would I.

I got to know other guys in the ward, and found that one of them was a Sergeant in my Company. For goodness sake, none other than Ready. His head was bandaged on one side, so I didn't recognize him at first. On line, he was as tough as he looked. His name was actually Ruffin, so he was known as Ruffin-Ready, and then we dropped the Ruffin part. It was sad to see him like that. Slump-shouldered and told not to be moving his head a lot, he wasn't the same guy. He had sharp features and was almost bald, a rugged combination. Hardy said he looked like Dick Tracy without hair. On line, he packed a P-38 in a German black leather holster cinched across his chest.

I recalled that on that attack over the Our, he came running past us going to the Aid Station, holding a blood-soaked bandage to his cheek. He was cussin and saying he'd just been nicked. It turned out his cheekbone was broken in two places, and they were concerned that it might have an effect on his eye. I found him sitting alone looking out the window. A steady rain was falling. It looked like the spring thaw might be setting in. Sensing there was somebody in the wheelchair beside him, Ready turned to look. "Buddy; it's you, huh?"

Was he ever surprised. He couldn't believe I was there. We did a light embrace and he perked up, said it was good to see me, and asked what happened. I told him and said I was okay. Gee-whiz, gritty ol' Ready. He asked about some of the guys in the Company, and I was glad I could tell him that enough of the ones we knew were still hanging in when last seen. As we talked about them, it sort of made me nostalgic to be back with the Company again. Crazy, considering how the day-to-day fear ate away at you, but you knew it was the same for everybody else; we shared it all—brothers. Ready was a perfect example. Nothing he wouldn't do for guys in his platoon; nothing they wouldn't do for him.

Ready, Jonesey and I buddied up and also made friends with a black guy in our ward, Josh, who had been with the all-black tank battalion that actually had liberated Bar-le-duc. We had some good pinochle games. I had recovered enough from the blurred vision and dizziness that I also was able to enjoy the luxury of reading again. Read some short stories by Joseph Conrad, also some by Thomas Mann, sea stories of the one, and, while the other wrote subtler stuff, it read well. The nurses were nice to us, except for one, a short woman with a happy bottom and a big voice, who acted like she was our Top-Kick She took offense easily, and one joker greeted her with a lusty after-dinner fart. She'd come by at ten o'clock and, without a minute's warning, yell, "Lights out!" And, bang, out they'd go, right in the middle of a card game. One night, Jonesey called out, "Hey guys, how do yah spell alleygator?" We shouted out the letters and that was the last we saw of her.

10.

Six weeks passed pretty quickly, and it was getting close to the time when we were to be going back to our outfits. Josh had contacted a Priest whom he'd became acquainted with when his outfit came through there and got rid of the Germans. He invited Josh to dinner at his home, and Josh asked if he could bring a couple of friends. Ready couldn't make it, but Jonesey and I went. The Priest had quite a few relatives and the table was very festively set, with a lace tablecloth and fine chinaware. They were somewhat reserved, but very polite. So were we. We got the feeling they were sort of upper class. With what little French Jonesey and I knew, we let Josh do the talking. We didn't do a whole lot of toasting, but—man!—there was a drink between each of the courses. Good at first, but the further along we got, the stiffer the drink, and by the time they brought out the dessert, I was hanging onto the edge of the table. The food was very tasty, the seafood soup a meal in itself, though after the third course, I couldn't tell you what the rest of it was, though the taste was superb. We thanked them for their generosity, several times. I was so unsteady on my feet, Jonesey and Josh had to guide me back to the hospital, Josh finally putting my arm around his shoulder. Wow.

Josh kept close tabs on what was going on, and one bright morning he came over and told me we were going back to our outfits. We got a new issue of clothes, some of it salvage, but, after a few days' wear up there, everything would look like salvage anyway. It so happened that the hospital staff was to have their weekly dance the night before we were scheduled to leave. We thought it might be nice to have our arms around a girl before taking off, but the staff raised a stink about that. "Absolutely no outsiders! We know these girls *personally*." Jonesey wasn't leaving, but he said he was going to crash the dance. "Let 'em try to throw me out!" I had no idea how that might work out. Ready wanted me to tell the guys he was hoping to make it back, and he told me to keep my goddam head down.

I had a warm double handshake with Josh, and off we went to our separate trucks. I slept through a series of long windy truck rides with a bunch of guys mostly from other outfits. We ate cold K-rations along the way, like they wanted us to get ourselves used to how things were going to be again. At last reaching an assembly area somewhere in Germany, we were issued packs and M-1s, and marched off. Boy was I ever out of shape. Crisp as the air was, it took no time for me to work up a sweat. The last thing I remember was the guy behind me asking, "Hey, fella, you okay?" I came to sitting in a ditch beside the road, held up by a Medic, and pulling back from smelling salts. It was funny how you could black out, wake up, and not know where the hell you were. You don't know you've been out.

11.

That was the beginning of an odyssey which took a number of turns through the rear echelon, one more troublesome than the other. Got myself a real snoot full, and then some. The difference going back this time was that I was fully aware of what was happening.

However, no complaints about how it started out. I'd been trucked up to the assembly area, but was sent back from there by ambulance. At the first stop, which I think was the Regimental Clearing Station, a Doctor (our guy, the only one who paid much attention to me) said they were probably a little hasty at putting me down as well enough to return. I didn't want to think I wasn't—at first. But, then, I did begin to feel kind of achy, and, as I sat there waiting for the Doctor to look me over, I also became somewhat woozy, the sensation I'd had when they initially brought me to with the smelling salts. After a while, it felt like somebody had thrown me against a rock pile. When the Doctor left, I was given a shot, some pills, and told that, with a little rest, I'd be fine.

I finally recognized some of the guys who were with me on the second ride back. One was Hardy's Platoon Leader, a replacement Lieutenant none of us expected to last, but he caught on quick. With Hardy in charge, he had to. He had his arm in a sling and looked like he was wasting away; he said it was more from nerves than the shrapnel he'd picked up. He had put Hardy in for a Bronze Star. When I told him he already had one, the Lieutenant said he deserved an oak leaf cluster on it. There was a kid looking blankly out the window. I asked him how he was doing, but he didn't answer. I could see from his expression he was probably pleading psycho, legitimately; he looked scared as hell.

Our next stop was at a schoolhouse. The doctor looked at my tag and wrote something on it after giving me a perfunctory exam. He had given me a cuff below the kneecap, and my lower leg popped up. That done, he insisted I be placed on a stretcher. I was laid on the floor at the front of a classroom. I looked over toward the blackboard and saw a guy on the floor there who was in serious shape, his leg amputated just above the ankle, the bandaged stump blood soaked and covered with a wire cage. (Most likely had it blown off by a mine.) Looking at him, I got up—what the hell was I doing on a stretcher?—but an attendant, a big Black guy, insisted I really ought to get back down. He lit me a cigarette, and, to show he didn't mean to be unfriendly, he also gave me a shave, of all things.

Things went downhill from there. Not having eaten all day, I arrived at the next place, hungry as a bear. I asked the ward boy, a skinny little Pfc, to get me something to eat, and he said it was past chow time and made a remark about all of us guys being such chow

278

hounds. There was a Sergeant roaming around, and I asked him, "How about some bread and water?" But he didn't hear me, at least made like he didn't. He was a big husky, good-looking guy with long blonde hair, wearing the spiffiest ODs, and making a play for the nurse with the flashing eyes. I had wondered at first, what the hell was a guy like him doing back here. Now I knew. I saw others (orderlies, I guessed) wearing shiny new combat outfits, complete with camouflage field jackets. Maybe why we were given salvage. The doctor finally came by, looked at my tag and moved on. I didn't even get time to ask him to get me something to eat. Hey, a piece of hardtack will do. And so it went. I wondered how a seriously wounded guy might have survived the trip back.

I finally wound up at a hospital outside Paris in a place called Garche. It had been a World War I hospital with a new section added on. No joy there either. It looked like I was in with a bunch of flunkies of one kind or another. We were parked in the corridor, and the guy in the bed behind mine had an ear infection that he was picking on so it wouldn't heal. They kept giving him antibiotics, and he kept a-pickin. He was with an anti-aircraft unit; said they never hit a thing. He himself never fired at so much as a fly. Another guy had gotten himself a dose, and he came in to have himself circumcised. For entertainment, one day they brought in a group of young girls who were doing a pathetic ballet for us, but the teacher stopped it when she saw the guy with the circumcision holding his bandaged groin. On another occasion, a guy was bothering a woman, a rather pretty one at that, who was down on her knees washing the floor. He kept goosing her and wouldn't let up, until I kicked his ass and almost had a fight on my hands.

That's the kind of situation it was. I was awfully impatient to get the hell out of there. Before I left, who should they bring by to cheer up the troops, but Sonja Henie, the ice-skating queen, shepherded around by a four-star bigwig, General Lear. There was a picture of their visit in the papers. She always had a beautiful dimpled smile. I was told she once had one for Hitler.

12.

Going into my second week at this place, I'd had my fill. I pleaded with the doctor to get me released. They hadn't done anything for me, and I didn't think I needed to have anything done. I said if I stayed any longer I would have a problem. I could feel it coming on. Who knows; I might kill somebody. That was good enough to get me shipped out. The only trouble was the amiable Doc didn't read me right. He couldn't understand why I wouldn't just relax and do nothing while I waited for the war to end.

So what did he do? He put me down for LA, limited assignment. (With a note that said, 'Make sure this guy doesn't get any weapons.') And where did I get assigned? To an Air Corps Repple-Debble, from which I'd be sent to a rear echelon Air Corps outfit. Goldbrick heaven! I couldn't blame the Doc. He thought he was doing me a favor. The RD I got shipped out to was the one located in that Rothschild Chateau near pre-war exclusive neighborhoods in Paris, like the Trocadéro. And who did I meet there, but my old friend Pistol Pete, the A-rab/Dago.

A few strings pulled, and Pete had long since gotten himself into a Transport outfit, where he could keep his black market business rolling. The more he got away with, the more daring he became. But he was finally caught ripping off a load of medical supplies, with all kinds of prime drugs, including morphine, which would have been a big hit for him. He'd been taking the truckload from Forward Storage, and so he worked out a deal with the Adjutant's Office, whereby he'd accept the lesser charge of misbehavior before the enemy—unintended. (I'd never heard of such a thing, but, of course, you couldn't believe all that Pete said.) His lawyer pleaded innocence (faulty orders from Quartermaster) and told Pete the case could be settled for a trip to a DTC, a detention center, where he'd serve a month and walk. So here he was sending a raft of stuff over the Chateau wall and doing a flourishing business in GI uniforms, long-johns, blankets, bedding, mattresses, belts, shoes, boots, soap, towels, silverware, radios, mimeograph machines, cameras, pistols, carbines, medals—no end of things he could lay his hot hands on. He had to expand his black market trade to compensate for losses in his whorehouse business, set back when he got stuck with a covey of girls whose heads had been shaved for consorting with the Germans. Their hair grew back, but not their esteem among the local trade, and they were even shunned by cohorts.

I found a number of former infantrymen, who had also been put on LA. I was able to pick them out because they were generally skinny looking and quiet. Occasionally, they wore the patch of their former outfit on their right shoulder. Some had just fallen in with the soft life you got in the Air Corps rear echelon. Others weren't comfortable with it. But all of us were glad to be out of the line of fire and have hot water and electric lights. A crusty old Sergeant said it seemed like what most guys did while they waited for reassignment—actually while trying to delay it—was debauch themselves in one way or the other: going to the whores, drinking, gambling, fighting, stealing, feasting on good Air Corps food, playing softball, or just pissing away the time doing nothing. They enjoyed a dogfight. Better yet, one afternoon, a couple of dogs got hung up and squealed bloody murder. Finally, some guy personalized it and poured a pail of cold water on them.

Don't get me wrong; we didn't hold anything against them. With time on your hands, it was easy to fall in with that kind of thing. It happens. But, dismissing the newspaper hype that glorified combat, wouldn't these guys maybe think for a minute that there were men on line still getting shot, and having a pretty miserable time of it? Oh well, let it go. How could you have an idea of what it was like up there, unless you'd lived it? How could you *tell* what it was like, even if you had? They showed the guys movies. Why worry? John Wayne was going to win the war. Already had; events just hadn't caught up.

The cadre officers, unlike ours, were easy to approach, so I asked to get assigned as quickly as possible—anywhere; at this stage, I wasn't going to be particular. No bitterness; I just wanted out. They couldn't understand me, and I told them I had a hard time understanding myself.

13.

Again, those Officers thought they were doing me a favor. Like the Doctor at Garche, they looked at my record and wanted to do well by me. I went to a France-based Air Transport outfit that had flown the gliders bringing paratroops into Normandy during the Invasion. Those had to be pretty gutsy pilots flying those motorless winged boxes, which didn't always make it to the ground and often crashed when they did. However, since that time, the outfit simply had nothing to do, and the Air Corps didn't know what to do with them. They wanted to be shipped back to the States, but others had priority.

Meanwhile, they were living high on the hog; but I mean high, eating Air Corps chow (steak once a week) and, having made friends with the locals in the town just outside their base, they regularly had dinner parties with them, which provided access to great chefs, also women whose men had either been killed, wounded, imprisoned, or disappeared, after going into the Underground. They invited me to one of their Friday night dinners at the Townhall. They supplied the pork chops and the proud chefs brought them in, trays shoulder high. The chops were gourmet spiced, grilled to perfection, a la cognac flambant, and were greeted by a rousing "Huzzah!" I'd never tasted anything like it.

I had a lot of respect for the pilots, though, not having much to do, most of them primarily drank and partied. Some had skied in the winter, and now played golf. During the snows of the Break-Through, while we were on the slopes of Luxembourg, they were on the slopes back here. I didn't care much for the enlisted men, and they didn't care much for me. There was a fat Texan who liked to toss his rope in my path to get me lassoed at the ankle. I told him to knock it off. There was no one I could especially get friendly with. But once I was assigned to Supply, I got to know the Sergeant there, and he was a good guy. He even taught me how to drive a six-by-six, double-clutching and all.

The Major came to me one day and said he noticed that I had been awarded the Purple Heart. How come I wasn't wearing it? (In the Air Corps you *wore* your medals? Well, ribbons, I guess.) I told him I never got the thing, so he said he'd put in for it on my behalf. Well, that turned out to be a break, because he sent my records in, and, since they had to go back to my former Division, I learned that they got lost. To be expected if you went from Air Force to Infantry—like a foreign country. So technically, I didn't belong anywhere.

Great! When the Major gave me the news that he had a tracer out, I was as much as on *my* way out. Packed up that night, I took off. My first thought was that I'd head for LeMans, and see if I could find Fleurette. I'd hitched my way to Paris, and, sitting at a café sipping wine, a young girl comes up to me with her father. They had noticed my shoulder patch. Our division had been the one that liberated Paris. They didn't care for the piss poor, watery wine I was drinking, so they took me to their neighborhood café and ordered a bottle of full-bodied Bordeaux and crêpes. Since the girl had learned English in school, we were able to have ourselves a little conversation. I thanked them and hoped they would excuse me. I had to be leaving.

Leaving, but where to? Fleurette might by this time have gotten herself another guy, maybe a GI. She was too nice a girl not to have found somebody. So all that way for nothing but bitter disappointment? And what if we did get together? We couldn't go out at night. At some point, I was bound to be stopped by the MPs, and they'd have questions. Could they get me for desertion? From what outfit? Did I have one? The Major surely would have had me reported A-Wall. After all this, me winding up in Detention, subject to court-marshal? Don't know what all the authorities might do to Fleurette for hiding a fugitive. Defenseless Fleurette. I know I was probably pushing it, but something inside was telling me *where*— dammit it all—I really did want to go. Indeed, had to. But should I be going there? The guys would be great, but the Officers might have a problem accounting for me.

I was so depressed, I went back to the neighborhood café, had myself enough wine to make me sleepy, and asked the barkeep to give me an overnight bed. He was dubious, but I laid some hundred franc notes on the bar, and he said he'd have coffee for me in the morning.

I was up early. Gosh, the French make good coffee. I shook off the headache, bought a baguette and a bottle of wine and hit the road east. The driver of the six-by-six who picked me up wanted to know, "Where do you mean, east?" I pointed to my shoulder patch, soon to come off.

"Infantry, huh?"

I nodded.

"And yah know dey still fightin out dere?"

"Yeah, been there before."

"Dass why I wondered." He gave me a funny look. "You sure?"

I said I had friends and asked him to take me as far east as he went, and I'd find my way from there, knowing that just then it had to be the way for me. I felt I could spill out enough bullshit to have them take me in. When the driver dropped me off, he wanted to know: did I know what I was doing? For sure? I told him I fell out so I could belong again, and left him scratching his head.

Crazy, of course, like I'd learned my stupidity from the Army's, but I'd learned something about myself too. Given a choice, I preferred situations where people would do their best to cope when things were bad. There were risks all over. But I'd made it before, and, back with my buddies, I'd make it again. There was the irreplaceable need of a sense of belonging. To put it in its simplest terms, I just felt I had to be with guys I understood—and who understood me. You look to the future, but you live in the now. The big thing is how.

ABOUT THE AUTHOR.

Growing up in the Depression, the youngest of three sons in a working class family, Syd Joseph Krause, a railroad demurrage clerk, could not have had the remotest dream that he might one day go to college, much less become an English Professor (MA, Yale; Ph.D. Columbia), who would publish numerous articles on major American Authors in learned journals, also a book (*Mark Twain As Critic*) with Johns Hopkins Press and become General Editor of *The Novels of Charles Brockden Brown*—America's first professional novelist—for which he did a "Historical Essay" and "Historical Notes." Following Fulbright Professorships at the Universities of Copenhagen and Tübingen, he returned to Europe on a number of occasions for lectures in Holland, Germany (East and West) Coimbra (Portugal), Rome, and Warsaw. What actually launched him on this career was the GI Bill of Rights, resulting from his participation in

a Defining Event of the Twentieth Century, World War II, when in
the fall of 1944 he joined the Fourth Infantry Division and was with
an on-line Company during two of the bitterest campaigns in the
Fourth's history: The Battle of Hürtgen Forest and the Battle of the
Bulge. He wrote an account of a post-Bulge battle he was in, which
appeared in a collection of *War Stories* by members of the Fourth.
As he thought about how men of his generation who survived the
War were passing, Krause went to a journal he'd written shortly after
discharge, and decided to do this novel dedicated to the memory of
survivors who have passed, as well as those lost in combat, hoping
to leave a record of what the War was like for them.

Printed in the United States
58344LVS00009B/132

9 781425 925796